WARMASTER 4: SORROWVALE

MELISSA MCSHANE

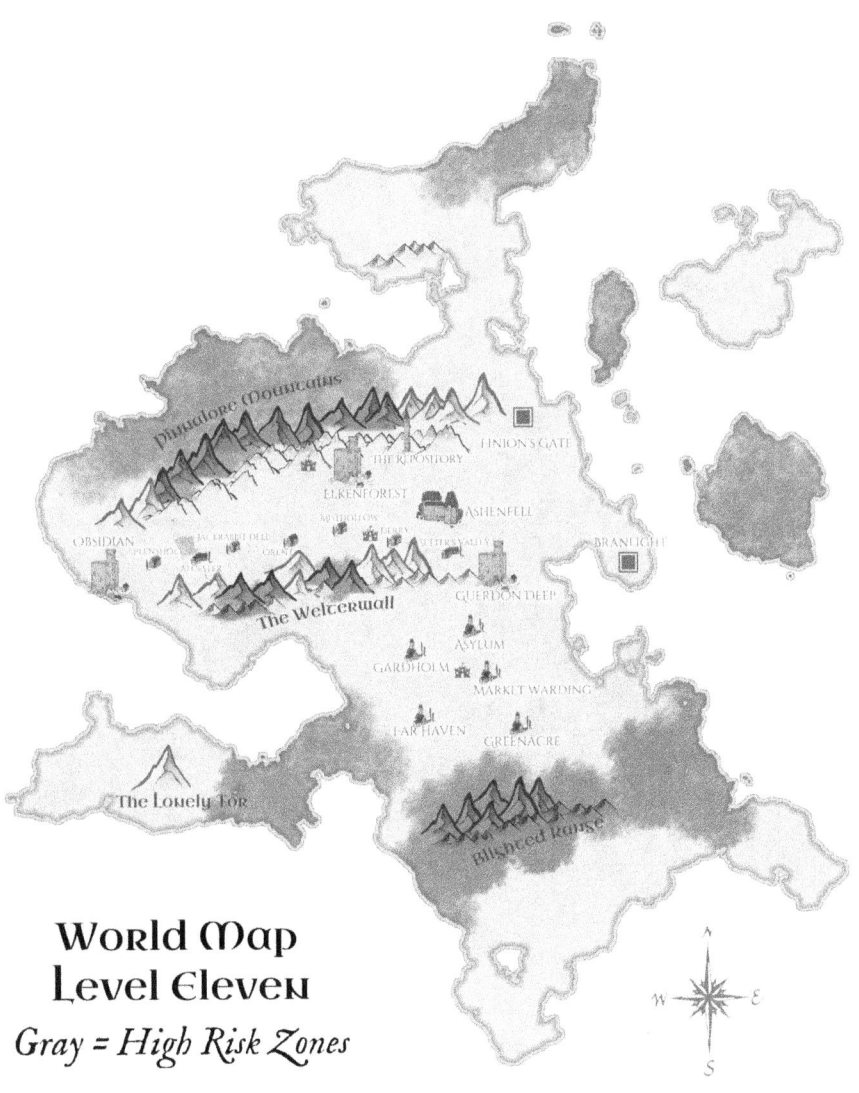

World Map
Level Eleven
Gray = High Risk Zones

CHAPTER ONE

Setting out on a new adventure, a new journey, usually invigorated Aderyn. She loved traveling with her friends, talking or joking, listening to Isold sing or walking in silence. The promise of something unexpected tugged at her heart, and even the possibility of fighting monsters couldn't dampen that. Today, as evening drew near, she couldn't summon up enthusiasm for anything.

The light of the setting sun flickered through the dense pines, casting fragments of shadow that pointed the way toward their unseen destination, a thousand miles away. They'd only walked for five hours that afternoon, but it felt like twice that, thanks to their new companion. Companion. That was much too friendly a word for what Jessemia was. "Burden" was better. "Whining misfortune" was even more accurate.

"I don't think we're going to find a better spot than this," Owen said. "Let's camp over there. The trees don't grow quite so close together."

That was the signal for everyone to set their knapsacks on the ground, even Aderyn, whose **<Knapsack of Plenty>** weighed almost nothing despite everything she'd loaded it with that morning. She stretched out her back and legs anyway. They'd left the road behind an hour ago, and the forest stretched out forever in every direction, as far as Aderyn could tell. She was grateful for the **[Map Access]** skill, though if she was separated from her friends, the map wouldn't guide her nearly as well as her **<Wayfinder>** could. The magic item given her by her grandfather led her to whatever her heart desired most and had already saved her life a few times.

Behind her, Jessemia let out a little whimper, then, when that failed to draw a reaction, whimpered more loudly. Aderyn ground her back teeth together. She had tried throughout the afternoon to remind herself that Jessemia was leaving her home and her father for an uncertain future. That Jessemia, despite being level six, had never really adventured before, since her father had hired higher-level adventurers to team with her and unnaturally boost her leveling. That the woman had been coddled and spoiled her whole life. But all those things kept bringing to mind their results: that she and her friends were stuck with an entitled, whiny, ineffective Pathseer for the next eight weeks. Nothing about the situation cheered Aderyn.

Livia was digging through her knapsack. "Why does the thing always sink to the bottom?" she muttered.

"Because it's made of solid bronze?" Weston suggested.

"Stop being reasonable. That's my thing, reasonableness." Livia came up with a bronze cube the size of Weston's fist, engraved on all sides with what looked like stylized V's. "Give me a minute."

"Why are we stopping? There's no inn," Jessemia said. "I demand an inn."

Aderyn caught Owen's eye. She didn't need **[Read Body Language]** to recognize the frustration expressed by the thin, taut line of his lips, pressed together to hold back a retort.

Livia stopped at the center of the clear space and held out her hand at arm's length. "Stand back," she said, "I don't know how far it will need to extend to fit all of us." With her thumb, she pressed the side of the <**Soldier's Friend**> bronze cube displaying four tiny tents.

A distant fanfare played, and Livia was suddenly at the center of a whirlwind that looked like half a dozen small humanoid figures dashing about faster than the eye could follow. The breeze the whirlwind kicked up blew Aderyn's hair wildly and made the pine branches dance and rustle their needles. Such a peaceful sound—

Behind her, Jessemia let out a piercing shriek, shattering Aderyn's calm. "What is that? What are those *things?* They're going to tear the forest apart!"

"Shut up," Weston said wearily. "It's magic setting up our camp for us. Did you want to pitch your tent yourself? Because I'm sure we can arrange that."

"I don't know how to pitch a tent," Jessemia pouted. "You're mean to suggest I should have to figure that out."

The whirlwind subsided, and now Livia stood, windblown and ruddy-cheeked, in the center of a ring of four tents, next to a merrily burning fire. She returned to stow the cube inside her knapsack. "Let's eat," she said. "Fresh bread from an Obsidian baker, apples, and cold roast chicken. I love the first night out from a city. We eat so well."

Aderyn was already rummaging in the <**Knapsack of Plenty**> for the foods Livia mentioned. "Here, somebody start water boiling for tea. I think we could use a hot drink."

Owen walked around behind Jessemia and removed the smallest of their iron pots from her knapsack where he'd put it to punish her. Carrying the extra weight had shut her up, but only temporarily. Jessemia flinched away from him. "Don't touch me."

"Don't flatter yourself." Owen handed the pot to Livia to fill with summoned water and then knelt beside Aderyn. "It still amazes me what we can fit into this thing," he said as she withdrew an entire roast chicken from the knapsack.

Aderyn handed him a couple of long loaves of bread, white and soft with a crispy brown crust that smelled deliciously of yeast. "I think foods stay fresher in here, too. Not enough that I'd want to store meat in it indefinitely, but I bet we could keep that chicken in it for a day and not notice a difference."

"It would be an interesting thing to test," Isold said. He accepted the portable spit from Aderyn and set to work wedging the uprights on either side of the neat little firepit ringed with stones. "Though I'm not sure we want to risk rotting meat ruining that magic item."

Aderyn took the apparently empty knapsack and stowed it in her tent at the foot of the bedroll Owen had laid out for her. "No, the experiment's not important enough to take that chance."

As she emerged from the tent, her eye fell on Jessemia, who stood alone at the edge of the campsite clutching her knapsack. Unexpected pity struck her, and she said, "Why don't you put your things away, Jessemia, and sit by the fire? It's been a tiring day for all of us."

Jessemia startled and hugged her knapsack tighter. "Put my things where?"

"In your tent. That one." She pointed at the tent across the small clearing from hers. "Then come have some dinner."

Jessemia glared at her as if Aderyn had slapped her. "I don't have to do what you say."

"I think I made it clear that you do," Owen said. He took the knapsack from Jessemia and tossed it into her tent. "Aderyn is trying to make you feel comfortable because that's the kind of person she is. I, on the other hand, am a monster, and I don't give a damn about your comfort. Go get settled, if you want. Dinner is here when you're willing to behave like a civilized person." He walked wide around the seething Jessemia and sat next to Aderyn by the fire, putting his arm around her shoulders.

Jessemia let out a little outraged squeak. Then she hobbled rapidly into her tent and tried to slam the tent flap closed. It fluttered shut with a sound like a single giant wing flapping once, *flumph*.

Livia chuckled. "I guess the prospect of an eight-week trip through the wilderness isn't enough to change her."

"I think Aderyn is the one who said changing her would take nothing short of *polymorph*," Owen said, giving Aderyn a squeeze. "Weston, you want to carve?"

Isold accepted a drumstick absently. His attention was on Jessemia's tent. "She's never had to walk this far before," he said.

"No, but she'd better get used to it fast. Tomorrow will be even longer." Owen tore into a wing and chewed enthusiastically. "It's a little dry, but still good. Too bad we've never seen any wild chickens. Though Livia would just turn them into paste trying to kill them with *stone sphere*."

"I told you, I have a plan," Livia said. "Two plans, in fact."

"That only fills me with twice as much dread."

"No, it's fine, I swear. Look." Livia drew the **<Wand of Sleep>** from its sheath on her knapsack. "This has a range of about a hundred feet. I'll put the prey to sleep, and then it's just a quick slash to the throat—"

"Oh, *ergh*," Aderyn said with feeling.

"What, and shooting or knifing fleeing prey is better? This way, they don't feel a thing."

"I'll admit I think that's a clever solution. Just—don't tell me the other one, all right?" Owen took another bite. "Isold, is something wrong?"

"I'm concerned that Jessemia hurt her feet walking for so long," Isold said. "Those boots of hers look brand new, and even good boots can leave blisters."

"So what?" Weston said. "She has to toughen up sometime. It's not like we can shorten this trip for her comfort."

"I was thinking more that she'll slow us down." Isold finished off his drumstick and set the bone aside. "I wish I hadn't sold the **<Wand of Minor Healing>**. If I heal her feet completely with the new wand or the **<Healing Stone>**, they'll be as tender as they were this morning, and I'm not going to waste our healing magic fixing her feet every day. There must be some middle ground." He rose and went to Jessemia's tent, where he spoke in a voice too low for Aderyn to make out.

"Go away!" Jessemia screamed. "None of you care if I die! Well, I don't need you. So leave me alone!" She burst into sobs that were audible through the tent wall.

Isold didn't move. He again murmured something, then spoke a little louder to be heard over the sobbing. "You'll be in much more pain if you try to walk all day on those feet. I can do something about that. Or do you enjoy hurting?"

The sobbing abated slightly. After a moment, the tent flap opened just a crack. Isold knelt in front of it and brought out the <**Wand of Healing**> he kept thrust through his waistband. The scent of raspberries filled the air, and then the tip of the wand glowed green with phosphorescent liquid that bubbled from it. Isold lowered the wand, blocking Aderyn's view, but in only a few seconds he stood up and tucked the wand, no longer glowing, back into his waistband.

"But I still hurt!" whined Jessemia. "You didn't do it right. You left me wounded on purpose!"

"If I heal you entirely, your feet will never toughen to withstand a full day's walk," Isold said. "What I did will allow calluses to form, and eventually they'll stop hurting. Now, I suggest you eat something—"

"I won't eat with *kidnappers*," Jessemia declared. "And you people are no better than Brigands. Maybe you *are* Brigands and that bitch Eleora sent me off with you so I'd be killed far from anywhere anyone will ever find my body and get revenge!"

"Wow," Owen said, loudly enough to reach Jessemia. "Are you a writer? Because that sounds like a bestselling novel to me."

"You're talking nonsense. And I wouldn't eat with you if it was a choice between that and being killed and devoured by a monster." Jessemia emerged from her tent and stalked toward Owen, who held a couple of hunks of fresh bread in one hand and a waterskin newly filled by Livia in the other. "You're a disgusting, lying, no-name fake Fated One, and someday you'll be sorry you treated me like this."

Owen took a deliberate bite of bread and chewed slowly. Aderyn could tell he was giving himself time to control his first response, which she was sure wouldn't have been violent, but probably would have been scathing. He washed the bread down with water and stood. Jessemia was tall for a woman, and Owen wasn't a lot taller, but Jessemia took half a step back as if he intimidated her.

"I'm guessing you've never been truly hungry," he finally said. "I don't much care if you refuse to eat. It might do you good to understand hunger. But if you slow us down by fainting because you didn't take care of your physical needs, I won't promise to stop for you. And then you can find out if being killed and devoured by a monster really is better." He held out a hunk of bread.

Jessemia stared at it. Then she slapped it out of his hand.

Aderyn drew in a furious breath and started up from her seat. Owen held up a hand to stop her that said *I've got this*. "Your decision," he said calmly. "You want to eat dirty bread, that's up to you. But Aderyn went out of her way to buy that bread, and you owe her an apology for wasting her effort." He took another step toward Jessemia, forcing her to back up again. "And this is your one warning: you can insult me all you like, because I don't care what you think of me, but insult Aderyn and I'll tie a rope to your feet and drag you to Guerdon Deep. Understand?"

Jessemia swallowed. Owen did not look like he was joking. She glanced once at the others, then at Aderyn. "I'm sorry," she said in a petulant, not-very-sorry voice. Then she ducked back into her tent without picking up the bread, which was now dusted with soil and a few dead pine needles.

Aderyn let out a breath. "You shouldn't threaten things you wouldn't do," she told Owen.

"You think I wouldn't?" Owen returned to sit beside her. "Well, you're right. I'd hog-tie her first."

Aderyn laughed. "She's awful," she said, but in a low enough voice that Jessemia couldn't hear. Aderyn disliked the woman, but they had to travel together, and there was no sense being antagonistic. Not that Jessemia showed any such restraint.

CHAPTER TWO

Livia brought Owen and Aderyn tin mugs of hot tea that smelled deliciously of blackberries. "It hasn't even been a full day and I'm exhausted," she said, settling in beside Weston and leaning against his broad shoulder.

Isold sat across from them cross-legged and held out a hand as if to caress the fire, warming himself. "It will get easier," he said.

"You really think so?" Aderyn said, disbelieving.

Isold shrugged. "She's lonely and miserable and only knows one way to interact with people, which is by whining or shouting to get her way. But I don't think she's stupid."

"So you think she'll learn to behave differently?" Owen tossed a couple of pine needles into the fire, where they browned and curled instantly. "That's more optimistic than I can be."

"Or me," Weston said. "And I still believe Livia will learn to love sunrise."

"Which is way more reasonable than expecting our 'guest' to become a decent human being," Livia said.

"I hope Isold is right," Aderyn said. "Sometimes I feel sorry for her. Who knows what kind of a person she might be if she wasn't arrogant and spoiled?"

"We're never going to find out," Owen said.

Aderyn was afraid he was right.

His words felt definitive, a curse on their journey, and no one spoke for a few minutes. Then Isold began singing, and Aderyn's heart eased, because it was a familiar lullaby her parents had sung to their children. They had sung it as a duet, and now Aderyn took up the harmony and sang with Isold. Her voice wasn't more than passable, and it definitely couldn't compete with the Herald's, but the intertwined melody and harmony sounded just right as darkness rose up around their little group.

When the song ended, Owen kissed Aderyn and said, "That was beautiful. Isold, was there magic in your song? Because I feel unexpectedly peaceful."

"Just the magic of music." Isold tilted his head back and smiled at the night sky, barely visible between the pines.

"Sing something else," Weston suggested. "Something sad."

"Why would you want something sad while we're all here together?" Livia asked.

"Because melancholy music when you're content is more intense." Weston leaned forward, propping his elbows on his knees. "Sing something heartbreaking."

Isold shrugged and cleared his throat. The new song wasn't one Aderyn knew, but it made her heart ache with longing for some nameless thing she could never have. Weston was right; listening to a sad song with her sweetheart's arm around her made that gesture feel even more intimate and loving.

Her gaze fell on Weston, who looked so intent he might have been trying to wrestle the music into submission. He caught Aderyn's eye and twitched his head, the smallest motion, in the direction of Jessemia's tent. Aderyn surreptitiously looked that way.

The tent flap was open, and Jessemia's shadowy figure sat in the doorway, leaning forward so her face was mostly visible. With her expression not contorted by rage or petulance, she was actually very pretty. Aderyn looked away before Jessemia noticed her watching. She wished **[Read Body Language]** worked on people other than her partner, because she dearly wanted to know what Weston thought Jessemia's behavior meant. Or what Jessemia was thinking right then.

At the end of the song, Owen said, "I've never heard anything like that before. And Weston is right. It's like the best kind of heartbreak. I realize that doesn't make sense."

"It makes perfect sense," Aderyn started to say, but a yawn interrupted her. "Excuse me. I think I need to turn in."

"I agree. Let's get some sleep." Owen rose and offered Aderyn a hand up. Aderyn cast a quick glance at Jessemia's tent. The shadowy figure in the doorway was gone.

She sat at the end of her bedroll and pulled her boots off. "Do you really think Jessemia isn't going to change?" she asked Owen.

Owen paused with one boot in his hand. "Don't you? She's so wrapped up in believing she's important she doesn't have any room in her head for learning what the world is really like. Or discovering her place in it."

"I think that's sad."

"So do I, honestly. What a waste of human potential." Owen lay on his back and stared up at the tent roof. "But we can't force change on her, and it's true I don't actually care if she changes or not."

"I guess I feel the same." Aderyn lay down next to him and took his hand. "But it's still sad. She doesn't have anyone who really cares about her. Even her father treated her like a pet rather than a daughter."

"This really bothers you, doesn't it?" Owen scooted closer and took her in his arms.

"I have a family who cares about me, brothers and a sister and parents and my grandfather, and I have you, and I have our friends.

All of that means so much to me I can't help imagining what it would be like to lose it, or not to have it at all. So I feel sorry for Jessemia even though I know, logically, she probably doesn't deserve my pity."

"You have a loving heart and a great capacity for compassion," Owen said, kissing her lightly on the forehead. "It's natural you'd see Jessemia's side."

Aderyn snuggled closer. "And you have a strong instinct to protect others, especially me, and I find that endearing. What does 'hog-tie' mean?"

"What, you don't have hogs in this world?"

"Don't be silly. Of course we do. But nobody tries to restrain them by tying."

"Well, if Jessemia mouths off to you, I'll demonstrate." He kissed her once more. "Good night."

"Good night. I love you."

She fell asleep almost immediately, and woke, disoriented, to find Owen, not sleeping beside her, but shaking her foot to wake her. "Get up," he said. "Jessemia's gone."

Aderyn scrambled to sit up and grabbed her boots. "When did this happen?"

"I'm not sure. Livia said Jessemia was in her tent at the start of Livia's watch, so either Jessemia sneaked past her or she took advantage of the moment when Livia woke me for my turn. Livia's waking the others. We need to decide what to do."

Outside, Livia and Isold stood near Isold's tent. Weston wasn't there. "He's looking for tracks," Livia said when Aderyn asked. "She's not a good Pathseer, and I doubt she has the ability to conceal her passage. Weston will find her. Or her trail, maybe."

"We can't count on her incompetence," Isold said. "She does have Pathseer skills, however underdeveloped."

"What I want to know is why we care," Livia said. "Let her go back to Obsidian. We won't get experience for her quest, but let's balance that against the possibility of eight weeks' undisturbed travel."

"If I thought she could find her way back to Obsidian, I'd say good luck and good night," Owen said. "But we're several miles from where the road begins, and it's far more likely that she'll wander until she dies. And contrary to popular belief, I'm not really a monster, and I won't condemn anyone to that fate." He sighed deeply. "We have to go after her. Aderyn, can the <Wayfinder> help?"

"Sure." Aderyn pulled out the orb with its concentric metal rings and warmed it in her cupped hands. She relaxed and filled her mind with images and memories of Jessemia, letting those flow through her until her entire body focused on one thing.

The <Wayfinder> didn't glow.

Aderyn shook it gently, though there was nothing to jostle or dislodge to make it work. Again, she tried to make Jessemia her heart's desire, and again, the ball remained inert.

"I don't understand," she said, though she had a horrible suspicion. "I know it's not broken." She let her heart fill with memories of Owen, and the large spike at the front immediately turned rosy pink that grew redder as she turned to face him.

"You think the <Wayfinder> knows your heart's not in it?" Livia said.

"That's my fear." Aderyn tried once more, this time recalling the moments she'd had sympathy for Jessemia. Still the ball remained inert. "I hope Weston finds her trail."

"Weston is stumped," Weston said as he emerged from the woods around the camp. "I found her trail and followed it to a stream, where she lost me. I didn't think she knew enough to use running water to obscure her trail. Which is ironic, given that I'm not a Path-seer and I was having plenty of trouble following her, since I don't have the [Tracking] skill."

"Then what can we do?" Aderyn put the <Wayfinder> into her purse. "She may be good at concealing her path—"

"Running water aside, I think she was lucky, not skilled," Weston said.

"All right, she was lucky, but my point is that being able to hide her tracks doesn't mean she knows anything about wilderness survival. We have to find her."

"None of us are Pathseers, Aderyn," Owen pointed out. "Weston can find our camp again, and you can use the <**Wayfinder**> to do the same, but if the rest of us try to search the forest at night, we'll end up as lost as Jessemia."

"As of level eleven, I have a skill called [**Find Object**]," Isold said. "That would take me directly to her if I was familiar with an object she has on her. But the only objects I'm aware of are her boots, and I didn't pay attention to them to the degree that skill requires."

Livia said, "Wait. I can use *scry* to locate her." She disappeared into her tent and came back holding a mirror the size of her two spread palms. The mirror was dark beneath the moonless sky and all the pines, but Livia muttered a few nonsense words and it flashed brightly as if a sunbeam had struck it. Everyone gathered around to look.

At first, Aderyn thought the mirror was still reflecting the sky and the pine branches. Then she saw movement, purposeful movement like someone walking fast, someone whose outline was irregular and white in places. Aderyn finally recognized the white patches as Jessemia's bleached leather vest, and from there identified her face and tousled chestnut curls.

Livia scowled. "Well, that's not helpful. She could be anywhere. Give me a second." She spoke again, a complex tangle of syllables, and the view expanded outward as if they were birds in flight watching the land below. After only a few seconds, though, Jessemia was lost to view, obscured by the trees. "And that's even less helpful," Livia said, lowering the mirror.

"I can't think of anything else to try," Owen said.

"This is my fault," Aderyn exclaimed. "If I had better self-control—"

"Do *not* blame yourself for that woman's foolishness," Owen said, taking her by the shoulders. "It's not your fault if your heart fails to truly care about someone selfish and arrogant who doesn't respect you or anyone else here."

"But—"

"Shh. Something's coming," Weston said, holding up a hand.

They all fell silent. After a few still moments in which Aderyn heard nothing but the night breezes through the trees, the sound of muffled footsteps became audible. Before anyone could draw a weapon to face this threat, Jessemia walked into their camp. Her hair was a tangled mess with pine needles stuck in the curls as if she'd rubbed her head against several branches, there were smudges of dirt on her face and hands and streaked across her formerly white vest, and she limped slightly. Her boots, Aderyn noticed, weren't even a little water-stained, which, if Jessemia had waded through a stream for any distance, said something about the quality of the material and the manufacture.

Jessemia stopped at the edge of the circle of tents. Her usual mulish expression was muted with tiredness, but her voice was as sharp and as whiny as ever. "I suppose you would have let me die out there. You didn't even bother coming to look for me."

"Did you want us to?" Isold asked.

"*No*," she said, and that one word was packed so full of disdain it overflowed. "I want to go home. I know *you* won't take me, because you're all mean and cruel."

"Nothing's stopping you," Owen said. "Why did you come back?"

"None of your business." She brushed past him and headed for her tent.

"Jessemia," Owen called after her.

Jessemia stopped. Her shoulders were hunched and tense, and

both hands were clenched. She didn't turn around. "Go ahead, mock me," she said derisively. "When I come into my destiny, we'll see who's mocking who."

"That was good tracking, finding your way back here in the darkness," Owen said.

Jessemia said nothing, but her shoulders tensed even more. Then she pushed through her tent flap and let it fall shut behind her.

CHAPTER THREE

The others all looked at Owen, whose gaze was fixed on Jessemia's tent. "Was that a compliment?" Weston asked in a low voice. "I'm sure it wasn't a compliment."

Owen shrugged. "She got lost trying to find the road to Obsidian, and then she found her way back here. That's deserving of recognition."

"One compliment isn't going to change her," Livia said. "Pandering to her pride is what made her what she is."

"Yeah," Owen said. "You're probably right. Look, why don't you all go back to sleep, and I'll finish my watch."

"I'll stay with you," Aderyn said. "You'd only have to wake me again in half an hour, and it will take me nearly that long to fall asleep."

When she and Owen were alone, she put her arms around his neck and said, "That was a generous thought."

"Livia's right, it won't make a difference."

"Not to her. But it says good things about your character that you were able to say it." She kissed him lightly. "And maybe complimenting her on actual achievements *will* make a difference."

"Hey, you were the one who wanted us to use *polymorph* on her." Owen smiled and drew her closer. "I still don't really care what happens to her, you know. But she's a human being, under all that arrogance, and that will keep me from leaving her to be devoured by wolves."

"That, and the promise of a ten thousand experience reward," Aderyn said.

"Mmm. I love the sound of that."

They separated to walk the perimeter, small as it was. The camp was quiet once more, but when Aderyn passed Jessemia's tent, the door flap twitched shut as if a hand had closed it more securely.

WHEN ADERYN LEFT HER TENT THE NEXT MORNING, Weston had lit the fire and started water boiling for coffee. Jessemia huddled near the fire as if the morning was freezing cold instead of chilly and fresh. Aderyn ignored her and helped herself to more of the bread, still soft. She found a stick and impaled a wedge of cheese on it to toast over the fire until it was nearly runny, then folded the bread around it and took a huge bite. Fresh bread and melted cheese was her favorite breakfast while they were on the road.

She caught Jessemia watching her, though the woman ostentatiously looked away when Aderyn turned. Jessemia's expression, petulant and scornful, made Aderyn want nothing more than to go on eating in front of her. She suppressed her ignoble impulse and said, "Do you want something to eat, Jessemia?"

"*He* said he wasn't going to wait on me," Jessemia said, jerking her head in Weston's direction.

"That's because I'm not your servant," Weston said. He was cutting up the remains of the roast chicken and stirring them into a pot of porridge.

"If you don't like porridge, you can have bread and cheese like me," Aderyn persisted. "It's not hard."

Jessemia sneered. "I'm used to eggs."

"What, while you're adventuring? How did your team manage that?"

"I don't know. That's not something the Fated One needs to worry about." The sneer became audible.

"It's not going to kill you to toast cheese over the fire," Aderyn said. The urge to slap Jessemia was growing stronger. "And I like it better than porridge." She took another bite of her meal. It had started to cool, but the flavors still combined wonderfully.

Jessemia eyed the bread and cheese. Then she idly picked up a stick and poked the fire with it. Aderyn said nothing. Jessemia helped herself to a chunk of cheese and awkwardly wedged it onto the stick.

"Keep an eye on it. If it starts to melt, it can fall off the stick into the fire," Aderyn said.

"I don't need your help," Jessemia retorted.

Aderyn shrugged and went on eating. She caught Weston's eye as her friend tipped ground coffee into the hot water. Weston looked as sour as if he'd tasted the bitter powder straight.

Jessemia squeaked. Aderyn glanced her way just in time to see the cheese fall from Jessemia's stick into the flames. She said nothing, though she was tempted to offer to cook the cheese for Jessemia, not because she wanted to help but because she couldn't bear the thought of food going to waste.

Jessemia, her lips pressed tightly together, picked up another piece of cheese and set about toasting it. This time, she managed not to lose it in the fire. Aderyn helped herself to some of the shredded chicken. Maybe this was a good omen for the day.

Owen emerged from their tent with his mess kit and filled his bowl with porridge. He sat beside Aderyn and dug in silently. Jessemia watched him warily. She ate her bread and cheese without a word, but Aderyn could tell she was waiting for Owen to say something.

"Nice day," Owen said. "Though it looks like rain is coming."

This was so banal Aderyn knew he meant to offer Jessemia a chance to respond politely with something equally inane, like a peace offering. But Jessemia ignored him with the kind of studied indifference that said she still hoped for his gory death.

Isold and Livia joined them around the fire. Weston handed Livia a mug of coffee, which she drank without opening her eyes. "More," she said, holding out the mug.

"You're not one of those people who can't get started in the morning without coffee, are you?" Jessemia said scornfully. "Aren't you embarrassed to be so dependent?"

Livia, her eyes still shut tight, snapped her fingers. A gout of water dropped out of the sky onto Jessemia, soaking her head and sending rivulets of water over her shoulders and back. Jessemia shrieked and leaped to her feet, shaking herself so water flew everywhere and made the fire hiss. Aderyn stifled a laugh.

"How dare you!" Jessemia raged. "I'm the Fated One! You'll regret treating me that way when I come into my destiny."

"Sure I will," Livia said. "Thank you, dearest," she said to Weston as he handed her the refilled mug.

Jessemia let out another strangled noise of fury and stomped away to her tent. "I will not apologize," Livia said.

"No one expects you to," Weston said.

"I'm surprised she's maintaining the Fated One belief," Aderyn said. "You'd think after everything that's happened, she'd realize the truth."

"She needs to cling to something to keep herself going," Isold said. "It's been less than twenty-four hours, and she's been told that fantasy for years. It's going to take more time than that."

"Just so she keeps walking," Owen said. "Though on that note, I've been thinking maybe we need to alter our course. The plan as it stands is to avoid any civilized outposts, villages and towns and the like, so we can maximize the number of monster encounters we have. We might gain more experience taking quests, but with Jessemia along, quests become more complicated. We certainly can't drag her into a dungeon she's underpowered for."

"So why do you want to reconsider that?" Weston asked.

"If she doesn't toughen up, she will definitely slow us down. Maybe we should stop in more towns at first, give her time to rest. If quest opportunities arise, well, we don't have to take them. And with luck, the ten thousand experience from **[Escort the Spoiled Darling]** will compensate for our losses elsewhere."

"It's a good idea," Aderyn said. "And I'm not saying that because I like real beds. These inns in the middle of nowhere never are very comfortable."

"I agree on both counts," Livia said.

"Then I take it you want me to plot us a new route," Isold said. "I'll do what I can, but my **[Map Access]** is spotty in this area."

"We don't have to stay at inns every night, so I'm sure it's fine," Owen said.

Jessemia didn't appear again until the meal was over and Owen called her name. Aderyn was impressed that he only had to call twice to get her out of her tent. "We all take turns cleaning up, morning and night," he told her. "You help Livia wash dishes."

"That's beneath me," Jessemia said. "You're mean to make me do chores. And I don't know how to, anyway."

Owen said nothing. Jessemia's glare faltered, but she stood her ground. Finally, Owen said, "As I said, we all take turns. Livia will teach you what to do."

"I refuse," Jessemia said. "You can't make me."

"Can't I?" Owen said. His tone was mild, but the look in his eye was hard and promised nothing good.

Jessemia tilted her head to face him more directly. "No."

Owen pursed his lips thoughtfully. "You're right. I can't."

"What—" Jessemia's mouth fell open. Then she laughed. "I knew you didn't dare force me. You're weak."

"I can't make you do anything you don't want to do," Owen continued as if she hadn't spoken. "I'm not going to stand over you with a whip and force you to wash dishes. Did you like your breakfast?"

"Did I—what are you talking about?"

"Because if you don't work, that's the last meal you get." Owen still sounded perfectly calm. "Your choice. Help with chores, or see how long you can go without food."

"You wouldn't dare."

Owen took a step forward, forcing Jessemia back. "I am getting tired of repeating myself," he said. "I don't care what happens to you. As far as I'm concerned, you're nothing but an escort mission worth a lot of experience to me and my team. But we're going to Guerdon Deep regardless, and we plan on earning plenty of experience along the way, with or without you. If you travel with us, it's on my terms, not yours."

Jessemia's cheeks were blotchy red with anger. "You—"

"Save it," Owen snapped, shutting her up. "Either help with dishes, or don't, but do it in silence. Nobody here cares about your complaints." He turned his back on her and went back to disassembling the spit.

Jessemia stood frozen where he'd left her, her chest heaving with angry breaths. Aderyn, who'd been packing the <**Knapsack of Plenty**>, watched her fight her inner battle and couldn't guess who the victor would be. Finally, Jessemia stalked to where Livia had summoned water to wash the pots and mess kits and snatched up someone's dirty tin plate. Aderyn stopped watching. Though she didn't like Jessemia, seeing her humiliated made her uncomfortable, like Aderyn's observation made the humiliation worse. Even though Jessemia had brought it all on herself.

Owen brought the pieces of the camp spit to Aderyn and

crouched beside her as she stowed them in the knapsack. "I'd never hit a woman in anger," he said, "not in any circumstance other than battle, but she's testing my limits."

"You're doing the right thing," Aderyn said. "And I love you for your patience."

"I don't feel very patient. More like on the brink of shouting."

"It's what you do that matters, not how you feel."

"My mom always said something like that. You're both very wise." Owen gave Aderyn a hand up. "It's going to rain later. Do you want me to carry your rain cape so you don't have to dig for it?"

"That would be nice, thanks."

By the time they rearranged their loads, Livia and Jessemia had finished washing up, and they all stood outside the ring of tents as Livia used the <**Soldier's Friend**> to break camp. This time, Jessemia didn't shriek, though she did cringe as the whirlwind snatched up the tents. When they set out, Jessemia again straggled behind despite Weston's efforts to make her walk with the others. Aderyn saw his face after she'd rebuffed him a fourth time, and her heart sank. If Weston, normally the most cheerful of them, fell into a terrible mood, that boded ill for the rest of the day.

They walked, rested, walked again. The overcast sky meant the air never warmed, and Aderyn was grateful for her padded coat. She didn't look back to see if Jessemia was keeping warm. Her earlier unwilling sympathy for the woman had evaporated. She'd pissed Owen off, she'd insulted Livia, she'd made Weston angry—as far as Aderyn was concerned, Jessemia didn't deserve any consideration.

Rain began falling about an hour after their midday meal. Aderyn's rain cape was of thin oiled leather that mostly covered her coat, all but the bottom three inches of it. She liked the way the rain tapped on the hood, though to be honest she felt that way because she was conscious of how it kept her dry, not because the tapping wasn't annoying.

Between the noise and the tapping and her lingering irritation over Jessemia, she didn't at first realize they were being followed. The smell of rotting meat came to her nose in whiffs, and when she finally realized she'd smelled it more than once over the last quarter mile, she said, "What is that stink?"

"No idea," Weston said from farther back. "Jessemia, walk closer."

"I don't have to—" Jessemia began.

"*Get down!*" Weston roared.

A huge brindled gray shape flung itself at Jessemia, who screamed and cowered. Weston darted forward to intercept it. Half a dozen more of the creatures loped toward them from the rear and the side. Aderyn Assessed them as she rushed to join him.

Name: Wylding Wolf
Type: Magical Beast
Power Level: 10
Attacks: Bite, Claw x2
Vulnerable to: none
Resistant to: none
Immune to: none
Special attack: confusion

The wylding wolf sows chaos and disorder in its path. It emanates an aura that can confuse its prey, causing victims to become disoriented. Those affected by this confusion behave erratically, sometimes being unable to defend themselves against the wylding wolf, sometimes turning on their allies. Wylding wolves travel in packs of 6 to 8 wolves and work as a team to take down powerful prey. You should feel less self-congratulatory about "powerful" and worry more about "prey," there.

She was about to shout a warning to Weston when she saw him lower his sword and stand still, swaying as if dizzy, as the first wylding wolf bore down on him.

Chapter Four

Jessemia's scream harmonized with the wolf's howl. [**Keep Pace**] dragged Aderyn forward as Owen sprinted toward Weston, but they weren't going to reach him in time. Terrified, she reached within herself, hoping instinct would help where knowledge failed.

The blue lines of [**Discern Weakness**] slid over the monster's rangy body, pinpointing spots on its belly and throat. Another spot, identical to the blue vulnerable spots but yellow, was centered on the wylding wolf's forehead, connected by a fine white line to a similar spot on Weston's chest. Aderyn's palm itched to touch it. Instinct told her this was related to her new skill [**Compel**].

She imagined herself grabbing hold of the yellow spot on Weston's chest and tearing it free. Her fingers closed around something rough and warm, and with the overarm throw Owen had taught her, she tossed the warm yellow spot to strike Owen.

The wylding wolf twisted in midair and leaped, not at Weston, but at Owen. Owen ducked and tumbled to put himself on the wolf's far side from Aderyn, who took advantage of its distraction to strike one of the blue points of light on its belly. For a moment, she heard chiming bells somewhere nearby and wanted to search for them, but a whiff of the stinking monster brought her to herself.

"Don't let them distract you," she boomed out with [Amplify Voice]. "Watch each other! Go for the soft tissues, and—" With a grunt, she delivered a finishing blow. "Keep away from their claws!"

Congratulations! You have defeated [Wylding Wolf]. You have earned [4300 XP]

Isold sang, filling Aderyn with courage and a new sense of competence. *Thunderstomp* knocked three wylding wolves down, and Weston, recovering from his confusion, vaulted over the nearest one to plant a knife deep in its neighbor's eye socket. Again Aderyn saw the system message and blinked it away. She ran with Owen to meet another of the slavering monsters, which rolled over and presented its belly in surrender, whining "Don't kill me!"

Aderyn lowered her sword. She'd never seen anything so pitiful. Then someone screamed her name, startling her. She discovered she was on the ground, her sword five feet away from her, and Owen was shouting at her to wake up. Stunned, she got to her feet.

A new scream startled her again. Jessemia was backed against a tree as a wylding wolf approached her. Aderyn located the yellow spots connecting the two and tore the one centered on Jessemia's chest free. Everyone else was fighting, so with a groan, Aderyn clutched the yellow spot to herself.

Immediately the monster's attention focused on her. Aderyn scrambled to pick up her sword. With a leap, the monster knocked her over, pinned her, and snapped at her throat. Aderyn got her sword between herself and the monster's jaws before they could close on her. Drops of saliva that felt like burning coals dripped on her neck and cheek. She didn't have breath to spare to scream.

Then the monster yelped in pain and drew back. Jessemia stood behind it, her sword extended and dripping with blood where she'd stabbed the wolf. Aderyn took the opportunity to scramble from beneath the wylding wolf. Anger that Jessemia hadn't paid attention to the Warmaster's instructions was crowded out by relief that she wasn't going to die horribly. When the wolf turned on Jessemia, Aderyn once more wrenched its attention to herself. Every time, **[Compel]** became more difficult, like trying to drag something out of a cooling tar pit.

This time, though, she was ready for the monster. She maneuvered it around to where Owen could use **[Outflank]**, and in just seconds he severed its spinal cord with the <**Deadly Blade**> in his off hand. When the system notice faded, Aderyn cast about for another enemy. No living wylding wolves remained. Several bloody bodies sprawled between the trees, one of them crushed by *stone sphere* and then impaled by *iron spikes*. Weston sat with his back against a tree, breathing heavily, while Isold crouched over Livia, whose right arm was bloody. Green light bubbled up and over her wounds, casting both their faces in an eerie green glow.

"Everyone all right?" Owen called. "Aderyn?"

"It caught me in its compulsion effect. Sorry," Aderyn said.

"I know we've always said we should appreciate what we have when we have it, but I cannot help thinking that when we reach level thirteen I will be capable of breaking such a compulsion easily," Isold said.

"Why didn't I get any experience?" Jessemia exclaimed.

Everyone stopped what they were doing to stare at her. "Um... because you didn't kill anything?" Aderyn said.

"I did so. I saved your life. I should have gotten experience for that." Jessemia pulled up a handful of weeds and wiped blood off her sword.

"You did distract it, and I'm grateful, but you didn't land the final blow." Aderyn glanced at Owen, wondering if he was going to intervene.

"I always get experience in fights. It's why I'm advancing so quickly. You must be doing something wrong."

"You're not in our team," Owen said. "So unless you manage to strike the finishing blow on a monster, you won't get experience."

Jessemia's mouth fell open. "But—that's not fair! How am I supposed to level if I don't get experience?"

"Once you reach Guerdon Deep, you can partner with teams of an appropriate level and you'll advance that way," Isold said, sounding kinder than Aderyn felt.

"That's not what Papa says. He says it's my destiny to be the Fated One, so anyone who teams with me will be rewarded. And all my other teams loved me." Jessemia smiled. "You really should add me to your team. I will draw monsters to me for us to fight and level fast. Just like now."

Irritated, Aderyn said, "You're so wrapped up in yourself you don't understand anything, do you? You're not the Fated One. Owen is."

Jessemia's smile became smug and pitying. "That's what he told you so you'd sleep with him, huh? I'm sorry, which of us doesn't understand anything?"

Every drop of sympathy Aderyn had ever had for Jessemia evaporated. She started for the woman, fists raised. "Owen won't hit a woman, but I've got no such reservations. Maybe if I beat—"

"Don't, Aderyn," Owen said. His tone of voice made her stop before she could hit Jessemia. She gazed up at him as he put his hands on her shoulders and drew her into his embrace. Then he kissed her so sweetly she forgot there was anyone in the world but the two of them. She kissed him in return, running her fingers through his hair and down the back of his neck, until he kissed her one final time and took her hands gently in his. Jessemia was staring at the two of them, her expression shocked.

"I don't expect you to recognize love when you see it," Owen said, his voice as gentle as his touch. "Maybe Aderyn is right that you're to be pitied more than disliked. I'm sure you only attacked that wylding wolf because you thought it was a good target, since it was distracted by attacking Aderyn. But whatever your motives, you saved her life, and I'm grateful. Thank you."

He extended a hand to Jessemia, who stared at it like she didn't know what it was. She looked from his hand to his face. For the space of a breath, she looked confused. Then she brushed Owen's hand aside and walked away.

Owen lowered his hand. "Let's keep moving. We've got a few more hours until sunset." He strode after Jessemia, stepping around wolf corpses until he was in the clear.

Aderyn joined him shortly afterward. Jessemia still walked in the lead, though not far enough ahead she was in any danger from another surprise attack. Aderyn leaned in close to Owen and said, "What game are you playing?"

"No game," Owen said. "She saved your life. I was too far away to reach you, and I was sure you were dead—those things seemed attracted to you."

"Oh. That was **[Compel]**. It—" A yawn overtook her. "It requires effort to use, not like **[Outflank]** or **[See It Coming]**. I had to stop the monster going after Jessemia. Twice."

"And now I regret my gratitude. If you only needed your life saved because you'd already saved hers—"

"It doesn't matter, sweetheart." Aderyn sighed. "Why does two days feel like twenty?"

"That was quite the battle, regardless of any complicating factors." Owen hugged her briefly with one arm around her shoulders. "I'm torn between wanting more of them and wishing we never see another monster. When I saw you fall..." His embrace tightened.

"It's fine. Nobody died. We move on."

"I'm sad we won't sleep in a real bed for another three nights. Now that it's over, I'm shaking. I could use the comfort of being held."

"We can do that anyway. And more, if we don't care about everyone hearing us."

Aderyn shuddered. "I don't want Jessemia knowing what we're up to. She'd act so snide about it, and cheapen our love. I'm good at waiting."

"I'm not. But I'll do as you want, because I love you." Owen took her hand, and they walked on.

By sunset, Aderyn's weariness had grown until she was barely putting one foot in front of the other. As soon as camp was set up, Owen guided her to sit in their tent and took the knapsack from her. "Lie down. I'll bring you food."

"I'm not an invalid. I can help."

"You called me Borrus just now and asked if I could come out to play. I don't think you've been fully conscious for the last half mile." Owen smiled. "And I don't think I even look like your brother."

"You don't. Borrus is dark-haired and he has our mother's dark blue eyes. Did I really say that?"

"You really did." Owen finished arranging his gear and gave Aderyn a little push. "And I changed my mind. I'll set food aside and you can eat when it's your turn to watch. Unless you think you need more sleep than that?"

"That really would be too much. Thank you."

She lay down and fell almost instantly asleep. When Owen shook her awake later at the end of his watch, she felt refreshed and hungry. She ate the last of the roast chicken while Owen walked the perimeter, then bade him good night and took his place.

CHAPTER FIVE

The trees were more widely spread here, and Isold had told them they would leave the forests behind in a day or two for the wide plains that spread out between the Pinnalore Mountains and the Welterwall. The air was already drier and warmer than Obsidian, though not at after midnight. Aderyn checked each tent, her own personal ritual to assure herself all her friends were safe where they should be. It was foolishness, because it wasn't as if any of them would sneak away, but this was her little family, and the thought of anything happening to it made her heart ache. So, every night, she checked.

Aderyn bypassed Jessemia's tent without looking in, telling herself Jessemia wasn't part of the family and the entitled snob didn't deserve her care. Then she mentally berated herself. Jessemia wasn't evil, and it mattered that she arrive safely at their destination, if only because of the experience reward.

The tent flap lay open a few inches, and Aderyn stopped there and peered inside, waiting for her eyes to adjust.

"I didn't figure you for someone who peeps at women," Jessemia said from the darkness.

Aderyn flushed. "I'm not. I was making sure you were all right."

"Afraid I'm going to run off again?"

"No. Just being courteous."

"Like you care what happens to me." Jessemia's bitterness filled the air like coffee grounds. "I know you hate me. You all hate me."

"I don't hate you." Aderyn wished she could make that claim for all her friends, but that might be a lie.

"You don't want me here. You think I'm incompetent. You're jealous of me." Jessemia sounded like she was winding up to proclaim a very long list.

Aderyn cut her off. "That's ridiculous. Why would we think you're incompetent *and* be jealous of you?"

"Because you know I'm the Fated One, and the Fated One does things that people don't understand. So you think less of me because I don't know how to wash a stupid tin plate, as if that mattered to my destiny."

Aderyn shook her head. Instead of challenging Jessemia, she said, "How did you decide you're the Fated One?"

"Papa studied the stories of the time before the level cap," Jessemia said. "He knows everything about it. And he realized that all the signs that proclaim the Fated One's identity describe me. Come from beyond the lands we know—Obsidian is as far from civilization as it's possible to get. Dancing on the knife's edge—I've always been good with a sword."

Aderyn had seen Jessemia fight and doubted this statement, but she said nothing.

"This was even before I got the Call," Jessemia said. She was sounding more excited and less petulant by the moment. "So when the system made me a Pathseer, Papa started generating quests. At first, I went into the wilderness with my chosen companions, who guarded me and found the right kind of monsters around Obsidian. Then he created quests just for me that I could do by myself. I've leveled faster than anyone ever has!"

Again, Aderyn wasn't sure this was true. She and her friends had reached level eleven in a matter of weeks, and that had to be faster than Jessemia. "Why does leveling fast matter?"

"I—what do you mean?" Jessemia sounded genuinely puzzled.

"I mean, it's not like your levels are more meaningful, or you get more skills, just because you gained them quickly. The only point to leveling fast is to get yourself out of the safe zone so you can have real adventures sooner."

"I wouldn't expect *you* to understand," Jessemia sneered.

Aderyn sighed. And they'd been doing so well. "Fine. You leveled fast. What's the goal?"

"To achieve the Fated One's destiny, of course!" Jessemia made it sound like Aderyn was mentally deficient not to have figured this out.

"And that destiny is... what?"

"Well, I," Jessemia said, and fell silent. "It will be evident when I achieve it."

"So you don't know what the Fated One is supposed to do in achieving his—all right, or her—destiny? No idea what responsibilities or tasks it includes?"

"Of course not! That's ridiculous." But she didn't sound certain.

"I see." Aderyn didn't know why she'd started this conversation, which was now both boring and pointless. "All right. I guess there's nothing more to say."

"So you believe me?"

Aderyn didn't think Jessemia should be that enthusiastic. Her eagerness embarrassed Aderyn. "Um, no, of course not. I just understand you a little better now."

"It doesn't matter what you believe. I am the Fated One." Jessemia sounded smug again. Aderyn felt weariness creeping back into her bones.

"Thanks again for saving my life," she said, and turned away.

"Why do you let that man boss you around? He's mean and horrible and he doesn't care if I die." The pouting sound was back.

"I don't let him boss me around," Aderyn said, irritated all over again. "I follow him because he's a good leader and he cares about his team, and I listen to his suggestions because I love him and that's how love works. And if he really didn't care if you died, you'd be dead already." She crossed the campsite rapidly, not caring where she went, just wanting to get away from Jessemia.

She stayed well away from the tents, just in case, until it was time to wake Weston for the final watch. Then she returned to her own tent and curled up beside Owen, who woke briefly and put his arms around her. She let him hold her and tried to stop remembering Jessemia's careless, stupid words. They were too stupid to matter, and it wasn't as if Aderyn was going to revisit every interaction she'd ever had with her sweetheart, looking for signs that he was bossy and a bully. No, it was Jessemia's perception of him she wished she could change. Owen had gone out of his way to help her, and she didn't realize she ought to be thankful.

"Aderyn, why aren't you asleep?" Owen murmured.

"Why aren't *you?*"

"Because you keep twitching. Did something happen that keeps you from relaxing?"

"Just stupid Jessemia. I don't know why I let her get to me. She doesn't know how lucky she is to have you looking out for her."

"Is that what I'm doing? Damn, I must be slipping. Where's the rope? Let me show you what hog-tying looks like."

Aderyn laughed. "I'm serious, Owen. She's so—what is it you always say? Clueless? She's so clueless she doesn't even realize how crippled she is as an adventurer, let alone as a Fated One."

"So stop worrying about it. We can't change her however we treat her, so we shouldn't worry about if we fail." Owen kissed her, his lips warm on hers. His hands worked their way beneath her shirt. "I changed my mind. I can't bear waiting for a real bed."

"What happened to doing what I want?" Aderyn slipped her hands around his waist and caressed the smooth skin of his back.

"Oh, according to popular opinion, I am a selfish monster who doesn't care what others think, and I intend to relax you my way, whatever you may say to resist me." He kissed her cheek, then returned to kissing her lips.

"A selfish monster, huh?" Aderyn kissed him back. "Then I guess I shouldn't say anything at all."

ANOTHER RAINSTORM THE FOLLOWING MORNING, THIS one harder, made them all decide on a late start. Aderyn huddled in her tent with Owen and watched the campfire. It continued to burn regardless of the rain that made it hiss and smoke. "I guess it makes sense a magical fire would be proof against rain," she said absently.

"I'm glad for the alarm spell on the camp boundaries," Owen said. "I mean, I wouldn't trust our lives to it, and standing watch is smart, but at times like this I really don't want to walk the perimeter."

Aderyn's gaze shifted to Jessemia's tent, pitched opposite theirs. The tent flap was open, but Jessemia wasn't visible. "I wonder what she's doing."

"Who, Jessemia? Probably plotting some other way to make my life hell." Owen's arms encircled Aderyn from behind, and he rested his chin on her shoulder. "I still haven't forgiven her for her ingratitude over you saving her from the wylding wolves."

"She doesn't know about **[Compel]**, so she doesn't know she should be grateful. Besides, she saved me as well."

Owen sighed. "I don't know how you manage to be so relentlessly forgiving of that woman. It might be a mistake. Suppose she takes advantage of it, and you end up hurt?"

"I'm not *that* forgiving," Aderyn protested. "And I don't always explain away her bad behavior. She makes me angry sometimes. I can just see her side occasionally, that's all."

"Well, don't expect me to follow suit. I love you, and I love your optimism, but I don't believe Jessemia has it in her to change. She's got no motivation to."

Aderyn couldn't think of a response. Owen had a point, but— no, he was right, and Aderyn needed to stop giving Jessemia more credit than she earned.

They watched the rain in silence until the downpour tapered off and the sun peeped out of the clouds. Rays of light struck the wet tents and their guy ropes, beaded with rain, and made everything shiny and fresh. Aderyn emerged from her tent and stretched. "It's not that late a start, is it? Livia, what's the time?"

"Almost ten-thirty," Livia said from inside her tent. Aderyn heard the rustling sound of people hastily donning clothing and armor and smiled. So Livia and Weston had taken advantage of the sound of the rain to conceal other activities.

She walked over to Jessemia's tent and said, "Jessemia? You should start packing up. We will want to be on the road soon."

Jessemia didn't respond. Aderyn twitched open the tent flap a fraction and peeked inside. Jessemia was gone.

Aderyn instinctively looked around, though they'd camped in a wide clearing with no cover for anything larger than a fox. "Jessemia?"

"Isn't she in her tent?" Owen said as he came up behind Aderyn.

Aderyn shook her head. "Jessemia! Where are you?"

Owen squeezed his eyes shut and cursed. "She has to have left before dawn. We'd have seen her otherwise. Weston, was Jessemia in her tent when you stood watch?"

Weston approached, doing up the laces of his trousers. "I don't know. I didn't check the tents. It was starting to rain, so I didn't figure anyone would go anywhere in that weather."

"Which is a reasonable assumption. And now we have to track down our missing bundle of experience." Owen ran his hands through his hair impatiently.

"Well, don't look at me," Weston said. "There's no way I can find her after this rain. Too bad the Pathseer is the one who's gone, because it would take a Pathseer to track someone in this mess."

"I'll get the <**Wayfinder**>," Aderyn said.

She extracted the steel ball from her <**Purse of Great Capacity**> and held it in her hands, warming it without activating it. The concentric rings of different metals, copper and silver and brass, quivered with pent-up energy as if it knew it was going to be called on to do its job soon. Aderyn sat with her legs crossed under her and thought of Jessemia, of her petulant face in its near-permanent scowl, her tangled chestnut curls, her increasingly dirty clothes that were completely unsuited to the wilderness.

To her relief, this time the <**Wayfinder**> worked, its main spike warming to a rosy glow in seconds. Aderyn rose and left her tent, walking slowly with her head down over the ball. Just as slowly, she turned in a complete circle near the firepit, concentrating on Jessemia. When she was certain she had the right direction, she called to the others. "I can find her. I hope."

"Are we sure we want to?" Livia asked. "Seriously, now. This is the second time she's run away, and while I agree we don't want to leave her out here to die, isn't there a limit to how much effort we're required to put in to dragging her ass to Guerdon Deep?"

"We won't leave anyone behind, including the spoiled darling," Owen said. "And this is a dangerous area for anyone on their own regardless of their level." He put a hand on Aderyn's elbow. "Let's go. Maybe this won't take long. I'm not sure she could get far in the rain."

Aderyn nodded and started walking.

She was rarely aware of her surroundings when she was focused on the <Wayfinder> and needed someone, usually Owen or Isold, to walk with her and keep her from running into trees. Keeping her heart's desire centered on Jessemia was particularly hard. The ground was muddy and shifted unpleasantly underfoot, raindrops from the tree branches dripped on her constantly, and since her head was bent, most of those raindrops went down her collar. She considered pointing out to Owen that for once she wasn't making excuses for Jessemia. When they found the woman, Aderyn intended to make sure she knew just how stupid she'd been.

The <Wayfinder> continued to warm and grow brighter, but it wasn't until Isold said, "Jessemia!" that Aderyn realized they'd reached their goal. She lowered the metal sphere and rotated her neck to ease the stiffness.

They had arrived at a small stream that wove its way between the trees, burbling as its path took it over piles of river stones that changed its tune. Jessemia stood with her hand on a tree trunk, as casually as if she'd been out for a stroll in some rich person's pleasure garden. But her hair was more disheveled than usual, soaking wet and plastered to her head, and her shirt and vest were similarly soaked through. Dead needles clung to her boots as if she'd trudged through drifts of them. She looked exhausted, and some of Aderyn's irritation faded.

"Are you out of your mind?" Owen demanded. "I mean, literally out of your mind? Because only a crazy person would go out in the rain like that. Were you that desperate to escape us?"

Jessemia had looked uncertain, but at Owen's words her chin firmed up and her head tilted in a challenging way. "Of course you'd assume that," she said. "Obviously I'm too stupid to come in out of the rain, is that it? Well, that's fine. I'm stupid. Now I'm going to get changed before you drag me off on this miserable journey again."

She stalked away, but Owen grabbed her arm and brought her to a halt. "You already know I don't care one way or the other what you think of us. But going out alone is risky. You may not care what happens to us, but you can't be so foolhardy as to not care what happens to yourself."

Jessemia yanked her arm out of Owen's grip. "It's none of your business what I do. Leave me alone, you bully." She walked away, increasing her pace until she was almost running through the trees.

CHAPTER SIX

Aderyn watched Jessemia go. That had been a strange interaction even by Jessemia's standards. She hoped the woman was at least headed back to camp.

"Owen," Weston said, "look at this." He pointed at a depression on the bank of the stream. "Something was here. Something big. It came to the river to drink."

"What do you mean?" Owen squinted at the mark. "What was it?"

"I don't know. Could have been an animal, but I doubt it. More likely some monster. And—" He stepped back and surveyed the surrounding trees, then reached high and plucked a shred of fabric from the place where a thick branch sprouted from an even thicker trunk. The fabric was dirty, but still obviously blue silk. "Jessemia was up there."

They all stood in silence for a moment. "Up in the tree," Aderyn said. "Why would she do that? Do you think she saw the monster?"

"I don't know. It's too big a coincidence if she came out here for some other reason and stumbled on a monster. And how would she have avoided being attacked?" Weston rubbed the scrap of fabric between finger and thumb. "If I could track it, I could tell where it came from, and where it went. But—"

"But, what?" Owen asked.

Weston shook his head. "I find it hard to believe, but it's possible Jessemia tracked it out here and watched it until it went away."

"That's crazy," Livia said. "Why wouldn't she tell one of us? She's not a strong enough fighter to face anything big by herself."

"She might not have had time," Isold said. "Suppose she heard it and decided to follow it... though I can't imagine why she would care."

"Unless it was a threat to our camp," Aderyn said.

The others stared at her. "You mean, she was protecting us?" Owen said.

"I don't know. That might not be true. But it's possible, right?" Aderyn didn't know where this theory came from. Maybe Owen was right, and her desire to make excuses for Jessemia was irrational.

"It's possible," Owen said, "but really unlikely. And I'm not sure it matters."

"It matters if it means she did something unselfish." Aderyn sighed. "I'm sorry. I'm making up stories now. I don't know what Jessemia was thinking."

"I don't know if it's all that unlikely, Owen," Isold said. "She wouldn't explain what she was doing out here, and that might mean she was embarrassed at having pursued a threat that ended up being nothing."

"All right," Owen said, "all right. It's possible. But I don't see what we can do about it."

"I'll talk to her," Aderyn said. "Maybe she'll be open with me."

"She doesn't respect you any more than she does the rest of us, but go ahead and try," Owen said.

They returned to the camp to find Jessemia changed into dry clothes, combing her hair. She wouldn't look at any of them. "I'm packed, not that you care," she said.

"Let's get moving, then," Owen said.

Aderyn waited until the **<Soldier's Friend>** had finished its work and everyone had set out. Then she dropped back to walk beside Jessemia, who as usual lagged behind. "Why did you leave camp this morning?"

"Like you care," Jessemia sniffed. "Don't pretend I matter to you. I don't believe it."

"Were you following a monster?" Aderyn persisted. "Something you thought was a threat to the camp?"

Jessemia shrugged. "Why would I do something that stupid? You must be stupid yourself to imagine a story like that."

Aderyn ignored the pulse of anger that shot through her at Jessemia's dismissive words. "I don't think it's a story. Jessemia, why didn't you tell anyone? We would have helped."

Jessemia was silent.

"Look," Aderyn said, "I don't know for sure what happened. But if you went out there to protect us from a threat, I appreciate it."

"I don't care," Jessemia said. "Stop trying to be nice to me. I know it's a lie."

Aderyn gave up. "Fine. You don't care about gratitude, that's fine. But I know what happened, and I think you're embarrassed because you've been rude and awful and now you've done something nice. Don't bother doing anything like it again."

She ran to catch up to Owen, who walked point. Owen said, "Well?"

"You were right. She's a terrible person who doesn't know how to accept thanks."

"I wish I'd been wrong. Imagine if your perception of her was reality."

"That's never going to happen," Aderyn said.

She stayed away from Jessemia all that day and into the next, feeling unexpectedly humiliated and hurt whenever she saw the woman. Humiliated, because she'd defended Jessemia to her friends, insisted she was capable of change, and she'd been proven completely wrong. It didn't matter that no one would criticize her or make fun of her for her mistake; she was deeply embarrassed, as if she'd exposed her innermost self to the world and had it savaged.

She was walking near Owen when he slowed to a halt. "What's that up ahead?"

Aderyn squinted. "Looks like an animal. A dog or a wolf."

"A dog," Owen said. "And it's hurt. Listen to its whining." He drew his sword. "Like I believe someone's pet is lost out here, miles from any settlement. It's an illusion."

"Cave bladders," Aderyn agreed, drawing her own sword and scanning the treetops.

"Watch out for an attack," Owen shouted. "In the trees—cave bladders!"

The "dog" vanished. In the next moment, something big and blubbery swung out of the trees on its fat tentacles. Its greenish skin glistened wetly, turning Aderyn's stomach. Then they were surrounded.

Aderyn waited for Owen to tumble past into a position for **[Outflank]** and then swung at one of the grotesque tentacles. Her sword glanced off the tough hide, but it swiveled toward her, exposing its enormous, vulnerable eyes. She thrust at the closest eye, making the cave bladder squeal in pain as she impaled it. It jerked away right into Owen's reach. With another powerful thrust, Owen skewered it through the other eye, making blood and fluids gush.

Congratulations! You have defeated [Cave Bladder]. You have earned [1000 XP]

The sound of screaming, human rather than monstrous, distracted Aderyn. Owen darted past her. "Jessemia's bolting," he shouted. "We have to stop her before she runs into any more of these things."

Aderyn raced after him, **[Keep Pace]** dragging her along rapidly until she caught up. Jessemia had dropped her sword and was fleeing right into the embrace of a cave bladder that swung out of the trees practically on top of her. Owen leaped and tackled Jessemia, bringing her down inches from the cave bladder's tentacles. Aderyn put herself between them and the monster, waiting for her moment. The cave bladder hauled itself into the trees, and for a moment, Aderyn thought it was retreating. Then two of its tentacles lashed out, wrapping around Aderyn and squeezing.

Her sword fell from her hands as her arms were bound to her side. She gasped, but no air reached her lungs. She couldn't even cry for help. Distantly, she was aware of Owen smacking the tentacles impotently with his sword blade, but her brain was fogging over and she couldn't remember where she was or why her chest hurt so badly.

Then a rush of energy filled her body, and she found herself climbing free of the cave bladder's hold as if its tentacles were slippery. She saw Livia nearby, chanting and gesturing as she cast *loose bonds*. Aderyn sucked in a wonderful lungful of air that stank of cave bladder and ran to put herself out of its reach. A system defeat notice appeared, and then another one popped up as Owen pierced one of those giant eyes all the way to the brain behind it.

And then the fight was over. Aderyn retrieved her sword and rubbed her ribcage. No ribs were broken, to her surprise. It had felt like the cave bladder intended to squeeze her until she shattered.

She walked to where Livia was casting *drench* to clean cave bladder guts off Owen's arms. "Is everyone all right?" Owen called out.

"We're fine," Isold said. "Though I didn't realize cave bladders were immune to certain mind-affecting skills, so it's as well there were only three of them."

"Three? It felt like a dozen," Aderyn said. Now that the fight was over, she remembered the sight of the monsters silhouetted against the sky and shuddered. True, she and her team were better equipped to fight them than they'd been the first time they encountered the creatures, but the cave bladders' horrible skin and grasping tentacles and enormous bulging eyes were the stuff of her nightmares.

Owen turned on Jessemia, who stood nearby, breathing heavily and looking panicked. "You shouldn't have run," he said. "Cave bladders pick off anything that flees. They're drawn to that movement."

"Like I knew that," Jessemia pouted. Her lips were trembling. "None of you care if I die. I have to take care of myself."

Owen closed his eyes, visibly fighting for calm. Then he said, "We won't let you die. I know you think I'm a monster, but I'm not inhuman, Jessemia. You shouldn't think that."

"You say that," Jessemia said, "but you've never done anything to prove otherwise. I hate you." She stomped away, through where the rest of them gathered, and stopped about fifteen feet from Aderyn, her arms wrapped around her chest and her body shaking.

Aderyn started toward Jessemia, but Isold put a restraining hand on her arm. "Don't," he said in a low voice. "She's angry and embarrassed that she did the wrong thing, and she's furious that Owen rescued her. She needs to deal with those emotions by herself."

"Oh," Aderyn said. "But—"

"No, Aderyn. Let it go." Isold's normally calm voice sounded strained. "There's nothing you can do to fix this."

"I don't want to fix her."

"Don't you?"

Aderyn didn't have an answer for that.

"WE COULD LEAVE HER IN THE NEXT TOWN," ADERYN TOLD Owen the next day as they walked at the head of the group. The trees had thinned to the point that you couldn't really call it a forest anymore, more like a plain with plenty of available timber. "She'd be safe there."

"And we wouldn't get ten thousand experience," Owen pointed out. "Call me mercenary, but I do kind of love experience."

"I also love not listening to her whine. And not listening to her complain about the food. Also, did I mention that I hate the whining?"

"I thought you were sympathetic to her plight."

Aderyn rolled her eyes. "I still am, but I'd be a lot more sympathetic if she was somewhere else to be safely pitied."

"We can endure. Isold! Is something wrong?"

"Not as such." Isold usually walked near the middle of the group, where everyone could hear his inspiring battle music easily, but now he advanced to join them. "We'll reach Plensholt in a few hours. Well before dark."

"Yes, but I didn't think anyone would gripe if we stopped early. You sound like you have something on your mind."

"Well." Isold cleared his throat. "We aren't likely to get many rooms to suit our team's needs. I wondered if we might take just two. Men in one, women in the other."

"You... um, why? That's sort of a strange request."

"I realize it inconveniences the couples, and that you might have expected privacy. I can only say that I would prefer it to be otherwise."

"Isold, you only talk like that when you're hiding something behind elevated language," Owen said. "You'll have to be more specific."

"I was hoping to avoid that. It's a delicate matter."

"Oh!" Aderyn said. "Did you want... no, that can't be right. If you wanted privacy for yourself, this is the opposite. Isold, please just tell us."

Isold cleared his throat again. "I'll need you to promise not to overreact."

"Isold!" Owen said, then lowered his voice as Isold shushed him. "Fine. Just tell us before the suspense kills us."

Isold glanced over his shoulder as if gauging how far away everyone else was. "Last night, I had a visitor. When I finished my watch and returned to my tent, Jessemia was there. In my bedroll. Wearing not a stitch."

Aderyn gasped. Owen let out a snort of laughter. Isold glared at them. "This is not funny."

"It's not," Owen agreed. "I apologize. I take it you booted her out the door?"

"With a great deal of delicacy and tact," Isold said. "I judge Jessemia to be rather fragile in her ego, and if she had meant her visit as a mark of her genuine interest in me, I would have been hard pressed to turn her down without hurting her."

"You don't think it was sincere?" Aderyn said.

"Not even a little. I have, with no false modesty, a great deal of experience with receiving come-ons much more direct than that. She clearly meant to seduce me to her side, gain my support against you, Owen, and use that attachment to drive wedges between all of us. Which meant a different kind of tactful rejection."

Aderyn had seen Isold angry before, but never like this. His marvelous voice, always melodic, was hard and flat without a hint of music. "That's horrible," she offered.

"It's sexual harassment is what it is," Owen said, sounding nearly as angry as Isold. "What do you want us to do?"

"Sexual harassment, what an appropriate phrase," Isold said, and a little of his anger fell away. "If not for my sense that she is too naïve and ignorant to realize the magnitude of what she tried, I would say we should leave her at the first possible safe place. But she is in most respects an innocent, and I choose not to take offense as deeply as I might."

"Yeah, but we can't spend the next seven weeks keeping her out of your tent, Isold," Owen said. "I mean, sure, we can get only two rooms in Plensholt, but that just pushes the problem back a step."

"I intend that as reinforcement of the conversation I plan to have with her tonight. I feel confident I can convince her that she has no chance with me and should stop trying." Isold glanced around again, prompting Aderyn to do the same. Livia was still some distance away, with Weston and Jessemia bringing up the rear. "I apologize for the disruption."

"Don't apologize. You shouldn't have to put up with being treated like a thing," Aderyn said.

"I appreciate your support. I half feared one or both of you would think I should have been thrilled at the prospect of another sexual encounter. But there's nothing exciting about knowing the person you're sleeping with sees you only as a means to an end." Isold nodded in farewell and retreated to his usual position.

"I feel awful," Aderyn said when he was out of earshot. "I did sort of think that at first. I mean, Isold likes sex, and he finds pretty much every woman attractive in her own way—but I understand him, I think, about being used."

"Yes, and I honestly don't see the appeal. Of Jessemia. She's too selfish." Owen strode faster. "Let's get to Plensholt and see if it's even a problem. We might find ourselves sleeping in a hayloft."

CHAPTER SEVEN

Plensholt wasn't as tiny as Aderyn feared. She'd expected a handful of farm houses, maybe a tavern or a store, with a token wall whose existence would trigger the system's protections against the most aggressive monsters. Instead, the friends began encountering farmsteadings well before Plensholt came into sight, big stone houses and barns surrounded by fields of grain. Farm workers eyed them cautiously, and when Aderyn Assessed them, she discovered they were almost all retired adventurers, none of them lower than level nine. Her first impression of these farms as vulnerable to monster attacks died.

By the time the light was ruddy and the path through the farmlands had become a real road, Plensholt and its wall were visible in the distance. **[Improved Assess 2]** showed nothing more than the town's name and status as a village. Maybe settlements this small didn't have more information for the skill to reveal. Aderyn examined it by eye instead. The ramshackle wall stood no more than five feet tall, built of the same stones that separated the farmsteading properties. It wouldn't deter a serious assault, but again, its purpose was likely just to define the village for the system's purposes.

There wasn't a gate in the wall, either, just a gap wide enough for a farm wagon to pass through. A woman wearing hardened leather armor stood beside the gap. She idly spun a wrist-thick staff in her hands, back and forth, blocking and parrying an imaginary opponent. Aderyn Level Assessed her.

Name: Sessa

Class: Staffsworn (retired)

Level: 10

When Owen was within speaking distance, she said, "What's your purpose, travelers?"

"Travel," Owen said. "We're on our way to Guerdon Deep and hoped to spend the night in Plensholt."

Sessa grounded her staff and examined the companions. "You'll find rooms at the Lone Pine. Don't start trouble and you'll find none here. Plensholt is full of retired adventurers who take exception to wild sorts thinking they can disrupt a peaceful community. Got it?"

"We do." Owen saluted her. "Which way to the Lone Pine?"

"There's only one street. You'll see it." She stepped ostentatiously to one side as if opening the nonexistent gate. "Welcome to Plensholt."

There was only one street, and the shops of Plensholt lined up neatly along it. Aderyn assumed they were shops. Only a couple of them bore signs advertising what was available inside. However, all of them were busy with people entering and leaving in a way Aderyn associated with business rather than home life.

The Lone Pine was obvious because it was one of the few buildings bearing a sign, and that sign was of a caricature of a pine tree with arms and legs, quaffing a tankard of ale. The delicious smell of roast beef wafted from its open door, rousing Aderyn's appetite, though it was still a few hours to sunset and a reasonable dinnertime.

Inside, the dimly-lit taproom smelled even better, with the scent of good dark ale twining with the roast beef. Only two women sat at the bar, far enough apart it was clear they weren't together. One glanced at the friends as they entered and then returned her attention to her mug.

A portly woman in a white apron came around the end of the bar and met them halfway across the taproom. "What can I do for you?"

"We would like rooms for the night," Isold said. "And a meal."

"Fair enough. How many rooms?"

"Just two, if they're big enough."

The woman nodded. "Two beds to a room, big enough to sleep two each. That good enough for you?" She sounded skeptical, like she thought Isold was stingy for wanting to pack each room as full as possible.

"That will work, thank you. That smells delicious. Is it dinner?"

"It is," the woman said with a smile that revealed a charming dimple. She let out a piercing whistle, and the door beside the bar swung open, revealing an attractive young woman whose dimple matched the woman's. "Celia, show these folks upstairs. Rooms two and six. That'll be twenty silver for the rooms and another six for dinner."

Aderyn paid, reflecting that the exorbitant exchange rate they'd paid to convert their Obsidian coin to standard still hadn't eaten much into what was left of their five thousand gold after paying off Virros the Rock and equipping themselves for the overland journey. Still, it was better they conserve their money. Obsidian to Guerdon Deep, Guerdon Deep to Finion's Gate—if they didn't have the opportunity to earn money along the way, the <**Purse of Great Capacity**> would be as flat as it appeared by the time their journey was over.

She trailed along at the rear of the group, her hand in her purse, counting coin by touch. The Lone Pine and the other buildings reminded her of Far Haven, which was a bigger town than Plensholt, but had the same rustic, comfortable feeling. Pine paneling gave the inn a homey look and a reassuring scent, and the brightly colored woven carpet that ran the length of the second floor hall made the inn look more like someone's home than a public building.

The upper floor was warmer than below, as if it clutched the heat of late summer to itself. None of the doors were numbered, but the girl, Celia, opened the first door off the stairs, then continued down the hall to open the last door on the right. "Hope that's enough room," she said, sounding as skeptical as her mother.

"It suits us, thank you," Isold said with a friendly smile.

Celia blushed and cast her eyes down, then hurried back down the stairs. Owen shook his head in mock despair. Aderyn expected him to joke about Isold's potential to leave a trail of broken hearts across the plains to Guerdon Deep, but he just said, "I think we're safe to leave our things here. Everyone get settled, and let's see about some drinks before dinner."

In the women's room, which was as stuffy and warm as the hall, Jessemia dropped her knapsack on one of the beds and declared, "I hope you don't expect me to share a bed with one of you."

Aderyn and Livia exchanged glances. "Wouldn't dream of it," Livia said. She dug around in her knapsack for a hairbrush. "Aderyn, is there water in that pitcher? I want to wash up a bit."

Aderyn checked. "No."

Livia summoned water that fell in a splash into the pitcher and basin. "Too bad *drench* is so cold," she said, scooping water to splash on her face.

"I refuse to use that water after you," Jessemia said, a whine edging her words.

"I could provide you with your own shower," Livia said, raising a hand as if to cast a spell.

Jessemia squeaked and fled.

Livia sighed and made room for Aderyn at the basin. "I take it our cramped quarters are to keep her from going after Isold."

"You know about that?"

"Know about what? You mean, she tried something already?"

Livia wiped her face with the tail of her shirt. "I just know she's been eyeing Isold like he was a fortress she was bent on conquering."

"Yes, this is to help Isold discourage her. Sorry you don't get privacy."

"It's fine. I don't envy Isold. Jessemia's a viper."

Aderyn washed her face and then borrowed Livia's hairbrush to tidy her hair. "You don't think she's more pitiful than evil?"

Livia shrugged. "Pitiable, maybe. She's too ignorant to be truly, maliciously evil. But selfishness can still hurt others. She gets no sympathy from me."

"I guess I'm too much an optimist. I keep thinking, suppose she could change? She'd be so much happier."

"You can't make people change, Aderyn. That has to be their choice." Livia accepted the hairbrush and put it away. "But you have a good heart to wish that for her after everything she's done."

"That's better than being foolishly optimistic, I guess."

She and Livia found the others seated at a table downstairs. All but Jessemia, who sat alone at a table on the other side of the room, ostentatiously ignoring the team. The men didn't look like they cared that they were being ignored. Aderyn sat beside Owen and drank deeply from the tankard of dark ale at her place. "This is really good," she exclaimed. "I didn't expect high-quality food and drink from such a small village."

"A small village populated by mid-level retired adventurers," Isold said. "The innkeeper, Gladyn, is a level twelve Spiritsmith. I imagine her skills are easily turned to brewing excellent ale."

"I didn't think to Assess her," Aderyn said. She took another drink, relishing how smoothly it went down. "I'm so glad we stopped here."

"I wish—" Weston glanced at Livia, then at Jessemia. "It's not important."

"I apologize for disrupting this night," Isold said.

"Don't you apologize," Aderyn said. "It's that stupid woman's fault."

"I will talk to her before we retire tonight," Isold said grimly. "That should resolve the matter."

The door to the kitchen banged open, and the most delicious aroma filled the taproom. The young woman brought a tray to their table and passed out plates of roast beef, piles of roasted root vegetables, and small loaves of bread split down the middle and spread with fresh butter. "Is your friend not joining you?" she asked, glancing at Jessemia.

"She isn't—" Owen jerked as Aderyn gently kicked him beneath the table. "That is, she prefers to eat alone."

The girl looked like she thought this was strange, but said nothing more. As she left to serve Jessemia, Aderyn said, "We should at least act like we're united. I mean, doesn't it make us look weak if we're not on friendly terms?"

"Yeah, you're right," Owen said. "And it's ungentlemanly of me to snipe at Jessemia to outsiders." He picked up knife and fork and attacked his meal. "This is incredible."

Aderyn agreed. The beef was tender and juicy, the vegetables had a honey glaze that was just the right amount of sweet, and the bread, while clearly of this morning's baking and therefore not warm, was soft and delicious.

The taproom door slammed open, startling Aderyn into fumbling her fork. A handful of men, dressed in the haphazard manner that meant they were adventurers, strolled into the room and approached the bar. The innkeeper, Gladyn, looked up from where she was polishing glasses. Her smile became fixed, the expression of someone not sure what welcome she ought to give a newcomer.

"Ale," the man at the head of the pack said. He had a strong, pleasant voice almost as nice as Isold's, but bass rather than tenor. "And whatever delicious meal I smell."

Gladyn's expression relaxed a little. "Certainly. Have a seat, you and your friends."

Aderyn reflexively Assessed the man, and froze. She gripped Owen's thigh beneath the table. "That man," she said, Assessing the rest of the newcomers as she spoke. "What class do you see?"

Owen glanced at the man. "Swordsworn. Level fourteen. Why?"

Aderyn shook her head. In a low voice, she said, "They're all Brigands."

CHAPTER EIGHT

Owen's hand closed more tightly on his belt knife. "All of them?"

Aderyn nodded. "What do we do?"

"Nothing," Owen said. "They haven't done anything overtly evil, and they believe their true class is still a secret. We keep an eye on them—"

Weston swore softly. "Jessemia."

Aderyn swiveled. The Brigand spokesman was standing next to Jessemia's table, speaking to her in a voice too low for Aderyn to make out the words, but Jessemia was smiling and laughing and tossing her chestnut curls in a coquettish manner. "We have to warn her," Aderyn said.

"How?" Weston said. "If we reveal that we know these fellows are Brigands, that will probably start a fight, and from what I can see, they're all level thirteen or fourteen. And there are nine of them. Even if we won that fight, we'd destroy this inn, and I don't want to do that to the nice lady who brews such fantastic ale."

"I doubt Jessemia's in any danger," Owen said. "If the Brigands came in incognito, they don't intend mayhem. That guy will flirt with her, and frankly I am fine with someone else keeping her occupied for a while."

"But—" Aderyn cast another, less overt glance at Jessemia and the Brigand. He had taken a seat next to her and was beckoning for ale for both of them. "You're both right, I know. It just feels wrong."

"If I'm wrong, and the Brigands want to start a fight, we'll reevaluate," Owen said. "Now, enjoy your meal. We'll keep an eye on Jessemia, just in case, but I really think everything is going to be fine."

Aderyn tried to eat, but the food no longer tasted quite so appetizing and her stomach felt full of acid. She made herself take a few more bites, out of respect for the cook's genius, but then she pushed her plate away and drank down the last of her ale. Jessemia was laughing at something the Brigand was saying. The man had his back to Aderyn, but he was broad-shouldered and had long brown hair he wore tied back with a leather thong at the nape of his neck. Either he was charming, or Jessemia enjoyed flirting, or both—but it didn't matter, because Owen was right, there was no danger.

She waved at the girl for another drink. With Brigands around, she didn't want to get drunk, but the ale was really good, and two could be her limit. With luck, it would settle her stomach. The Brigands seated themselves at tables near their spokesman—their leader? —who sat alone with Jessemia at her table. None of them did anything overtly evil, but Aderyn felt uncomfortable anyway.

She drank in silence, listening to the others talk about nothing much, and set her empty mug down just as Isold said, "I will ask Gladyn if she would like me to perform tonight. If we're wrong, and hostilities arise, I will be in a position to soothe spirits."

His words reassured Aderyn. So she wasn't the only one worried.

Isold spoke to Gladyn, then left the room, returning a few minutes later with his drum. The fireplace was empty at this season, but he drew up a stool in front of it anyway and started tapping his drum, testing the sound before going into a merry ballad with a mildly ribald chorus. The music soothed Aderyn's spirits, though her stomach still hurt.

The Brigands all became alert when Isold began singing, all except their leader, who was still intent on Jessemia. When the song ended, the Brigands hooted and stomped their approval, and a few of them called out requests for other songs. They didn't act at all as Aderyn expected an evil class to behave. Well, even Brigands benefited from neutral ground, and tearing up an inn meant not getting its services.

Just as Aderyn returned her attention to Jessemia and the Brigand leader, Jessemia looked around. She caught Aderyn's eye and smiled, a nasty, triumphant expression that irritated Aderyn. As if she cared whether Jessemia captivated someone.

As the hours passed, Aderyn's stomach continued to ache sharply, and her tension increased until even her favorite songs performed by Isold couldn't calm her. She couldn't stop watching Jessemia, whose flirtation had progressed to casual caresses, the touch of a hand, all things that to Aderyn seemed like a really bad idea to exchange with a Brigand. It wasn't as if Jessemia knew that's what the man was, but he was a stranger, and didn't she have the least sense of caution?

Fingers brushing the back of her hand made her jump. "Aderyn, go to bed," Owen said quietly.

"What? Why?"

"You're wound so tight I'm afraid you're going to snap. I thought you were going to let this go." He closed his hand on hers. "Sleep. They'll leave soon, and everything is going to be fine."

"I can't go while Jessemia is with that man."

"Sweetheart, Jessemia is not your responsibility. She's enjoying herself for the first time since we left Obsidian. Sure, he's a Brigand, but he's not hurting her, and it's not like we'll see him again."

Aderyn closed her eyes and let out a deep breath. "You're right. Thank you. I love you."

"I love you, too. Get some rest."

The room's stuffiness hadn't eased after the sun set, but the one small window that looked out over the even smaller stable yard could be pushed open to let in a night breeze. Aderyn undressed to the shift and drawers she wore to sleep in and settled into the bed she would share with Livia. Her stomach's burning had diminished since she'd left the taproom, and she drew the thin blanket over her shoulders and curled up around the remaining ache, drifting off almost immediately.

Her sleep was restless, though, as first Livia, then Jessemia came to bed. They didn't light the room's lamp, but the lamp burning in the hall shone into Aderyn's face, disorienting her into believing day had come. When the room was finally dark and still, she fell into disturbing dreams that felt real until she jerked awake and realized she'd been dreaming. Every time she woke, her stomachache got a little worse, until she dragged herself out of a nightmare in which she was fighting monsters with her friends' faces and her belly burned so badly she couldn't fall back asleep.

She drifted in and out of awareness, hoping the pain would subside, until she finally woke fully and knew it wasn't indigestion, she was genuinely ill. For a moment, she lay on her back, considering her options. There was a chamber pot under the bed, but she didn't want to share the room with the stench of her vomit and she didn't want to make Livia wait on her by emptying it, not when she was sure that throwing up would make her feel better enough to manage it herself.

She fumbled into her clothes in the darkness and, boots in hand, eased past the door into the hallway. Someone had extinguished the lamp that had woken her earlier, but light spilled up the staircase from below. Wincing at the terrible stomach pain, which had begun to throb in a way that told her she only had minutes before her body would eject whatever burned inside it whether she wanted to or not, she sat at the top of the stairs and pulled her boots on. Then she made her way down to the first floor and went looking for the back door.

She immediately knew she was worse off than she'd realized. Not only did her stomach hurt, her vision was clouded and her joints ached. Cold sweat broke out along her hairline. She rested one hand on the wall for balance and, clutching her stomach with her other arm, followed the now-nauseating scent of dinner to the kitchen. She had no idea how late it was, but the fires had been banked and the kitchen was empty of people, so she guessed it was between midnight and four o'clock.

Fumbling through the darkness, she finally found the door and burst out into the cool summer night. Her stomach was twisting itself into a tangle of burning, acidic pain. She stumbled forward, aiming for the outhouse, but before she was halfway there her stomach lurched. She fell to her knees and her body tried to turn itself inside out with vomiting. She lost track of time as she convulsed there in the stable yard. There was nothing but pain and endless retching.

When finally her stomach calmed, Aderyn gasped for breath and dashed tears from her eyes. Her skin felt so painfully sensitive the light wind raised all the hairs on her arms and made her shiver, though sweat still beaded her forehead. Her joints ached terribly, so even though the stink of vomit nauseated her further, she crouched there on hands and knees for a while, breathing slowly and not too deeply and mustering her strength. Then she pushed herself upright and got to her feet.

Dizziness briefly struck her, but her vision cleared almost immediately. Her empty stomach felt much better. It couldn't have been food poisoning, because no one else was sick, so it was just bad luck she'd picked up a stomach illness somewhere. Aderyn hoped no one else would get sick. Likely how she felt now was a temporary remission, and she'd be laid up for a day or so. How awful if everyone got it.

She took a step to return to her bed, but the dizziness struck her again, so she closed her eyes and breathed deeply, regaining her balance. When she felt steadier, she opened her eyes, only to see furtive motion at the corner of the stable yard, where the stalls formed part of an L with the inn as the other stroke. Curious, Aderyn focused on that corner. For a moment, nothing moved, but Aderyn didn't think, even in her illness, that she'd imagined it. Then something—no, someone—moved, and light from the setting quarter moon shone on chestnut curls and a pale face.

Jessemia.

Forgetting her illness for the moment in her curiosity, Aderyn crossed the stable yard to the stalls. "Jessemia, what are you doing out here?" she whispered, and then wondered why she had spoken so quietly. There wasn't anyone else there except one piebald mare drowsing in her stall.

Jessemia jumped and spun around. "What are *you* doing here?" she demanded in a normal voice. "Were you spying on me?"

"I came outside to—I wasn't feeling well." Aderyn stepped closer. Not only was Jessemia fully dressed, she had her knapsack at her feet. "Are you going somewhere?"

"You can't stop me," Jessemia said, sounding as if she'd won a prize. "None of you can."

"Stop you doing what?" Aderyn glanced around, but still saw no one else.

"I'm leaving. Hadrus is going to take me away from all this and escort me to Obsidian." Jessemia folded her arms across her chest. "So go back inside. This is none of your business."

A different kind of cold sweat broke out on Aderyn's brow. "Jessemia, who is Hadrus? That Brigand leader?"

"The—what?" Jessemia's forehead puckered in a frown.

"They're Brigands. All of them. I don't know what that man told you—"

"You're making it up. I Assessed him. He's a Swordsworn." The frown gave way to a pout. "You're just jealous that he likes me."

Aderyn grabbed Jessemia by the shoulder. "Jealous? Why would I care? I'm telling you, whatever this Hadrus said, he doesn't want to take you to Obsidian."

Jessemia wrenched away. "Let go of me. I'm going with him, and you can't stop me. Go tell the bully if you want. I'll be gone before you get back."

Aderyn almost left. Her stomachache was coming back, her whole body ached, and Jessemia's ignorance and stupidity infuriated her. But she knew as clearly as if she could see the future what awaited the woman if she went off with those Brigands. "They'll use your body as they choose and kill you when they're done with you," she said bluntly. "If you believe otherwise, you're a fool. Come back inside before it's too late."

Jessemia was looking past Aderyn. "They're here," she said triumphantly. "You just want me to suffer. That's why you lied to me about Hadrus. He's funny and nice and he wants to help me."

Aderyn turned. Three dark figures approached from beyond the stables. The moonlight silvered their hair so the blond one looked like he was glowing. Aderyn gripped Jessemia's arm. "We need to run."

Again Jessemia pulled free. "You run. I'm going." She ran toward the Brigands. Aderyn cursed under her breath. Then she ran after Jessemia.

The Brigands stopped a few feet from the stables like they were waiting on Jessemia and Aderyn to reach them. Aderyn could make out their confused expressions as they looked at her, then at each other. She wished she had her sword, though what she thought she could do against three level fourteen Brigands without the rest of her team to back her up, she didn't know.

Jessemia was putting her knapsack on as she ran, which turned her run into a stumbling gait. "You came!" she exclaimed.

"What's that one doing here? Who is she?" the blond Brigand demanded. "A Warmaster?"

"She's nothing. Just ignore her," Jessemia said.

"I'm coming with her," Aderyn said.

Jessemia turned on her, outraged. "I said go back inside!"

"You know two is better than one," Aderyn said, addressing the blond Brigand. "Won't your leader Hadrus agree?"

"Does Hadrus know about this, then?" the blond Brigand said, his expression clearing. "Heh. Sounds like him, the randy dog."

"Right," Aderyn said, wishing her head was clear. She had a feeling she was doing something stupid, but all she could see in her inner vision was Jessemia disappearing with a bunch of men who saw her as a victim. "Hadrus. Let's go."

The Brigand sized her up. He smiled, a cruel, lascivious grin. "Never knew a woman so eager," he said. "Maybe you and I can have some fun later."

Aderyn managed a smile she was sure made her look ill. Jessemia glanced from the Brigand to Aderyn in confusion. "You don't want her," she said. "She's nobody. I'm the one Hadrus is going to take back to Obsidian."

"Sure he is," the Brigand said. "But, like she says, two is better than one. Come on, then."

Jessemia lifted her chin and walked ahead of the Brigands, deliberately putting space between herself and Aderyn. The three Brigands followed her, jostling each other and talking in low voices. Aderyn could only hear them when their talk turned into sniggering laughter now and then.

She was sure now she'd made a mistake, but her head had started throbbing and she couldn't remember what she should have done instead. She followed as close as she could manage and hoped she wouldn't have another vomiting seizure. Maybe she couldn't remember what the right thing was, but she was certain showing weakness to these men would be fatal.

CHAPTER NINE

After a few paces, the Brigands caught up to Jessemia. None of them laid a hand on her, and briefly Aderyn considered whether she was wrong about their intentions—but no, that was impossible. They just had instructions to deliver Jessemia to their leader unmolested. And now they were guiding their unwitting captive out of the village. Aderyn expected them to go around to an unmonitored section of the low wall, but instead they walked straight down Plensholt's one street to the gap in the wall.

Aderyn rubbed fog out of her eyes and searched for a guard, a sentry, even a random wakeful person who might see them and raise the alarm. But the gap was empty. Her roving eye fell on a lumpy inert form off to the side, in the lee of the wall. Just as she realized it was human, she heard one of the Brigands laugh and kick a stone out of the road so it struck the person. Whoever it was didn't react. Aderyn's stomach revolted for a different reason.

She wished she could grab Jessemia and run with her back to the safety of the inn, or even point out the dead guard Jessemia clearly hadn't seen. Part of her raged that she was walking voluntarily into captivity and violation and death, all for the sake of a woman who didn't care what happened to her. Her head hurt enough that the inner voice was muted. Distantly, she hoped her friends would wake early and follow—though could even Weston find her, when he had no [Tracking] skill?

As her inner battle raged, she went on putting one foot in front of the other, only barely aware of her surroundings. From the position of the setting moon, they were heading west and a little north, which was mostly the way to Obsidian, but Aderyn was certain Hadrus had no intention of taking Jessemia to that city.

She smelled wood smoke, and a few minutes later, they entered one of the copses that dotted the plains. Firelight flickered over the trees nearby, and Aderyn quickened her step until she was just behind the Brigands. Fire meant safety—no, not this fire. She shook her head to dispel the fog that persisted in clouding her vision.

She didn't realize they'd come into an open space and didn't stop walking when the Brigands did. She bumped into the blond one and stepped back as he turned on her, snarling, "Watch it."

"Well, look at this," a soft, drawling voice said. "You came."

"Of course I did, darling," Jessemia said, hurrying forward to embrace the Brigand. Aderyn recognized his broad shoulders and long brown ponytail, but she hadn't seen his face until now. He wasn't handsome, with a thick, ridged scar that crossed his left cheek from the corner of his eye to below his jaw, but his smile gave him a roguish charm—at least, until you saw his eyes, which were hard, with heavy brows. At the sight of those eyes, Aderyn's heart sank. There was no way he intended to keep whatever lying promises he'd made Jessemia, which meant both Aderyn and Jessemia were in serious trouble.

Hadrus's gaze fell on Aderyn, and his smile vanished. "Who's this?"

"You wanted her too, right?" the blond Brigand said. "Two are better than one, huh?"

"Really." Hadrus walked forward, bringing Jessemia with him

because she was clinging to his arm. "A Warmaster. She wanted to come?"

"She said—"

"Shut up, Carel," Hadrus said. He took Aderyn's chin in his hand and tilted her head back to examine her. He was very tall, easily as tall as Weston, though not as heavily built. "What in thunder is your game, girl?"

"I'm not letting you take her," Aderyn said, trying to sound assertive. Her stomach was starting to hurt again, though, and she probably only sounded weak.

Hadrus smiled again, an expression that curled up on the side opposite his scar. "You think you can stop me?"

Aderyn swallowed and said nothing.

"Stop you?" Jessemia said. "She wants to keep me from going home, but you won't let her keep me here, will you, darling?"

"Oh, we're going back to Obsidian, never fear," Hadrus said. "There's too much waiting for us there."

Jessemia shot Aderyn a triumphant glare. "See? Hadrus, dearest, leave her here. We don't need her."

Hadrus removed Jessemia's hands from his arm. "I don't see why I should. After all, as Carel says, two is better than one. I'll find a use for her." He thrust Aderyn away from him. "Bind them both. And no touching, understand? This one's papa will want his darling daughter back unharmed, and the other one—" He grinned again. "She's looking a little under the weather. I want her well enough to appreciate the attention I'll give her."

Through the laughter of all the gathered Brigands, Jessemia exclaimed, "What? What are you talking about, darling?"

"Spare me," Hadrus said. "You're stupider than I thought."

Hands gripped Aderyn's arms and bound her wrists in front of her. She didn't fight. That would be pointless even if she hadn't felt about to throw up again. Jessemia did struggle, prompting two more Brigands to hold her as a third tied her hands together and another took her sword and belt knife. She shrieked in outrage that turned to fear as the ones holding her groped her body. Aderyn shouted, "Leave her alone! Didn't you hear him?"

"I don't mind my men having a little fun," Hadrus said as Jessemia burst into tears. "They know how far they can go. And what I'll do if they go even a step over that line."

"What do you want with her?" Aderyn asked, not expecting an answer.

But Hadrus surprised her. "Ransom," he said. "Jessemia's doting papa is wealthy enough to pay anything to get her back. We'll go to Obsidian and collect a fat reward. You, on the other hand—" He smiled that nasty curved smile again. "I doubt anyone's interested in paying for a useless Warmaster. You'll have to satisfy me another way."

The blond Brigand, Carel, dragged Aderyn, stumbling, to sit at the base of a tree. The Brigands holding Jessemia shoved her so she hit the ground near Aderyn with a cry that turned into tears. Both of them took up a guard position near the two women. Aderyn watched in a haze as another Brigand kicked dirt over the fire and the rest settled on the ground to sleep.

"Stop crying," she told Jessemia. "That won't help."

Jessemia kept weeping, curled in on herself like she wanted to make herself disappear. Aderyn's stomach hurt enough that she felt no sympathy for her. She just wanted not to have to listen to the sobs, which grated on her raw nerves. "I mean it, Jessemia. Shut up, or I'll vomit on you and you'll know what true misery is."

"I hate you," Jessemia gasped between sobs. "If you hadn't come, Hadrus would—"

"You have got to be kidding," Aderyn said. "How stupid are you? Hadrus played you. He wanted a hostage, and you walked right into his hands. I—" She swallowed. It didn't help. "Oh, crap," she said, and lurched away from the tree to vomit.

The Brigands guarding them swore. "She's really sick," the

bearded Brigand said. "I thought Hadrus was just playing with her when he didn't take her immediately."

"Guess he knew what he was doing," the black-haired Brigand said. "Hey, pull it together, girl. You don't want to have to sleep in that."

Aderyn heard all this faintly over the sound of her retching. When she finished, she wiped her mouth and said, "You're so considerate."

The Brigands laughed, a surprisingly not-cruel sound, though Aderyn thought anyone who could be amused by someone else's suffering didn't get any points for not being awful. "Hey, let's take them over here," the bearded Brigand said. "I was kidding about you having to sleep in it. Wouldn't want you to stink when you're finally well enough for Hadrus to make you his woman."

"So kind," Aderyn managed.

The black-haired Brigand got her to her feet, not roughly, and led her to a nearby tree, away from her vomit. His companion hauled the still-crying Jessemia to a standing position and dragged her, struggling, to sit beside Aderyn. Aderyn leaned against the tree and tilted her head back, breathing heavily. She felt like she'd vomited up her intestines that time.

"Jessemia. Jessemia," she said, speaking more loudly to get the woman's attention. "Stop crying. I'm not kidding. They'll go on tormenting you if they know they can get that reaction."

"Stop talking to me," Jessemia sniffled.

"Gladly." Aderyn curled up on her side. There was nothing she could do in this condition except try to sleep and hope that would cure her. Probably sleep was out of the question, between Jessemia's sniffles and the hard ground and the watchful gaze of two Brigands, but she had to try.

The next thing she knew, sunlight shone through the tree trunks, and she smelled wood smoke again. She awkwardly got into a sitting position, using her bound hands to push herself up. Brigands moved through the camp, most of them involved in skinning and butchering a small deer. Hadrus sat beside the fire, idly poking it with a long stick. Aderyn wiped drool from her cheek and leaned back against the tree. No one was watching them at the moment, but the Brigands all moved with a graceful alertness to their surroundings that told Aderyn they would notice if she tried to stand, let alone run.

Jessemia still snored gently beside Aderyn. Her hair was tangled and dirty, with pine needles matted where she'd lain on that side first. Looking at her, Aderyn's anger rose. This idiot woman had gotten them both captured, and she had the nerve to sleep as peacefully as if they weren't surrounded by dangerous enemies. When they got out of this, Aderyn was going to make her regret her stupidity.

Hadrus looked up at that moment and caught Aderyn's eye. He smiled and rose, dusted himself off, and sauntered toward them. "Feeling better?" he asked.

Aderyn did feel better, but admitting it would seal her fate. She swallowed and tried to look pale and in danger of vomiting again. "Like you care," she said, weakly, then brought both hands up to cover her mouth.

Hadrus took a step back, but he was still smiling. "I hope you're well enough to walk. I'd hate to kill you when you offer so... much... potential."

Aderyn nodded and visibly swallowed again.

Hadrus crouched beside Jessemia and put a hand gently on her shoulder, shaking her. Jessemia blinked and looked up at him. "Hadrus?" she said in a soft, sweet voice that irritated Aderyn. "You didn't mean it, did you? About ransom? You were just joking, weren't you?"

Hadrus stroked her cheek with the backs of his fingers. "You really believed all that nonsense I fed you, didn't you?"

Jessemia's smile fell away. "Nonsense?"

"Why in thunder would I care about a random young woman I

met in a tavern?" Hadrus said. "You're pretty enough, I suppose, but nothing special."

"But I'm the Fated One! I told you. They kidnapped me and forced me to leave my home—you said you'd help!" Jessemia, for a miracle, wasn't crying, but her face was white with shock.

"My dear, I care exactly nothing for your delusions," Hadrus said. "You'll earn me a nice, fat ransom, and then you can go." He stroked her cheek again. "Though maybe we will have a little fun before you leave us."

Jessemia jerked away from his touch. Hadrus laughed. "Not right away," he said. "I'll give you some time to think about whether you want to come to me voluntarily." He stood and dusted invisible dirt from his hands. "We'll eat soon, and then I hope you're both ready to walk. Obsidian is four days' journey from here, and you may have noticed we don't exactly have horses." He walked away, whistling.

Jessemia struggled into a sitting position. "I don't understand," she said, quietly. "He told me he wanted to help."

She sounded so confused Aderyn didn't swear at her like she wanted to. "He lied to you, Jessemia," she said instead. "What did you tell him? That your father would reward him for helping you return?"

Jessemia nodded.

Aderyn stopped herself before she could say anything about how Jessemia's father Liander of the White was impoverished after the faction war that had resulted in White faction's fall from power. If the Brigands heard that, they'd kill Aderyn and Jessemia, probably after violating them, and Hadrus would be the first in line.

"I'm the Fated One," Jessemia said, still in that confused voice. "This isn't supposed to happen to me. They were going to help me level up on the way back."

That did it. "You idiot," Aderyn said in a low, cutting voice. "You're not the Fated One. That's a delusion your father planted in your head. You've been spoiled and pampered your whole life to the point that you're nothing more than a crippled Pathseer who can barely fight and can't use any of her skills properly. We are in this situation because you're so arrogant you didn't realize you were being played. You were eager to stick it to Owen, weren't you? I guess we should be grateful that you only plotted to run away instead of selling us out to those Brigands to ambush us. How can you be so stupid?"

Jessemia stared at her, her whole face slack in astonishment. "That's not," she began, then paused, bit her lip, and continued, "Hadrus promised—"

"*Shut up* about Hadrus," Aderyn said. "He *lied* because you were an easy mark, don't you get it? And now we're both going to be raped and killed and left where no one will ever find our bodies. Is that what you wanted?"

"I didn't want this!"

"Then maybe you shouldn't have been a stupid, arrogant cow," Aderyn spat. "I wish I'd gone back inside when you told me to."

"Why didn't you?" Jessemia asked.

Her voice was faint, but it sounded like a genuine question. Aderyn let out a deep breath and wished her stomach hadn't started to hurt again. "Because I knew what they would do to you," she said, "and I couldn't let even someone as stupid as you to go off to that fate alone. And now I'm just going to die with you."

Tears filled Jessemia's eyes, but she didn't burst into noisy sobs. She turned away from Aderyn and leaned against the tree trunk, all in silence.

Aderyn closed her eyes. So much for her compassionate impulse.

CHAPTER TEN

Aderyn concentrated on not vomiting again, though there wasn't anything in her stomach but bile. She knew she was sick because she didn't feel hungry despite her empty stomach. She'd need to choke something down or she wouldn't have the strength to walk anywhere.

To distract herself, she watched the Brigands. Hadrus had returned to sit by the fire, where the butchered deer turned on a makeshift spit. He was in profile, the unscarred side of his face toward her. In that pose, without his terrible smile, he was almost handsome. Aderyn shuddered at the thought and Assessed him, choosing the Full Assessment. The more information she could gain about him, the... well, "safer" probably wasn't on the table, but she'd take any advantage she could get.

Name: Hadrus

Class: Brigand

Level: 14

<u>Skills</u>**: Assess (10), Awareness (14), Climb (11), Conversation (12), Sense Truth (11), Spot (14), Survival (8), Swim (2), Knowledge: Geography (9)**

<u>Class skills</u>: Improved Weapon Proficiency (14), Improved Armor Proficiency (10), Knowledge: Monsters (9), Dodge (14), Parry (12), Improved Bluff (14), Trip (10), Deception (8), Disarm (7), Intimidate (11), Charge (6), Two-Weapon Fighting (4), Misdirect (5), Basic Map Access (4), Overrun (2), Demoralize (4), Sunder (2), Shatter Confidence (1)

<u>Skill Alert</u>: Intimidate (11), Demoralize (4), Shatter Confidence (1)

Aderyn had never heard of the last two skills. She examined each in turn.

[Demoralize]: Use [Intimidate] to lower an opponent's defenses.

[Shatter Confidence]: When [Demoralize] is successfully used, this skill induces temporary fear in an opponent. Increased ranks in this skill intensify the induced fear, sometimes causing an opponent to flee.

That those skills were highlighted in red meant Hadrus was either skilled with their use beyond whatever ranks he had, or he frequently depended on them in combat. Aderyn felt cold when she thought about him using them on her friends. Then she remembered there was a chance her friends would never find her, and she swallowed again to keep the bile down.

She Assessed the two remaining skills she didn't recognize.

[Deception]: Makes someone proficient in telling believable lies. Countered by [Sense Truth] or experience in seeing through illusions magical or mundane.

[Misdirect]: Distracts an opponent from awareness of someone's true class by turning their attention elsewhere. Countered by [Sense Truth]. Efficiency is improved when this skill is used in conjunction with [Deception].

Aderyn contemplated this. She had seen through the Brigands' concealment because she was a Warmaster, not because of her [Sense Truth] skill; clearly Jessemia's [Sense Truth] wasn't high enough for that. But lies weren't effective when someone knew the truth. So it didn't matter what her friends' [Sense Truth] ranks were, because she'd warned them what to expect, and [Deception] and [Misdirect] wouldn't affect them.

The thought of her friends made her chest ache worse than her stomach. How long would it take them to discover she was missing and not just in the privy or out for a walk? With Weston not having the [Tracking] skill, they might not be able to find her. Tears pricked her eyes and she ruthlessly blinked them away. The Brigands weren't paying her any attention at the moment, but she refused to show weakness.

The smell of roasting meat made her queasy. It also roused her thirst. She might be close to dehydrated after all the vomiting without drinking any water. She weighed the need for a drink against reminding the Brigands she existed. Thirst won out.

She struggled to her feet, which tingled from her sitting on them, and approached the fire. "I need water."

Two of the Brigands, one of them Carel, stopped their bantering discussion. "What makes you think we care what you need?" Carel said.

"Your leader wants me well. That means food and water. Unless you'd rather I was sick on you?" Aderyn tried to keep that from sounding too sarcastic. There was still a chance they'd change their minds about needing her and slit her throat.

The Brigands exchanged glances. Then the other one took a waterskin from his belt and stood so he could hold it to her lips. She supported it as best she could with her bound hands and drank gratefully. Her tortured stomach subsided.

When he removed the waterskin, reflexively she said, "Thank you." Immediately she felt stupid. Thanking her captors, that was ridiculous.

The Brigands laughed as if they saw the stupidity in it, too. "Sit," Carel said, unexpectedly without malice. "Food's ready."

The smell still nauseated her, but Aderyn choked down the meat anyway. The moment it hit her stomach, she knew it was a bad idea. All the soothing effect of the water vanished, and her insides began to burn again. She took a few bites of bread the Brigands had probably stolen from Plensholt. It didn't help.

The other Brigand left the fire and quickly returned, steering an unresistant Jessemia to sit next to Aderyn. Aderyn glanced at her. Jessemia was very pale, and her eyes were red-rimmed, but she ate venison without complaint. Her silence unnerved Aderyn, which surprised her as she'd spent so much time wishing Jessemia would shut up.

Her stomach roiled, and she rose as quickly as she could and rushed to the trees, where she vomited up her meal. It smelled even worse the second time around. When she finished, she wiped her mouth and tried to get her breathing under control.

"More water," Carel said from beside her. She drank and again felt better, stronger and more able to endure the ache in her joints.

"What's your game?" she asked.

The blond Brigand laughed. "You're a beauty," he said. "It's too bad you might sick up on me, because I'd love to take you back into the trees for a little one-on-one time. Maybe once Hadrus tires of you. He bores easily."

She remembered how often Owen had called her beautiful, and tears came to her eyes again. Carel noticed and laughed more heartily. "Don't think that moves me. Cry all you want. It won't change anything."

Aderyn spat on the ground near his feet, wishing she dared spit in his face. He only laughed harder and walked away. Aderyn leaned against the tree, pillowing her head on her arms. The rough bark hurt, but it was a distraction from her body's continuing pains.

Behind her, Hadrus shouted, "Let's get a move on. We've got ground to cover."

Aderyn pushed herself upright. She wasn't bound too tightly, but her wrists were sore and her shoulders ached from holding that position. She watched the Brigands dismantle their camp around Jessemia, who still sat motionless beside the fire. Then Hadrus strolled to her side and hauled her up, making her cry out in pain. "Ready to walk?"

"Leave me alone," Jessemia said dully, with none of the petulance Aderyn was used to.

Hadrus chuckled. "Sure," he said. Then he pulled her to him and kissed her hard, making her squirm and make protesting noises trying unsuccessfully to get away. Hadrus let her go only as far as continuing to hold onto her arm. "That's a taste of what you'll get," he said with a lopsided smile Aderyn hated. "I'll give you some time to think about it. I love giving a woman a few days of anticipation."

Jessemia wiped her mouth violently with her sleeve and glared at Hadrus, but said nothing.

Hadrus shouted, "Time to go! Let's form up around our guests. Wouldn't want them to fall behind or get lost."

Nine Brigands surrounded Aderyn and Jessemia, and Carel prodded Aderyn into motion. Wishing she had the power to kill every one of them with her desires, Aderyn set out.

Her stomach ached, but not as badly as before, and she didn't yet want to empty it. Worse was her continued mental fogginess and the pain in her joints and her general weariness that made walking torture. She reminded herself of the probable consequences of failing to keep up and managed to go on putting one foot in front of the other. Jessemia remained silent, for which Aderyn was grateful.

She soon fell into a fugue, barely aware of her surroundings, not knowing how long they walked between rests. She had the feeling the Brigands didn't stop to rest nearly as often as she and her friends did while they were traveling, but that might have been her illness wishing she didn't have to walk at all. At some point, she was handed a chunk of bread and some venison, which she forced herself to swallow. Again, her stomach protested, but not as strongly as before, and she kept this meal down.

After a while, she realized the sun was shining in her face, making her squint. She roused herself to look around and saw nothing but more plains and more scattered trees. Just then, Hadrus roared, "Time to camp! Let's see about making our guests comfortable."

The copse they camped in was almost identical to the one from the previous night. Aderyn sank down next to a tree, utterly grateful for the hard ground and the knuckle of the tree's root digging into her bottom. She was sweating, though it hadn't been a hot day, and she ached all over, and her food sat like a lump of lead in her stomach. Maybe she should induce vomiting. It might make her feel better.

Jessemia sat beside her, watching the motions of the men starting a fire and disappearing past the trees to hunt for dinner. Nobody was paying attention to the women, but there was no point trying to escape, even if Aderyn hadn't been ill and exhausted. There was nowhere to go that the Brigands wouldn't find them.

Jessemia abruptly said, "They're not going to let us live, are they."

Aderyn was too tired to yell at her for her stupidity again. "No."

"And they'll rape us first."

"Yes."

Jessemia let out a long breath. "I was so stupid."

"You were." Aderyn was too tired for tact, either.

Jessemia fell silent. Aderyn leaned her head against the tree trunk. The bark caught at her hair, pricking her scalp with tiny twinges of pain as she moved.

"I'm sorry," Jessemia said.

It was the first time Aderyn had ever heard her sound genuinely contrite. Ignoring the throb of sympathy that pulsed through her, she replied, "Sorry won't change anything. It's not going to free us. Or did you think you could apologize and make everything all right?"

"I don't know what I thought," Jessemia said, sounding as weary as Aderyn felt. "This shouldn't have happened. I don't understand. Hadrus sounded like he really cared."

Aderyn's heart throbbed again, and she took pity on Jessemia. Sort of. "He has a skill called [Deception] that makes his lies believable. And it's not like you're very introspective. You're too caught up in thinking of yourself to pay any attention to others."

"Oh." Jessemia said it as if they were having a normal conversation and Aderyn had just told her the time. "I didn't know. Is that really true?"

"How can you not know?" Aderyn swallowed more harsh words. Instead, she said, "It's true. You're self-absorbed, and it—" Again, she stopped herself before she could say *It's going to get you killed*.

"Oh," Jessemia said, again as if this was the most ordinary, obvious thing in the world, and fell silent.

Aderyn surveyed the camp. Only five Brigands, including Hadrus and Carel, remained in camp. Hadrus sat beside the fire and gazed into its sprightly flames as if he could control them like a Flamecrafter. Five, nine, either way it was too many for Aderyn to fight alone even if she'd had her sword. Her heart ached with longing for Owen and the others to burst into the clearing and take Hadrus's head off.

Time passed. Aderyn dozed off, exhausted enough to ignore her various pains. She woke after a while when Jessemia prodded her and said, "Something's wrong. Nobody's come back with a kill."

Aderyn blinked and sat up. Hadrus had risen and was pacing the clearing. "Where are those lazy bastards?" he shouted. "They know not to stray from camp after dark, even if it means coming back empty-handed."

"I'll go look for them," Carel offered.

"And stumble around in the dark and get lost yourself?" Hadrus said. "You'll stay here. Dig out what's left of the rations and feed the women. They'll return eventually. Garman has his Pathseer abilities, so they won't stay lost forever, unless they're afraid of the reaming I'll give them when I see them." He returned to sit by the fire. Carel shrugged and gestured to one of his fellows to bring his knapsack, and both of them rummaged around and started pulling out dried meat, fuzzy cheese, nuts, and more bread.

The sight of food made Aderyn's stomach ache again. She was pretty sure if she vomited one more time, she'd turn a corner and start recovering. She walked a few paces away from Jessemia and knelt, swiftly jabbing a finger at the back of her throat before she could think too hard about what she was doing.

When she finished throwing up, she did feel better. She got to her feet and regarded the camp. No one was paying attention to her, and she considered walking away, deeper into the copse—but it wasn't big enough for her to hide in, and eventually someone would find her and bring her back, possibly hurting her to convince her running was a bad idea.

Out of nowhere, a system message flashed across her vision.

**Congratulations! You have defeated [Gidion the Brigand].
You have earned [8000 XP]**

Aderyn sucked in a startled breath. Her friends were near. She kept her face concealed. If Owen and the others were out there picking off Brigands in secret, she didn't want anyone here guessing the truth by seeing her elated expression.

A few more agonizing minutes passed. Aderyn's every sense was on alert, listening, watching, waiting for the rumble of *thunderstomp*. Another system message flashed.

**Congratulations! You have defeated [Rollo the Brigand].
You have earned [8500 XP]**

Too bad system messages weren't directional. She would love to be able to track her friends' progress, to know where they were.

Distantly, a loud noise shook the trees, echoing like a shout through a canyon. It *was* Isold's **[Shout]**.

**Congratulations! You have defeated [Eddus the Brigand].
You have earned [8000 XP]**

The Brigands in the clearing all came alert, some of them leaping to their feet and drawing weapons. Hadrus rose more slowly, his head tilted to catch the last echoes of **[Shout]**. "We're under attack," he said, as calmly as if this was no surprise. "Be ready."

A crack of thunder out of a clear evening sky startled Aderyn. The ground rumbled, and a wave of rolling earth slammed through the clearing, knocking Aderyn and all the Brigands who were standing over. She landed on her bound hands and suppressed a cry of pain. *Thunderstomp.*

With a shout, three figures burst into the clearing. Firelight reflected off the blades two of them wielded. Aderyn pushed herself to a sitting position and shouted, "*Owen!*"

CHAPTER ELEVEN

Owen was on the first downed Brigand before the man could draw his sword. The Brigand screamed as Owen's <Twinsword> found its mark and pierced him through the heart. The system message that appeared gave Aderyn new hope.

**Congratulations! You have defeated [Lister the Brigand].
You have earned [8000 XP]**

Weston lunged at the one Brigand who'd been alert. The Brigand parried Weston's first strike and pressed the attack. The other Brigands were almost as quick to respond, though, and Owen was drawn into a clash of swords with the bearded Brigand who'd mocked Aderyn the previous night.

Something slim and silvery shot toward Aderyn, flying so smoothly it had to be *telekinesis*, and embedded itself point first in the earth at her feet. In her confusion, it took her a moment to recognize her own sword. Then she slung her bound hands around it, pressing the rope to its edge and sawing away. She was in too much of a hurry to care if she cut herself, and a couple of shallow nicks later she was free. She rubbed her wrists briefly before snatching up her sword.

She started toward Owen, intending to provide him with [Outflank], but after a few steps she stumbled to a halt. Her vision blurred occasionally, and she ached so much lifting her sword was impossible. She cursed her weakness, but she would be a liability. Instead, she propped herself against the nearest tree and studied Owen's opponent. The man loved big, sweeping slashes that had all the power of his not inconsiderable strength behind them, and he was prone to catching Owen's blade against his and shoving Owen off balance. Aderyn saw how those slashes left him open on his right side, noted that he became off balance himself in the moment after shoving, and discovered with [Improved Assess 2] that his [Advanced Weapons Proficiency] was too low for level thirteen. He was big, and he used his size to overpower his opponent.

She knew the instant the <Twinsword> carried her observations to Owen, because he stopped engaging his opponent closely and began using his <Deadly Blade> to deflect the man's sword instead, thrusting with the <Twinsword> at his unprotected right side. But in the next moment, Hadrus joined the fight, and Owen had to defend against both.

Aderyn clenched the hand not holding her sword so tightly her fingers were numb. Weston had downed his first opponent nearly as fast as Owen, fast enough that the system message had overlapped the first. He was now fighting Carel, who was almost as good a swordsman as Owen. Both Owen and Weston looked close to being overwhelmed.

Ropy tentacles of mud emerged from the ground, entangling Carel. Carel stopped attacking Weston and struck at the *immobilize* spell, severing a few tentacles that were immediately replaced. Weston's slim blade pierced one of the tentacles and continued into Carel's chest.

**Congratulations! You have defeated [Carel the Brigand].
You have earned [9000 XP]**

"Weston!" Owen shouted.

Weston raced toward where Owen fought a defensive battle against his two opponents, both blades deflecting blows, but Hadrus was pressing the attack, and Aderyn saw at once Weston would be too late. She pictured Owen dead at Hadrus's hand, and rage swept over her, obliterating her lingering symptoms of illness. She ran at Hadrus, furious strength filling her, and struck him from behind.

It would have been a glancing blow if not for **[Outflank]**. Instead, she skewered him low on his back, near his kidney. Hadrus howled and turned to face her. "You dare fight me?" he shouted.

Fear took the place of anger. Even as she remembered the skill **[Shatter Confidence]**, she dropped her guard and backed away. Hadrus followed her. His sword was bloody—she didn't remember him hitting Owen, and natural fear joined the induced fear of Hadrus's skill. "I'm going to gut you," Hadrus snarled, "leave you bleeding and dying, and then I'm going to drag your friends to where you can see me kill them as the life leaves your body."

The temporary strength her rage had given her had died, leaving her weak and sweating again. Hadrus's threat seemed very real. Aderyn raised her sword to a defensive position anyway. If she was going to die, she wouldn't go without a fight.

Hadrus raised his sword for a finishing blow. Then another clap of thunder split the sky, and Hadrus stumbled forward almost onto Aderyn's blade. Confused, she stepped back rather than pressing the attack. Livia stood there in her wrestler's stance, drawing back her arm for another blow. Her fist glittered like mica in the firelight —*stone fist*, more powerful than *thunder punch*, but more wearying for Livia. At the moment, Livia looked fierce rather than tired.

Then a hand gripped Aderyn's shoulder, and Owen put her gently to one side. "I've got this," he said.

Hadrus took a few more steps away from Owen and shook his head as if regaining his senses. He brought his blade up in time to catch Owen's next strike and dodged the thrust of the <**Deadly Blade**>. "You're bold," he said. "Which of the women is yours? Did I steal something that belongs to you?"

Owen struck again with a ringing clash of metal on metal. "Only a sick bastard thinks of women as property. I'll be doing the world a favor in getting rid of you."

"More bold words." Hadrus's lips peeled back in a snarl. "I promised I'd kill you in front of the useless Warmaster. So much for your rescue." He thrust, and Owen wasn't fast enough. Owen grimaced as Hadrus's sword scored him along the hip, below his brigandine.

Aderyn frantically studied Hadrus's fighting style. He was good, maybe as good as Owen despite the difference in their weapons skill ranks. He fought with a tight, contained style that left no easy openings, no holes in his defense for Owen to exploit even with [**Two-Weapon Fighting**]. He was slimmer than Owen, but taller, and had a longer reach he used to his advantage. Owen had to come in close to hit him, putting himself in the way of those powerful blows.

Weston had engaged the bearded Brigand and was trading blows while Livia circled them, looking for an opening. Aderyn hadn't seen Isold anywhere, which frightened her almost as much as watching Owen fight Hadrus. At least it didn't look like [**Shatter Confidence**] had worked on Owen.

As she thought that, Aderyn came to her senses. Hadrus was just a man, not some terrifying monster, and [**Shatter Confidence**] might have worked on her once, but she wasn't going to let Owen die because she was afraid.

She Assessed Hadrus once more, focusing on the fuzzy yellow ball of light attached to his chest that was linked to a matching one on Owen. With some effort, she wrenched the light from Owen's chest and drew it swiftly to herself.

With a startled oath, Hadrus spun around to face her. Aderyn smiled and beckoned to him with her sword. Hadrus took a few stumbling steps toward her, then with a snarl he advanced at speed, raising his weapon for a powerful two-handed blow that would split her skull.

Owen struck from behind, thrusting deep into Hadrus's back and making the Brigand scream in agony. Aderyn dove in beneath his guard and drove her sword into his gut, twisting the blade so it went as deep as she could manage. Hadrus stared at her in astonishment. "You're nothing," he croaked. "How could you—"

Aderyn said nothing. She shoved him backward off her sword so he fell to the ground, clutching the terrible wound. She didn't move until Owen took her in his arms and held her tight. Then she embraced him, shivering convulsively in the aftershock of combat.

**Congratulations! You have defeated [Hadrus the Brigand].
You have earned [10,000 XP]**

"He's dead," she murmured, unnecessarily, just as another system message appeared.

**Congratulations! You have defeated [Arondo the Brigand].
You have earned [8000 XP]**

"Where's Isold?" Livia exclaimed.

Owen's grip loosened. "He was right behind us."

Aderyn counted back. "There's still one Brigand out there. He was hunting for food."

"Isold!" Weston shouted.

"I could use some help," Isold called out from within the trees.

Owen steered Aderyn toward the sound of Isold's voice. Thanks to **[Read Body Language]**, Aderyn saw he was dealing with the lingering effects of his fear for her and needed to feel she was safe. Her heart ached for what he'd endured while she was kidnapped, though probably she should save that sympathy for herself as the one actually kidnapped and threatened with violation and death.

They found Isold and the remaining Brigand a few dozen paces into the copse. Isold looked tired. The Brigand's sword lay at his feet, and he stood immobile, his jaw slack, his eyes unfocused. "[Hypnotize]," Isold said. "Someone should finish him off."

"Aderyn?" Owen said.

Aderyn shook her head. Now that the rush of combat had passed, she again felt her aching joints and her near-exhaustion. "I killed Hadrus. That's enough."

"I'll take care of it," Weston said, circling around to face the Brigand. Isold stepped back. The Brigand blinked as if waking up, but Weston didn't wait for him to recover his sword. With one swift motion, he stabbed the Brigand through the heart. The man sagged and collapsed atop his sword.

Congratulations! You have defeated [Garman the Brigand]. You have earned [8000 XP]

Welcome to Level Twelve

"Aderyn," Owen said, then, "Aderyn!" He took her in his arms as her knees buckled. "What did they do to you?"

Aderyn shook her head. "I've been sick with some kind of stomach illness. I haven't kept anything down for more than twenty-four hours now."

Owen held her close and said nothing. His heart beat rapidly, and his breathing was labored. She closed her eyes and welcomed his embrace.

"Jessemia," Isold said.

Aderyn looked up. Jessemia stood a few feet away. She'd found a knife to cut herself free and looked wary. Owen released Aderyn, though he kept a protective hold of her shoulder. "What happened?" he said.

"Jessemia," Aderyn began, then didn't know how to go on. Her earlier anger was a shadow of itself, faded into near-nothingness after the terror of the fight.

"I wanted Hadrus to take me to Obsidian," Jessemia said in a small voice. "Aderyn followed me."

Owen's sudden rage tensed his muscles and tightened his grip painfully on Aderyn's shoulder. "You idiot," he said, his voice unnaturally quiet. "You trusted a Brigand's promises and you nearly got Aderyn killed. That's it. I'm done with you." In a louder voice, he said, "Let's see what we can take off these bastards and find a place to camp."

"Weston and Livia will do it," Isold said. "You need healing."

"I'm fine."

"Owen," Aderyn said.

He glanced down at her, and his expression softened. "Stay with me," he said.

"Of course," Aderyn reassured him. "I need you. It's been—" Unexpected tears filled her eyes. "I haven't let myself dwell on what they planned for us."

Owen clasped her hand so tightly she exclaimed. "Sorry," he said.

"Sit," Isold said. "I don't know how you're still upright with that wound on your hip, and it looks like someone tried to cut your arm off at the shoulder."

Owen gingerly lowered himself to the ground. "Battle rage," he said. "I'm feeling the pain now."

Aderyn sat beside him as Isold used the <**Wand of Healing**> on Owen's wounds. Her stomach ached, this time with welcome hunger, and she wanted nothing more than to sleep until she woke up healthy. To distract herself, she called up Advancement on her Codex to see what level twelve had given her.

Name: Aderyn

Level: 12

Class: Warmaster

<u>Skills</u>: **Bluff (9), Climb (9), Conversation (12), Intimidate (7), Sense Truth (13), Survival (7), Swim (1), Knowledge: Monsters (9), Knowledge: World Lore (2), Knowledge: Demons (1)**

<u>Class Skills:</u> **Improved Assess 2 (20), Awareness (13), Knowledge: Geography (9), Spot (12), Discern Weakness (18), Dodge (11), Improvised Distraction (10), Outflank (14), Draw Fire (6), Keep Pace (13), Amplify Voice (10), See It Coming (8), Basic Weapon Proficiency (Swords) (7), Read Body Language (5), Basic Map Access (3), Compel (3), Spot Weakness (1)**

Movement drew her eye, and she watched Jessemia take a few steps toward her and Owen. Owen ignored her so blatantly it was obvious it was on purpose. "Are you still feeling sick?" he asked Aderyn. "Is that something the wand can cure, or the <Healing Stone>?"

"I'm sorry," Jessemia said.

Owen fixed her with a cold, implacable glare. "I don't give a damn whether you're sorry or not. You should start walking. It's a long way to Obsidian."

"I can't do that," Jessemia said. "Please don't leave me behind."

"Oh, so now you want our company?" Owen's grip on Aderyn's hand tightened. "You've run out of chances, Jessemia. I wish I could say I can't believe you trusted the promises of a Brigand, but unfortunately, I can totally believe it."

Jessemia's eyes were bright with tears. "I didn't know he was a Brigand."

"Maybe not, but how stupid do you have to be to believe some stranger you met in a tavern cares about you?" Owen got to his feet and drew Aderyn up with him, steadying her with an arm around her waist. "I'm serious. You're no longer welcome to travel with us."

"Owen," Aderyn said.

"Don't defend her, Aderyn. She nearly got you killed."

"I know, but we can't leave her here to die."

"Sure we can. She brought this on herself." Owen showed no sign that he cared that Jessemia could hear every word. Tears trickled down Jessemia's face.

Aderyn put her arms around Owen's neck and held him close. "You were afraid for me, and that makes you angry," she whispered. "But we're not Brigands. Jessemia was stupid, and we were both in danger because of it—no, listen to me," she said as Owen tensed. "Leaving her to die is too much. For my sake, sweetheart."

Owen shook his head in resignation. "You're too nice a person."

"I guess. But I'd hate myself forever if we left her."

"We can't have that." Owen kissed her.

"Aderyn convinced me. Get your things," he told Jessemia. "And be grateful one of us has compassion."

Jessemia wiped her eyes and silently walked away.

CHAPTER TWELVE

"Sit here," Owen said, guiding Aderyn to a place beneath a thick-trunked tree. "We'll sleep soon. You're sure you're feeling better?"

Aderyn nodded.

"You'll rest, and in the morning you'll be recovered. These stomach bugs are nasty, but at least they don't last more than a day or so." He kissed her again and walked back to the fire, saying something Aderyn couldn't hear to Weston, who was rifling through Carel's belt pouch. Sighing, she closed her eyes and tilted her head back.

She drifted, not quite conscious, until Owen returned and helped her stand. Her joints still ached, but her stomach no longer felt like food would lie in it like a stone, and most of her pain came from weariness rather than illness.

They walked only a short distance, leaving the copse behind, before Livia activated the <**Soldier's Friend**>. Aderyn wearily entered her tent and sank down onto the bedroll Owen laid out. She was asleep before he joined her.

When she woke, it was full daylight, and she was alone. She sat up and stretched. A few lingering aches were all that remained of her illness, that and a gnawing hunger roused to painful heights by the smell of hot porridge and coffee.

She lifted the tent flap. Livia sat beside the fire, drinking from a tin mug, with Weston eating porridge beside her. Aderyn said, "It must not be as early as it feels if Livia is awake."

"You're well," Livia said. "What a relief. And I'm so glad we found you."

"How did you do it?"

"You left the <**Wayfinder**> behind," Isold said as he emerged from his own tent. He held the metal orb out to her. "You never said how difficult it is to use it for more than half an hour at a time."

"I didn't think of this," Aderyn said, accepting her precious magic item. "I'm glad. I was sure we were lost for good."

Livia's smile vanished. "No thanks to that stupid woman. Is it true she voluntarily went to that Brigand?"

"She believed his lies. It was—" Aderyn shut her mouth. She didn't know why she was defending Jessemia.

"I haven't seen her this morning," Isold said. "She ought to eat before we get on the road."

"I'd just as soon we left her in Plensholt," Livia said. "Let her make those people regret meeting her. And then we could be free and happy. I don't even care about the loss of experience."

Weston ladled up porridge into a tin plate and passed it to Aderyn. "There's honey too."

Aderyn ate cautiously at first, but when her stomach failed to rebel, she dug in happily. She didn't love porridge all that much, but it suited her abused stomach perfectly.

"Where's Owen?" she asked between bites.

"Scouting. One of those Brigands we defeated ran when Isold used [**Shout**] on him, and Owen wanted to be sure the fellow didn't return seeking revenge," Weston said.

Aderyn set her empty plate aside and regarded the one tent flap that wasn't open. "Give me a minute," she said.

She didn't know how to alert Jessemia that she was there, since you couldn't exactly knock on a tent door. Then she remembered that Jessemia had nearly gotten her killed and decided she didn't care about politeness. She pushed open the tent flap and stepped inside. Jessemia huddled on her bedroll, curled into a tight ball with her arms hugging her knees. Her eyes were open and she was staring at nothing.

"Come have breakfast," Aderyn said.

Jessemia shook her head.

"If you don't eat, you can't keep up, and I might not be able to stop Owen leaving you behind a second time," Aderyn said. "As it is, I think he might leave you in Plensholt."

"You all hate me," Jessemia said. Her voice wasn't petulant for once; she said the words like she was making a flat statement about reality that no one would dispute.

"I don't hate you," Aderyn said.

"You should." Jessemia closed her eyes.

Aderyn groaned and grabbed Jessemia by the arm, hauling her up. Jessemia didn't resist, which was good because she was taller than Aderyn by a few inches. "Stop feeling sorry for yourself. It's pathetic and contemptible and a backhanded way to get people to take care of you. You're alive, I'm alive, nobody hurt us, and it's time to move on."

Jessemia blinked at her. "Aren't you mad at me?"

Aderyn sighed. "I don't know. You were almost fatally stupid, but I got myself into that mess. I didn't have to follow you. So if I blame you, I have to blame myself as well. Better to just accept that we were both stupid and move forward."

"I don't understand." Jessemia's brow furrowed. "I haven't been nice to any of you. You don't owe me anything. Why did you follow me?"

"I told you. I couldn't let you go off to die." Aderyn felt unexpectedly weary, as if this conversation sapped her energy. "If you don't understand that, maybe you really are past changing." She turned to go.

Jessemia said, "Thank you."

Aderyn had never heard her say anything in the least grateful before. After a moment's stunned silence, she said, "You're welcome." Then she left the tent and walked back to the fire. Jessemia followed her and sat beside her.

Weston and Livia had been bantering, but they fell silent when Jessemia sat down. Then Weston scooped up a plate of porridge and handed it to her. Jessemia accepted it and ate slowly while Livia glared at her. Finally, Livia said, "We ought to leave you in Plensholt."

"I understand," Jessemia said.

Aderyn looked up at Owen's approach. He glanced over all of them, his gaze passing over Jessemia without interest, and ended by smiling at Aderyn. "I don't think that Brigand is coming back," he said. "At least, there isn't anyone but us out here for miles. Let's get on our way. We won't want to stop in Plensholt for long."

No one spoke. Jessemia set her empty plate aside and rose. "Thank you for rescuing me," she said to no one in particular.

"We didn't," Owen said flatly. "We rescued Aderyn. You were just a lucky bystander."

"Stop," Aderyn said. "You know we would have gone after Jessemia if she had been the only one taken."

"That is not a given," Owen said.

"Of course it is. You're not evil and you're not cruel." Aderyn put a hand on his arm. "I know you're angry, but you can't let that spill over into hating someone. That only hurts you."

"I'll stay in Plensholt," Jessemia said.

"You don't have to," Aderyn began, but Jessemia cut her off.

"You didn't want me along, I know," she said, "and I was—" She drew in a sobbing breath. "That Brigand didn't care anything about me. I thought I was special, and you all didn't see it, but he treated me like a thing he could use for his pleasure, and that showed me everything I believed about myself was a lie. So, you were right."

"Don't expect me to contradict you so you'll feel better about yourself," Owen said. "You're selfish, arrogant, and oblivious to reality. I don't believe that's changed just because you were captured and threatened with rape and death."

Jessemia shook her head. "I spent all night thinking about who I am. Those teams my father found for me—they were just humoring me, weren't they?"

"Probably," Owen said.

"And I'm not really the Fated One."

"No."

"Then I—" Jessemia breathed in deeply again and let the air out in a long stream. "I shouldn't let you go on taking me with you. I can at least do that."

Aderyn shifted uncomfortably. She didn't like Jessemia, and the thought of her no longer being a part of their group was a relief. But she'd never thought the woman could humble herself at all. What might Jessemia end up being if she really had changed?"

"Then it's settled," Owen said. "You can stay with Gladyn at the Lone Pine while you figure out what work you can do in Plensholt."

Jessemia nodded and returned to her tent. Aderyn watched her go and wished she didn't feel so unsettled about Owen's decision.

Food and sleep revived Aderyn, and she felt only a little achy as she walked beside Owen. The memory of being a captive had faded with the sunshine and fresh air, and while she was sure the memories would trouble her for a while as she fell asleep at night, for now, everything was fine.

She watched Owen now and then, admiring his strong profile and how his blond hair curled around his ear. She didn't think she was being obvious about it, but then he said, "Do I have a twig in my hair or something?"

"I'm glad to be with you again. I was so afraid."

Owen's jaw tensed. "We took far too long figuring out what had happened. I thought you'd gone for a walk when you weren't at breakfast, and of course I didn't care enough to track down Jessemia. Then we heard about the dead guard, and neither of you were anywhere we could find you, and I made a leap of logic based on how friendly Jessemia had been with that Brigand leader. I didn't know why you would have gone with her, and I was terrified that the Brigands had killed you because you were an impediment to their plans. You were still on the team roster, so it wasn't a rational fear, but still."

"I think we were lucky all around. Hadrus—the Brigand leader—he enjoyed taunting us with what he planned to do, so he never got around to doing anything."

"That's not as reassuring as you probably hope." Owen took Aderyn's hand in his. "And now, what about Jessemia?"

"She was really scared and I think that made her see sense. Don't be mad."

"I'm getting over it." He sighed. "Her change of heart won't last. But it doesn't matter. We'll leave her in Plensholt and never have to think about her again."

"I guess."

Owen gave her a skeptical look. "You don't think it's a good idea?"

"It is, I suppose. I just—"

"Aderyn, she's a burden even if she isn't going to whine anymore, which as I said is likely not a state of affairs that will persist long. Why shouldn't we leave her somewhere safe that she won't interfere with our plans?"

Aderyn shrugged. Her face felt hot, though she didn't know why this conversation made her embarrassed. "You know I've always felt it was unfortunate that she was raised the way she was—coddled, told she was special, given everything she ever wanted. She's never had the chance to discover who she could be. We could do that for her."

"You're kidding. We can't fix everything that's wrong with her. And that assumes she's willing to change, which I doubt."

"I know. I'm just being softhearted again."

They walked in silence for a while, still holding hands. Finally, Owen said, "Why does this matter so much to you?"

"What, Jessemia? I don't know. I just—Owen, I have a class everyone thinks is worthless. Even you only gave me a chance because neither of us knew any better. So I understand, a little, what it's like to be the subject of other people's assumptions. Everyone thinks Jessemia is a joke. What if she could be more?"

"You can't possibly compare yourself to her. You don't have a selfish bone in your body." Owen squeezed her hand gently. "Okay. I think I get it. But she's got a lot of bad habits to overcome, and we can't make that happen."

"No, but we can give her a chance. Show her what it's like to be a confident person who isn't self-centered and ego-driven."

Owen threw his head back and groaned at the sky. "Why do I feel like you just came home with a stray dog?"

"I don't understand. Why would I bring a stray dog home? They're feral and covered in parasites."

"It's just a thing kids try in my world." Owen stopped and kissed Aderyn. "She can stay with us. But I'll set the rules. If she chooses not to obey, well, there are a lot of little villages between here and Guerdon Deep."

Aderyn returned his kiss. "Thank you. It's the right thing to do."

"I'm not totally convinced of that," Owen said, "but I trust your instincts, whether they're about fighting or about other people. Jessemia is lucky to have you as a defender."

That made Aderyn uncomfortable. "I didn't know that's what I was doing."

"You spoke on her behalf. That's a way of defending someone."

"That's true." Aderyn thought about that for a while. "I guess if

I want her to be different, and I'm the only one who feels that way, I am defending her."

"Nothing wrong with that, sweetheart. And you're a good person to care so much." Owen hugged her briefly. "I'll tell her when we stop for lunch. But I'm not going to go easy on her. No accommodations for her sake. She does as I say or she leaves."

"That's reasonable. If she's going to change, she has to be challenged," Aderyn said.

CHAPTER THIRTEEN

They stopped to eat when the sun reached its zenith, grapes and what Owen called beef jerky from the <**Forager's Belt**>, hunks of cheese wrapped in cloth, and fresh water summoned by Livia. Nobody spoke. Jessemia sat a little ways away from the others and nibbled her food.

Owen ate a few final grapes and said, "Jessemia."

Jessemia looked up. Her eyes were reddened as if she'd been crying. She didn't say a word.

"You made a mistake," Owen said. "It could have cost you and Aderyn your lives. Do you have anything to say about that?"

"I apologized to Aderyn," Jessemia said in a dull voice. "She said it wasn't enough. I don't know what else to do."

"My mom always says when you screw up, you have to apologize and do what you can to make restitution. What are you going to do, Jessemia?"

Jessemia frowned. "I don't understand."

"You've apologized," Owen said. "How are you going to make things right?"

"I don't..." Her voice trailed off, and she got an intent look that said she was considering. "Aderyn said I was too self-centered to realize Hadrus was lying to me. I don't want to be like that anymore. I want to think of other people first. But it doesn't matter. I'm staying in Plensholt."

"That's up to you." Owen leaned forward so she had to look him in the eye. "Aderyn convinced me to give you another chance. You can stay in Plensholt if you want. Or you can travel with us."

"Owen!" Livia exclaimed.

"I thought we were finally rid of her," Weston groaned.

Aderyn was watching Jessemia rather than her friends, and the look of humiliation that crossed Jessemia's face sent a stab of sympathy through her. "Stop," she said. "She's a person, not a thing. She didn't injure you, she hurt me, and that gives me the right to say how we're going to treat her. And I say she should come with us."

Jessemia's mouth fell open. "You want me to stay? After what I did?"

"You can't make restitution if you're in Plensholt," Aderyn said.

"But there are still rules," Owen said. "You do as you're told, because we're experienced adventurers and you're not. No more complaining about things you don't like. No special treatment—you pull your weight like all of us. And you stay out of the way when we fight. Understand?"

Jessemia nodded. "Thank you."

"Don't thank me, thank Aderyn," Owen said, rising and dusting off his posterior. "Let's move on. I've decided we'll stay one more night in Plensholt. Aderyn still doesn't look well."

Aderyn started to protest that she felt just fine, but she caught Owen's wink and realized what he really had in mind for that night in Plensholt. The idea of cuddling with Owen—of more than cuddling—sent a nice warm rush through her.

"You're not worried about Isold?" she murmured when they were on their way again.

"Jessemia is cowed enough I doubt she'll make advances," Owen murmured back. "Whether Isold has changed his mind, I don't know."

"No. That's not possible. Is it?"

"He didn't say anything against Jessemia staying with us, and he's as kindhearted as you are. Though he's also conscious of interpersonal relations, so I don't actually think he'd act on any desires he might have developed for Jessemia, not when that could make travel awkward. And I don't really care. All I want is to spend the night with you, naked and sharing a bed, and everything else can go to hell."

"Don't all those rooms have two beds? We'll be wasting space." Aderyn pretended to be concerned.

"I know you didn't just suggest that you want us to share with someone else," Owen said with a smile. "I don't swing that way."

Aderyn laughed. "I guess we waste space, then."

RAIN FELL ON AND OFF FOR TWO DAYS AFTER THEY LEFT Plensholt. To the north and east, the plains stretched out before them, empty of anything but the occasional firs. To the south, the terrain rose gently until it became hills that extended all the way to the Welterwall, several days' journey away. Aderyn suspected the weather was keeping the monsters under shelter, because nothing attacked.

She kept an eye on Jessemia, who spoke only when spoken to and who huddled into her rain cape miserably. Jessemia walked near the center of the group now, next to Isold, who ignored her. So did Livia and Weston. Owen spoke to her only to give her instructions when they camped. Aderyn didn't exactly regret the impulse that had led to her arguing for Jessemia to stay with them, but her friends' reactions made the atmosphere chilly and uncomfortable. She would have welcomed a monster attack.

When Weston said, "There's a building over there, at the top of that rise," her heart leaped as if he'd said something more exciting. She looked in the direction he indicated, but saw nothing but trees and hills.

"I don't see it," Owen said.

"It blends in with its surroundings a bit, but it's clearly not natural." Weston shielded his eyes and squinted. "A stone tower."

"Huh." Owen pursed his lips in thought. "Maybe we should check it out."

"It could be something interesting," Aderyn said. "Like a dungeon. Or a forgotten settlement."

"It's not like we're in a hurry," Livia said.

"True. Weston, how far away is it?"

"Maybe two hours' hike," Weston said.

"Then let's do this," Owen said.

They all walked faster, Aderyn thought because of the prospect of something breaking up the monotony of the day's travel. They soon left the plains behind for the low hills, which weren't steep enough to slow them. Trees grew here and there, pines whose needles shone wetly under the intermittent rain, as well as the occasional cedar. After a few of these rises, Aderyn saw it: a tower whose gray stonework covered in moss did blend, as Weston had said, with the surrounding evergreens. Enough trees surrounded it that Aderyn couldn't make out its size, though it didn't seem much taller than the trees. But it was close enough to Assess.

"Hold on a bit," she said, stopping so she wouldn't trip on a root or stone as she read aloud.

Name: The Lonely Gard

Type: Standard dungeon, advanced, victory condition variant B

Power Level: 15

Inhabitants: abominations, monstrosities

Traps: none

Reward: 3500 gold plus random treasure drops (70% mundane, 30% magical) and the Phoenix Stylus

Weston whistled. "Level fifteen. I think that's a bit much for us."

"I guess, but we can still take a look at it, right?" Aderyn said. The idea of coming this far and not at least seeing the dungeon clearly disappointed her. Besides, it might give them something to talk about that would break the dour silence.

"Why not?" Owen said. "It's about time for lunch, anyway."

"You want to eat next to a dungeon?" Livia exclaimed.

"It's not as if it's going to come to life and attack us." Owen looked suddenly worried. "Dungeons can't do that, right?"

"There are no records of a dungeon capable of influencing the world outside its confines," Isold said.

"Yeah, and there were no records of a sapient dungeon, either, but Winter's Peril and Gamboling Coil said otherwise."

"I really don't think it's possible for the dungeon to grab us and make us enter," Aderyn said. "And I'm hungry. Come on, let's look at it!"

The others followed her through the trees as she hurried along. The closer they got to the Lonely Gard, though, the less eager Aderyn became. The silence among the trees worried her. There were no birdcalls, no rustling of small animals through the undergrowth, not even a wind blowing through the pines to make the needles rub together. All she heard was her and her friends' footsteps crunching over the dry needles and kicking up small stones.

She came out from beneath the trees and stopped. A small cleared area, no more than twenty feet wide, spanned the distance between the tree line and the base of the tower. Massive stones made up the foundation of the tower, big enough Aderyn couldn't imagine them getting to this place by any means short of magic. The door was equally massive, big enough to let three people carrying three other people on their shoulders through at once.

But the dungeon's intimidating presence wasn't what had

stopped her. A man lay crumpled on the ground six steps from the dungeon door, face down, blood saturating his left leg and stiffening his hair. One hand was missing, and a rag was tied tightly around the stump. She couldn't tell if he was breathing.

Isold pushed past her, muttering, "Sorry," and knelt beside the man with the <Healing Stone> in his hand. "He's still alive, but only just." With his free hand, he parted the man's hair, revealing a deep gash with purpling edges. He laid the stone against the wound. Green light welled up from within the man's suddenly translucent skull as if he'd swallowed a hundred fireflies. Aderyn held her breath. The green light flickered, steadied, flickered again. Isold pressed the <Healing Stone> harder against the wound. His eyes were closed, and he was muttering to himself words too quiet for Aderyn to hear.

Then the glow faded. The man remained motionless. Aderyn's chest hurt from not breathing as she willed him to move, to sit up, even to let out a breath. Isold sat back on his heels and rubbed blood off the <Healing Stone> on his trouser leg. He put a hand on the man's shoulder and gently shook him.

The man shifted and stretched out his maimed arm. His back rose and fell with a deep breath. He let out a moan of pain and said something garbled that Isold leaned closer to hear.

Isold took the maimed arm in his hand. "I'm afraid the <Healing Stone> won't regenerate lost limbs. All I can do is heal the wound so it won't hurt. And your leg is badly broken—I see bone poking out. It will hurt to have it set, but if you can endure a little longer, the pain will pass."

The man again said something too incoherent for Aderyn to understand. Isold nodded to the others. "Help me get him on his back."

After Livia cut the man's knapsack straps and removed the bag, Weston and Owen gently turned the wounded man as directed, while Aderyn set to cutting the trousers away from his broken leg. That looked nasty, with the shattered end of the bone sticking out. She couldn't imagine how he'd gotten out of the dungeon on that leg.

Isold quickly healed the stump of the man's arm, then, with some effort, realigned the broken bone. That procedure made the man cry out and then faint. While Isold wielded the <**Healing Stone**> a third time, Aderyn Assessed the man.

Name: Crillon

Class: Stalwart

Level: 12

A Stalwart. That explained a lot. No one else could have survived those injuries. Aderyn tossed aside the bloody remnant of Crillon's trouser leg. "Let's see about making him more comfortable," she said to Weston and Livia. She noticed Jessemia standing nearby, her face pale and worried, and was grateful the woman hadn't, in Owen's words, freaked out at the sight of the badly wounded man.

Aderyn and Livia went through Crillon's knapsack and, as Weston lifted him, folded a spare shirt into a pillow and spread the man's half-cloak beneath him, protecting him from the wet ground. Crillon came to as Weston laid him gently down. He worked his mouth a few times before whispering, "Who are you?"

"We found you outside the Lonely Gard," Aderyn said. "Do you remember what happened?"

Crillon raised his maimed arm to touch his head where he'd been injured, and froze. "My hand—I remember. The weirdling bit it off. It tore Amabel's throat out—she killed it, but at such cost—" His eyes flew open, and he sat up. "Where's the <**Phoenix Stylus**>? Where is it? I didn't—oh, no, if I lost it after everything—"

"It's here," Isold said. He held out a silver rod about the same size and shape as a charcoal pencil. Golden traceries moved over its surface, deepening to red at their edges like thin flows of molten ore. The rod came to a sharp point at one end and was rounded at the other.

Crillon snatched it from Isold's grasp and clutched it to his chest, weeping. "It has to be worth it," he sobbed. "Thank you. If I'd died here, everything would be lost."

"That sounds like a story worth listening to," Owen said.

"Let me rest a bit longer, and then I—" His face paled. "I totally forgot about Coralie. I need to get back to her—she won't have started worrying yet, we weren't gone all that long, but—"

"Who's Coralie?" Aderyn asked.

Crillon shook his head. "If you help me return to her, I'll tell you everything as we go. I'm already in your debt, but I'm sure we can pay you something for your help."

"Don't worry about that," Owen said. "Where is she?"

"I'll show you. And... thank you." Crillon tried to rise, his legs and arms shaking, and Weston gave him a hand up. "Thank you again."

"Are you sure you're ready to walk?" Weston asked.

"I just need a few minutes," Crillon said. "But I'd drag myself on that broken leg if I had to."

"What's so important you'd injure yourself further?" Isold asked.

"If I don't," Crillon said, "our town dies."

CHAPTER FOURTEEN

With Crillon's arms draped over Owen and Weston's shoulders, they made their way slowly across the hills, heading east. Crillon's heavy breathing and stumbling gait made it impossible for him to speak, however impatient Aderyn was to hear his story. But after only a hundred paces, he was able to walk unsupported, and half a mile farther along he was moving as easily as if he'd never been injured. Aderyn knew Stalwarts were capable of sustaining great damage and had tremendous recuperative powers, but she'd never seen them in action before.

Eventually, Crillon said, "We're from Alcester, which is about two days' journey from here, I think—I've never been good with directions. That was what Jeddro did—he was a Pathseer—I can't believe he's gone." Crillon's last words came out choked, and it took him a minute before he said, "Sorry. I'm weaker than I thought if I can't bear up under the loss of my companions."

"There's nothing weak about mourning a loss," Isold said. "I take it you had a team that died in the Lonely Gard?"

Crillon nodded. "We'd been together since level six. Well, that's misleading. We were all born in Alcester, we all got the Call around the same time, and we were all in the same caravan that took us to the safe zone to begin adventuring. We separated after reaching Gardholm, but once we leveled up to six, we wanted to return home to defend our town. So we teamed up, and—the rest isn't important. Typical adventuring stuff, monster battles, quests, a few dungeons."

"How big is Alcester?" Aderyn asked.

"Bigger than any of the sanctuary cities, but smaller than Setter's Valley. You're wondering how much defense a town out in the Plains needs, huh?"

"I was, yes. Were you the only adventurers there?"

"Only ones not retired. Which is why we were called on when disaster struck." Crillon rubbed the stump of his wrist absently. "Some change in the environment poisoned Alcester's water supply. A corruption at the source, it turns out—there's a Tidecaller in Jackrabbit Dell who came to look into it. He couldn't do anything about it, because pulling more water out of the system just increased the poison influence."

"And that means death for a community," Owen said. "No water, no life."

Crillon nodded. "We've got enough spellslingers who can cast *drench* that it's not an immediate death. But that's a very temporary solution, and we had another option. Coralie said—she's a retired Spellcrafter who lives in Alcester—she said she could make an artifact that would remove the poison from the water. It won't eliminate the source of the corruption, but it will negate its influence."

"Sounds like a quest to me," Livia said.

"The mayor of Alcester issued the quest—escort Coralie through the creation of the artifact. That was five days ago. Oh, there's the stream. I was afraid I was going in circles." He pointed at a wide stream cutting across the hills about a hundred paces ahead. "Our camp is upstream from here."

They turned to follow the stream, which smelled fresh and cool and less muggy than the waterlogged air. Owen walked just behind Crillon. "So, what was the quest? What's out here?"

"The artifact we need is a **<Stone of Purification>**," Crillon said. "Obviously I don't understand the details, but it requires a perfect river stone that's been bathed in water infused with pine and mint. Once that's done, the Spellcrafter uses the **<Phoenix Stylus>** to inscribe what Coralie calls 'instructions' that tell the stone how to recognize the poison. We came out here because it's the closest large stream to the Lonely Gard. Coralie was going to treat the stone while we were gone, see about cutting down on the time the quest takes."

He held up the **<Phoenix Stylus>** so it caught the afternoon light. "This will save our town. I know Jeddro and Amabel and Fillicia wouldn't regret the sacrifice of their lives to make it happen." His voice was hoarse, and his eyes shone with unshed tears.

Aderyn couldn't think of anything to say. He'd lost his closest friends, lost his hand, and he still only thought of saving his home. Maybe it was better not to say anything.

Crillon sped up. "Coralie? Are you still there?"

"Of course I'm still here, you wandering ape," a querulous female voice said from somewhere ahead. "You've only been gone a few hours. What did you think—"

The trees thinned out near the stream, enough that Aderyn could see where someone had dammed it off to create a small pool. Beside the pool sat an elderly woman with iron-gray hair bound up tightly at the back of her head. She held an iron bar attached to a hand grip across her lap. An enormous pile of stripy gray fur next to her lifted its head, revealing that it was a cat curled up at her side. Aderyn couldn't understand why Crillon and the others had left her alone and undefended. She didn't look as if she could give anything a fight.

The woman stared at Crillon's stump. "What in *thunder* happened to you?" she whispered. "Crillon, where are the others?"

"The Lonely Gard was even more difficult than we imagined,

between some bad luck and not expecting how dangerous the monsters would be," Crillon said. "The others are dead, and I would be too if not for these adventurers. They saved my life."

"You mean Amabel—" The woman, Coralie, released her grip on the iron bar and covered her mouth. "My granddaughter—"

"I'm so sorry, Coralie," Crillon said. "I tried. It's what I do, protect them, but the final boss, the weirdling, was almost too much. Amabel knifed it between the ribs just before it killed her. She and I were the last to survive. But we beat the dungeon, Coralie, and I got the <**Phoenix Stylus**>." He held the silver rod out to Coralie.

Coralie took it with a shaking hand. "At such a cost," she whispered. She wiped her eyes with her other hand and then rested that hand on the fur pile that was the cat. "But it's pointless. I can't complete the <**Stone of Purification**> creation."

Crillon dropped to his knees. The cat stretched and wandered over to him, nudging his remaining hand. Crillon ignored it. "What do you mean? That's the thing you needed, right?"

"And I'll be able to inscribe the instructions with it. But there's one more step, and with just the two of us, it will be impossible to do." Coralie idly spun the stylus between her fingers as if it was an ordinary stick.

"What step?" Owen asked.

Coralie cast her gaze down as if embarrassed to look at him. "The ones who saved Crillon's life. Thank you. The last element I need is a crystal prism from the Icebright Caves. Crillon and I alone can't handle it. And our town will suffer and die for our failure."

Owen laughed. Coralie's head snapped up. "Are you mocking our pain?"

"I'm laughing because that was an almost perfect play on my sympathies," Owen said. "You could just ask, you know."

Coralie's eyebrows raised. Sharp blue eyes stared Owen down. "Most people aren't moved by altruism."

"I'm not most people," Owen said. "You need to get to the Icebright Caves, we can take you there."

Those sharp blue eyes shifted to fix on Aderyn, and then on the other friends, ending with Jessemia, who squirmed and wouldn't meet Coralie's gaze. Coralie said, "You speak for everyone? Bold of you."

"I don't usually, not without discussion, but in this case I know we're all in agreement," Owen said. "Right?"

"We're all from towns in the safe zone that could easily find themselves in Alcester's predicament," Aderyn said. "Where are the Icebright Caves, anyway? They sound cold."

"The name refers to the many [Prismatic Crystals] that grow there," Coralie said. "The Caves themselves are at the base of the Welterwall, not high enough on the slopes to be cold year round. From here, it's a three-day journey south by southwest. Still interested?"

"I haven't heard anything to change my mind," Owen said.

Aderyn was ready for the system message that appeared.

A new quest is available: [Clean, Clear Water]
Escort Coralie the Spellcrafter to the Icebright Caves. This quest is part of the quest chain [A Town's Salvation]. Accepting this quest makes the rest of the quest chain available.
Accept? Y / N

All around her, her friends gestured to accept the quest. "Do you need to inscribe the stone here, or can it be as we travel?" Owen asked.

Coralie cocked her head and examined the sky. "I can't do it while I walk, if that's what you're asking. The magic won't take long, but best we get a fresh start in the morning anyway."

Owen unslung his knapsack and set it on the ground at his feet. "Sounds ideal. Do you mind if we set up camp near here?"

Coralie ran her fingers over the gray cat's fur. The creature stretched and arched its neck to be scratched. Despite its size, it was muscular rather than fat, and Aderyn could easily imagine it smashing through any wall that got between it and the food dish. "You will save our home. Do whatever you like."

Aderyn set down the <Knapsack of Plenty> and stretched. While Livia examined the nearby terrain, looking for a good place to use the <Soldier's Friend>, she Assessed the elderly Spellcrafter.

Name: Coralie

Class: Spellcrafter (retired)

Level: 17

Aderyn had never seen a Spellcrafter of such a high level. Well, maybe she had, because she'd been too low a level to see her grandfather Marrius's skills and level, and he was a powerful Spellcrafter too.

Out of curiosity, she turned Skill Assess on the elderly woman. What skills might someone who'd reached level seventeen have, and with what ranks? She read the list that appeared silently, then counted. Twenty class skills! The long, long list stunned Aderyn. Coralie's skill ranks were higher than she would have guessed, too. It must be that retired adventurers, while no longer receiving level advancement, could continue to earn skill ranks. No wonder Coralie had proposed making the <Stone of Purification>. Aderyn couldn't begin to imagine how many magic items and artifacts she'd created over the years.

A distant fanfare heralded the appearance of their camp. Crillon took a step backwards in astonishment, but Coralie chuckled. "You're more than you appear, if you've got one of those," she said. "May I see it?"

Livia handed the bronze cube to Coralie, who turned it over in her hand, examining it. "Good work," she said. "There aren't many of these around. Never mind the level you have to be to have the skill to make it, the components are difficult to find and in some cases bloody. Take good care of it, young woman."

Livia nodded and put the thing away in her knapsack.

"And I'll sit by the fire while I do this, if you don't mind," Coralie said, rising somewhat stiffly from her seat beside the pool. "I'm not as young as I once was."

Aderyn collected Owen's knapsack as well as her own and stowed them in their tent. Livia followed her. "I didn't think about offering a tent for Coralie and Crillon," she whispered. "Too late now, I guess."

Aderyn looked past her at where Coralie was settled by the fire with her odd iron rod beside her. "Let's see how the day goes. I wonder if she'll let me watch?"

She crossed the camp to the fire and said, "What is it you have to do?"

Coralie held a smooth, oval stone in her left hand. The stone was big enough her fingers barely curled around its edges. "Warmaster," she said, drawing the word out like she was examining it for flaws. "Your class generally retires early. I've never seen one of you higher than level five. How is it you've achieved level twelve?"

Aderyn took this as an invitation to sit across from her. The cat, sensing a potential lap, wandered over and rubbed its head against Aderyn's hand. Aderyn wasn't fond of cats, but she had to admire this one's persistence. "My partner and I discovered what makes a Warmaster successful. With a partner, I have someone to use my skills on behalf of, and he and I support each other."

"Interesting. Wait a moment." Coralie dipped a hand into her belt pouch and removed a pair of glass lenses set into a gold wire frame. She settled the glasses on her nose so the lenses caught the fire-light, revealing an iridescent sheen that made them slightly opaque, then hesitated. "These <**Eyes of Insight**> reveal someone's skills and ranks. May I use them on you?"

"You could have done it without telling me," Aderyn said.

"I could," Coralie replied, "but deceiving allies is the fast track to an evil class, and even though I'm retired, I believe in being honorable when it comes to adventuring matters. May I?"

Aderyn nodded.

Coralie focused her sharp blue gaze on her through the lenses. "You have skills I've never heard of," she said, "and your ranks are much higher than your level would account for. Is that what you mean by your partner supporting you?"

"We have paired skills that advance at the same time, like [Keep Pace]. And some of my skills affect his, like how [Improved Assess 2] and [Discern Weakness] make him a better sword fighter. And the reverse is also true." Aderyn petted the cat's head, and its purr vibrated through her hand and up her arm.

"Astonishing." Coralie removed the <Eyes of Insight> and extended them to Aderyn. "Tell me what you see."

The request unexpectedly embarrassed Aderyn. "Oh, I, um, can see your skills and ranks already. [Improved Assess 2]. It's a class skill for Warmasters."

"No kidding." Coralie's expression became one of respect. "I see. That all makes you a tactician."

"Yes."

"Unbelievable. What a waste of a good class, if everyone assumes you're worthless." Coralie put the lenses away in her belt pouch and picked up the <Phoenix Stylus>. Her matter-of-fact attitude impressed Aderyn. She was so used to defending her supposedly useless class it was refreshing to meet someone who took her explanation in stride. If that was something that came with age and experience, getting old might not be so bad.

CHAPTER FIFTEEN

Coralie ran her fingers idly down the <**Phoenix Stylus**>. "Just shove him away if he's annoying," she said.

"What? Oh, the cat." Aderyn realized she'd been scratching behind the cat's ears for a while now. "He's, um, big."

"He's twenty pounds of muscle and two ounces of brain, is what he is," Coralie said. "Come here, Gustavio. This is Prince Gustavio Strongpaws, fiercest mouser in the Plains and the biggest softy you can imagine. I said *here*, you dummy." She snapped her fingers at the cat. Prince Gustavio Strongpaws ignored her.

"I never knew a cat that was smart enough to come when it was called," Aderyn said.

"Hah. He knows. See the way his tail twitched when I said his name? He's happy where he is and he knows I'm not serious in needing him. Cats are like that. Fortunately, he's not as dumb as I suggested, and he obeys when it matters. You don't like cats, do you."

Aderyn shrugged. "I don't hate them. I'm just not a cat person."

"That's good, because he likes you, and Prince Gustavio Strongpaws is an excellent judge of character. Which one's your partner? Your team leader?"

"Yes. Owen."

"Jacob Owen Lindberg, that's a strange and unnecessarily long name. I'm guessing you're lovers?"

Aderyn blushed. "He's my sweetheart, yes."

"I've always believed in being direct. Lover, sweetheart, comes down to the same thing, doesn't it?"

Aderyn noticed the golden lines on the surface of the <**Phoenix Stylus**> had grown brighter and now glowed like real gold in sunlight. "Those aren't hot? It looks like they should burn your hand."

Coralie glanced at the stylus. "Just an effect of the magic warming up. Excuse me, I have to concentrate now. You can watch if you stay quiet."

Aderyn nodded and knelt up so she could see clearly. Coralie held the <**Phoenix Stylus**> above the surface of the stone so the tip was a fraction of an inch from it. The golden lines moved downward as if drawn by gravity until they piled up at the tip of the stylus. A line of pure white light shimmered into being, connecting the stylus's tip and the stone's barely-curved top face. Coralie held the stylus in that position for several seconds. When Aderyn glanced at her, swiftly so she wouldn't miss anything, she saw Coralie's eyes were closed and her lips were moving in soundless speech.

Then Coralie lowered the stylus to rest on the stone and began writing, golden lines that sizzled with energy. Except the writing wasn't in the language Aderyn knew, and it wasn't pictures; it looked like fragments of letters, connected in ways that made sentences impossible to read. Some of them were great swooping spirals, while others were staccato lines so sharp no human pen could write them.

Aderyn became aware of others gathered around, all of them silently watching Coralie draw, or write—it was impossible to say which. She herself was breathless at the beauty of the Spellcrafter's work. The stone was alive with color as the fresh strokes of hot gold cooled to red and then to black, like metal removed from a forge and left to cool in the afternoon air.

Finally, Coralie lowered the stylus. She was breathing heavily and perspiration beaded her forehead. "Earthbreaker," she said. "Can you cast *drench?*"

"I can," Livia said.

Coralie silently extended the hand holding the stone away from the fire. Livia cast the spell, making a gout of water splash over Coralie's hand and arm. Coralie shuddered with the cold, but made no sound. She rubbed the stone off on her trouser leg, leaving a dark smear like soot, and displayed the stone. The curves and lines she'd drawn were now etched into the oval face, and golden light pooled and shifted in the crevices as if it were liquid metal confined by the grooves. "It's done, or at least that step is done," she said. "And I'm exhausted. I need a few hours' sleep."

Aderyn and Livia exchanged glances. Coralie looked like she intended to lay her bedroll right between the tents. Sure, she was a powerful retired adventurer, but she was also someone's grand-mother, and to Aderyn the thought of an old lady sleeping without shelter felt wrong.

"You can share a tent with me," Jessemia said.

Aderyn and Livia's shared look became one of astonishment. Jessemia wasn't meeting anyone's eyes, but her voice was firm. "There's plenty of room for both of us," she added.

"Well, that's very kind of you," Coralie said. "If you're sure you don't mind."

"I want to help," Jessemia said. "Let me take your bedroll."

When the two women had disappeared into the tent, Livia said in a low voice, "Did that just happen?"

"Jessemia's not a bad person," Aderyn said. "And she said she wanted to learn to think of others."

"Yes, but I didn't believe she meant it." Livia eyed the tent door.

"I still say she's a lost cause. One act of kindness doesn't make someone an unselfish person."

"No," Aderyn said, "but it's a start."

THEY GOT AN EARLY START THE NEXT MORNING, EATING quickly and packing quickly. Even the <**Soldier's Friend**> seemed to work more rapidly than usual. No one said anything, but Aderyn was sure they all felt the urgency of the quest. She imagined her home town of Far Haven stricken by drought or poisoned water, how quickly that would devastate the community, and hoped if it ever happened, someone would be in a position to do what she and her team were doing for Alcester.

After a quick, private discussion, Owen had offered Crillon the final slot on their team roster. "I know it's not the same, and we can't take your friends' place," he'd said, "but if anything goes wrong, we'll be more effective if we're officially a team." Crillon had just nodded and silently accepted the invitation when the system presented it.

Neither Crillon nor Coralie had been skeptical of Owen's explanation about Jessemia, that they were escorting her to Guerdon Deep as part of a quest. Even though that was perfectly true, Jessemia's continuing silence and her lack of interaction with the team made it look like a lie. Aderyn had to admit Jessemia looked more like a prisoner than a guest or a friend.

So she walked beside Jessemia that morning and tried a number of conversational openings. Jessemia responded to all of them dully and let them drop as soon as possible. Finally, irritated, Aderyn said, "Damn it, Jessemia, you're acting like we're taking you to your own execution!"

Jessemia glanced at her, startled at her eruption. "What does 'damn it' mean? I've never heard that before."

"It's a swear word Owen invented, or something. I learned it from him, anyway. I think it has to do with the void demons come from." Realizing they were edging up on forbidden information about Owen's origins, Aderyn said, "Anyway, the point is, you're acting like you're terrified of us. No one's going to hurt you."

Jessemia bowed her head. "I know none of you like me."

Aderyn couldn't tell her that wasn't true. "Do you want us to like you?"

"I don't know. I want you not to hate me, but I know that won't happen."

Impatience surged through Aderyn. "If you keep behaving like a kicked puppy, it definitely won't. People don't like that behavior. That whole timid hangdog attitude. It makes them feel like they're being manipulated to be nice to someone so they'll stop acting that way."

"It does?" Jessemia straightened. "I didn't think I was doing that. I don't expect anything from any of you."

"Well, that's not how it seems. You need to have self-respect or no one will ever like you, that's what my father says. He says self-respect is the key to confidence, and confidence is attractive no matter your appearance."

"Oh." Jessemia fell silent for several paces. Then she said, "What do I need to do to gain your forgiveness? You said, make restitution, but I can't go back and make those bandits not capture us. So, what do you expect?"

"I—" The question caught Aderyn off guard. "I guess all I really want is for you to stop whining and complaining and expecting special treatment. And you've done that."

"I might go back to that, though. You can't know."

"Sure I can. At least, I choose to believe you've changed. Don't you think so?"

Jessemia shrugged. "I've been trying."

"Then be proud of that effort." She thought about telling her to stop cringing when Owen spoke to her, but given how hostile Owen had been and how distant he still was, that would only humiliate her further. "And try not to dwell on the past."

"I don't. But I can't not remember." Jessemia sounded unexpectedly angry.

"I don't know what else to tell you, Jessemia," Aderyn said, feeling angry herself. "I know you made a bad start of things, but most of that wasn't your fault. You didn't ask for a father who treated you like a pet, or for teams who babied you and lied to you about what it meant to be an adventurer. Maybe—I can't believe I'm saying this, but maybe you need to think of yourself as a victim of your circumstances, too."

"A victim?"

"Not in the sense that you aren't responsible for your life. But who knows who you might have been if those things hadn't happened? And I choose to believe that person is inside you somewhere, and it's possible for her to take control. I don't know, maybe that's nonsense. But I don't think so." Aderyn's cheeks were hot, and she wished she hadn't been so open. Still, who else would tell Jessemia the truth?

"A victim," Jessemia replied, sounding thoughtful. "If I—"

"Aderyn, come and look at this," Owen called.

"Sorry," Aderyn said, and hurried forward to Owen's side.

Owen, Weston, and Crillon stood at the top of the next hill, looking down into the small valley. It was empty of all but a few solitary pines and covered with long yellow grasses and several shrubs Aderyn didn't recognize at that distance. Animals milled about, eating the grass and ignoring the shrubs. The wind from the east had picked up, sending waves of motion across the valley as the grasses bent and tossed.

"Antelopes," she said. "You want to hunt them? Livia's gotten good at picking stragglers off with the <**Wand of Sleep**>."

"Not that. Farther south." Owen pointed.

She followed the line of his arm and stiffened. Something moved through the tall grass near the base of the hills opposite. It was striped a dull tan and cream that blended with its surroundings, and its head was unusually bulky, making up about a third of its entire body. Its casual, lithe movements reminded Aderyn of a snake stalking its prey. Without being prompted, she Assessed it.

Name: Greater Chimera

Type: Abomination

Power Level: 11

Attacks: Bite x2, claw x2, gore, breath attack

Immune to: poison

Resistant to: blunt force

Vulnerable to: none

Special attacks: *stinking cloud* **breath attack**

A monstrous combination of goat, dragon, and lion, chimeras are a true abomination created centuries ago by powerful Bonemenders who wielded their powers recklessly in a true case of "just because you can doesn't mean you should." The chimera's violent nature stems from its subconscious awareness of its own unnatural state and desire for revenge against its creators. Its vestigial wings

Aderyn stopped reading and peered at the distant shape. She could barely make out bumps along its sides that might have been small wings.

Its vestigial wings allow it to make long, gliding leaps rather than true flight, but that's small comfort when it's bearing down on you from above. A chimera's dragon head breathes out a gas that paralyzes the victim just long enough to be disemboweled. Though chimeras are nearsighted, they have an excellent sense of smell, can track any land-based creature with ease, and hunt in packs. Where there's one, there are three more you haven't seen. Maybe you should take a look around now.

"Power level eleven, though," Weston said. "It shouldn't be a challenge for six of us."

"If there was only one, sure," Owen said. "I count three. That one, and two to its left. They're going after those two antelopes on the fringes of the herd."

Weston shielded his eyes. "Four. There's another on the right. Well, crap. That's too many."

"We'll have to either work our way wide around the herd, or wait for the chimeras to leave," Crillon said. "And I'd bet on them taking their sweet time about hunting and eating. We can't afford a delay."

"I can plot us a route to take us around," Weston said. "Better if we had a Pathseer, but it will have to do."

"We do have a Pathseer," Crillon said.

An uncomfortable silence fell. Finally, Owen said, "Jessemia's only level six. Her skills aren't high enough."

"She could try," Aderyn said. "She could help Weston."

"It's not a burden I want to put on her. She's not a member of our team." Owen turned to Weston. "See what you can do. We'll warn the others."

By this time, Livia was approaching, followed by Isold, with Coralie and Jessemia trailing behind. Weston nodded and ran west along the ridgetop.

"Where's he going?" Livia asked.

Owen summed up the situation and added, "We'll need to stay close together. Chimeras hunt by scent, so if the wind changes, we could be in trouble."

Swift movement in the valley below drew Aderyn's eye. The chimera she'd Assessed darted forward and leaped high, snapping its small, batlike wings open so it glided through the air. Its prey lifted its head and then started to run, but it was too late. The chimera's lion jaws fastened on the antelope's throat and ripped through it with a spray of ruby blood.

A ripple of movement spread through the herd as the nearer

antelopes reacted to their fellow's death. Then the herd was in motion, bounding east. The other chimeras sprang after them. Two brought down prey. The third missed its strike and breathed out a cloud of greenish-brown gas from its dragon head that enveloped a fleeing antelope. It froze mid-stride, teetered for a moment, and then fell over, paralyzed. Aderyn shuddered at how the chimera sauntered over to the fallen antelope and tore its belly open, as casually as if it had all the time in the world.

"Start moving," Owen said. "We'll meet up with Weston. They might be too preoccupied with eating to care about us, but we won't take chances."

CHAPTER SIXTEEN

They hurried westward, staying low along the ridge though Aderyn remembered her Assessment and didn't think the chimeras could see them at that distance. Soon, the chimeras were out of sight as well, and Aderyn was about to ask if they should head south when she saw Weston loping toward them.

"There's a safe route up and over the hills," he said, "except the southern side is sheer and rocky, and we'd have trouble getting down. So we'll have to take the route closer to that valley. It's still far away, I hope far enough away, but we won't be able to keep an eye on the chimeras to know if they've been fooled."

"It's risky however we do it. We'll stay out of sight and hope that's enough." Owen gestured to Weston to lead the way, and they rearranged their walking order, with Owen and Aderyn behind Weston, Coralie and Jessemia in the middle watched over by Crillon, Isold just behind them where his song would be audible to everyone equally, and Livia bringing up the rear.

The walk was pleasant, almost peaceful, but Aderyn couldn't stop watching the eastern hills, waiting for chimeras to make their bounding, gliding leaps over the crest. Since Owen was doing the same, she didn't think it was paranoia. The wind continued to grow stronger, whipping Aderyn's hair in its long tail around her face and flattening the grasses. It wasn't just blowing from the east anymore, but came in short gusts from the south as well. Aderyn welcomed those, as they blew her hair away from her face and cleared her vision.

She was so preoccupied with watching the horizon and occasionally brushing hair out of her eyes that she didn't at first realized the wind had changed again. It wasn't until she caught sight of the flattened grasses that she understood the wind was now coming from the west. She grabbed Owen's arm. "The chimeras are downwind of us."

"I know. There's nothing we can do but keep going, and hope we're far enough away." Owen concealed his anxiety poorly. Aderyn guessed he was wishing they'd taken the closer route, the one that would have allowed them to watch the chimeras. Now, if the monsters attacked, they'd have very little warning.

They ran now, dodging the small shrubs that grew here and there across the hills. Aderyn saw in passing that they were poison ivy. No wonder the antelopes avoided it. She did the same, though it wasn't as if she intended to stop and fondle the leaves with her bare hands. Would chimeras be affected by poison ivy? Despite her fear, she couldn't help being amused at the thought of luring a chimera close to a poison ivy shrub and rubbing the leaves all over one of the hideous faces. She must really be addled to consider it.

She glanced once more at the crest of the eastern hills, and her heart pounded once in terror, so hard it hurt her chest. A sleek, tan-and-cream form with a bulky front end stood at the top of the rise, looking down at them. Then it bounded down the slope, half running, half gliding, on a direct course for its prey.

Aderyn shouted a warning and drew her sword. The others drew in close, protecting Jessemia and Coralie. Owen drew his sword as well and shouted, "Watch for the others!" before racing to meet the oncoming monster. Aderyn, drawn rapidly along by **[Keep Pace]**, hurried with him. She forced herself to slow as Owen's **[Overrun]** carried him into the chimera and past it, knocking it off balance so Aderyn had time for **[Discern Weakness]**. Lines of blue light slid over its deformed body, becoming blue points at several locations: the lower belly, the chest, each of the three throats.

Aderyn struck low, aiming for the belly and scoring a hit along the creature's left flank. The chimera screamed and clawed at her, but **[See It Coming]** had her well out of the way of the strike before it landed. She swung again, connecting more solidly, and then Owen was there, slashing at the lion's throat. The chimera backed away just in time to avoid taking more than a fine red line across its throat.

"Do we have to slit all three throats?" Owen shouted.

"Don't know," Aderyn called back. "Better stick to hitting the heart!"

Isold's battle song filled the air with **[Inspire Courage]**, raising Aderyn's spirits. It harmonized with the deep rumble of *thunderstomp*. When the earth didn't tremble beneath Aderyn's feet, even Isold's song couldn't stop her feeling afraid, because it meant more than one chimera was attacking, and they might be in serious trouble.

The chimera facing her reared up and threw its dragon head back. Aderyn didn't need **[See It Coming]** to know what that meant. "Poison gas!" she shouted, and threw herself to the side. Owen backed away and rolled to get out of the way of its breath weapon. In the next moment, he'd vaulted atop the chimera's broad back and brought his sword plunging down between the muscles of its shoulders. The dragon head closed its jaws, gas leaking from its mouth, and the chimera twisted desperately to get at the annoyance perched behind its heads.

In its moment of distraction, Aderyn leaped forward and aimed a thrust at the blue dot over the monster's heart. With a scream of effort, she drove her blade deep into the chimera's chest. It jerked, reared up again, dislodging Owen, and fell into spasms at Aderyn's feet.

Congratulations! You have defeated [Greater Chimera].
You have earned [8000 XP]

Owen sprang to his feet. "Aderyn, watch out!"

Aderyn turned, leaping backward instinctively. A cloud of gas that stank of rotting oranges, sickly sweet, enveloped her. She took a few more staggering steps, trying to get clear of the cloud, but her legs wouldn't obey her, and her arms were numb, and she fell, dropping her sword and landing painfully on the **<Knapsack of Plenty>**.

A giant three-headed shape loomed over her. She tried to scream, but her lungs felt nearly as paralyzed as the rest of her, barely able to inflate to take in air. Dizziness claimed her, and her eyes fogged over. In that state, the shouting and screaming and hissing roars mingled into one horrible sound she would never forget.

Through the fog, she vaguely saw the three-headed shape get knocked to one side like someone had tackled it. Fuzzy-edged silver tangles floated in front of her face. They were pretty, and distantly she thought they meant something important, but her brain was too muddled to remember.

Someone knelt beside her, and she knew she ought to warn the person to stay out of the gas, but she couldn't speak any better than she could breathe. She felt herself lifted, not by hands but by a force that carried her aloft. *Telekinesis.* That was Livia beside her. They couldn't let Livia be paralyzed, because who would knock the chimeras down with *thunderstomp* if she was incapacitated?

She drifted down to lie on matted grasses that were soft but had sharp edges like barely blunted razors. Again, someone knelt beside her, maybe Livia, maybe not. Her air-starved brain raged at her to think clearly. She might be paralyzed, but that didn't mean she couldn't act. Unless it did. Why was thinking so hard?

"Is she going to die?" That was Jessemia.

"The paralysis isn't permanent." Coralie, sounding confident. Then, more sharply, "Get down, girl!"

A roar, not the chimera's roar but the sound of fire devouring a forest, nearly deafened Aderyn, which irritated her because her hearing was practically the only thing that still worked. Heat caressed her skin, and Jessemia screamed. Something landed on top of Aderyn, not a chimera because it didn't disembowel her, but something heavy and soft. She heard sobbing from whatever the thing was.

"Sorry about that, but it was almost on top of us," Coralie said. The stink of burned hair came to Aderyn's nose. All right, two things still worked.

"What *is* that?" Jessemia demanded.

"A [Fireblast Rod]," Coralie said, sounding smug. "My own invention. Shoots a stream of fire that will seriously discourage any attacker it doesn't outright kill. Guess chimeras aren't immune to it."

The heavy thing moved and sat up. Aderyn guessed it had been Jessemia, taking cover from the [Fireblast Rod]. If it had killed a chimera outright, she no longer wondered at Coralie's ability to defend herself when she was alone. She tried to say, "Use it again," but all that came out was "Ooseeugin."

"She's coming out of it!" Jessemia exclaimed.

Aderyn realized breathing had become easier. She tried to move her arms, but all she could do was twitch her fingers. She told herself to be grateful for that.

Silver letters, these clear and sharp-edged, appeared in front of her vision.

Congratulations! You have defeated [Greater Chimera].

You have earned [8000 XP]

She had killed one. Coralie had killed one. There was that most recent system defeat notice, and those foggy silver tangles had been another. Aderyn's brain still wasn't working properly, but she could still add to four.

"Areyahdud?" she mumbled. *Are they all dead?*

Jessemia and Coralie apparently didn't speak Mumble. "Just rest," Coralie said, patting her shoulder. "It's almost over."

As she said this, more silver letters appeared.

Congratulations! You have defeated [Greater Chimera].
You have earned [8000 XP]

Five. One they hadn't seen. Aderyn was too numb to feel as afraid as that number should have made her. She concentrated on wiggling her fingers and then her toes. Gradually, the numbness retreated, and she was able to move her arms at the elbow and her legs at the knee. Her vision returned, and she blinked, relieving her dry eyes—she'd never truly appreciated blinking before—and saw Coralie and Jessemia staring down at her. Jessemia looked worried. Coralie looked calm.

Footsteps swished the grass, and Owen knelt beside her, taking her hand in his. "Are you recovered?"

Aderyn tried to shake her head *no* and couldn't. She squeezed his hand and worked her jaw a few times. "I'm getting there," she managed, and while the words weren't clear, they were intelligible.

"That was close," Owen said. "Weston caught a lungful of gas too, or the edges of one. He wasn't as thoroughly paralyzed as you, but he couldn't fight. Crillon and I killed the one that gassed you, Livia pulverized a third, and Isold used **[Suggestion]** to force the other one to attack its friend, weakening it so I could slit its throat. Turns out you do only need one slit throat to take a chimera down."

"And Coralie blasted the mind-controlled one with that rod of hers," Livia said. "I would not want to come across you in a dark alley. There's not much left of it but some burned hairs and a couple of splintered bones."

"It is quite powerful," Coralie said, again sounding smug.

"Level seventeen Spellcrafter," Owen said. "I'm impressed."

The numbness had faded from Aderyn's arms and chest, and she struggled to sit up. Owen helped her, then kept his arm supportively around her shoulders. "That was something," he said. "We were lucky."

"I feel lucky," Weston said. He was rotating his arm like he was working feeling back into it. "Aderyn, you're all right?"

"I don't think I can walk yet, but I'll be fine soon." Her hips still felt stiff and incapable of supporting her, but the numbness was fading faster now.

"While Aderyn recovers, I will harvest these monsters," Isold said. "They have bezoars used to generate illusion effects such as invisibility and multiple images, and the goat horns can be ground and used as a component in several potions."

"Everybody take a rest, then," Owen said. "But let's make it quick, Isold. I don't want to hang around these bodies for long."

Isold nodded. He drew his belt knife and knelt beside the nearest chimera.

Aderyn leaned against Owen and drew in a deep breath, then coughed at the stink of burnt hair. "I'm fine," she assured Owen.

"I'm just selfish enough to want you never to rush headlong into danger," Owen murmured, stroking her hair. "But you wouldn't be the woman I love if you didn't."

She smiled. "I remember my mother telling you we'd look out for each other."

"Which we have."

Aderyn caught Jessemia's eye. The woman was watching her and Owen with a thoughtful expression. She turned away when she realized Aderyn had noticed. Aderyn thought back. "I think Jessemia tried to protect me," she said.

"How could she do that? She's level six. She'd be more likely to get herself killed."

Aderyn watched as Jessemia walked away. "I don't know," she said, "but I think she's not who she used to be, after all."

CHAPTER SEVENTEEN

The next few days' travel was uneventful except for the travelers accidentally walking through a grove of scimitar trees on the second day. It was an immature grove, and the trees' slicing blades waved wildly in the air without connecting with anyone. Aderyn thought they were cute, and said so.

"The full-sized trees are nightmarish," Isold said. "A scimitar tree has enough awareness to direct its attacks at whatever threat is nearest, and its skill is as great as a Swordsworn of that tree's power level. Their bark is iron-hard, so weapons do less damage, and to my knowledge the only way to effectively deal with one is to uproot it or burn it."

"All right, sure, but look at how adorable that is," Aderyn said, pointing at one of the smaller trees. Its flailing limbs tipped with shining black blades sliced the air impotently. "I mean, sometimes it connects with its own branches. Besides, isn't it true that the young of every species are cute in their own way? My mother says it's so their parents won't devour them when they are nuisances."

"My mom said something like that, only she was talking about her own children," Owen said. "Aderyn, come on. Maybe these saplings can't hurt us, but no sense giving them the opportunity. It's kind of cruel, too."

Aderyn followed him out of the grove to where the others waited. "Should we raze the grove? Those trees will eventually grow up to be a danger."

"I was going to, but you've made me see them as helpless babies, thank you so very much," Livia grumbled.

"Ignore what Aderyn said, and let's destroy them," Owen said. "Any ideas how?"

"It's fine," Livia said. She took a solid stance and bowed her head, breathing in deeply. A low groan issued from her lips, growing louder and higher-pitched as the seconds passed. The ground beneath the scimitar trees shuddered. Then it rippled, making the trees seem to dance. One sapling tore free of the ground, then another, and in the next moment, all their roots were exposed. Deprived of their support, the scimitar trees leaned against each other or fell over.

Aderyn covered her mouth with her hand, suppressing a cry.

"Don't say a word," Livia warned. "They're not sentient enough to feel anything like what you're imagining, suffocation or slow death or whatever. Tell her, Isold."

"Save your pity for the people who would have been their victims," Isold said. "Even if they had consciousness, they are still evil creatures. You're letting your imagination get the better of you."

"I know," Aderyn said. "I'm sorry. You're all right, and I need to control myself."

Congratulations! You have defeated [Scimitar Tree, Juvenile]. You have received [100 XP]

They waited for the last of the system defeat notices to disappear before moving on. Aderyn felt unexpectedly discouraged. Not because they'd killed the scimitar trees, because she knew that was for the best. No, it was because she'd felt inappropriately bad about it.

Some monsters started out cute and grew to be vicious, slavering killers—all right, pretty much all monsters started out that way. Isold had said once there was no glory and no honor in killing something that couldn't fight back, but there had to be a line between slaughtering helpless young and waiting for them to grow old enough to be dangerous.

"Stop thinking like that," Owen said.

"You don't know what I'm thinking."

"I do. You feel guilty about sympathizing with monsters. Don't worry about it."

Aderyn turned on him. "And what happens if I let my sympathies get in the way of protecting my friends, Owen? What about that?"

Owen didn't react to her outburst. "You won't. I have faith in you."

His calm response made her feel guilty again, this time about lashing out. "I'm sorry. I didn't mean to yell."

"I understand." Owen took her hand and squeezed it lightly before letting her go. "You're compassionate and you have a good imagination. It's easy for you to imagine yourself in others' shoes. Even those others who are monsters and don't wear shoes. Remember the misthounds?"

Aderyn sighed. "You're right. I'm afraid it's a weakness."

"Or it might be a great strength. It depends on how you use it."

Aderyn considered that as they walked. No, she was sure it was more a weakness than a strength. But it wasn't one that affected her often. She never hesitated to finish off a wounded monster, or to take advantage of Isold's [Fascinate] or [Hypnotize] to kill the creatures he rendered helpless. She'd just have to be careful, that was all.

The Welterwall loomed ever closer as they walked. Not as tall as the Pinnalore Mountains, they still made a gray-brown mass against the sky like a row of jagged teeth. Aderyn's father and mother had adventured there for over a year when they were level thirteen and spoke often of the monsters they'd killed and the quests they'd completed. From their stories, Aderyn knew each of the mountains had names, but she only remembered the three largest: Gendon's Peak, Mount Formidable, and Sage Mountain. It was Sage Mountain they headed for now, tall and stark with slopes unsoftened by trees or snow.

On the third day, the hills became steep and rocky, and the going was slower. Coralie, who'd been carrying Prince Gustavio Strongpaws around her neck like a fur collar, put him down and used her <Fireblast Rod> as a cane to help herself along. Aderyn watched this in some dismay. She couldn't help imagining the rod going off accidentally and blasting one or all of them with terrible fire.

Weston was clearly thinking the same thing, because during one of their increasingly frequent rests, he crouched beside Coralie and said, "Would you mind if I carried you?"

"Mind? You'd better believe I would," Coralie said. "But I'm not stupid and I'm not proud. I know I'm slowing us down. So I can endure a little humiliation." She eyed Weston and added, "The system should have made you a Stalwart. Crillon's a good boy, and he's as strong as a Stalwart ought to be, but you'd be the stuff of legends."

"My father said the same when I got my Call," Weston said. "He's a Stalwart, and we all assumed it's what I would end up being, but instead I followed in my mother's footsteps."

Coralie got wearily to her feet. "You remind me of Prince Gustavio Strongpaws," she said. "To look at him, you'd think he was nothing but an ungainly ball of muscle. But I've seen him walk the ridgepole of a three-story house and leap off to land as lightly as a Spider, and I've seen him pass through gaps in fences you'd swear he couldn't fit his head through, much less the rest of him. We aren't any of us what we seem, to some degree or another."

"I like how unexpected that makes life," Weston said, hoisting her to sit straddling his shoulders.

With Coralie taken care of, they walked more quickly, but it was still nearly nightfall before the elderly Spellcrafter said, "We're near. Can you hear that? The crystal song?"

Everyone held still. The wind blew lightly across the shrubs that grew along the slopes of the hill. Aderyn heard nothing but the high-pitched whine in her ears that sounded whenever no other noise was audible. Then she realized it was coming from outside her head. The longer she listened, the more complex the sound became. One note became two, two became five, always in perfect harmony.

"The crystals sing in the early evening," Coralie said. "The Herald I traveled here with, decades ago, said they responded to the last rays of sunlight. In any case, it's as good as a beacon to help us find the Icebright Caves." She nudged Weston, who gently set her down and handed her the <**Fireblast Rod**>.

With Coralie now in the lead, they clambered up steep slopes, sometimes using their hands to pull themselves over rock outcroppings, occasionally sending showers of loose pebbles rattling down the stone walls. Aderyn grew so focused on putting one hand, one foot, in front of the other that it surprised her when she bumped into Weston, climbing just behind Coralie.

Ahead, a cave mouth yawned, taller than Weston and twice again as wide as it was tall. Light glittered inside it, though Aderyn saw no crystals, prismatic or otherwise. The song was louder now, harmonizing with itself as beautifully as Isold could have managed.

"I must remember this tune," she heard Isold mutter from down the slope.

"We've got half an hour of daylight left. Plenty of time to find an appropriate crystal," Coralie said.

Owen grabbed her shoulder and brought her to a halt. "We need to check the cave out first."

"It's not dangerous. There's nothing in there a monster would want." Coralie smacked the butt of her <**Fireblast Rod**> twice against the stony ground. "And if there is something there, I can make it have a really bad day."

"We don't have to go to that extreme. Let Weston check it out."

Coralie grumbled, but nodded. Weston slid past her and clambered lightly up to the cave mouth. A narrow rock ledge protruded beneath the opening, as perfectly situated for someone to stand and look inside as anything Aderyn could imagine. Weston flattened himself to one side of the cave, then slipped inside, his passage making no noise. The crystals' song continued as sweetly as before.

A tremendous roar, shrill and deep at the same time as if many voices made it, shattered the peaceful evening, sending a flash of fear through Aderyn. From deep within the cave, Weston shouted, "*Shit!*"

Owen started forward, but Weston burst from the cave, waving his arms and yelling, "Get back! Get back!"

Aderyn backed away, too off balance to draw her sword. The others clustered around, and Aderyn had the sudden mad thought that if whatever had alarmed Weston could use magic, they were all neatly grouped to be decimated by *fireball* or *stone sphere* or *icy blast*.

Weston bounded lightly down the slope and turned, breathing heavily, to face the cave. "I don't think it followed me," he said. "It was right there in my face, close enough to give me a shave, so there was nothing stopping it from following me. I don't know why it didn't."

"What was it?" Owen asked.

Weston drew in a deep breath, calming himself. "It moved too fast for me to get a good look at it. It was big, though. Had a head like an insect, with pincers as big across as my arm span." He spread his arms wide to demonstrate. "Golden-brown chitin and I don't know how many legs."

Owen and Aderyn exchanged glances. "I'll go," Aderyn said.

"Wait," Owen said. "We shouldn't take unnecessary risks.

Coralie, you said these were the Icebright *Caves*, caves plural, right? Can we find another of them?"

Coralie shook her head. "There are multiple caves, yes, but only one of them opens to the outside. The rest are an internal cave system."

"I'll be careful," Aderyn assured Owen. "I always am."

Owen nodded. "Weston, go with her. Get both of you out of there if it turns out the creature is faster than **[Improved Assess 2]**."

Aderyn and Weston scrambled up the slope, moving slowly. Weston was as silent as always. Aderyn felt sure everyone for a mile around knew she was coming, between her heavy breathing, the scrape of her boots on the stone, and the rattle of dislodged pebbles.

When they were a foot below the cave, Weston whispered in Aderyn's ear, "See if you can pull yourself up and look over the threshold. It was tall enough it might not notice movement that low."

Aderyn nodded. She grabbed hold of the ledge and hoisted herself up to where she could hook an elbow over it. The sparkling was more noticeable this close to the cave, and she could see individual crystals fracturing the sunlight into rainbows that were caught by other crystals and refracted again and again. In full daylight, the cave would be blinding. Aderyn blinked away tears and stared deeper into the cave. She still saw nothing moving. Fortunately, **[Improved Assess 2]** didn't depend on whether her imperfect perceptions noticed a monster or not.

The message that appeared made her heart skip faster.

Name: Clapperclaw
Type: Magical Beast
Power Level: 16
Attacks: Claw x2, bite, special attacks
Immune to: fear effects, poison, elemental wind damage, elemental water damage
Resistant to: mind-altering effects, edged weapons damage

Vulnerable to: bludgeoning damage

Special attacks: pounce, rake, rend, fear aura

The monstrously oversized briar beetle Clapperclaw achieved its stature over years of exposure to the radiant energy of the Icebright Caves' [Prismatic Crystals]. Its temper is erratic and its behavior unpredictable. It has been known to slaughter entire adventuring teams and completely ignore others. Since it's impossible to know how it's feeling at a given time, your only hope is to snatch a crystal and retreat immediately, as Clapperclaw will perceive your presence with its excellent hearing, but will not pursue an adventurer beyond the mouth of its cave.

If you aren't already convinced that this encounter is too much for you, consider its special attacks. Clapperclaw can *pounce* by leaping vertically into the air and landing with its full weight on its prey. If it catches hold of an enemy with its front claws, it can *rake* with its hind claws, often disemboweling the prey with this attack. If *rake* doesn't finish the victim off, once Clapperclaw has two claws on its enemy, it can *rend* the prey by pulling hard in opposite directions. It won't matter, because you'll be wetting yourself in terror thanks to its *aura of fear*. Time to contemplate whether your need for a [Prismatic Crystal] is as great as you thought!

CHAPTER EIGHTEEN

Aderyn slid down from her perch, her heart pounding, and made her awkward way over the rocky slope to her friends. "It's a named monster called Clapperclaw," she said. "Power level sixteen with half a dozen attack types, and it gives off a fear aura I think Weston and I caught the edge of." She was sure her heavy breathing was due to more than exertion.

"It wasn't there before," Coralie said. "I swear it. Though that was fifty years ago. It never occurred to me that anything might live in that inhospitable cave." Her voice shook with suppressed tears. "I guess that's it."

"This isn't over," Owen declared. "I refuse to give up before we've tried. Level sixteen, huh? The Sarnok was level sixteen."

"And it nearly ate us for breakfast," Livia said, "or had you forgotten?"

"All right, that was difficult, but my point is that we used skill and cunning to defeat the Sarnok, which means there are other ways than going head to head—"

"Head to toe. That thing is enormous," Weston said.

"Let's forget about irrelevancies for now, Weston." Owen gazed at the cave mouth, which sparkled less as the sun went down. "We'll camp somewhere away from here and approach this fresh in the morning."

They made their way back down the mountain. Aderyn welcomed the need to pay attention to where she put her hands and feet. She felt the memory of the giant bug press down on the back of her neck as if it was watching her. Even having only seen its Assessment, the memory terrified her. Owen was mad to think they had a chance against it.

The campsite they found was flatter than its surroundings, but not by much. If not for the <**Soldier's Friend**>, Aderyn was sure the tents would have slid down the mountainside. As it was, the whole camp looked off-kilter, like she had her head permanently tilted to the left. Livia had with some effort made a more level area for the campfire, which burned as cheerfully as if it didn't know the challenge they faced.

They sat around the fire as darkness fell and ate in morose silence. Aderyn re-read Clapperclaw's Assessment in memory, making herself focus dispassionately on the details. About the only advantage they had was its vulnerability to bludgeoning attacks, which meant Livia's *stone fist* and *stone sphere* would be more effective than usual. But Isold's mental attacks wouldn't work as well, and the chitin Weston had mentioned was probably the reason for its resistance to bladed weapon attacks. Pounce, rake, and rend sounded so awful she didn't know how to counter them.

But what worried her most was that fear aura. That could mean anything from unnerving her and her teammates to making them flee in terror. Without knowing the specifics, it was more dangerous than all the rest.

She pulled her legs up and rested her chin on her knees, hugging her shins. Owen glanced her way. "Don't fall into despair," he said.

"I'm trying not to, but then I remember what [**Improved Assess 2**] said about how it pounces on people before disemboweling them and tearing them apart. I don't know how to counter that."

"It's not solely your responsibility."

"I'm the Warmaster. My class is meant to figure out tactics. It's at least somewhat my responsibility." Aderyn sighed. "I wish I'd seen it, because now my imagination has come up with all sorts of nightmares."

"It was shaped like a praying mantis, if that helps," Weston said. "Partly upright, I mean. But thorny all over. The pincers were twice as wide as its head. I didn't think about it at the time, but now I don't know why it didn't overbalance with those attached to its head."

Aderyn pictured a thorny praying mantis and didn't know why she'd ever found those insects appealing. "At least it doesn't have a venom attack."

"That's a better way to look at it," Owen said. "There are a lot of ways this could be worse. It could be completely immune to bladed weapons. It could read our minds to know where we are."

"It could have been willing to chase Weston beyond the cave," Isold said. "We would likely not have been able to get away in time, not on that terrain."

"And maybe the pouncing thing is irrelevant," Owen said. "Coralie, how big is that cave once it opens up?"

"I don't remember the details after so many years, but I'm sure the roof isn't more than thirty feet high." Coralie sat with Prince Gustavio Strongpaws on her lap, petting his soft, short fur. "Some of the deeper caves are bigger than that. There was one we couldn't see the ceiling of. But that first cave is fairly small."

"So it's possible, if Clapperclaw is that big, it wouldn't be able to jump high enough for a pounce," Owen said. "Aderyn, were the rake and rend abilities dependent on pounce?"

"I'm not sure. I think those were a matter of it grabbing hold of its prey, and pouncing only made grabbing easier. So not being able to pounce is a disadvantage, but not as big a disadvantage as it could be." Aderyn reviewed the Assessment again. "I'm intrigued by how the Assessment said Clapperclaw sometimes won't attack. Maybe we could figure out what makes the difference and take advantage of that."

"Maybe we don't have to kill it at all," Weston said. "If the point is to grab a crystal and get out, well, we have the <**Cloak of Mists**>, or Livia can make herself invisible."

But Coralie was shaking her head. "It can't just be any crystal," she said. "I have to identify one that will resonate with the <**Stone of Purification**>. That takes time."

"That's too bad," Crillon said. He'd been quiet until now, but his voice was strong. "It would be a shame to kill the creature."

Everyone stared at him. Crillon returned their regard unflinchingly. "I'm serious. It seems to attack only when someone intrudes on its home, it doesn't pursue its prey past those boundaries—I don't think it's vicious. Not the way those chimeras were."

"Huh," Owen said, in the tone of voice that said he was thinking hard. "You may have something there."

"All right," Livia said, "maybe it's not vicious. But it's still in our way, unless you've given up on the idea of saving your town."

"I didn't say we shouldn't, I said killing it would be a shame. If it wasn't mindless, we could maybe talk it into giving us access." Crillon bowed his head. "I guess I'm just tired of seeing death everywhere."

Aderyn didn't know how to respond to that.

"Let's sleep on it, and see what the morning brings," Owen said.

Snuggled up with Owen in their tent, Aderyn said, "And I thought *I* was inappropriately soft on monsters."

"I don't know if he's wrong," Owen replied. "If we could communicate with it—"

When he didn't go on immediately, Aderyn said, "It's big, but it's still an insect. I don't think they have enough mind for communication."

"I know, but—well, maybe you're right. Good night." He drew her close and kissed her.

With the memory of Clapperclaw fresh in her mind, Aderyn took a while to fall asleep, and when she did, she dreamed of thorny praying mantises of a normal size swarming their camp. She tried to speak to them, but all she heard in return was buzzing.

The following morning was gray with overcast, and the air smelled sharp and damp like an oncoming storm, though the clouds weren't right for rain. The weather suited Aderyn's mood. She wasn't discouraged anymore, not the way she'd been the previous night, but she still didn't know how to defeat Clapperclaw, and that made her snappish and disinclined to speak to her friends.

Finally, Livia grabbed her by the arm and dragged her out of earshot of the camp. "Stop being cranky. That's my thing."

Aderyn couldn't help laughing. "I'm not cranky, I'm disgruntled."

"Same thing, different word. You're not helping matters." Livia scowled at her. "It's all right if I do it, because everyone's used to me being out of sorts in the morning. But your mood is affecting the others because you're usually so relentlessly positive. You want this to fail, go on being cranky. Disgruntled. Call it what you want."

Stunned, Aderyn said, "You think I have that kind of influence?"

"Aderyn, everyone knows you're the one who figures out our enemies' weaknesses. If you lose hope, why should any of them bother?" Livia patted her shoulder. "Cheer up, even if you don't feel cheerful. I think we'll figure this out."

"That's unexpectedly optimistic of you."

Livia shrugged. "The stakes are higher than usual. I keep thinking how I'd feel if it was Asylum facing destruction. I'm not sure what I would do if it meant making the ultimate sacrifice."

Aderyn was used to Livia being pragmatic, but this was the first time she'd said anything like this. "I don't know, either," she said. "And I'm going to do what I can to make sure it doesn't come to that."

"That's more like it." Livia patted her shoulder again. "Now, I need at least one more cup of coffee before we face almost certain death."

Shortly after, they broke camp and returned to the Icebright Caves. This time, they searched until they found a place with a direct path to the cave mouth, less strewn with rubble that didn't require much scrambling to traverse. The lack of sunlight meant the cave didn't sparkle as it had the previous night. It lay in shadow, looking deeper than before.

They gathered in a loose group behind a nearby boulder. Owen said, "Let's review what we know. Clapperclaw has several specialized attacks that depend on it getting a claw on someone. That means we stay mobile so it doesn't have a chance to use those attacks. It has an aura of fear, but we don't know the details, which makes that its most dangerous attack. It does not appear to have any unusual or powerful senses aside from its hearing. It won't leave the cave. And it may or may not choose to go after intruders. Did I miss anything?"

"It's immune to fear and poison, resistant to mind control and bladed weapons, and vulnerable to bludgeoning damage," Aderyn said. "Our best bet may be to protect Livia while she hammers it."

"That's one approach," Owen said. "What else might we try?"

"We could keep it busy while Coralie searches for the crystal," Weston said. "But that exposes her to danger, and she's the only one who can complete the item creation."

"Figure out what causes it to attack or not," Crillon said.

"Identify its other weaknesses," Aderyn said. "I didn't see it to use [Discern Weakness]. I think the first thing we should do is give me the <Cloak of Mists> and have me go in there—"

"Aderyn," Owen said.

"It makes sense, Owen. We need as much information as we can get if this is going to be successful. And I doubt it can detect an invisible creature."

"The <**Cloak of Mists**> only makes you hard to see," Owen pointed out, "not invisible."

"That's good enough. I don't have to go far, and I'll run if it spots me." Aderyn held out her hand to Weston. "But I need to do this now before I lose my nerve."

Owen sighed. "Find out what you can, and quickly."

Swathed in the <**Cloak of Mists**>, Aderyn climbed the ascent and pulled herself up and over the lip of rock before the cave mouth. Her heart was hammering and her breathing was labored, so she crouched there for a minute until she was calmer. She felt anxious rather than afraid, so either Clapperclaw's fear aura didn't extend this far, or it had to be an intentional attack. Neither of those possibilities reassured her.

Finally, she stood and took a step forward, testing. Nothing happened. She heard no noises from within the cave, smelled nothing foul, and nothing moved. She continued to walk forward into the dimness. She couldn't take light with her, not even Livia's *orb of light* that would hover beside her, because Clapperclaw might realize the light belonged to possible prey. Weston had said it wasn't hard to see inside the cave, so she hadn't wasted worry on that.

Now she understood what Weston had meant. Crystals grew randomly from the walls and ceiling, more thickly the farther she went. They glowed with a soft radiance that would have been imperceptible from a single crystal, but from their massed ranks was brighter than the light of the full moon. If Aderyn hadn't been so nervous, the light would have enchanted her.

Beyond the opening, the cave extended as a tunnel, no wider or taller than the entrance. Aderyn revised her guess as to Clapperclaw's size downward. Or maybe that was why it hadn't pursued Weston; it was too large. That thought made her shudder.

She picked her way across the tunnel floor, which was mostly clear but littered here and there with fallen crystals. She didn't want to kick those and make a noise that would draw Clapperclaw's attention. The crystals ranged in size from no bigger than her pinky to the length and breadth of her forearm. The fallen ones gave off as much light as the ones protruding from the walls, which Aderyn found interesting. She'd subconsciously assumed it was some quality of the caves that gave them their luminescent properties, something they only maintained while they were connected, but apparently not.

Ahead, the passage widened, and Aderyn slowed her steps, listening, watching. She still smelled nothing, not pleasant or unpleasant, just a dry, dusty sensation in the air as if of a long-shut-up room. The glow increased, suggesting a greater mass of crystals beyond where the passage came to an end some fifteen feet away. Aderyn crept to the passage opening and, flattening herself against the wall, peered around the edge.

CHAPTER NINETEEN

Based on what Coralie had said about the caves deeper in, Aderyn had expected something vast and deep. This cave, while large, failed to meet that expectation. Aderyn guessed it was only about a hundred feet from where she stood to the far wall, and maybe a little longer in the other dimension. Crystals grew in clumps or in glorious solitude all over the walls and ceiling, shedding their soft light over the dark form curled up in front of another, larger exit.

Aderyn gazed at Clapperclaw for a few breathless seconds. The creature was more terrifyingly monstrous than she'd imagined. Golden-brown chitin turned purplish by the crystals' radiance shone in the low light, studded all over by sharp spurs like thorns on a rose stem. Its segmented body rose and fell with its breathing, revealing a dozen jointed legs beneath its fat abdomen that was similarly armored. Its head rested atop its massive forearms, the pincers of its jaw oversized and gleaming sharply along the inner edges. Aderyn couldn't see the forearms clearly, but she thought they were spiky, too. It was the most horrifying monster she'd ever seen.

She realized she was wasting time and, stepping to where she had a clear view of its abdomen where she assumed there would be some weak spots, Assessed the creature. Immediately, as if [**Discern Weakness**] had been waiting impatiently for her to come out of her fugue, blue lines crisscrossed Clapperclaw's body, sliding and shifting until they focused into blue dots of light. Aderyn despaired at how few there were. Most of Clapperclaw was haloed in a red aura, indicating strength against weapons. Blue dots appeared at every ridge of the carapace where the armor plates fit together and over one another, and more dots glowed at the joints of its massive forelegs. That was all.

Aderyn called up Clapperclaw's Assessment again and saw nothing had changed. In despair, she tried focusing on part of the information [**Improved Assess 2**] gave her, the part she worried most about: Clapperclaw's fear aura. She thought this only worked on adventurers' skills, but it was worth trying.

To her surprise, the words "fear aura" glowed brighter and pulsed three times before enlarging into a new block of text:

Fear aura: This ability varies by creature possessing it along three dimensions: intensity, range, and control. Intensity refers to how much fear the aura causes; range refers to how far the effect goes; control refers to the intentionality of the effect. Would you like to Assess the target creature for more information? Y / N

Relieved, Aderyn selected Y and again Assessed Clapperclaw.

The target creature exceeds authority limit for this skill. Choose another target.

"Damn," Aderyn whispered, then clapped a hand over her mouth. It was too late. Clapperclaw roared and shot up, and up, rising to a height of fifteen feet and getting its lower limbs underneath it. Its heavy head swung back and forth as if it was scenting the air. Aderyn froze. She knew she ought to retreat, but the sound of the roar and the sight of the creature's pincers as they clacked slowly open and closed terrified her.

The monster shifted its enormous bulk and took a few steps, not in Aderyn's direction. The plates of its carapace shifted and slid as it moved, their edges scraping across the chitin and sending up a noise that made the crystals hum discordantly. Aderyn came out of her stunned stillness and realized this was her chance to run. With superhuman will, she turned her back on Clapperclaw, though every nerve screamed at her not to. She hurried, less cautiously, back through the passage and out into the sunlight, thrilling at the brightness of day even though the sky was still overcast and it wasn't all that bright.

She bounded down the slope to where her friends waited and was caught up by Owen when she nearly tripped in her haste. Owen hugged her. "We heard it, and we thought the worst had happened. Did it see you?"

"No, but I made a mistake and it heard me. I guess its hearing really is exceptional." Aderyn calmed her breathing and stepped away from Owen. "And the system taunted me with the chance to learn more about its fear aura and then said Clapperclaw is too high a level for that. Or for me to find out about it at level twelve, maybe."

"Did you not learn anything, then?" Weston asked.

"I saw its weak spots. There aren't many." Aderyn explained what [Discern Weakness] had revealed, including how much of Clapperclaw was protected. "I have a guess about the fear effect, no thanks to the system. The roar terrified me every time I heard it. [Improved Assess 2] says a fear aura has a range, an intensity, and intentionality. I'm guessing the roar is what carries the fear aura, which means its range is limited to hearing distance. And since it didn't make me flee in mindless terror, I think the intensity is worse the closer you get, but not devastatingly so."

"That's a reasonable guess. I'll take it," Owen said. "Tactics, Warmaster?"

Aderyn nodded. "We really have no choice but to go in fast and hit it hard before it reacts. Plenty of bludgeoning attacks to throw it off balance so our swords will have an effect."

"And if we can go in quietly, that will help us get the drop on it," Owen said. "Any ideas about that?"

"I'll go first," Weston said. "If I use the <**Cloak of Mists**>, I can get into position for [**Improved Sneak Attack**]."

"The rest of us aren't stealthy, though," Aderyn said. "If you get into position and Livia makes our first attack with *stone sphere* or some other bludgeoning attack, it won't matter if Owen and Isold and I make noise."

"What about me?" Crillon said. "You'll need me to soak up damage while the rest of you hit it."

Owen shook his head. "You're sitting this one out. If the worst happens, and Clapperclaw kills us, someone has to get Coralie and Jessemia to safety. And you can take more damage than any of us."

"But—" Crillon stopped. "No. You're right. We have to plan for the worst."

"Keep the <**Fireblast Rod**>, too," Owen went on. "You'll need it for defense. We can't risk it being lost in that cavern."

Coralie looked like she'd been about to offer it, but she subsided. She sat against a rock and welcomed Prince Gustavio Strongpaws onto her lap. The cat had stayed close throughout their trip up the mountain, as if he knew how serious the situation was.

"Then it sounds simple," Owen said. "Weston sneaks inside, Livia pummels the monster, the rest of us go in after. Clear?"

Aderyn was watching Jessemia, who looked frightened, and on impulse she said, "Weston, take the cloak, and everyone make your final preparations. Jessemia, can I talk to you?"

She drew the woman aside and said, "What's wrong?"

"What happens to me if you all die?" Jessemia asked. "I know it's selfish of me to think that way when you're about to attack that monster, but..."

"It's natural to fear for the future," Aderyn said. "If the worst happens, go back to Alcester with Crillon and Coralie. They'll have to evacuate the town and they'll need a good Pathseer to help."

Jessemia let out a choked laugh. "I'm not a good Pathseer. I'm a joke."

"Then you'll have to discover how to be what they need. I think you can do it." Impulsively, Aderyn hugged Jessemia, who didn't return the embrace. "And you can figure out the rest as it happens."

She left Jessemia standing alone and returned to Owen's side. Shrugging out of the <Knapsack of Plenty>, she showed the <Wayfinder> to Coralie. "This will take you back to Alcester if necessary. But I think everything will be all right."

When she stood, her friends had shed all but their essential gear and were waiting for her. The sight brought unexpected tears to her eyes, not because she was afraid for the future, but because she had gone into danger beside them so many times. This was just one more fight—the most dangerous fight of their lives, but she couldn't think of anyone she'd rather face danger with.

"Weston," Owen said.

Weston climbed swiftly up the slope and disappeared into the cave. Owen waited a few seconds, then gestured to the others to follow him, as if he already wanted to remain silent. Aderyn ended up at the end of their procession, with Isold's lanky frame immediately in front of her. She wasn't frightened anymore. They'd succeed, or not, but either way they would do it together.

When she entered the cavern, Weston was already gone—or maybe she just couldn't see him thanks to the <Cloak of Mists>. It didn't matter. She was already counting seconds until the agreed-on time when Weston would be in position and Livia could attack.

But she was only halfway down the passage when she heard a roar that made her bones quiver. "That's it," Owen said. "Go, go!"

Livia was already sprinting for the big cave, which frightened Aderyn more because Livia always insisted she was no runner. Weston must be in trouble. Aderyn ran after her, outpaced by long-legged Isold and keeping up with Owen thanks to [Keep Pace] tugging at her calves.

They burst through the mouth of the cave and kept running. Ahead, Weston was dodging Clapperclaw's front legs with their razor edges and spikes as they tried to impale him. Clapperclaw roared again, that strange high- and low-pitched sound, and terror struck Aderyn, sending her fleeing through the cavern.

Get away get away sang a terrified chorus in her head. Something in her path tripped her, and she landed hard on both outstretched hands. Pain shot through her arms, and a more natural fear that she'd broken a bone filled her. The thought cleared her head. She was still afraid, but not as horribly so. She breathed deeply, crouched on hands and knees, until she felt steadier. Then she got up and hurried back to the fight, hoping her moment of weakness hadn't been fatal for someone.

Clapperclaw's scream rang out once more. This time, Aderyn's fear was distant, as if she'd passed through terror to a place where it couldn't affect her anymore. Weston, however, broke and ran. The monster's front leg slashed down, and Weston cried out as it stabbed him in the back, slicing through the back of his leather jerkin and the shirt beneath and sending blood spurting. Weston fell, not trying to catch himself.

Aderyn screamed his name and dashed forward. Owen shouted and threw himself between Weston and the foreleg that once again descended to stab through him. He blocked the foreleg with crossed blades and managed to shove it to one side as Isold grabbed Weston and hauled him to his feet. Aderyn swung at the first joint of the foreleg, cutting deep but not severing it. Clapperclaw screamed in pain and swung its other foreleg at Aderyn, knocking her backward and tearing her jerkin but not wounding her. Aderyn kept her balance only barely and darted back out of reach.

Behind her, Livia chanted, and *stone sphere* slammed into Clapperclaw's shoulder, knocking it back a step or two. The plates of its carapace flared, and some cream head-sized gobbets of pus dropped from beneath its armor to hit the ground. Clapperclaw screamed again and raced for Livia, who barely had time to cast *stone fist* before it was on her. She stood her ground as its pincers reached for her, letting fly with a tremendous punch to Clapperclaw's jaw that staggered it. Livia pressed the attack, punching again. Then she screamed as Clapperclaw's razor-edged foreleg swiped across her chest, shoving her away and cutting deep into her flesh as it did.

Aderyn swung at the other foreleg's lowest joint, all she could reach, and then had to run out of its reach as it swung at her. Livia lay curled on herself beneath Clapperclaw's body, its inability to see at that angle the only thing that had saved her. Aderyn sheathed her sword and ran as fast as she could, sliding beneath the monster's body to drag Livia to—not safety, nowhere was safe, but to where Isold could heal her. But Isold was busy with Weston and barely acknowledged Aderyn. "I can't sing yet," he said tersely.

Aderyn nodded. Barely fifteen seconds into this fight and half her team was down. She drew her sword and looked around for Owen, expecting to see him moving into position for **[Outflank]**. They might all be dead, but they could go down fighting.

Instead, she saw him kneeling beside Clapperclaw, picking up—oh, gross, he was handling the lumps of pus! And Clapperclaw had just seen him and had whipped around to dive on him. "Owen!" she shrieked.

Owen dropped what he held and sheathed his <**Twinsword**>. With the <**Deadly Blade**> in his off hand, he leaped for the monster's segmented carapace and climbed to where its back became vertical. Clapperclaw went mad, twisting and bucking and shrieking, trying to dislodge Owen. Aderyn saw his intent and ran for the lower section of its back, watching the monster gyrate and waiting for the moment when its movements exposed a gap between segments.

Owen was still hanging on, miraculously, the knife poised to stab just as Aderyn intended. Clapperclaw arched its back, a gap appeared —and Owen, rather than inserting the <**Deadly Blade**> and stabbing Clapperclaw to whatever it had for a heart, reached inside and withdrew an handful of pus. Aderyn's stomach revolted. She was distracted enough that she missed her own opportunity at the vulnerable spot. Cursing herself, she prepared for another blow.

Owen let go and dropped to the ground. "Stop!" he shouted. "It's not what we thought!"

Clapperclaw twisted around and bore down on Owen. Aderyn screamed his name and flung herself at him. Owen held up the hand holding the cream-colored mass so it was between himself and the monster.

And Clapperclaw lowered its head with its terrible pincers and, with a plaintive cry, gently plucked the thing out of Owen's hand and folded it between its forelegs.

CHAPTER TWENTY

"What—" Aderyn gasped. "Owen, what just happened?"

"It's not what we thought," Owen repeated. "Look."

He walked over to where another blob of pus lay. Aderyn, feeling squeamish, followed him. "Oh, Owen, that's disgusting, don't—" she said as he bent to scoop it up.

"Take a look," Owen said, offering it to her. "You're the one that said all baby creatures are cute out of self-defense. Don't tell me you've changed your mind?"

Aderyn looked. It wasn't a handful of pus. It was a grub, cream-colored and with a dozen tiny foot stubs waving helplessly in the air. Lidless black eye spots reflected the eerie glow of the crystals so they appeared luminescent themselves. It wiggled as if trying to right itself.

Owen carried the grub back to where Clapperclaw could take it. The monster had already returned the first grub to the safety of the carapace, and as it accepted the second one, it crooned, a low sound the crystals resonated with, this time pleasantly. "This explains everything," Owen said. "Why it attacks sometimes but not always, and why it's so fierce when it does attack. It's got babies to protect."

"All right, but why didn't it attack you when you took one of them? Shouldn't it have reacted even more violently?" Aderyn watched Clapperclaw pick up the remaining grubs and stow them away.

"I took a chance on it—her—being smart enough to see that I didn't kill the grub when I could have." Owen put his arm around Aderyn. "I guess it worked out."

"What would you have done if it hadn't?"

"Died screaming, probably. Can we just be grateful it worked?"

Aderyn tried to calm the hammering of her heart. "And you get upset when *I* risk myself."

"That's my prerogative as a protective male," Owen teased.

Footsteps sounded, and Weston came to stand beside them. His jerkin and shirt were still in bloody tatters, but he moved as easily as if he'd never been injured. Livia and Isold followed him. "That was the kind of experience I hope never to repeat," Weston said.

"Hold still while I cast *repair*, unless you like the unkempt ruffian look," Livia said. Her voice was hoarse the way it got when she was suppressing her emotions, and Aderyn could see the look in her eyes as she touched Weston that said he wasn't the only one his near-death had affected.

They all looked up at Clapperclaw, who had settled down on her hind legs but whose upper body was still upright. Her forelegs cradled the final grub close to her chest, and again she crooned. "That's so sweet," Owen said.

Aderyn shuddered. "I think we've reached the limit of my compassion for baby monsters. Grubs are not sweet."

"Your inappropriate sympathy has infected me, then," Owen said, nudging her gently with his elbow.

"That is a lot of grubs," Weston said. "Do you suppose this cave complex is overrun by hundreds of Clapperclaws? I have trouble believing it."

"[**Improved Assess 2**] said Clapperclaw got to be this size over years of exposure to the **<Prismatic Crystals'>** radiant energy," Aderyn said, trying not to think of hundreds of grubs crawling over the walls. "If her babies leave to find their own homes, they likely won't get very large."

"Briar beetles are only the size of a large dog in their natural state," Isold said. "And they fight for dominance whenever territory is at stake. Clapperclaw would have incentive to send her offspring out into the world."

"So, does this outcome mean it—she—is going to let us move freely in here?" Livia said.

"I don't know how long her tolerance will last," Owen said. "I wouldn't bet on it being forever. She's still a giant bug, and who knows how intelligent she actually is. She might forget who we are after a while. And mothers are known to be overprotective of their young, so there's a chance she might decide we're a threat, after all."

"So we'd better get moving, is what you're saying," Weston said.

When Coralie entered the cave, Clapperclaw shifted her weight, but otherwise remained still. "Don't worry, I won't approach," Coralie told her. "Not that you understand what I'm saying." She withdrew the engraved stone from her belt pouch and cradled it in both hands. "Now, let me see…"

"I had a thought," Isold said, "when the crystals resonated with Clapperclaw's cries. How do you find the right crystal?"

"I see what you're getting at," Coralie said. "The stone makes the right crystal sing. You're thinking if the resonance is increased, the sound will stand out better?"

"Yes," Isold said. "Will it work?"

"It means that instead of trying to… let's say 'wake up' the right crystal among all these dormant ones, we'll have woken all of them and the right crystal will sound out of tune. It should be much easier to hear." Coralie ran her thumb over the incised design. "And it will sound extraordinary."

Aderyn and Owen gathered with Weston and Livia at the mouth of the passage, sitting comfortably. Crillon and Jessemia sat behind them, since Coralie had said "This isn't something anyone should miss." Isold and Coralie stood near the center of the cave. Off to the side, Clapperclaw regarded them curiously—at least Aderyn wanted to believe Clapperclaw felt curious about these strangers who had invaded her home.

Isold breathed rhythmically, rolling out his shoulders and his neck to loosen the muscles. Then he sang a single high note, holding it for only two seconds before changing to a different note a step lower. With every note, Aderyn waited for the sound she remembered so clearly, the music of the **\<Prismatic Crystals\>** resonating through the cavern.

On the fourth note, the sound changed. Clapperclaw was singing along, matching Isold's note exactly but an octave lower. Isold smiled, but didn't stop singing.

The sixth note did it. As Isold and Clapperclaw sang, the crystals picked up the music and filled the cavern with it. The sound rang through Aderyn like a bell, making tears come to her eyes with how beautiful it was. She clasped Owen's hand and closed her eyes so nothing could distract her from the song.

Distantly, she heard footsteps as Coralie walked through the cave. It felt like no time at all before a different note joined the marvelous sound, not quite discordant but clearly not matching the rest. "This is it," Coralie said. Aderyn opened her eyes to see the elderly woman snap one of the crystals free from the wall near Clapperclaw, who continued to regard Coralie with interest.

Coralie dropped the unfinished stone into her belt pouch, then hesitated. "If I put them together, the noise will be deafening."

"I'll take it," Isold said.

With the stone and the **\<Prismatic Crystal\>** separated, the music gradually faded away. Owen stood in front of Clapperclaw and bowed. "You probably don't understand most of what I'm saying, but this is how we show thanks," he said. "Good luck to you. We'll spread the word about you so maybe you won't be plagued by adventurers."

Clapperclaw let out an eerie keening cry. Then it bowed its upper body and folded its forelegs beneath itself.

Aderyn grabbed Owen's arm and pulled him away. "Let's not push our luck."

"Did you see that, though?" Owen sounded awed. "I know she understood."

"I also know we didn't get experience for defeating her, which means we *didn't* defeat her," Aderyn said. "Which suggests she could still be a threat. And if she did appreciate how we treated her, we don't want to put her in a position where she might feel she needs to destroy us, after all."

"You're so sensible," Owen said.

They hurried down the mountain and back into the foothills, making good progress so by the time sunset came, they were well away from the Icebright Caves and in a comfortable place to make camp. Once the **<Soldier's Friend>** had done its work, Coralie found a comfortable place to sit and pushed Prince Gustavio Strongpaws away when he tried to sit on her lap. "Somebody take this nuisance. It's not much of a **<Stone of Purification>** if it's got cat hair embedded in it."

Jessemia picked up the cat and staggered under his weight before finding a comfortable position for him. The cat put his front paws on her shoulder as if helping to support his weight and watched Isold avidly. He'd been quick to learn about Isold's **<Forager's Belt>** and the delicious beef jerky it produced. Aderyn wouldn't have guessed Isold to be a cat person, but he certainly was a soft touch when it came to Prince Gustavio Strongpaws.

"Is it all right if we watch?" Owen asked. "It's a lot of people staring."

"It doesn't disturb me," Coralie said. "But this part is boring." She laid the crystal on her lap and cupped the engraved stone in both hands. Bringing it to her lips, she breathed out over its surface, the stream of air going on longer than Aderyn thought was humanly possible. As Coralie breathed, the lines on the stone, already awash with glimmers of gold, glowed brightly. It reminded Aderyn of blacksmiths working the bellows to make the forge fire burn yellow-hot.

Swiftly, Coralie shifted the stone to one hand and picked up the <Prismatic Crystal> with the other. It was as fat around as the hilt of Aderyn's sword and blunt at both ends. The last rays of the sun struck the crystal and sent rainbows shooting everywhere. Before the yellow glow could fade, Coralie touched one blunt end of the crystal to the surface of the stone.

Light burst from the crystal, pure white light not refracted by the prism. Aderyn threw up a hand to protect her eyes from the brilliance, but the moment was over before she could do more than blink. When she could see clearly again, the prism was colorless, the rainbows it shed were gone, and the stone glowed with the same radiance the crystals in the cave had. The light in the grooves was silver instead of gold.

"Wow," Owen said. "How does it work?"

"I'll show you, if you've got a pot and some water," Coralie said.

Livia summoned water into the largest pot and set it near the old Spellcrafter. Coralie gathered up a handful of dirt and cast it into the pot, then two more handfuls until the water was murky. "Not something you'd want to drink, eh?" she joked. She stirred the water with her hand, then lowered the <Stone of Purification> into it.

Congratulations! You have completed the quest [Clean, Clear Water].
You have been awarded [10,000 XP]

Aderyn expected a flash of light, or for the water to boil, or something else dramatic to accompany the system notice. But nothing happened except that Coralie said, "I need a mug."

Weston handed her a tin mug. Coralie dipped it into the pot and drank thirstily. Then she upended the mug, and the rest of the water spilled out on the ground, a pure, clear stream of it. Coralie again dipped the mug and poured out more clean water.

Aderyn gasped and leaned over to look into the pot. No dirt remained. The water was clear enough to see all the way to the bottom, where the silver traceries on the stone glimmered. "That's amazing."

"We'll put that where it will catch the corrupted water, and it will support Alcester until someone comes up with a more comprehensive solution." Coralie cracked her neck and stretched. "That took a lot out of me. I think I'd better lie down for a bit."

"Let me help you," Jessemia said. "I can lay out your bedroll."

"Thank you, dear, that's very kind of you," Coralie said, a little louder than necessary. Aderyn watched her go into Jessemia's tent. What had that been about, that strange emphasis as if pointing out Jessemia's action? Surely Coralie didn't know why Jessemia wasn't fully accepted by Aderyn's team? And even if she did, why would she have drawn the conclusion that Jessemia was trying to change—or believe that she already had?

Everyone else set about making dinner or settling camp. Owen said, "I'm going to walk the perimeter, if you want to join me, Aderyn?"

They walked wide around the camp, wider than the *alarm* magic covered, just in case. Nothing stirred. It was a peaceful, beautiful evening. Aderyn thought back to how the day had begun, how she'd anticipated dying, and said, "Do you think tonight is more beautiful because of the near-disaster we had?"

"Yes. I always appreciate the quiet beauty of nature after we've survived something awful." Owen took her hand. "Weston nearly died. Livia was badly injured. Isold said it was a near thing for both of them. And I wasn't nearly so certain as I looked, holding that grub and hoping with all my heart that I wasn't about to die."

"Livia and I talked about making the ultimate sacrifice this morning. About how this quest means life or death for an entire town, and what we'd be willing to give for the sake of all those strangers."

"I never know the answer to that. I was pretty cavalier about accepting this quest in the first place, not even discussing it with the rest of you." Owen looked troubled. "I wonder now if that wasn't prideful rather than altruistic."

"Maybe a little. But none of us would have wanted to turn it down, so really, you were just a little quick off the mark." Aderyn squeezed his hand. "I don't know if I want to give my life for strangers, but I don't think I could have walked away and abandoned Coralie and Crillon."

"I feel the same."

They walked in silence until they finished the circuit and returned to camp, where the soup pot boiled. The delicious smell made Aderyn finally feel like everything was back to normal.

As they ate, Crillon said, "The quest is complete. What will you do next?"

Owen glanced at Aderyn. "I sort of assumed we'd escort you all to where the stone has to be placed," he said. "But that's up to everyone."

Livia spoke from where she leaned against Weston's broad shoulder. "I want to see how this ends."

"So do I," Weston said.

"I intend to tell this story when we return to civilization," Isold said. "It would be an unsatisfying tale if it didn't have an ending."

"I should probably protest more, but I don't know if Coralie and I alone can make it all the way back." Crillon tipped up his soup bowl and drank down the last drops of broth. "Thank you."

A new quest is available: [Purify the Source]
Accompany Coralie the Spellcrafter to the source of the river
that supplies Alcester and see the <Stone of Purification>
placed correctly. This is the culmination of the quest chain [A
Town's Salvation].
Accept? Y / N

Aderyn accepted the quest and watched it shrink down to a glowing blue dot in the right-hand side of the Codex display. "How far a journey is it?"

"The source is just outside Alcester," Coralie said. "Five days' travel from here, maybe a little less."

"Then let's get some rest," Owen said, "and hope the next journey isn't as eventful as the one that brought us here."

CHAPTER TWENTY-ONE

Aderyn knew from experience that the system was aware of what happened in the world. Dungeons had communicated with her like people. Her Assessments were increasingly chatty and casual, just as if the system was sharing information with a friend. But she wouldn't have guessed the system paid attention to their conversations and responded to their idle wishes.

On the other hand, their journey to Alcester was peaceful, almost boring, with no monster attacks and no spontaneous quests or mysterious dungeons throwing themselves in the adventurers' way. The weather was clear and beautiful. Livia's *sleep* wand helped them kill two deer without a struggle. No one argued; no one got sick. It was exactly as if the system had heard Owen's hope for an uneventful trip and decided to grant them an unofficial reward for their hard work and sacrifice.

Rain didn't threaten until the fifth day, when they came over a final rise to see the town of Alcester lying before them. It was as large as Coralie had said, with hundreds of little thatch-roof buildings, and didn't look at all as if it was poised on the brink of disaster. A wide river, big enough to require a bridge to cross it, ambled past the town on its way through the Long Plains.

"It ends up in Lake Aristel," Crillon said as they stood watching it from above. "The Tidecaller from Jackrabbit Dell said it's only a matter of time before the corruption builds up in the lake to the point of killing everything that lives in it or drinks from it. So it's not just Alcester in trouble. In case you were wondering how much of a difference this quest makes."

"Then we should go directly to the source," Owen said.

They walked northwest until they reached the river, then continued west along its banks. Different trees grew there, fragile-looking willows with their limp, dragging branches, other trees Aderyn didn't recognize with hand-sized leaves and rich brown bark. The trees didn't look as if they'd fallen ill with corruption, but Crillon pointed out the brown edges of the leaves, how the willow branches were starting to curl up at the ends. The knowledge made all of them walk faster, though in practice they were hobbled to Coralie's slower pace.

The trees grew thicker the farther they went until they were walking through a beautiful little forest. Thunder rumbled in the distance, and Aderyn felt spatters of water strike her cheek. She welcomed the rain. Its purity felt symbolic of what they meant to do.

The river narrowed until it was narrow enough to jump. Coralie walked beside it with her head bowed, muttering to herself as Prince Gustavio Strongpaws strolled beside her, meowing occasionally. Finally, she stopped and slung her knapsack off. "This is it."

The spot Coralie had picked didn't look different from the rest of the riverbank. If there was corruption, it wasn't visible, though Aderyn was willing to trust Coralie and Crillon's word. She certainly wasn't going to drink from the river there.

"Is there something special you need to do?" Owen asked.

Coralie squatted and dug through her knapsack. "Here it is," she said, bringing out the <**Stone of Purification**>. She took a couple of steps so she stood beside the river and then tossed the stone into its depths. She rubbed one hand on her trousers. "That's all."

"You mean... it's done?" Owen said.

Congratulations! You have completed the quest [Purify the Source].
You have been awarded [15,000 XP]

Congratulations! You have fulfilled some of the requirements for the quest chain [A Town's Salvation]. You have been awarded a partial reward of [7000 XP].

"I guess that means it is," Aderyn said. She felt suddenly tired, the way she always did right after completing a complex or dangerous quest. The feeling would pass, but at the moment, all she wanted was a meal and a quiet bed.

"Let's hurry to Alcester," Crillon said. "By the time we get there, the remaining corruption will be gone, and we'll be able to give them the good news."

Owen bent and scooped up a handful of water to drink. "This is the best water I've ever tasted. Too bad you can't bottle and sell it."

Crillon and Coralie exchanged glances. "That's a strange notion," Coralie said, "but not a bad one."

"Is bottling river water a thing from your world?" Aderyn whispered to Owen as they all headed back downstream.

"Yes, and I'm afraid I've just introduced the concept of artesian water snobbery to Alcester." Owen sounded both alarmed and amused at once.

"I don't know what that is, but I'm sure they're so grateful for any water they won't mind if it turns into that artesian thing," Aderyn said with a smile.

When they were within sight of Alcester again, Aderyn Assessed the city to keep her impatience in check. The completion of the water quest had invigorated her, but there was no point to running, since the purification effect had to work its way downstream.

Name: Alcester

Status: Town

Government: Elected mayor, town council

Civilization level: 8

Resources: Spiritsmith x1, Spellcrafter x1, Windwarden x2, Flamecrafter x1, Earthbreaker x2, Bonemender x1; Crafters level 8; Hospitality level 8; Food supply level 9

Alcester is a farming community founded by adventurers who left Obsidian for a quieter, more orderly life. Its position along the Fairford River allowed it to grow rapidly, making it the second-largest town in the Long Plains. Visitors to Alcester are warned that the citizens, while polite to strangers, view them with suspicion, particularly those who come from Obsidian. It is Alcester tradition that their way of life is superior to all others, so its people are both suspicious *and* smug. If you intend to settle here, be prepared to be referred to as "the foreigner" for at least the first fifteen years of your stay.

When Aderyn got to the end of the Assessment, she was glad she hadn't read it aloud. Coralie and Crillon were nice, but they might take offense at the system's characterization of their home town. Besides, she and her team weren't staying, so it didn't matter—that, and she hoped having helped save Alcester would incline people to like them.

Alcester was unnaturally quiet, though people thronged the streets. With a closer look, Aderyn realized most of them gathered in loose groups near dry fountains, carrying pots or large vases. Her team passed near one of these groups, near enough to see a tired-looking Windwarden casting *drench* repeatedly, filling the containers people held.

"That's got to be brutal," Livia murmured to her. "*Drench* is one of the most basic spells a spellslinger can cast, so it's not normally exhausting, but no one's ever established how long you can go on casting it before you fall over. These people are desperate."

Watching the little groups, Aderyn was seized with a desire to run through Alcester, screaming the news that their town wasn't doomed —but Coralie had insisted they tell the mayor first and let her spread the word.

Most of Alcester's construction was single-story basic wattle and daub, with thatch roofs, but Aderyn knew this kind of construction well enough to tell when the owners were using it to make a state-ment. The fact that all those cottages had fine glass windows added to her skepticism. Her suspicion that someone wanted Alcester to look unnaturally rural was confirmed when they came to the center of town and discovered dozens of brick buildings with slate shingles. Shops with extremely modern plate glass storefronts, the kind of glass Aderyn had only seen in large cities, and raised sidewalks flanking the hard-packed dirt street told Aderyn that Alcester liked its amenities and wasn't shy about flaunting them.

Coralie led them to the only three-story building in town and entered without knocking. The man seated in a comfortable-looking chair just inside the door glanced up from the book he was reading, did a double take, and shot to his feet. "Coralie," he said. "Did you— were you successful?" He glanced over the others. "And who are these strangers?"

"I need to speak to Rashana," Coralie said. "Right now. But... yes."

The man's whole body sagged, and he closed his eyes and breathed out heavily in relief. "She's in here. Go ahead. I—"

"Don't," Crillon said. "The poison may not all be gone yet. We need to give Rashana the information and let her make the announcement."

The man nodded. He resumed his seat, but left the book on the floor where he'd dropped it.

"In here" was the first of three doors opening off the tiny

entrance. Coralie pushed through it and kept going so the rest could follow. It wasn't much of a room; there was a battered desk and an equally old bookcase filled with books and a couple of lacquered wooden boxes, latched but not locked. The fraying carpet's pattern was no longer visible due to decades of wear. The only beautiful thing about the room was the painting hanging behind the desk, which showed an ethereal white city nestled into dark mountain valleys Aderyn thought might be fanciful. Surely no real place could be so dreamlike.

They'd caught the woman seated behind the desk napping, her chair tilted back to rest against the wall, her feet propped on the desk. She blinked and sat up when they entered. "Sorry," she said, rubbing her eyes. "I haven't gotten much sleep lately." Then she gaped. "*Coralie.*"

Coralie dumped Prince Gustavio Strongpaws on the desk, disrupting the few books that lay there. "It's done," she said bluntly. "I created the <**Stone of Purification**> and we placed it in the river. The effect has already started making its way downstream."

Rashana looked like she'd been turned to stone. Prince Gustavio Strongpaws batted at the arm she'd propped on the desk that looked like it was all that was holding her up, then rubbed his face against it. Rashana unfroze long enough to stroke his head, though she didn't look like she knew she was doing it.

"It feels so anticlimactic," she said. "How long before we can turn the fountains back on?"

"Give it two more hours, just in case." Coralie leaned against the desk. "Sorry. I'm exhausted. I hate old age."

"Sit." Rashana stood, but Coralie waved her away.

"I'll go home now. But these people will need lodgings," she said.

Rashana focused on the others for the first time. Her expression grew wary. "I don't recognize them. Crillon, where are the others?"

Crillon shook his head. "They didn't make it out of the Lonely Gard."

Rashana sucked in a breath and put a hand on the desk for support again. "No. Crillon, I'm so sorry. Coralie, you lost Amabel —I don't know what to say. I never imagined that might happen."

"None of us did. We did our best, but sometimes... anyway. This team—" Crillon gestured— "saved my life and helped us fulfil the quest. We owe them everything."

"Of course." Rashana focused on Owen. "You're welcome here. Give me a minute, and we'll take you to the inn and arrange for your stay. No charge, obviously." She visibly gathered herself and tried a smile that looked ghastly. "Thank you."

"We were happy to help," Owen said. "Please don't feel you have to put yourself out. I can tell it's been a stressful time, and we don't want to add to your burden."

"Nonsense. This is a time of rejoicing." Rashana came around the desk and offered her hand to each of Aderyn's team, one at a time. "We'll overcome this tragedy. Crillon, let me go with you to tell your team's families what happened. You shouldn't do this alone."

Aderyn had forgotten that everyone who'd died in the Lonely Gard had relatives here. If it was a time of rejoicing, that wasn't true for everyone.

Chapter Twenty-Two

Three hours later, Alcester was in the middle of a town-wide celebration. People danced and sang in the streets, children chased each other through the crowds, and the fountains sprayed beautifully fresh, clean water higher than Aderyn thought was usual.

The inn, which didn't seem to have a name, overflowed with excited, happy men and women all on the fast track to serious inebriation. Aderyn sat with her tankard at the table her team had secured in the corner of the taproom and watched with peaceful pleasure. She was too tired from the events of the last several days to want to stand on the table and sing and dance like some of the drinkers, but the joy the other patrons exhibited made her quietly joyous as well.

Owen put his arm around her shoulders and hugged her. "You're quiet. Anything wrong?"

She shook her head. "Just the aftereffects of completing a long, dangerous quest. And the anticipation of a lovely night with you."

Owen let out a relieved breath. "I was afraid you were too tired. I didn't want to push and make you feel sex was a duty."

"Never that." She leaned into his embrace.

Across the room, Jessemia sat alone at the bar. Aderyn watched as an attractive man sat beside her, leaning in to say something. Aderyn saw his smile. Jessemia's lips moved, and the man's smile wavered. Then the man collected his beer and walked away. Jessemia went back to looking into her mug, her head bowed.

Impulsively, Aderyn stood. "I'll be back."

She dodged merrymakers, smiled and shook her head at someone who asked her to dance, and took the seat next to Jessemia that the man had occupied. Jessemia glanced her way, then back at her mug.

"You're not feeling sorry for yourself again, are you?" Aderyn said. "Because that's unattractive and self-centered, and I know you don't want either of those things."

Jessemia smiled and shrugged. "No. I was thinking of Crillon's team, and how he had to tell their parents and loved ones they're not coming back. And I was thinking, if something happened to us on this journey, Papa would never know what happened to me." She laughed briefly. "I guess that is sort of self-centered."

"No, I get it. It's natural to think of what might happen, or to consider ourselves in others' places." Aderyn signaled for another beer and drank deeply. A stray memory came to mind, and abruptly, she said, "What were you doing in the woods, that morning before we fought the cave bladders?"

"When?" Jessemia reddened.

"I know you remember. You went out alone and claimed it was nothing, but Weston saw something big was out there, a monster of some kind. What happened?"

Jessemia wouldn't meet Aderyn's eye. "I heard something near the camp and decided to track it. I wanted to prove I was a good Pathseer despite what you all thought. I don't know what it was, because I'm bad at identifying monsters—something furry, as big as a bear but with fangs like daggers and a dark blue pelt."

Aderyn shook her head to indicate she didn't recognize it.

"Anyway, it caught my scent and chased me, and I led it away from the camp and climbed a tree. It lost interest in me quickly and went away. I was too embarrassed to admit I really was as terrible a Pathseer as you all believed, so I was rude. Sorry." Jessemia's face was dull red, and her hands trembled.

"You protected the camp," Aderyn said. "That was good of you."

"Was it?" Jessemia sounded startled.

"Of course. You risked your life to take that monster away from where it could hurt anyone."

"Sure, but you all probably could have killed it. I only did all that to protect myself from being laughed at."

"Even so, that action helped others." Aderyn took another drink. "You have changed, you know. Maybe not the way you expected, but you never complain about the food or the travel anymore, and you let Coralie share your tent. How do you feel?"

Jessemia stared into the depths of her mug again and didn't speak. Aderyn waited. Finally, Jessemia said, "I still don't know if I'm who I want to be. I'm not even sure who that is. And the truth is, my first impulse after asking Coralie if she wanted to share my tent was annoyance that I wouldn't have my space to myself. So I don't know how much credit I should take for that, or for the monster thing."

"My mother says it's not how we feel, it's what we do that counts," Aderyn said. "There was this one time when I was young and my mother had a large order to fill—she's a Spiritsmith—that was for a disease cure. She made us children help make the deliveries. I was eight and I thought it was the most tedious thing ever. But I helped, because that's what we do in my family. And I remember there was one home I took the cure to where the mother was so grateful she cried and gave me a little iced cake as a thank you. I felt so guilty because I'd been resentful of the work."

She shook her head slowly as memory returned. She hadn't thought of this in years. "So I told my mother how I felt, and she said, 'Was that woman's family helped less because you were resentful instead of eager?' I've never forgotten that."

"Don't people know when you're serving them out of spite or bitterness?" Jessemia asked.

"They do, mostly. But they're still helped. It's like—" Aderyn groped to explain something she barely could put into words. "It's all right not to be enthusiastic about sacrifice, is what I'm saying. We're human, and that means we aren't perfect. But we do our best and hope it's enough. The thing is, you didn't let your annoyance leave Coralie without shelter. And that's worthy of something."

"Huh." Jessemia drank the last of her beer. "So it's about not giving in to those impulses, not about trying to completely eliminate them."

"That's a better way to say it. It's impossible to be completely without negative traits, I think. Maybe Isold is close to this. He's the most genuinely good person I know."

Jessemia blushed again. "I agree."

Aderyn guessed she was thinking about her unsuccessful seduction. Isold must have been even more tactful than he'd said.

Jessemia stood. "I think I want to get some sleep. Thank you."

"For what?"

"For thinking I'm worth saving." Jessemia was gone before Aderyn could respond.

Aderyn sat staring at Jessemia's empty mug until someone sat down beside her. "Sorry, I have a sweetheart," she said automatically.

"I'm glad to hear it," Owen said. "What were you and Jessemia talking about?"

"Things. You know, she really does want to change. I mean, I've said that before, but that was always my hope for her. This time, it's her hope for herself."

"Once we get to Guerdon Deep—"

"That's a long way for her to be helpless," Aderyn said. "Couldn't we do something about it?"

Owen's eyebrows rose. "You're serious."

"Of course. How can we give her confidence?"

"Let me think about it," Owen said.

THEY LEFT ALCESTER AT DAWN THE FOLLOWING DAY
under a light rain that grew heavier as the day progressed. Aderyn
trudged beside Owen and let her mind drift. It had been a glorious
night, and she hadn't thought of anything but her sweetheart, but
now that they were on their way again, she couldn't help thinking of
Jessemia and her desire to be something better. She wasn't sure Owen
had taken her seriously in wanting to help Jessemia, which annoyed
her because usually he did what he could to support her. Well, she
already knew she was the only one who believed Jessemia could
change.

Late on the second day, during a rare pause in the rainfall,
Weston stopped. "Those are dire hawks, and they're headed our
way." He pointed at the distant shapes of birds.

"Let's get ready to welcome them," Owen said, drawing his
sword. "Jessemia, stay near Isold and don't run. Dire hawks are faster
than you can imagine and they're drawn to fleeing prey."

"Can I help?" Jessemia asked.

Owen regarded her closely for a few seconds. Then he said, "Not
at your level. Stay out of the way, don't run, and you'll be fine."

Owen's matter-of-fact tone surprised Aderyn. He hadn't been
dismissive or disdainful of Jessemia at all. Jessemia nodded and
moved closer to Isold.

Aderyn drew her sword as well. They'd fought dire hawks before
and nearly been overwhelmed because the monsters were faster even
than fade dogs and capable of diving attacks that were enhanced by
their speed. Now, though, she knew their tactics, had Assessed their
weaknesses, and was prepared to counter them.

The dire hawks came on quickly, seven of them flying in a loose
group. When they were close enough for the team to hear their

hoarse croaks, Livia let fly with *iron spikes*. The hail of metal shot through the flock, striking the three dire hawks in the lead and making them scream in pain and fury. As one, the flock wheeled and dove.

Aderyn held her ground. The tingling warning of her skill [**See It Coming**] showed her the ghostly shape of a dire hawk that hurtled toward her, backwinging to claw her face. Then the real dire hawk was there, nearly as large as a human and with a ten-foot wingspan. It clawed at her, but Aderyn had stepped out of the way and swung her sword at its neck. Blood flowed, and the dire hawk jerked and flapped awkwardly trying to get aloft again.

Aderyn thrust at its chest, impaling it left of center, then had to retreat a few paces to get out of the way of its wildly beating wings with their sharp, powerful leading edges. The dire hawk croaked again, but weakly, and hit the ground. Aderyn dodged the wings and brought her sword down in a powerful two-handed thrust that impaled the dire hawk behind its head.

Congratulations! You have defeated [Dire Hawk]. You have earned [3325 XP]

Two identical system notices appeared in quick succession. The remaining dire hawks ascended a good distance, circling overhead like carrion eaters. Aderyn was aware that Livia was down and Isold was tending to her, but she didn't dare take her attention off the monsters. She waited for them to move again, balanced on the balls of her feet.

One dire hawk dove. Aderyn had time to wonder why it was alone when the second dove, and the next, and the next, all of them flying at erratic intervals.

And all of them were diving at Jessemia.

Aderyn recalled the way the team was positioned, how it looked like they were protecting Jessemia, and cursed. Even as she thought that, she grabbed hold of one of the four fuzzy balls of yellow light attached to Jessemia and hauled it to Owen with **[Compel]**.

Immediately she saw the problem. With all the dire hawks' attention on Jessemia and the speed at which they were moving, Aderyn couldn't tell which of the yellow lights came from which creature. The one she'd chosen first belonged to the one farthest back, and the one who'd dived first had almost reached Jessemia, who stared up at it in shock. Screaming with the effort, Aderyn gathered up all three of the remaining lights and dragged them to the closest target. Herself.

The leading dire hawk swerved in midair, slowing for a second or two. Its confusion saved Aderyn, who managed to get her sword into position before it dove on her. She blocked its terrible talons with her blade, then stumbled backward as the second dire hawk attacked.

The third dire hawk's scream became a choked gurgle as Weston's thrown dagger took it in the throat. It flapped away, but that left Aderyn facing two deadly enemies. Then Weston was at her side, driving the second dire hawk away from its companion.

The one remaining monster clawed Aderyn's face. She saw the attack coming and dodged, not fast enough, and one talon raked her cheek. She thrust for the weak spot on its belly, but missed as it darted back, just as if it too had **[See It Coming]**. Aderyn was breathing heavily. Without her partner, she wasn't much of a threat. But she wasn't going to lie down and let it kill her.

The dire hawk screamed and turned its back on Aderyn. Jessemia stood there, her sword dark with blood. She held the weapon awkwardly, as if she'd never wielded a sword before, but her face was set in a determined frown and she raised her sword to block the dire hawk's furious attack. Aderyn took advantage of its distraction to drive home a thrust to the back of its neck.

Congratulations! You have defeated [Dire Hawk].
You have earned [3325 XP]

She wiped away the blood trickling down her face and winced at the pain when she touched the long cut. Jessemia looked stunned. She prodded the dead dire hawk with the tip of her sword. "That would have—" she began.

"Talk later," Aderyn said, and shoved past her to put herself opposite Owen, who was still battling his enemy. But before she could strike from behind, Owen drove his blade deep into the dire hawk's gut.

Aderyn blinked the system message away and turned, scanning the sky. No more vile monsters wheeled above, looking for an opening. Breathing heavily, she lowered her sword. She recalled the last time they'd fought dire hawks and how terrifying it had been. This could have ended much worse.

CHAPTER TWENTY-THREE

Owen left the monster he'd killed and hurried to her side. "That's deep," he said, touching her cheek beside the wound. "Let's get you healed. Is anyone else wounded?"

"I'm fine now," Livia said. Weston and Isold just shook their heads. Isold examined the tear and pulled out the **\<Healing Stone\>**. He cupped it in his hand and ran it over Aderyn's face. Green light shone at the edge of her vision, and warmth spread across her cheek to her jaw and forehead.

Owen turned away from Aderyn and approached Jessemia, who looked frightened. Before he could speak, she said, "I know you said not to fight, but everyone else was fighting the others, and I was afraid for Aderyn. I thought I could be a distraction."

"You're in more danger than we are because your fighting skills would be inadequate for monsters of this level even if you weren't crippled as a Pathseer," Owen said. "Getting that dire hawk's attention could have killed you."

He spoke matter-of-factly, with no rancor, but Jessemia cringed anyway. Then she straightened. "I didn't want to die," she said, "but I couldn't not help. I'm sorry if that was wrong."

Owen surveyed her for a moment. "You weren't wrong," he finally said. "Good instincts."

Aderyn heard all this in a blur. She wasn't in pain anymore now the healing was complete, but using **[Compel]** so often and so rapidly made her dizzy. "Thank you," she said to Jessemia's indistinct form. She blinked rapidly to clear her vision, and bone-deep aches took the place of the dizziness, as if she'd exerted herself to her limit.

"We'll wait for Isold to harvest the spleens, and then we'll get away from this mess," Owen declared. "Aderyn, sit down. You used **[Compel]**, didn't you?"

Aderyn nodded. "It's getting easier, but four times in four seconds is a strain."

"What's **[Compel]**?" Jessemia asked. She had a handful of grass and was scrubbing her sword blade clean of blood.

Aderyn hugged her knees and rested her head on them. "It forces an enemy to target the person I choose."

"You mean, so they don't go after a weaker opponent?"

"Right. It lets me, well, organize a fight."

"I didn't know that was possible. I thought Warmasters were—sorry." Jessemia looked embarrassed.

"So does everyone. I don't mind." She had minded, once, but with as skilled as she'd become, she no longer cared what others believed. More or less.

Jessemia's eyes widened. "They were diving at me," she said, "and then they went after you. Was that **[Compel]**?"

Jessemia sounded so astonished Aderyn's discomfort grew. "Yes," she said, feeling like she was admitting to something shameful.

"But you couldn't fight three dire hawks at once," Jessemia said.

"It was the only option," Aderyn said. "And I trust my teammates to defend me as I defend them."

Jessemia glanced at Owen before returning her gaze to Aderyn. "Thank you," she said quietly. "You didn't have to risk yourself for me."

"And you didn't have to attack that dire hawk," Aderyn said. "Thanks."

Again, Jessemia looked at Owen as if waiting for him to criticize. Owen said nothing. Finally, Jessemia turned away and walked to where Isold was expertly slicing into dire hawk abdomens, collecting the spleens that produced a valuable liquid used in speed enhancement potions.

"That was brave," Aderyn said.

"And you were daring," Owen said. He was still watching Jessemia. "But was taking on all three dire hawks really the only way?"

"There wasn't time to send them after separate targets. You're not yelling."

Owen startled. "Should I yell?"

"Jessemia did disobey your instructions to stay out of fights." The body aches were subsiding, though Aderyn knew from experience that they wouldn't go away entirely until she slept.

"She saw a threat and stepped in to counter it. That's not the same as thinking she can fight a level nine monster on her own. Like I said, she had good instincts." Owen laid a hand on Aderyn's shoulder. "And I think it's important to show her the difference between sycophancy and genuine compliments."

"Important?"

Owen sighed. "You want to help her change. I'm maybe a little more sanguine about how possible that is."

Aderyn smiled. "So I was right, is what you're saying."

"When it comes to people, you usually are," Owen said.

THE NEXT DAY, THEY ENTERED A FOREST, DENSE WITH FIRS and low-growing shrubs and ferns. At midday, the trees were a welcome relief from the sun's heat. Aderyn walked next to Owen and kept an alert eye out for threats. Cave bladders might no longer be terribly dangerous to her team, but she'd never forgotten seeing one silhouetted against the night sky, its fat tentacles and shapeless body a dark, threatening form.

Behind her, Jessemia said, "Something came through here recently."

The others stopped. "What do you mean, something?" Owen said, putting a hand on his sword.

"I can't tell. Sometimes I see tracks, but I don't usually know what makes them. I can tell the difference between an animal and a monster, though." Jessemia didn't shrink in on herself the way she usually did when Owen spoke to her. Aderyn hated that the woman was so afraid of her partner, though some of that feeling was annoyance that Owen had made himself so frightening.

Weston walked to Jessemia's side. "Show me," he said.

"I don't know—" Jessemia fell silent, eyeing Weston as if waiting for him to say something scathing as he usually did. Then she pointed at spots on the ground that didn't look unusual to Aderyn. "It was big, whatever it was, because its hooves dug deep into the earth. Deeper than a deer or a horse. And it went... that way." She pointed to the left.

"Huh." Weston crouched and examined the earth. "I see it now."

"Is it a threat?" Livia asked.

"I don't know." Jessemia gazed into the distance in the direction she'd pointed. "Maybe? I don't always notice a monster's tracks. That's probably because my skill in **[Tracking]** is so low."

"It's not your skill level," Aderyn said, "it's that you don't think to use it. You're waiting for it to work on its own."

"Isn't that right?" Jessemia's puzzlement was obvious. "They always told me to trust my instincts."

"'They'—you mean your former teammates?"

Jessemia nodded. "But maybe they only said that because I

wanted to believe I was special. To believe skills worked differently for me."

She didn't sound embarrassed at referring to her past, but Aderyn felt the sting anyway. "They weren't wrong. [Tracking] is as much a matter of instinct as it is thought. But you have to be active in searching for tracks in order for instinct to matter."

"How do you know that?" Now Jessemia sounded curious.

"My [Improved Assess 2] skill lets me Assess skills to learn more about them. Your [Tracking] skill is as high as it should be for your level, so I know you've practiced it, but your [Knowledge: Magical Beasts] skill is much too low. That's why you can see tracks but not identify what made them."

Jessemia nodded. "How can I change that?"

That was a question Aderyn didn't have a good answer for. "Encountering and fighting monsters is the only way I know. And we're in an area where most of the monsters are too powerful for you, so fighting them is dangerous."

"Maybe," Owen said. "Let's go after this one."

"Without knowing what it is?" Livia protested. "It could be too dangerous for *us* to fight."

"Then we don't engage. But we can at least see what it is." Owen turned to Jessemia. "If you think you can track it."

Jessemia bit her lip nervously. Then she nodded. "I can."

"Everyone stay alert and follow Jessemia," Owen said, drawing his sword. "Jessemia, don't get too far ahead. Let's go."

They walked through the woods with weapons ready. Jessemia didn't appear to be doing anything special, though occasionally she slowed to study the ground. Aderyn still couldn't see the tracks. She hoped Owen's confidence wasn't misplaced. Suppose this was something really powerful?

Then Jessemia came to a stop and held up a hand for the others to stop as well. "I can smell it," she whispered. "It smells of fire and ash. It's near."

"Form up," Owen said.

Weston had already moved ahead. Aderyn and the others followed him. The forest was so still it unnerved Aderyn, no bird-song, no chittering squirrels, not even the sound of wind in the branches. Weston's return relieved her mind of dire imaginings, hooved creatures that could cleave a skull in half or tear flesh to the bone.

"It's a burning stag," he whispered. "Looks like an ordinary deer, but its antlers are on fire."

"Let's get Jessemia and Aderyn close enough to Assess it," Owen said.

Jessemia looked pale, but she nodded.

As they crept closer, the smell of burning became stronger, and soon Aderyn saw glints of fire through the trees. When she finally saw the creature clearly, it was obvious Weston's description had been inaccurate in one respect: the burning stag was shaped like a deer, but it was half again as tall as an ordinary stag and built heavily. Aderyn was sure its mass was all muscle. Its magnificent antlers blazed with fire that ran like liquid down the prongs and over the top of its head. Aderyn Assessed it.

Name: Burning Stag
Type: Magical beast
Power level: 10
Attacks: Hooves x2, bite, gore
Immune to: elemental fire damage
Resistant to: none
Vulnerable to: elemental water damage (see below)
Special abilities: ignite, infect, summoning call

Burning stags are forest denizens who kill trees by sharpening their antlers on them, causing fire damage to the wood beneath the bark. Burning stags have been known to start forest fires intentionally, as this drives woodland creatures out of hiding and into their jaws. They cannot be harmed by fire,

but extinguishing their antlers confuses them and makes them easier to hit. Their bite carries a form of hoof and mouth disease that can be transmitted to any bitten creature and may be fatal. Don't be fooled by how pretty they are. Being gored by a burning stag is as bad as you're imagining right now.

Blue lines slid over the monster's body and coalesced into dots of blue light beneath the burning stag's chin and in a row along its underside.

"What do you see?" Owen whispered.

Aderyn started to answer, but Jessemia said, "It has three kinds of attack, it can't be hurt by fire but water confuses it, and it has a **[Summoning Call]** special ability I don't understand."

Owen glanced at Aderyn. Aderyn nodded. "Their bite carries disease, and **[Summoning Call]**... give me a moment." She Assessed the attack and added, "It can call others of its kind to join it. It doesn't say how many, but I'm guessing whatever's within earshot."

"Then we'll have to be quick," Owen said. "Livia?"

"Go as soon as the fire dies," Livia said, and snapped her fingers.

A mass of water five feet across appeared in the air above the burning stag's head. It hung there for a moment before crashing down over the monster's antlers, head, and forelimbs. The fire flickered almost to nothing, but didn't die. The burning stag reared up and screamed a terrible challenge, turning rapidly in search of its enemy.

Livia muttered and snapped again. More water drenched the burning stag. This time, the flames went out. Owen and Weston were off in an instant, with Aderyn lagging slightly behind so she could see where to go for **[Outflank]**.

The burning stag screamed again when it saw the three friends. This time, the sound was compelling, tugging at Aderyn's heart as if she could hear its **[Summoning Call]** and respond. Weston threw a dagger that pierced the monster's throat, but the attack was too late to stop it calling for help.

"It's fine, just take it down!" Owen shouted. He tumbled past the burning stag so he was opposite Aderyn and thrust at its belly with the <Twinsword>. The burning stag twisted away so Owen's blow didn't do more than score its flesh. Aderyn attacked, drawing its attention. It turned on her, giving Owen a clear shot at its flank. This time, his strike connected, and blood too red to be natural flowed.

Weston darted back and forth in front of it, dodging its occasional snapping bites. Aderyn spared a second or two to watch him. "It's too fast," she told him. "Wait for us to pin it down and then go for the throat."

Weston nodded.

Aderyn moved closer to the monster, though the smell of burning and hot ashes dizzied her. "Close in, keep it from moving!" she shouted.

Owen followed her lead. Aderyn gradually worked her way around the burning stag until she faced it. She felt the alertness [Outflank] always gave her that said Owen had moved to the rear when she moved to the front.

The burning stag screamed. This time, it was a strangled sound that didn't go farther than its attackers. It planted its forelegs in a wide stance and kicked out with its back hooves. Owen grunted and fell back. [Outflank] disappeared, making Aderyn's heart skip in fear for her partner.

Another scream shattered the air. This time, it was Jessemia. Aderyn couldn't lose focus to see what had frightened the woman. She pressed the attack, blocking the burning stag's antlers as it tried to gore her. Sharp pain shot through her shoulder as one of those attacks got past her defenses, goring her high on her right side. Though the fire was extinguished, the antler burned hot as a coal as it pierced her body. She gagged on the smell of her own burned flesh.

Weston took advantage of its temporary immobility to strike its throat. His blade struck true, and with [To the Heart] he drove the blade through the burning stag's throat in an upward motion that sent it all the way into the monster's brain. The burning stag struck weakly at Weston, tearing his leather jerkin but not reaching flesh. Weston withdrew his blade and the monster dropped lifeless to the ground.

Congratulations! You have defeated [Burning Stag].
You have earned [5000 XP]

Aderyn was already scanning the woods for Jessemia. Another burning stag with its antlers extinguished stood only fifteen feet away, motionless. Isold had a hand up palm first in front of the monster's face. His whole body was rigid. Jessemia stood behind him, staring at the hypnotized monster.

Aderyn and Weston hurried to Isold's side, preparing to kill the second burning stag before it shook off **[Hypnotism]**. Weston readied his blade for **[To the Heart]**, and Owen said, "Don't."

CHAPTER TWENTY-FOUR

"Don't?" Aderyn turned to see Owen limping toward them. The front of his brigandine was scuffed and marked by scrapes from the burning stag's sharp hooves. "What are you talking about?"

"Let Jessemia do it," Owen said.

Jessemia let out a squeak of dismay. "But you said—"

"Never mind what I said. Hurry, before it comes to its senses."

Aderyn and Weston exchanged skeptical glances, but Aderyn said, "Right at the base of the throat. Make it a powerful blow."

Jessemia nodded. She walked around Isold and raised her sword. The burning stag shook its head and reared up, preparing to attack her. Jessemia screamed in terror and thrust her blade at the vulnerable spot. The monster's momentum as it crashed down on her drove the sword deep into its head. Jessemia screamed again as it bore her to the ground.

Aderyn and Weston both dove for her, Weston to wrestle the burning stag's bulk off Jessemia, Aderyn to drag her to safety. Aderyn expected to see Jessemia covered in blood and unconscious. Instead,

Jessemia clung to her, her whole body shaking. Her leather vest was scuffed and torn by those terrible sharp hooves.

"Is it dead?" she asked, her voice shaking as badly as her body. Then her expression changed. "I killed it," she said faintly. "The system message—*I* killed it."

"That was impressive," Weston said. For once, his voice when he spoke to Jessemia didn't sound scornful or annoyed. "I can't believe you stood your ground like that."

"I was too afraid to do anything else," Jessemia said. "That's the first time I've killed a monster. Every other time, my teammates did the work and I shared in the experience." She sounded awed.

"You did well," Owen said. "It landed on you—are you injured?"

"No—" Jessemia felt along her ribcage and winced. "I suppose I am. It hurts when I move at the waist."

"Cracked ribs," Isold said. "Owen?"

"It caught me in the stomach with its kick. Felt like slamming into an iron girder," Owen said, gently prodding his abdomen. "It hurts like hell, so there's probably internal damage. And Aderyn— you're wobbling. Were you injured?"

"It gored me," Aderyn said, gingerly touching the charred hole in her leather jerkin. "The heat seared the wound so it didn't bleed." Saying that made her feel like gagging again.

"I will heal all of you, then, but let's get away from these creatures. Who knows if there are more of them within range of the **[Summoning Call]**?" Isold put a hand on Jessemia's elbow and steered her away from the bodies. Jessemia still looked stunned.

By the time they were far enough away that Owen declared them safe, the pain in Aderyn's chest had grown to a burning ache. She made Owen lie down for Isold to use the <**Healing Stone**> on him, holding his hand through the process. When he was moving easily, she let Isold pass the <**Wand of Healing**> over the hole in her chest, then waited patiently while Livia's *repair* spell fixed her jerkin. Weston handed her a hunk of bread and some of the delicious beef jerky from the <**Forager's Belt**>. "It's lunchtime," he said, "though with the excitement we've had it feels like it should be later."

Aderyn nodded absently. Her attention was on Jessemia, who sat very still while Isold healed her cracked ribs. She didn't look anything like the woman they'd met weeks ago in Obsidian. Her curls were a tangled mess, her clothing was scuffed and dirty, and her boots had lost their polish and now looked more like something an adventurer would wear. Aderyn wished [**Assess**] revealed character. It would be nice to know whether Jessemia had changed on the inside as well as on the outside.

Jessemia said something to Isold, who nodded and helped her stand. Weston handed them both food, and Jessemia clutched hers to her chest and walked over to sit by Aderyn. "How do I know when I will level?" she asked.

Startled at the directness of the question, Aderyn said, "Oh, well, it's not—leveling happens when the system decides you've gained enough experience. People have tried calculating the exact number, but they all came up with different results. So there's no answer to that question."

"Oh." Jessemia took a bite of bread. "I was hoping to see my skills improve."

"That happens as you adventure, not when you level," Aderyn said. "You'll gain new skills at each level, but the skill ranks go up the more you use a given skill. You can check your Advancement to see if that's happened." She could Assess Jessemia's skills herself, but it felt right to encourage her to monitor her progress.

Jessemia snapped her fingers next to her temple and said, "Advancement." Her eyes focused on a point about a foot in front of her face. She brightened. "My [**Tracking**], [**Knowledge: Magical Beasts**], and [**To the Heart**] all increased! What's [**To the Heart**]?"

"Didn't anyone tell you *anything?*" Aderyn exclaimed.

Jessemia blushed and looked at her feet. "They said not to worry about it. And Papa said the Fated One has a destiny and skills don't matter."

"But didn't you care?"

"I didn't think about it." Jessemia shrugged, but her face was still red. "I believed that was how adventuring worked. My other teams told me to stay out of danger and that I shouldn't be bothered with chores and things. I got used to it."

Aderyn tore off a hunk of beef jerky and chewed to keep herself from blurting out something harsh and critical, though she didn't know who she was angrier at, Jessemia for being so clueless or her former teammates for contributing to keeping her incompetent. When she got herself under control, she said, "They didn't help you at all. They just made you weak."

"I know." Jessemia finished her bread and wrapped her arms around her knees. "Is it too late for me?"

"No. Absolutely not," Aderyn said with more conviction than she actually felt. She believed it was possible for someone to make up lost ground by adventuring properly, but whether *Jessemia* could manage it... she'd been coddled and babied so much, and what if she couldn't break those habits? "But you have to want it. Otherwise you might as well settle in one of these villages and retire."

"I don't want that. I'm tired of being told not to try things." Jessemia's lips pinched in a tight line. "Do you still think I'm useless?"

"You're underpowered for your level. That's not the same as useless. And you killed the burning stag by yourself."

"Not really. Isold kept it hypnotized." The whine was back in Jessemia's voice.

"Stop that," Aderyn said. "Whining is unattractive and it makes you look weak, remember? The monster broke free of [**Hypnotize**] before you killed it, and you stood your ground and didn't run. You earned that kill."

"I'm sorry," Jessemia said. "I guess I have a lot of bad habits to break."

"You do," Aderyn said bluntly. "But you've already changed. And if you resist the urge to complain and look for special treatment, you'll go on changing."

Jessemia nodded. "I'll try."

"Good." Aderyn looked around. "Weston, will you explain to Jessemia what **[To the Heart]** is?"

Weston looked up from where he and Livia had been talking. "It's a skill that lets you make a single deadly strike at a key vulnerable point. Owen calls it a kill shot. What you did to kill the burning stag was **[To the Heart]**. Straight through the throat into the brain. I didn't know you had that skill."

"I never used it before," Jessemia said. She stood and walked away through the trees, her shoulders hunched.

"Jessemia, don't go out of sight," Aderyn called. Jessemia stopped about twenty feet away with her back to the others. Her shoulders quivered like she was crying. Aderyn rose, then hesitated. She didn't know what had brought that on, and she didn't know what she ought to do about it. Sometimes people needed space to experience emotions, without anyone else interfering, but was that what Jessemia needed right now?

Someone put a hand on her shoulder. Owen said, "What did you say to her?"

"It's not my fault," Aderyn said. "We were talking about skill advancement, and then she walked away."

"Huh." Owen patted her shoulder and then went to join Jessemia. He moved more easily now that Isold had healed him. Aderyn thought about following him. He was never gentle with Jessemia, and he might make things worse. But Owen was speaking to Jessemia in a low voice, not yelling, and Jessemia had turned so her face was partly visible, and she didn't look upset. Aderyn decided to leave them alone. Whatever Owen had in mind, it was worth letting him try. She watched them, though, just in case.

When they both turned to come back to the others, she sat and pretended she'd been looking elsewhere, though they must have seen her back away. Owen said, "We should see about making more progress before we camp. Jessemia will watch for tracks that might mean monsters we can kill. We haven't made a real push to gain experience yet."

Aderyn saw Weston and Livia exchange skeptical looks, but they said nothing. Isold said, "That will make a difference. Thank you, Jessemia."

"I'll do what I can, but—" Jessemia caught Aderyn's eye. Aderyn shook her head slightly, warning Jessemia that she was verging on whininess again. "I'll do my best," Jessemia said instead.

"Let's move out," Owen said. "We've got a lot of ground to cover before night."

THREE DAYS LATER, THEY LEFT THE FOREST BEHIND. None of the monsters they encountered were higher than level four, and all of them fled rather than attacking. Aderyn's frustration over not meeting anything worth experience came to a head when they startled a pack of misthounds in the early morning. "Why do we have such bad luck?" she exclaimed. "Go on, run," she shouted after the fleeing hounds. "I'm almost to the point of being willing to put in effort for the fifty experience each of you is worth!"

"We'll get there," Owen said. "Besides, they're too beautiful to kill."

"The village, or possibly town, of Jackrabbit Dell is northeast of here," Isold said. "We might see if there are any quests we can pick up."

"Would a village have anything worth our time?" Aderyn asked. "Plensholt didn't."

Isold nodded. "The plains are much more dangerous, our current problem notwithstanding, with higher-level monsters than are found near the safe zone. So even though their size makes them villages, they have very little in common with Gardholm or Far Haven."

"Let's head that way, then," Owen said. "Isold, you and Jessemia walk ahead and guide us there. Aderyn and I will take the middle."

The plains soon became low, rolling hills covered with dry end-of-summer grass and flowering bushes. At the top of each rise, Aderyn scanned the distant hills, hoping to see Isold's village. The land was empty all the way to the horizon.

"I can't imagine settling out here," she told Owen. "Everything's so empty." She checked her system map. The fuzzy dot of Jackrabbit Dell was only a day's walk away, and she should have been able to see it in the distance.

"Plensholt isn't more than five days' journey from Alcester, and it took six days to get from there to here," Owen said. "That's not a lot farther than Far Haven to Market Warding."

"I guess, but it feels so much more distant." They started up the slope of the next hill. This time, when they reached the top, Aderyn saw a thin gray trail of smoke rising into the air, barely more than a thread. "There it is."

"I love seeing new towns appear on the horizon," Owen said. "You never know what you'll find."

"You just like sleeping in a real bed," Aderyn teased.

"So do you." Owen clasped her hand briefly. "But really, the possibility of getting quests excites me. Killing monsters is fine, but a quest could be anything."

"I think that's only true for our team. We end up with secret quests, and unusual challenges, because you're the Fated One. Everyone else gets vermin extermination." Aderyn hesitated. "We can't invite Jessemia into our team, because the level difference is too big."

"Even if we could, we shouldn't." Owen pinched his lips tight in thought. "If Jessemia joined our team, it would cause the same problem as before—she'd level too fast and her skills would stagnate. It's too bad, because she's improved considerably. But it would end up hurting her."

"All right, but what if we end up taking quests in Jackrabbit Dell? She'd participate in them simply because she's traveling with us, but she wouldn't get a reward. That's unfair."

"I hadn't considered that." They reached the top of a hill, and now Jackrabbit Dell was visible as a dark blotch in a valley between two hills. "We'll have to figure something out. You're right, it's not fair. But I don't think it's safe to send her off on quests with no companions."

"That would be worse." Aderyn stopped for a moment to admire the view. "I hope there's something for us in Jackrabbit Dell. What kind of a name is that, anyway?"

"I guess there are a lot of rabbits in the valley," Owen said. "Livia should be pleased."

"Why should Livia be pleased?" Livia called out from where she and Weston walked behind.

"Jackrabbit Dell. Bunnies. Lots of bunnies," Aderyn said.

"Jackrabbits aren't bunnies," Livia said. "They're not cute, for one, with those long legs and enormous ears. They don't do anything but eat and shit and run."

"So you'd be all right with eating one," Weston said.

"If I liked tough and gamy meat, sure."

"Let's hope they have more to eat in that village than jackrabbits," Aderyn said.

CHAPTER TWENTY-FIVE

They crested the last rise before reaching Jackrabbit Dell well before sunset and paused there to let Aderyn Assess the village. It really was closer to being a town, she reflected, with a high stone wall shaped like a kidney bean surrounding it and many red-brick buildings.

Name: Jackrabbit Dell

Status: Town

Government: Elected council

Civilization level: 6

Resources: Spiritsmith x1, Windwarden x1, Flamecrafter x2, Tidecaller x2, Earthbreaker x2; Crafters level 6; Hospitality level 6; Food supply level 9

Jackrabbit Dell was founded by a team of adventurers who wanted to settle down together. It welcomes anyone who is willing to work hard and contribute to the economy. Strangers passing through Jackrabbit Dell are requested to visit the town council. The council claims this is a courtesy, but the truth is they want to know which classes of which level they can call on to do whatever tasks the citizens aren't interested in dealing

with. That makes you their stooge, but you'll get the experience, so in the end you'll be the one waving farewell. Even so,
beware what you agree to.

Aderyn repeated this to her friends. Weston said, "That could be
a problem."

"Why?" Owen said. "The important thing here is that this
confirms there are quests available in Jackrabbit Dell."

"Yes, but suppose they demand we do a quest we don't want to
do? We might be stuck here for a while." Weston came to stand
beside Owen. "I do not want to do a lot of fiddly little low-experi-
ence-reward quests, particularly ones we've been guilted into."

"Isold will talk our way out of that," Owen said. "Relax. It will
be fine. Think of a nice warm bed and a meal that isn't dried meat
and cheese."

Weston scowled. "You know where to hit me, don't you?"

"You are sort of predictable when it comes to food," Aderyn said.

Weston slapped his muscular chest. "I'll have you know it takes a
lot of work to maintain this physique. Healthy meals are part of
that."

"Nothing wrong with healthy meals," Owen said. "In fact, can I
have some of those grapes?"

They strolled down the rise into the valley. It wasn't as small as
Aderyn had expected, spreading out between the hills so it ran several
miles north and south and was more than a few miles wide. Outside
the town, farmland extended in both directions, with crops almost
ready for harvest. The sight of the waving grain and the gold-tasseled
ears of corn surprised Aderyn. She hadn't realized how late in the
year it had gotten. She loved fresh corn. Maybe someone had begun
harvesting already, and it was available at the inn.

The stone wall rose seven feet in the air. Unlike Plensholt,
Jackrabbit Dell had a gate, a big sturdy oaken thing studded with
iron and spiked on top. Aderyn couldn't help imagining what it
would have taken to bring the wood here, given that the nearest

forest was a day's travel away. Come to think on it, the stone couldn't be from around here either, or maybe the farmland had been rocky and the original settlers had dug up enough stone to build the wall. Either way, it was impressive construction.

Two men wearing mismatched armor lounged in front of the gate. They came to attention when the friends approached. Aderyn Assessed them, though she knew they were adventurers from their armor. Adventurers picked up pieces of armor from all over, and one of the ways to tell someone was high level without Assessment was observing their equipment.

Name: Calior

∞ Evalina

Class: Staffsworn (retired)

Level: 13

Name: Brist

Class: Swordsworn

Level 12

"Hey there," Calior said. "You coming from Obsidian?"

"We are," Owen said. "We hoped to stay the night here, maybe pick up a few quests."

"The Council is always ready to provide quests for visitors," Brist said. He smiled at Aderyn in a way that clearly said he found her attractive. Aderyn smiled back. She got no sense of menace off him, not the way she had off those Brigands, and even though she wouldn't encourage him, it was nice to be appreciated.

Weston stilled. "Someone's coming," he said.

Brist and Calior readied their weapons. "Did you bring trouble down on us?" Brist asked. He no longer looked friendly.

"It's coming from the north. We came from the west," Weston said. His head was tilted as if to catch whatever sound had reached his Moonlighter's ears. "Someone shouting."

Now Aderyn heard it, too—a long, drawn-out wail punctuated by shouts of *Help* and intervals of silence short enough that they had to be pauses for breath. She loosened her sword in its scabbard and watched the top of the hill.

A figure crested the hill and sped toward them, stumbling as her speed threatened to overbalance her and send her tumbling to the bottom. "Help!" she shrieked. "Something took my son! Somebody help me!"

Startled, Aderyn Assessed the woman as she ran.

Name: Tirla

Class: Spiritsmith (retired)

Level: 9

The guards came to attention, drawing weapons, but didn't leave their posts. Aderyn started forward, but Owen grabbed her arm and brought her to a halt. "Those guards think this could be a trick to draw them away from their post," he murmured. "Let's wait."

"But if it's serious—"

"A few seconds won't matter."

Tirla reached the base of the hill and broke into a run. She'd stopped calling for help and looked like she was pushing herself to her limit. When she staggered to a halt in front of the guards, she was breathing so heavily she couldn't speak. She was soaked from waist to ankle and covered in mud.

"Tirla," Calior said. "What happened?"

Tirla shook her head and held up a hand, asking for him to wait. In a few seconds, she straightened and gasped, "Something took Rhian. I think it was a dust witch. If we go now, we might catch it."

The guards exchanged glances. "Tirla—" Brist began.

"I wasn't asleep for more than twenty minutes. The creature is still out there." Tirla's breathing was slowing, but the intensity in her voice and posture made her sound as if she was still running. "Please, Brist. Come with me."

"You know we can't leave our posts," Brist said. "And we couldn't track a dust witch anyway."

"You're just giving up?" Tears filled Tirla's eyes. "He's not dead, I know it. Fine. You won't help, I'll find someone who will. Open the gate."

"Excuse me," Owen said. "Did you say your son is missing?"

"My son has been *taken*," Tirla said bitterly. "Calior, get out of my way."

"How do you intend to find him?" Owen asked.

Tirla shook her head. "I'll get my friends. We'll search the area." She didn't sound certain.

"A dust witch has glamours," Isold said. "Magical obscurations on its path."

"We can try the <**Wayfinder**>," Aderyn suggested.

"The skill [**Obscure**] will interfere with that item's magic," Isold said, shaking his head. "We will need a Pathseer to have any chance of tracking the creature."

"Nobody asked your opinion, stranger," Tirla spat. "We take care of our own. With enough of us, it won't matter that we don't have a Pathseer."

"I can do it," Jessemia said.

Tirla glanced at her, then gave her a longer look as she Assessed her. "You're level six. How good could you be?"

Jessemia straightened her shoulders. "Better than nothing, which is what you have now."

Aderyn regarded her in astonishment. Jessemia hadn't sounded this confident since she'd been humbled by the bandits. "Let her try," she said. "All of us together should be enough to tackle a dust witch." Since she had no idea what a dust witch was, she probably shouldn't be so assertive, but if the life of a child was at stake, they really didn't have any time to waste.

Tirla bit her lip. "I don't—you're strangers—"

"Strangers who want to help," Owen said. "Have these gentlemen pass the word in the town. They can get a rescue team moving along after us. Then, if we're wrong, you'll have someone to back you up."

Tirla glanced at Calior. Calior nodded. Tirla drew in a deep breath. "All right."

A system message appeared:

A new quest is available: [Rescue the Missing Child]
A dust witch has kidnapped Tirla's son Rhian. Locate him and restore him to his mother.
Accept? Y / N

Aderyn hesitated only briefly. She still didn't know how this would work if Jessemia wasn't their teammate. But a child's life was at stake. She chose Y.

You have accepted the quest [Rescue the Missing Child]. Set as primary quest?

This time, Aderyn chose N. She saw Jessemia moving her hands in the air as she, too, accepted the quest. If Jessemia could find the boy, even if Aderyn and her team did the rest of the work, she deserved experience for that success. Aderyn hoped the system knew a fair solution.

"Show me where you were when the boy was taken," Jessemia said. Again, she sounded as confident as if she were twice her level. Tirla nodded.

At the top of the hill, Tirla turned east and ran along the hill's crest rather than down into the next crease in the land. Bushes and brambles flashed past, surrounded by tall yellow grasses that reached Aderyn's knees. After a minute or so of running, Tirla swerved north to descend the hill into another valley. This one was much smaller than Jackrabbit Dell's and had a trickle of a stream running through it. Bushes grew thickly along the stream's banks, and the air was rich with the scent of water and green growing things.

Tirla came to a stop at a place where the stream bank was

churned up as if someone had crashed in and out of the water several times. "Here," she said, breathing heavily. "We were harvesting merry-wort, and then I woke up and I was lying half in the stream. The dust witch put me to sleep."

"Water, especially running water, is poisonous to dust witches," Isold said. "It's unlikely such a creature would come so close to a stream."

"I can't explain that," Tirla said. "All I know is that I was magically put to sleep, and when I woke, Rhian was gone. We've killed many dust witches over the years because they're common on the plains. They've stolen people before." Tirla began weeping. "I can't bear this. My boy is all I have left of his father."

"There are no tracks this side of the stream," Jessemia said. "Do you remember where Rhian was before you fell asleep?"

"No. It's all a blur." Tirla squeezed her eyes shut. "I think he was —yes, he'd crossed to the other side. He made a game of it, leaping from bank to bank."

Jessemia jumped awkwardly over the stream, though it wasn't more than three feet across. "Stay there," she said as Owen made as if to follow. "It will disturb the tracks."

"You found tracks?" Tirla exclaimed.

"Shoe prints. Your son's," Jessemia said distantly. Her attention was fixed on the muddy shore. "Nothing else."

"I know what it is!" Tirla said. "I'm not lying!"

"No." Jessemia backed away from the stream. "But if a dust witch can't touch water, it wouldn't have come this close to the stream. So its tracks will be farther back." She crouched and stared at the ground. "Isold, what else do you know about dust witches?"

"They appear to be gaunt, pale women," Isold said. "Their clothes are dull brown and shift constantly, obscuring their bodies like mists. They can cast glamours that confuse the eye and mind-affecting magics such as *sleep* and *bewitching presence*. They—" Isold glanced at Tirla and appeared to change his mind about what he meant to say. "They are, as I said, vulnerable to water. And they burrow into the ground to create their lairs."

"So they're not very heavy," Jessemia said.

"Not to my knowledge, no."

Jessemia straightened. "I see marks of something that passed here, barely disturbing the ground. I'm not sure **[Tracking]** is enough to follow it. But the creature was dragging something heavier that left a trail, and that is easy to follow."

"Dragging something heavier—you mean Rhian," Aderyn said. Tirla let out a choked cry.

"I assume so," Jessemia said. "Whatever it was wasn't moving under its own power—that looks different. The dust witch put both Tirla and Rhian to sleep and then carried the boy off." She pointed. "That way."

"Time to go," Owen said. "Jessemia, lead the way."

Jessemia nodded. She hiked her knapsack higher on her shoulders and set off across the plains.

CHAPTER TWENTY-SIX

They walked now instead of running, long strides that still felt to Aderyn like they were crawling. She told herself Jessemia was moving faster now than any other time she'd tracked a creature, but her rapidly-beating heart insisted they should go faster because a boy's life was at stake. She found herself speeding up until she was within a foot of Jessemia and then forcing herself to slow. Sometimes Owen put a hand on her elbow to restrain her, for which she was grateful. Despite her anxiety, she didn't want to interfere with what Jessemia was doing.

It struck Aderyn as ridiculous that they were following the woman who only two and a half weeks ago she'd considered useless and annoying. Even now, she wasn't totally sure she trusted Jessemia's abilities. Believing Jessemia had changed wasn't the same as being confident in Jessemia's skills, which were still lower than average. Unless—

Aderyn swiftly Assessed Jessemia, focusing on her skill ranks rather than anything else. She stumbled once—reading the Codex was difficult to do while walking—but had time to note that Jessemia's **[Tracking]**, **[Knowledge: Magical Beasts]**, **[Spot]**, and

[Awareness] were all higher than they'd been when they'd left Obsidian, high enough to be reasonable for a level six Pathseer. That was only partly a relief. Jessemia having the right skill ranks for her level was good, but she was still only level six. Aderyn told herself to stop worrying. There was nothing they could do about Jessemia's level, and saying something might destroy Jessemia's confidence and kill any chance they had of bringing Tirla's son home safely.

Jessemia led them over a few low rises, not steep enough to be called hills, and then slowed. "He's not being dragged anymore," she said, "but he's walking, and his footsteps are still deeper than the dust witch's. They look normal. I mean, like he's walking under his own power, not being forced."

"That would be the dust witch's *bewitching presence*," Isold said. "It is like [Charm], in that it persuades the victim that the dust witch is someone dear to him, a friend or lover or spouse. The difference is that [Charm] places an effect on the victim's mind that is not perceptible to any other person, whereas *bewitching presence* alters the dust witch so that anyone looking on it is affected. Rhian must have believed he was following someone familiar."

"Why are we talking? Rhian is in danger!" Tirla exclaimed.

"I want to be sure I'm following the right trail," Jessemia said. "We're losing the light."

The sun hung low in the western sky, casting their shadows in the direction they'd been traveling. "Does it confuse the tracks? The shadows, I mean?" Aderyn asked.

"A little," Jessemia said. "But mostly the problem is that I can't track anything this subtle in the dark. So we have to hurry, but if I go the wrong way, we'll waste daylight backtracking." She stepped from one side of their group to the other and then set off again without a word.

Despite what Jessemia had said, they moved more slowly now, slowly enough that their pace was closer to a walk than a run. Aderyn stopped watching Jessemia and instead scanned the horizon. The yellow of the dry grasses had deepened to gold in the warm light of sunset, and a wind had picked up, tossing the bushes that grew here and there and filling the air with the rushing sound of long grass rubbing against grass.

Suddenly, Jessemia stopped and threw up a hand in warning. "Something's wrong here. I don't know what. The footsteps disappear a few feet on, like Rhian vanished or flew away."

"Back up and let me take a look," Livia said. As Jessemia retreated, Livia shuffled forward, her feet dragging in the earth and pushing up furrows as if her feet were plows. She crouched a few feet away from the group and parted the grasses with both hands until the earth was visible. She muttered a few nonsense words that had no visible effect. Then she waved a hand, and the ground in front of her reared up like an ocean wave, revealing a hole barely big enough for a grown man to enter.

"I could use **[Excavate]** to dig the burrow up," she said, "but it will warn the dust witch that we're coming, and the thing might kill Rhian before we can reach him. We'll have to do this the hard way."

"Can you *scry* to see where he is? What the burrow looks like?" Owen asked.

Livia shook her head. "I tried that first. The dust witch cast a glamour over the area that blocks *scrying*. So we're going in blind."

"Can you fight?" Owen asked Tirla. "Because it might be safer—"

"I'm not staying behind when my son is at risk," Tirla said.

"Okay." Owen surveyed their little group. "Isold, the dust witch uses earth magic and mind magic, right? Is it immune to those things?"

"It is immune to mind magic, so I'm afraid I won't be much direct help, though I can still sing." Isold looked grim. "As to earth magic, I have no idea. It may be able to counter some of Livia's spells such as *hungry pit* or *thunderstomp*. Until Aderyn can Assess it, we are, again, going in blind."

"Then Aderyn and I will go first. Livia, you follow immediately behind, with Weston behind you." Owen looked at Jessemia. "I want you to bring up the rear."

"That's fine. I'm not much of a fighter," Jessemia replied.

"You're enough of a fighter to watch all our backs. If the dust witch has friends on the outside, I don't want to find out about it the hard way." Owen gripped her shoulder. "You'll be fine. Isold, you and Tirla stay to the rear, in front of Jessemia."

"I can fight," Tirla said. "And I brought a few potions and infusions I can do damage with."

"That tunnel is narrow enough we'll be going single file anyway." Owen's eyes narrowed. "Okay. You go in front of Weston. Everyone stay alert. Livia, pay attention for signs that the tunnel is going to collapse."

"Do you think that's likely?" Aderyn asked.

"I think it's an unlikely thing that is the most likely to kill us if it happens, which is why I want us alert for the possibility." Owen straightened. "Let's go."

The irregular hole crumbled at the edges, showering Owen and then Aderyn with dry earth as they passed through. Immediately, the passage sloped sharply downward into blackness. "Oops," Owen said. "Livia, some light?"

Livia chanted a few words, and an *orb of light* the size of a walnut flashed past Aderyn to hover just above Owen's shoulder, where it would illuminate the passage but not blind him with its soft glow. Owen stepped forward, and his foot rolled over the grit and dust that made up the floor. He flung out an arm for balance. "It's hazardous terrain," he called back to the others. "Watch your step."

Cautiously, placing each foot with care, Aderyn followed Owen down the slope. Dust rose with every step, drying the air and parching Aderyn's skin. The lack of moisture in the air and soil unsettled her. It was like all the water had been leached from the environment. Earth shifted beneath her feet, revealing a couple of shriveled, desiccated earthworms. She couldn't imagine anything natural living here.

The *orb of light* cast strange shadows ahead and behind, making their shapes bob and curve over the irregular walls. Aderyn realized the slope was decreasing just as it leveled out. She couldn't guess how far down they were, but it had to be fairly deep—and yet the burrow was still drier than the wind off the plains, not damp the way living soil was when you dug it up. It was easy to think of this soil as dead.

She saw the walls shift just as Owen stopped and brought his sword to the ready. "Watch out!" he shouted, and swung his sword.

Beyond Owen, the walls bulged and strained like bubbling ooze, but dry and shedding veils of dust every time they moved. Aderyn couldn't get past Owen for [Outflank], couldn't see any creatures to strike, just the undulating walls. She Assessed them anyway.

Name: Shambling Mound, Earth
Type: Formless
Power Level: 6
Immune to: elemental fire damage
Resistant to: bladed weapon damage
Vulnerable to: elemental water damage
Special attack: smother
Shambling mounds conceal themselves in the terrain matching their type and attack by engulfing and smothering their prey. That's pretty much all they do. More than enough, as far as you're concerned.

"Livia, get past me!" Aderyn shouted. "They need *drench!*"

She pressed herself flat against the wall, hoping she wasn't leaning into another shambling mound. Ahead, Owen stopped trying to swing his sword in the tight space and was thrusting at both sides of the passage. The shambling mounds surged and retreated in total silence, one advancing as the other avoided Owen's sword.

Livia shoved past Aderyn and pushed Owen to the side. With a gesture, she summoned water in a shapeless glob bigger than any

Aderyn had seen her produce before and flung it at one of the shambling mounds. Immediately it turned dark with water and sagged, dripping and sliding down the wall until it collapsed on the tunnel's floor. Owen withdrew his sword as Livia repeated this with the other shambling mound. "Watch out, they're not dead," she said.

Owen jabbed the first one. The sword went into the mud of the shambling mound's body with no resistance. "I don't know what it will take to kill a pile of mud," he said.

Congratulations! You have defeated [Shambling Mound, Earth].
You have earned [950 XP]

"I guess that was it," Owen said. He stabbed the other shambling mound, and another system message appeared.

Congratulations! You have defeated [Shambling Mound, Earth].
You have earned [950 XP]

Aderyn breathed deeply, willing her racing heart to slow down. Despite the water, the air still smelled dry. "I wish I knew how to tell where those creatures are," she said. "They have a smother attack we could have trouble defending against if they leaped on us."

"Those gave themselves away by moving too quickly," Owen said. "I don't think they're intelligent enough to ambush their prey. Still, everyone watch out."

Aderyn picked her way past the dead shambling mounds. The idea of stepping in the mud made her queasy, like it was entrails and blood rather than earth. Owen moved more slowly now, scanning the walls and floor for hidden monsters. Aderyn tried not to walk too close. She didn't want to be so far away she couldn't help him if something attacked, but too close and she'd impede his movement.

Then Owen let out a yelp as the floor disappeared beneath his foot. He flung himself backward, away from the pit that yawned wider and wider in their path. Aderyn shrieked and grabbed him under the arms, dragging him away, but the ground shifted under her feet and she scrabbled to stop her own slide.

Livia chanted something, and the earth shuddered and stopped moving. Then the ground bulged and rose, filling in the pit until the floor was smooth and unmarked.

You have received [1500 XP] for defeating the [Hungry Pit Trap].

Aderyn realized she was sitting with Owen sprawled half atop her. "Maybe Livia should go first," she suggested.

"If we're going to go on encountering terrain hazards, definitely," Owen agreed.

They shuffled around until Livia was at the head of the line and continued on. Livia moved confidently, but her shoulders were hunched with tension. "This is so unnatural," she murmured. "It's earth, but it's been killed. It's like walking through something's mummified corpse."

"Oh, don't say that," Aderyn said. "This place is creepy enough without those images filling my head."

"You think that's bad, try being me," Livia said tersely. "I almost can't bear this environment."

"Let's just keep moving, okay?" Owen said. "It's possible the dust witch knows we're here, which might mean facing greater challenges, depending on what other traps or creatures it has to send against us."

Livia stopped. "Like that one?"

Aderyn looked past Owen. They'd come to a place where the path forked in half, two passages that looked identical. "Can you tell which one to take?" she asked.

"I have the skill **[Tremorsense]**, as of level twelve," Livia said, "but it hasn't been working in this dead earth. I think it's time to try the <**Wayfinder**>. We have to be past where the dust witch obscured its tracks."

Aderyn drew the item from her pouch and held it in her cupped hands. At first, she feared it would fail the way it had the first time she'd tried to locate Jessemia. She'd never seen Rhian, didn't have any contact with him, and maybe that meant failure. But then she recalled all the many things she'd found without having seen them and told herself to stop whingeing, even silently. In the next second, the orb glowed, the spike turned pink, and as she turned from one passage to the other, its glow darkened to rosy red when she faced the right-hand passage. "There," she said.

"We have to go faster," Tirla demanded. "That dust witch might already—" Her voice cut off with a choked sob.

"I don't think the <**Wayfinder**> can locate—I mean, I think the person has to be alive," Aderyn said. She wasn't sure this was true, but Tirla needed not to give up.

"Let's move," Owen said.

The right-hand passage was narrower, as if the main passage had actually divided in half at the fork, and Aderyn shrank in on herself, trying not to brush against the gritty walls that shed showers of dust whenever she touched them. Her hair was full of dirt, her clothes and boots were grimy, and she imagined a long bath when this was over. She told herself this was an optimistic thing to think and not self-indulgent, because if this was over, they'd be back in Jackrabbit Dell with Rhian safely rescued.

No one spoke. The breathing of seven people in a narrow space and the sound of their footfalls filled the air. Aderyn tried not to think about suffocation, of being trapped underground. She wasn't claustrophobic, but it was impossible not to imagine the walls closing in.

Livia came to a stop. "There's light up ahead. Reddish light like a fire. A torch, or a campfire. And I think the space opens up."

"Aderyn," Owen whispered. "Can you sneak up there?"

"Not well," Aderyn replied.

"We need some idea of what we're facing. Weston?"

"I won't fit past you all. The passage is too narrow," Weston said.

"Then it's up to me," Aderyn said. "Scoot over. I'll do what I can."

She wriggled past Owen, then Livia. The tunnel stretched out before her, dark and apparently endless. She drew in a steadying breath and crept forward.

CHAPTER TWENTY-SEVEN

After about twenty feet, the passage widened, and distant firelight flickered over an opening a short distance away. Aderyn was terribly conscious of the patter of dry earth, which sounded like gravel on stone to her anxious ears, falling wherever she incautiously touched the walls. Her footsteps felt like they echoed, though that was impossible in that narrow space.

As she neared the opening, she walked closer to the wall, wishing she dared press against it for better concealment. From her vantage point, the space looked like a dirt cavern, something excavated roughly and left unfinished. The fire burned in a small pit, with sticks and broken branches lying in a tangle rather than built neatly. She saw no movement, no monster and no Rhian.

She cautiously poked her head around the edge of the wall. There were no furnishings. A couple of cages no taller than four feet, made of rough-hewn branches lashed together with hairy rope, stood against the wall where they couldn't be seen from inside the passage. Inside one, a boy of about nine or ten lay curled up, asleep or unconscious. Inside the other, a gaunt man stirred and sat up. "You've come," he rasped, his voice as dry as the walls. "Let us out." He coughed, then added, "Hurry before it comes back. Please."

Aderyn eyed him suspiciously. Then she Assessed him.

Name: Dust Witch

Type: Abomination

Power level: 14

Abilities: spellcasting, earth manipulation, [Obscure]

Immune to: elemental fire damage, elemental earth damage, elemental lightning damage, mind-affecting magic and skills

Resistant to: bladed weapon damage

Vulnerable to: elemental water damage

Special attacks: *bewitching presence*

A dust witch thrives on dead land, whether natural or created by it. In addition to their ability to cast earth-based spells, they are experienced with glamours and mind-altering magic that hide their path or trick their prey into believing they are an ally. Dust witches feed on creatures that they starve nearly to death, preferring dry food to, well, juicy, which is as disgusting as it sounds. Elemental water damage weakens them but does not destroy them; filling their environment with moisture deprives them of their earth magic abilities. You'll still have to overcome their glamours, but if you've gotten this far, you have a decent chance of surviving. Well, better than even. Probably.

In an instant, she made a decision. She walked toward the cage, slowly, pretending to survey the cavern. Even knowing what she did, [Improved Assess 2] didn't reveal the dust witch's true shape. She heard her friends following her and hoped Owen was paying attention to [Read Body Language]. "Where did it go?" she whispered.

"Out," the dust witch croaked. "I don't know where. Please, help me."

Aderyn glanced over her shoulder. Owen and Livia had entered the room. Aderyn widened her eyes, willing Owen to understand *It's a trap.* Owen caught her glance and slowed, raising his sword.

"Rhian!"

Aderyn cursed. Tirla dashed past the others to the cage holding the unconscious boy, screaming his name again. The dust witch sat up rapidly, gripping the bars of the cage. And tentacles of earth sprang up throughout the cavern, twining Aderyn and her friends in their grip.

Aderyn didn't react fast enough. The hard, solid earth tentacles bound her arms to her sides and squeezed so hard her eyes tried to burst from their sockets. Beside her, Owen had managed to keep his sword arm free and was hacking at the tentacles holding him. Livia didn't seem to be doing anything about the tentacles pinioning her arms, but in the next moment, the Earthbreaker flexed and the tentacles imprisoning her crumbled to dust.

Tirla struggled wildly against the tentacles imprisoning her, her thrashing growing weaker until she sagged unconscious in her bonds. Aderyn saw this in a daze. Her lungs couldn't expand, and she grew dizzier by the moment. Distantly, she heard chanting, and then the tentacles gripping her shattered into pieces that flew everywhere. She drew in a dust-filled breath and started hacking and coughing as particles filled her lungs. Livia supported her, saying words Aderyn couldn't understand.

"Water," Aderyn choked out. "The dust witch—the man—water weakens it—"

Livia nodded and snapped her fingers. A rush of cool air scented with water filled the cavern. The dust witch, temporarily trapped in the cage, couldn't avoid the mass of water that fell on its head. It shrieked in furious anger and shook itself like a dog coming out of a deep pool. The human disguise faded, revealing an even gaunter form swathed in pale brown gauzy veils. Their shredded edges fluttered in an unseen wind, making the dust witch's body blur.

The dust witch slipped between the bars of the cage with a terrifying grace. It snapped its fingers as Livia had done, but instead of water appearing, the fire went out, leaving the cavern in darkness except for Livia's one small magic light. Blinking in the sudden darkness, Aderyn pushed herself to her feet and drew her sword. More lights came on as Livia summoned several *orbs of light*. Aderyn turned to survey the cavern. The dust witch was gone.

"It's concealed itself," she shouted. "Watch the door!"

A scream snapped her attention to Jessemia, who stood in the doorway with her sword fallen at her feet. She appeared to be fighting an invisible opponent with her hands, batting and struggling as if wrestling. Isold also had his hands full trying to drag the invisible dust witch off Jessemia.

Weston and Owen raced to their aid, but hesitated rather than strike. Aderyn guessed they were afraid of hitting Jessemia or Isold by accident. Beside her, Livia chanted a string of nonsense syllables and swept her arms in an arc before her. The air shimmered, and the dust witch became visible. It had its hands around Jessemia's throat.

"*Drench* it again," Aderyn commanded, grabbing Livia by the shoulder. "Water weakens it!"

The gout of water this time was big enough to catch Jessemia and Isold as well, but it made the dust witch scream and release Jessemia. Weston and Owen struck at the same time. The dust witch impossibly dodged both blows and flew at Livia. Aderyn gasped and dove at the dust witch, forgetting **[Compel]** in her remaining lightheadedness, and got her arms around the thing's waist. It smelled terrible, of ancient dust and decay and things rotted beyond recognition. Aderyn bore it to the ground and tried to pin it.

The world changed. Instead of bare, dead earth, a grassy meadow stretched in all directions. A spring sun shone in the blue sky, and Aderyn watched two robins flap and flutter toward distant trees. It was all so beautiful she forgot—

Icy water poured over her head and shoulders, making her screech in surprise. She was on her hands and knees in mud churned up by *drench*. The dust witch was gone. Cursing, she got to her feet and dashed water out of her face. Tirla lay on the floor near Rhian, free of *immobilize* and stirring feebly. Isold knelt at the entrance, bubbling green light showing he was healing someone. Owen and Weston had the dust witch backed against the wall. By their hesitation, they weren't confident of their chances.

Aderyn picked up her sword from where she'd dropped it and advanced on the dust witch. Its form shimmered, and again it vanished. Owen and Weston lowered their weapons like they no longer had a target, as if the dust witch hadn't just gone invisible, it had made them forget about it as well. The creature's casual warping of their minds infuriated Aderyn. She rushed past her friends and struck the wall where she'd last seen the creature, thrusting with her sword until the tip grated on earth.

She'd hit something, though how solidly, she didn't know. The sound of *dispel magic* filled the air, and with a shimmer of the air, Aderyn was face to face with the dust witch. The monster threw back its head, shrouded in veils, and cackled, a hoarse, desiccated sound. It reached for Aderyn, ignoring the sword impaling it. Aderyn's instincts threw her backward. Being touched by the creature seemed a really bad idea. She tore her sword free of the dust witch's body and struck again, this time at its abdomen. It cackled again and advanced on her. Aderyn raised her sword for another blow.

Suddenly Owen was behind the dust witch, and Aderyn felt the strange pull of **[Outflank]**. As one, she and Owen struck, Owen aiming high, Aderyn going low. This time, the dust witch screamed and beat at the blade impaling its belly with ineffectual fluttering hands that looked like bundles of sticks bound at one end. A gout of water drenched all three of them, and then Weston was there, his dagger thrusting at the dust witch's throat. The creature gurgled as if drowning, and finally sagged, falling to the ground and bursting into a shower of dry, dead earth.

**Congratulations! You have defeated [Dust Witch].
You have earned [15,000 XP]**

**Congratulations! You have completed the quest [Rescue the
Missing Child].
You have been awarded [8000 XP]**

Aderyn gasped for breath, trying not to inhale bits of dust witch. She ached all over as if this was the end of a hard day's march. "The boy," she said.

Livia had wrenched apart the rough branches of the cage, and Tirla was sitting with Rhian in her lap, holding him and rocking back and forth. The boy looked dazed still. Aderyn reflexively Assessed him, fearing another trap, but **[Improved Assess 2]** didn't show anything suspicious.

Owen put a steadying arm around her shoulders. "Are you all right? It looked like a glamour got you."

"I'm fine. What about you? You lowered your sword."

"I forgot what we were fighting for a minute. Then I saw you stabbing the wall, and the illusion broke."

Aderyn scanned the room, counting. Everyone was still there, no one was hurt—no, Jessemia lay on the floor, her shirt drenched with blood. An icy fist gripped Aderyn's heart. She hurried to the woman's side, but before she reached her, Jessemia sat up, plucking at her bloody shirt.

"You stabbed me," she said to Owen.

"The dust witch moved out of the way, and I was careless," Owen said. "Are you healed? I apologize—I didn't realize what had happened until it was too late."

Jessemia regarded him with narrowed eyes. "That would be one way to be rid of me," she said.

Owen flinched. "I'm sure I deserve that. I really didn't mean to hurt you."

"I know. I was joking." Jessemia drew in a deep breath. "I've never been this close to death before. It's terrifying. This is what it's really like? Adventuring?"

"Sometimes." Owen extended a hand. "You fought well."

Hesitantly, Jessemia clasped his hand. "I didn't do much. I mostly just stood there and hoped someone would kill that thing. I can't believe I survived." She smiled. "And I gained a level when we completed the quest to rescue Rhian. Level seven. It feels different. Does leveling feel different at higher levels?"

"It feels different because it's the first one you've actually earned," Owen said.

Jessemia's smile became pensive. "It is, isn't it?" She released Owen and pulled her bloody shirt away from her skin again. "Is it whining if I say this feels awful?"

"Not at all," Owen said.

IT WAS FULL DARK BY THE TIME THEY RETURNED TO Jackrabbit Dell. Calior and Brist weren't on guard at the gate, but the man and woman who'd taken their place recognized Tirla and exclaimed over her grimy condition. They fell silent as Tirla explained about the dust witch and the friends' rescue of Rhian. Their appraisal of Aderyn and the others went from cautious to respectful, and they opened the gates without a word about entrance fees or cautions about behavior.

Tirla took them first to her own home. "I can't host you all, the house isn't big enough," she said, "but I want to get Rhian to bed immediately, and I owe you—well, everything. This will have to do."

She slotted thick glass vials and bulbs into a cleverly compartmentalized roll of cloth and handed it to Owen. "The yellow tubes will boost your speed, the blue vials will boost your strength. The bulbs with the green liquid are powerful healing agents, better even than a <**Healing Stone**>, but I'm afraid I only have two. The red bulb will give you a temporary boost of magic energy, but be careful when you choose to use it, because it will make you sick if you drink it when you're feeling fresh. And the purple ones in the prism-shaped vials are to pour over your weapons. A blade or an arrowhead dipped in that infusion will sicken an enemy, weakening it and disorienting it."

"This is really very generous," Owen said. "Thank you."

"Like I said, I owe you everything." Tirla wiped her eyes, smearing the remaining dust on her face into a thin layer of mud. "There's two inns, but if you go to the Raven's Rest and give Cinzus my name, he'll take care of you."

"Thank you again," Aderyn said. "I'm glad we could help."

"So am I," Tirla said.

Chapter Twenty-Eight

They got many skeptical looks as they walked through Jackrabbit Dell, annoying Aderyn until she realized how awful they must look, dusty or muddy or in Jessemia's case bloody. And of course no one would know what they'd accomplished that day. So she smiled politely at everyone they passed and told herself the story would spread soon enough. Not that she wanted to be famous, but she was just proud enough to want people to know they weren't scruffy no-name adventurers.

The Raven's Rest was the larger of the two inns, three stories of dull red brick with many small glass-paned windows. Remembering Alcester, Aderyn was wondering where the glass had come from, and whether carting it across the plains had been expensive, when they entered the inn and she Assessed the patrons. Then she changed her thinking. Almost everyone in the taproom was an adventurer or a retired adventurer, and there were enough high-level spellslingers to make the magical transportation of glass simple.

A bald man with a pot belly approached them, drying his hands on a towel. "How can I help you?"

"Are you Cinzus?" Owen asked. "Tirla the Spiritsmith told us to talk to you. She said we'd find good service here."

Cinzus eyed their grimy condition and clearly decided not to ask. "Of course. How do you know Tirla?"

"We helped her rescue her son from a dust witch." Owen plucked at his filthy sleeve. "It wasn't a clean job."

Cinzus's mouth fell slack. "I—well, that's unexpected. A dust witch? Are Tirla or the boy hurt?"

"Not anymore. Sorry if this is rude, but could we get cleaned up somewhere? And if you have rooms to rent, that would be great."

"Oh, of course." Cinzus still looked stunned, but he gestured toward a side door. "There are washrooms this way, and a bathing room. I'm afraid the bath's heating isn't working right now, so it may take a while doing it the hard way if you all want hot baths, but there's plenty of hot water in the washrooms. How many rooms do you want? I've got seven free right now."

"Four rooms," Owen said. "Thanks."

Cinzus led them up the back stairs to the third floor and began opening doors. "That's ten silver per room per night, and you can sleep as many people as you can cram into one, though with four rooms you won't have that problem." He looked as if he wanted to ask about their sleeping arrangements but was restraining his curiosity. Aderyn didn't feel the need to enlighten him.

She took clean clothes down to the washroom and stowed them in a cupboard, then stripped down and sluiced warm water over herself. The washroom was equipped with a spray hose, close enough to being a shower, and she rinsed and scrubbed her hair with the soap provided until the water ran clear instead of brown with dirt. Another cupboard held drying cloths, and she dried off and dressed and felt like she'd finally left the dust witch behind.

With her hair still damp, she opted not to take up bathing time and returned to the taproom. Weston was there, his long wet hair gathered back from his face, seated at a table covered with food.

When Aderyn exclaimed over the number of dishes, Weston said, "Cinzus insisted. He said if we'd killed a dust witch, we'd done more than serve Tirla and Rhian." He tore off a mouthful of roast fowl and chewed enthusiastically.

Aderyn sat and served herself a large helping of herb-flecked roasted potato wedges and a chicken wing and a couple of ears of fresh corn on the cob. "I feel slightly guilty about this, but not enough to turn the food down. This tastes incredible." Now that the tension of the quest was over, she was ravenous.

Owen and Isold entered then, and Owen sat beside Aderyn and kissed her cheek. "Are we conquering heroes, then?"

Weston shrugged. "I guess. It's strange. We did something difficult, but it feels like it was a responsibility we couldn't not take on, you know? And that means taking this kind of praise for it is... maybe not wrong, but not something we demand."

"Yeah, I get that." Owen dug into his own meal. "I'm mostly still feeling guilty over stabbing Jessemia, even though it was an accident. It's the kind of accident I never want to have, hurting a team member."

"Jessemia isn't part of our team, but I take your meaning," Isold said. "She knows it was an accident."

"Yes, but with as hostile as our relationship has been, it's awkward. Like I secretly still don't care if she gets hurt."

"That's not true," Aderyn protested. "You've always been fair to her, even when she didn't deserve it."

"I guess." Owen stripped meat off a chicken breast with his belt knife and forked up chicken and potatoes in one bite. "I'll get over it."

Livia joined them then, straddling a stool next to Weston and grabbing a plate. "This is impressive. I'd say I don't think we can eat it all, but the way I feel, I could eat it all on my own."

"Where's Jessemia?" Aderyn asked.

"Washing her shirt. I mended it for her, but it's still covered in blood."

Owen winced.

"It was an accident, Owen," Aderyn said. "Let it go."

"I don't think she holds a grudge," Livia said. "She acted like getting injured was a reasonable risk. I have to say she's actually turning out to be an adventurer. Or at least the beginnings of one. She's still a little whiny. But she's come a long way."

Aderyn finished off one ear of corn and started in on the next one. The kernels were juicy and sweet, perfect as they were with nothing added. She thought about pointing out that she'd been right about Jessemia's potential, but decided that would just sound smug.

"I wish we could officially team with her now," Owen said.

"Is that still the guilt talking?" Weston asked with a grin.

"No, just that I think she's taking her adventuring seriously. But I'm still convinced it would harm her to level artificially fast."

"Maybe there's something we can do about that," Isold said. "If we encounter lower-level monsters, we can guide her in learning how to defeat them. That will give her experience she earns herself, and she'll boost her skills as she fights."

"I like that plan," Aderyn said. "I want her to succeed."

"I admit I was skeptical of your optimism," Owen said, "but it turns out you were right."

Even though Aderyn hadn't wanted to brag, his compliment cheered her.

They were almost done eating when Aderyn realized Jessemia still hadn't appeared. "I'm going to look for her," she said, rising from the table. "Maybe she was more tired than hungry."

Aderyn knocked on Jessemia's door and, when she didn't immediately get an answer, pushed the door open a crack and peeked inside. The rooms they'd been given each had one bed big enough for two people, and Jessemia lay on hers, fully clothed and staring at the ceiling. "Don't you want food?" Aderyn asked.

Jessemia didn't look at her. "How damaged am I? As an adventurer?"

Aderyn entered the room and shut the door behind her. "Pretty damaged. But you've already improved a lot since we left Obsidian."

"I feel so stupid," Jessemia said. "I wasted so much time believing I was special instead of doing things that would actually make that true. I wish—" She blinked away tears. "I shouldn't blame Papa, because he only wanted what he thought was best for me, but it's not like he's an adventurer. He didn't know any better."

Aderyn thought that was more generous than Jessemia's father Liander deserved, but she held her tongue.

"But it is still partly his fault for arranging for me to level too fast," Jessemia went on. "And my fault for going along with the plan. It's not too late for me, is it? I mean, I gained a level on my own, the right way. That has to mean something."

She sounded so despondent Aderyn's heart went out to her. "It's not too late. You're making progress. And there are things you can do to improve your skills and gain experience too. We'll help."

"I'm not sure why you'd want to, given how badly I've behaved." Jessemia's tone became bitter, and she again returned her attention to the ceiling.

"Because you're trying to change, and that's deserving of respect," Aderyn said. "And don't feel sorry for yourself. That really is annoying. If you want to make amends, you can't do it by wallowing in the past."

"But I can't—" Jessemia seemed to hear the whine in her voice and pinched her lips tight as if capturing the rest of that sentence. "I mean, don't you all think about how awful I was to start? Shouldn't that make you not want to help?"

"People don't have to stay the same their whole lives," Aderyn said. "You want to be different, and you're doing what you can to make that happen. That changes how we see you."

Jessemia's cheeks reddened. "Isold told you what I did, didn't he. I'm so embarrassed. I don't know if I can face him again."

"He doesn't hold it against you. I know because he said so." Aderyn leaned against the wall. Now that she was full and clean, weariness had caught up to her. "Look, you can either go on dwelling on the past, or you can resolve to look to the future. It's your choice."

"I don't know if I can forget how I behaved, but maybe I shouldn't want to. Not if forgetting means I might do it again."

"I think you won't." Aderyn yawned. "I'm sorry, I'm really tired. You should get something to eat. Don't avoid the others, either. Just go down there and behave as if everything is normal, and see how they react."

Jessemia nodded and sat up. "Thank you. I haven't forgotten that I hurt you more than the others. If you can forgive me, that means I have hope."

"That's right." Impulsively, Aderyn hugged her. Jessemia didn't return the hug, but when Aderyn released her, she was smiling.

"Tell them I'm going to bed," Aderyn said. "I don't think I can keep my eyes open a moment longer."

She didn't bother lighting the lamp in her own room, just stripped off her clothes and dropped them on the clothespress rather than folding them away. She crawled into bed in her shift and drawers and was most of the way to being asleep when Owen came in. She sleepily snuggled up to him when he joined her in bed, enjoying the way his breathing warmed the back of her neck.

"Did you say something to Jessemia?" Owen murmured.

"I'm falling asleep, Owen. I can't remember."

"Well, she was polite and friendly at dinner. She almost wasn't the same person. So if you told her something to change her, you did well."

Aderyn yawned. "She changed herself. She just needed a reminder of that."

"I doubt she'd have changed if you hadn't been so constant in her defense. I hope she realizes that."

"Maybe. I guess." She yawned again. "Thank you for giving her a chance. Now, let me sleep."

Owen chuckled. "Good night, sweetheart. I love you."

She heard his words in a haze, and then she was asleep.

"WATCH OUT, IT'S GOING TO SPIT AGAIN!" ADERYN shouted.

Jessemia darted to the side, narrowly avoiding a line of sticky acidic fluid. Where the acid fell, it burned a sizzling black line that led back to the enormous digger beetle, which was longer than Aderyn was tall and fat and segmented like a sickly green pill bug. The digger beetle reared up on several of its hind legs and clashed its longer forelegs together with a crack that sounded like *thunderstomp*.

"The weak spots are the eyes and on its underside where the thinner plates covering its belly meet," Aderyn said, pointing with her sword. "When it rears up, aim for one of those. It's also weak along its armor plated back, but those spots are harder to hit. Remember you want to pit your strengths against its weaknesses."

Jessemia nodded. She darted forward to meet the creature's rush, feinted to its left, and when it reared up, she flung a dagger at its belly. The dagger struck one of the lines where the plates met and sank to the hilt. Jessemia shouted with delight.

"All right, that was good, but the dagger can't go deep enough. You'll need to use your sword," Aderyn said.

"Can't I aim for the eye?" Jessemia asked.

"You can, but your **[Thrown Weapons Proficiency]** still isn't high yet, and if you were on your own, trying to kill it with thrown daggers alone might get *you* killed." Aderyn advanced on the digger beetle and slashed at its head, getting its attention to give Jessemia time to draw her sword.

Jessemia balanced lightly on the balls of her feet, waiting for her chance. The next time it reared up, she plunged forward and impaled it right at its midsection. The digger beetle shuddered and collapsed.

"Seven hundred experience!" Jessemia exclaimed.

Aderyn had seen the system notices when her companions had killed the other digger beetles, so she knew how much they were worth, but Jessemia's excitement was cheering. "You must be almost to level eight. Be careful not to touch the blood, it's mildly acidic too."

"It's disgusting." Jessemia tore up handfuls of dry prairie grass and scrubbed her blade carefully. "You really do know everything about tactics. Is that from experience, or from your class?"

"A little of both. And I'm still learning." Aderyn waved at Owen, who'd chased the final digger beetle some distance away before killing it. "Digger beetles aren't very complicated in their tactics. Trample, spit acid, bite."

"Why does everyone think Warmasters are useless? It's obvious you're not."

"Because a Warmaster without a partner is close to useless. We need each other to thrive." Aderyn examined her sword blade for spots of digger beetle spit and found none. "And nobody understands that, so Warmasters go on being useless."

"That's so unfair!" Jessemia sheathed her sword with unnecessary force as if in emphasis.

"It is what it is." Aderyn shrugged. She smiled at Owen, who now approached. "But since I have a wonderful partner, it doesn't matter to me what others think."

"Am I a wonderful partner?" Owen asked as he joined them. "I like to think so. Jessemia, how many did you kill?"

"Two," Jessemia said. "With only a little help."

"You're getting the advantage of the Warmaster's vision, so don't be ashamed of that help." Owen clasped Aderyn's hand. "I'm sure it must feel like a slog, killing creatures worth so little after all that time getting experience for high-level monsters. We've been doing this for almost three weeks and you haven't reached level eight."

Aderyn squeezed his hand in warning. Jessemia could take that as a rebuke, a reminder of having artificially gained experience and levels in the past. But Jessemia just shrugged. "I'm in no hurry. I want to increase my skills."

"Which you have," Aderyn said. "Your [To the Heart] and [Acrobatics] are as high as anyone might expect at level seven, and you've increased [Thrown Weapons Proficiency] by two ranks in the last two weeks. That's remarkable."

Jessemia beamed. "You know, that feels really good. I can't believe I ever thought that unnatural leveling I was doing was satisfying. Well, I guess it really wasn't. Not as much as true success is."

Aderyn thought about saying more, decided it would be condescending, and kept her satisfaction about Jessemia's progress to herself.

Chapter Twenty-Nine

"Should we help Isold harvest these monsters?" Jessemia asked. Isold was crouched beside one of the fallen digger beetles, his hands wrapped in leather strips as he cut away the thin plating over its underside.

"He's the only one with knowledge of what to look for and how to do it safely," Owen said. "We can get the rest of these on their backs, make it easier for him."

The three of them hauled on the digger beetle Jessemia had killed until it rocked gently on the curve of its armored back. A short distance away, Weston did the same, while Livia used *excavate* to shape the earth around another so it rolled over. "I still say they're disgusting," Jessemia said. "But I suppose if they have valuable body parts, it's worth putting up with that."

"A Spiritsmith of the right level can turn the beetles' stomach acid into a universal solvent potion," Owen said. "According to Isold. The acid is more valuable because in general anyone fighting these monsters is too low a level to harvest it, so it's not commonly available. We'll make sure you get your share of the coin."

"Thank you. That's generous, given that we're not really a team."

"You killed two of them, so it's fair," Aderyn said. "I wish we were near a town where we could sell the acid and get it off our hands. I know Isold is careful, but I still feel superstitious about it." She gestured at the blackened, dead patches and strips of grass. "Imagine that happening to your skin. It would eat down to the bone in an instant."

"It's fine, Aderyn. Isold knows what he's doing." Owen steered Aderyn away from the corpse. "Sit and rest for a bit. You, too, Jessemia." He followed this up by sitting at the top of one of the many low rises in this part of the Long Plains and arranging his sheathed sword comfortably out of the way.

Aderyn sat next to him and surveyed the distant eastern horizon. The rises grew steeper in that direction until they could justifiably be called hills, covered with unexpectedly soft grass that was tinged with green even now that summer's end was nearing. Owen called this time the "dog days" of summer, though he didn't know where his world had gotten the name. Aderyn imagined the land panting heavily like an overheated dog, gasping for air. Today, a warm breeze stirred the air so it wasn't so hot, but the weather still made Aderyn long for nightfall.

"That fight was exhausting," she said. "But only because doing anything in this heat is exhausting. I'm actually looking forward to Guerdon Deep. So much cooler."

"Did you not like that city?" Jessemia asked.

"I didn't dislike it. But it's bleak on the outside, forbidding."

"And all the house interiors are gorgeous," Owen said. "All that color and comfort."

"Which is why I didn't hate it. But it's never going to be my favorite place to live."

"So, where would you like to live?" Jessemia leaned forward, looking interested.

"I guess I miss my home of Far Haven. It's funny, we've seen a lot of big cities now in our travels, but none of them have replaced my hometown in my heart." Aderyn dug in the grass with the toe of her boot. "Even though I see the advantages to living in a city."

"I miss home," Jessemia said. "But the closer we get to Guerdon Deep, the more excited I get."

"You'll have the chance to travel all over the Forsaken Lands, and when you go back to Obsidian, it will look different," Owen said.

"I guess it's strange for you, not having a home you can go back to," Jessemia said.

They'd revealed the truth about Owen, that he was from another human world somewhere beyond the demon void, a week ago. Aderyn had felt smugly satisfied that her friends considered Jessemia safe to trust with that secret, since many people would assume Owen was a demon based on his origin. Jessemia had turned out to be friendly and eager to help... all right, there had been the occasional backsliding into whining, but all Owen had to do was hit one of the iron pots with the flat of his sword, making it ring dully, and Jessemia would blush and fall silent.

The point was, Aderyn had been right, and she liked being right, especially when being right had so many other satisfying benefits. Like making a new friend.

"It was hard, the first few weeks after I learned I'm dead back in my own world," Owen admitted. "But I feel like I fit in here in ways I didn't back home. It's embarrassing to admit, but I like being special. Overpowered sword skills and Fated One and all."

"I can't believe I ever thought I wanted to be the Fated One, now that I know what it actually means." Jessemia hugged her legs and rested her chin on her knees. "And I also can't believe no one's ever thought to ask the question of what specifically the Fated One is supposed to do. To think Tarani's memorial has been sitting there for centuries, hiding its secrets."

"It's not like there are guides anywhere else," Aderyn said. "And if you think about how many potential Fated Ones believe the same thing, that it's a destiny that will just fall in their laps, it makes sense that any new Fated One would fall into the same mistake."

Immediately, she felt uncomfortable—after all, Jessemia had been one of those Fated Ones—but Jessemia didn't blush or act like she felt criticized. She just plucked blades of grass and held them up for the wind to blow them back toward where Isold was finishing his work.

Weston came up the rise just then. He'd untied his long hair, which whipped around his face as he combed through it with his fingers. "I figure we've got another five hours of daylight. You want to make camp a little early? We've had two battles today."

"That was exactly my thought," Owen said. "Where's Livia?"

"Turfing up the dead grass to give the earth room to breathe again. She said something about how the digger beetle acid offended her." Weston grinned and tied his hair back again. "I told her it's not like anyone's going to come through here to care, but she said if we only ever do things because of what others will think, we might as well have stayed in the safe zone."

"She's not wrong." Owen got to his feet and offered Aderyn a hand up, continuing to hold her hand after she stood. "Isold? You finished?"

"I am," Isold said. He unwrapped the tattered leather bindings from his hands and tucked them into his knapsack. "Livia, I think you've restored the landscape sufficiently."

Livia moved across the nearest hill, gliding through the ground like it was water. It looked like she was riding a wave of grassy earth. She stepped away from the wave and walked the last couple of feet toward them. "I reshaped it," she said. "That's more satisfying."

"You looked like a surfer gal," Owen said. "Riding waves of landscape."

"Do people in your world do that on ocean waves?" Aderyn asked. "I thought they didn't have magic."

"They have surfboards. I'm terrible at surfing, but it's exhilarating even if you suck at it."

Aderyn tried to imagine people standing on wooden planks atop the waves they'd seen off the coast of Obsidian and failed utterly. So much of Owen's experience was alien to her.

They continued east under the hot sun. The breeze turned into a wind Aderyn welcomed. She felt tired, but content—the good kind of tired that comes from a moderate workout and the rush of battle. Her leg muscles ached slightly as the gentle rises turned into steeper hills. Soon, they walked across the tops of the hills, looking down into narrow creases that widened into valleys. It felt like walking across the top of the world, though the valleys weren't deep and the hills weren't tall—more an illusion created by how far she could see across the hills.

After five minutes, at the top of a hill, Owen came to a stop. "What's that?"

Aderyn shaded her eyes against the sunlight. "It looks like a little house."

"It's a door set into the hill," Weston said.

"What does that mean?" asked Livia. "Is it a dungeon?"

"Let me see," Aderyn said. She couldn't see the door clearly at this distance, but it was still less than two miles away and well within the range of [Improved Assess 2].

Name: Goldenhallow

Type: Standard dungeon, intermediate, victory condition variant A

Power level: 6

Inhabitants: Magical beasts, aberrations

Traps: None

Reward: 500 gold, <Bracers of the Wind>

The Goldenhallow dungeon evolved to suit the nomadic communities of the Long Plains. Its relatively small monetary rewards reflect the dungeon's true benefit, which is earned

experience through defeating monsters. After it is completed, the dungeon resets in six days.

"That's amazing," Aderyn said after reading this aloud to her friends. "A cute little dungeon all the way out in the middle of nowhere."

"Dungeons aren't cute," Livia said. "It doesn't matter how adorable their entrances are, they're still full of monsters that want to tear your face off."

"It looks like a hobbit hole," Owen said. "All round and with grass growing up its hill. I have trouble imagining a dungeon behind that door. There ought to be a cozy room with a fireplace and Bilbo Baggins sitting down to second breakfast."

Aderyn couldn't think where to start asking questions, so she let Owen's moment of nostalgia for his own world go. Instead, she said, "Isold, what are <**Bracers of the Wind**>?"

"Hardened leather vambraces that generate a guiding wind, providing bonuses to thrown weapons and arrows," Isold said. "Specific enough to certain classes that they aren't worth much money, but they are valuable to adventurers in that narrow specialty."

"So Weston or Jessemia could use them," Aderyn said. "I think we should go for it."

"It's level six, Aderyn," Owen said. "We'll get barely any experience for its monsters, even if the level is an average and there are some power level seven or eight creatures."

"But Jessemia could benefit," Aderyn said. "She can take on most monsters of those levels, and we'll be there as backup. And it sounds fun!"

"You've been in the wilderness too long if you can describe a dungeon as 'fun,'" Livia groused. "Admit it, this is because the dungeon door looks like a dollhouse."

"I refuse to admit anything of the kind," Aderyn said loftily. "Jessemia, what do you think?"

"I think I'm not going to drag the rest of you into a dungeon solely for my benefit," Jessemia said. "I would like to try it, sure, but it doesn't seem anyone else will get anything out of it."

"Aderyn's not wrong," Owen said. "It might be good for you to gain experience—not the leveling kind, but life experience—in facing a dungeon, and this one seems pretty tame. But we wouldn't send you in alone. That would be foolish."

"I don't want to take the selfish route."

"Then it doesn't have to be selfish," Weston said. "I like the idea of those bracers. You clear the dungeon, we stand by for support, and I get the bracers and we split the rest of the reward."

"*You're* agreeing to this?" Livia exclaimed.

Weston shrugged. "Sure, why not? Dungeons are interesting. And that one is adorable."

Livia groaned. "You people are weird."

"Isold? You've been quiet," Owen said.

"I'm just considering the possibilities. The description said the true benefit was experience from monster defeats. That suggests we might be in there for some time." Isold was frowning at the distant door. "On the other hand, we're not on a deadline."

"Livia, how serious are your objections?" Aderyn asked. "Are you grousing for the sake of grousing, or do you really think it's a bad idea?"

"Oh, it's not a terrible idea. I just object to making dungeon-delving decisions on the basis of how cute a dungeon is. If you all want to, I'm in." Livia shook her head. "Why am I always the voice of reason? Shouldn't someone else take a turn?"

Weston hugged her, lifting her off her feet so she squeaked. "You'd be so disappointed if someone usurped your role as level-headed team mom."

"Put me down, oaf! And don't call me mom again. It's creepy." Livia ostentatiously dusted herself off.

"Jessemia? Are you good with this?" Owen asked.

"A little nervous, but yes," Jessemia said, not sounding nervous.

"Then we'll get closer, camp for the night, and take on Golden-hallow Dungeon in the morning," Owen said.

Aderyn had to restrain herself from skipping as they trekked down the valley toward the dungeon entrance. It had been a while since they'd attempted a dungeon, and this one looked much easier than Gamboling Coil had been. She still had nightmares of being stalked by the vampiric sanguisuge. Goldenhallow... all right, yes, it was cute, but that wasn't why she wanted to defeat it. Jessemia had been doing so well, both in advancement and in becoming a nicer person, and Aderyn wanted that to continue. And how better than to give her confidence in her ability to defeat a dungeon?

She examined the door as they drew near, not Assessing it but admiring it. The door was perfectly circular, surrounded by sod blocks from which colored specks of purple and white flowers grew. It wasn't precisely a dollhouse door, because it was clearly tall enough for even Weston to fit through easily, but it did look like a giant version of something a child might build in the woods to attract mythical fairies.

They camped thirty feet from the door, but Livia set their four tents, which all faced each other and the central campfire, at an angle so none of them had their back to the dungeon. This seemed strange to Aderyn at first. It wasn't like the dungeon was going to attack them, or send out monsters to tear up the camp in the middle of the night. But the more she thought about it, the more it felt right—like acknowledging the dungeon was going to affect them very soon.

She slept, and dreamed of carnivorous rabbits attacking fluffy golden sheep and carrying them away in their jaws despite being five times smaller than their victims; woke, and stood her watch, trying not to be distracted by the nearby door; slept again, and fell through dreams populated by round wooden dungeon doors that multiplied as she walked through and around them. By the time she woke for real at just before dawn, she was ready for the day's adventure to start.

They all seemed to feel the excitement. Even Livia woke early, though she needed three cups of coffee to force her eyes open. They readied their gear, broke camp, and gathered near the wooden door. Its doorknob was shaped like an acorn. Jessemia giggled when she saw it. Now she sounded nervous. "That's ridiculous."

"Dungeons take shape according to their surroundings," Isold said. "Though I admit there aren't any oak trees anywhere near here, so where the acorn motif came from, I have no idea."

"Go ahead and open the door, Jessemia," Owen said.

Jessemia put her hand on the knob, hesitated, then turned it and pushed the door open. It swung inward without so much as a creak of the hinges, just a faint whoosh of displaced air. Aderyn, who stood immediately behind Jessemia, sniffed. The air smelled neutral, not fresh and not stinking of monster.

"I don't think anyone's been in here for years," she said. "This is exciting!"

"It's just a dungeon," Livia said. "Go on, enter. I can't see from back here."

Jessemia walked forward, followed by Aderyn. The door opened on a hall wide enough for two people to walk side by side. It looked so ordinary Aderyn was disappointed: polished wooden floor, no windows, nothing interrupting the smooth perfection of the paneled walls. She checked the ceiling in case something clung to it, waiting for its moment to drop on them. Nothing. The corridor extended straight ahead past the limits of her vision.

The lights from outside dimmed and then disappeared entirely as Weston, at the rear of the group, closed the door. A second later, Livia summoned a handful of *orbs of light*, little walnut-sized glowing lights that floated around them and illuminated the corridor clearly, if not with as much brightness as daylight.

What it illuminated looked nothing like what Aderyn had seen. Walls of black stone, rough and coated in something that shone with an unhealthy luster, took the place of planed wood. The floor wasn't of polished wood anymore, but of irregularly-shaped flagstones fitted closely together so the spaces between weren't more than black threads making a crazy pattern across the floor. Despite the odd, sickly glow from the walls, the hall was so dim it made Aderyn squint, with even Livia's lights seeming swallowed up by the terrible dark stone. The smell of wet stone and decomposition filled the air.

Jessemia whispered, "What happened? Is this normal?"

"No," Owen said. "Aderyn, can you Assess this place?"

Aderyn swallowed. "Not from inside. But I think... I think my original Assessment was a lie."

A system message flashed across her vision. Instead of silver, the letters were the color of blood and quivered like something was restraining them.

YOU WILL NEVER LEAVE SORROWVALE, ALIVE OR DEAD.

CHAPTER THIRTY

"Sorrowvale?" Owen said. "Aderyn—"

"I know!" Aderyn exclaimed. "Everything I saw was false. Everything." She put her hands over her face, wishing everyone wasn't staring at her. She remembered the dungeon Assessment clearly. There had been no hint of a lie in those calm, reassuring letters. Nor, she realized, had there been anything chatty or confiding as she was now accustomed to seeing from the system's communications.

"Shouldn't you have known the Assessment was wrong?" Weston asked. "Sorry, I didn't mean that as a criticism, I meant—"

"I understand what you meant," Aderyn said. She drew in a breath and got herself under control. "Usually when someone or something conceals the truth of its Assessment, **[Improved Assess 2]** shows that. Not what's really there, but that the person is lying. But that only happens if the person is close in level to me. If they're skilled at **[Deception]** or a really high level, I'm as fooled as anyone." She swallowed again. Her throat kept trying to close up with fear. "I think this dungeon is a lot higher level than six."

Another system message appeared. The letters were still blood red, and their quivering made them look as if every stroke had been drawn by a shaking hand.

There is an exit.
There must always be an exit.
You will die screaming.

Jessemia whimpered. "Why is it doing this? I don't understand. Can't we just leave?"

"The door is gone," Weston said. "It's a dead end now."

Aderyn's heart beat faster. "I'm sorry. I'm so sorry. I should have known—"

"You had no way of knowing," Isold said. "This was a mistake we all made."

"It was too cute," Livia growled. "Now I wish I'd thought that through."

"Let's keep it together, everyone," Owen said. "It said there's an exit. I don't think that's a lie."

"Why not?" Jessemia demanded. The edge on her voice said she was close to panic. "It lied about everything else!"

"Because it's still a dungeon, and it has to have rules," Owen said. "Aderyn? Isold?"

"All dungeons have three things: a challenge, a reward, and an exit," Isold said. "This one can't be any different just because it's apparently evil."

"I've never heard of an evil dungeon," Weston said.

"Neither have I, but we've encountered sentient and even sapient dungeons, and sapient creatures can choose good and evil." Isold sounded as calm as if such a possibility wasn't terrifying. "However malevolent this Sorrowvale might be, it can't not have those three elements."

"The Goldenhallow assessment said victory condition variant

A," Aderyn said, and wished her voice wasn't shaking. "That means you win by finding the exit. I think maybe the thing about how there must always be an exit means that victory condition is in effect."

"Then I guess we'd better get moving," Owen said.

Aderyn grabbed his arm. "But we know nothing about it. We're going in blind. We don't know what monsters are in here, what traps we'll face—"

Owen removed her hand from his arm and clasped it. "At the risk of sounding critical, we're not in a position to learn any of those things unless you've developed the ability to Assess a dungeon from inside—stop looking like that! I told you it wasn't a criticism, just fact. We can only move forward, carefully, and watch out for hazards the way we always do. In fact, Weston, you come up here to the front, and Jessemia, follow behind him."

"There's no good way to do this, Owen," Isold warned.

"I know. Look, everyone, ignore the system notice. This dungeon wants to rattle us. We won't give it the satisfaction. Are we ready? Let's go."

Aderyn couldn't see clearly past Owen, who was right in front of her, but she didn't want to. Her aching heart told her that this was all her fault. She'd been fooled by the dungeon's appearance into a cocky assurance that it would be a simple afternoon's romp. As if dungeons were ever pleasant and nice no matter how they looked. And she'd relied on [Improved Assess 2] even though she knew it could be fooled. Hadn't the Diabolist Jedrek done just that, months ago?

She wiped self-indulgent tears from her eyes. This was stupid. It didn't matter that she'd screwed up, because they were here now and they needed to face what was in front of them, not dwell on how things should have been. Out of the corner of her eye, she saw Jessemia watching her, but the woman said nothing. For once, Aderyn would have welcomed Jessemia whining, because if Sorrow-vale was dangerous for her team, it was doubly dangerous for Jessemia at her low level and whining would have been justified.

The corridor stretched on for what felt like forever as they crept at the pace Weston needed to check for traps. A low noise like the wind wailing across a barren plain hovered just at the limit of Aderyn's hearing. She tried to ignore it, but the volume rose until it felt like a sawblade across her nerves, wailing and fading briefly and then returning.

"That could be a monster," Owen said, so firmly her fears diminished. "Everyone be ready to fight. We're coming up on a corner."

"How are you not terrified?" Aderyn said.

"Because I've seen enough slasher films to know how they turn out," Owen said. "Sorrowvale wants us frightened. But we're not babies. We've endured worse than some scary noises and what looks like an off-brand horror film set. We'll stay together, and it will be fine. Besides, there's no soundtrack providing cues for a jump scare."

For once, Owen's nonsense references to things she'd never heard of comforted Aderyn. He was right—they'd stay together, and together they could accomplish anything.

Weston rounded the corner and came to a halt. "It's a door."

They all crowded in around him, Aderyn thought because no one wanted to be alone at the back of the group. The door was of plain, deeply-grained wood with iron fittings and an oversized latch. Owen reached for the latch, but Weston grabbed his hand. "Give me a minute. We can't count on there being no traps in this place just because Goldenhallow didn't have any."

He surveyed the door thoroughly, finally running his fingers along the lintel as if checking for dust. "I think it's clean. I could be wrong. I don't dare assume anything about this place."

"We have to take chances sometime if we don't want to just sit here and wait for the dungeon to come after us," Owen said.

Weston turned the latch and pushed the door open. A breath of dead air escaped the room beyond, smelling of dust and wood rot though Aderyn still saw nothing but stone.

"Wait a second," Livia said, and sent half her lights flashing forward into the room. They lit up a dozen human figures. Aderyn involuntarily recoiled and put her hand on her sword. But when the figures didn't move, she took a closer look. All of them were identical shades of gray, and the lights playing over them didn't make them react.

"Statues," Aderyn said.

"Hopefully not living statues," Weston said, moving forward.

"Or statues who used to be people," Livia said.

Jessemia gasped. "Is that possible?"

"Some monsters can turn flesh to stone," Isold said. "I see nothing moving in here, though."

"It could be a magical effect," Livia said. "A trap."

"It can't be a trap in the wall, or they'd all be facing the same way," Owen said.

Sure enough, the statues were all oriented at random. Aderyn walked slowly to the statue of a woman wearing a hooded cloak over a full-skirted gown she didn't think was suitable for adventuring. The hood was pushed back on the statue's head so its face was fully visible. A chill numbed Aderyn's fingers at the sight. She'd never seen anyone look so terrified. Though the eyes were blank of pupil or iris, they were wide and startled, the mouth caught in a terrible frozen scream. Whoever had carved this statue knew human emotion perfectly.

"I think these are just statues," Owen said. "This guy doesn't look like an adventurer. His clothes are too fancy."

"Same here," Aderyn said.

Weston was prowling the walls, searching for traps. "There's another door that doesn't look like it's trapped. I don't want us caught off guard, though."

Aderyn's attention returned to the statue's face. A trick of the light made its blank eyes look darker. She leaned closer just as a dark liquid began trickling from the corners of the eyes over the statue's cheeks. Startled, she stepped back.

The statue reached for her.

Aderyn screamed and stumbled away. "They're attacking!"

Everyone backed away, avoiding the statues, and rushed for the door. Weston shoved past them all and rattled the knob. He swore under his breath and dropped to one knee, pulling out his lock picks.

Aderyn and Owen drew their swords and waited. The statues moved slowly, like people swimming through mud, their legs shuffling and their arms shifting a little at a time. The two closest to the friends were men, one dressed the way Owen was in a brigandine carved of gray stone, the other wearing the kind of puffy-sleeved shirt and leather vest Aderyn had seen the wealthy of Obsidian wear. Their faces were still frozen in terror the way the first one had been, as if they were the ones in danger of death. Black liquid seeped and ran from their eyes like oily tears.

"I don't think these swords will be much good against stone," Owen murmured.

"We have to try," Aderyn said.

A *stone sphere* shot past them to impact against the nearer statue. It shattered into a thousand sharp-edged pieces Aderyn flung up her free arm to protect her face against. "Sorry," Livia said. "I hoped magic stone might damage them." She stepped past, making Owen protest. In both hands, she held a massive hammer rough-hewn of granite. Taking a solid stance, she swung the [Elemental Hammer] at the statue's head.

The statue's head exploded the way *stone sphere* had. The statue never stopped moving. One hand closed over Livia's forearm, and she screamed and yanked away from its grip. Owen grabbed her and hauled her backward just as Weston shouted her name. "Keep working!" Owen shouted back.

"The door's open," Weston said. "Livia, what happened?"

"Everybody move!" Owen shouted. He dragged Livia, who was cursing between sobs of pain, through the door after the others. Aderyn, at the rear, felt the tug of stone fingers on her hair before she jerked free and slammed the door behind her. She kept going a few more steps before slowing to control her terrified breathing.

A system message appeared, again in quivering blood-red letters.

You have survived the touch of the stone children.
Mostly.
You have earned [10,000 XP]

Everyone surrounded Livia, who was clutching her left forearm with her right hand. "Don't touch it. It could be contagious," she warned Weston.

"It's spreading," Jessemia said. "You're turning to stone."

"I can feel my body fighting it," Livia grunted. "My natural affinity for the element versus its corrupted stone. I refuse to let it take me."

Aderyn approached. Livia's bare forearm was patchy with gray stone in the shape of a swollen hand. As she watched, two of the "finger" patches merged, growing larger. Aderyn drew in a startled breath.

"Yes, it's terrifying," Livia said with a tight smile. "It feels like wrestling an invisible opponent. But I love a good challenge."

"It's going to be all right," Weston said. "You're going to be fine."

"Being optimistic again, dearest?" Livia said.

"I was talking to myself. I had to leave a pick behind in that door."

"Which is practically like losing a family member," Owen joked. His voice was too strained for humor.

Livia gasped. The stone blotch spread a little farther. Weston grabbed her shoulder. "Fight it, Livia," he said in a low, urgent voice. "No one is as stubborn as you. Fight this."

Livia nodded, biting her lip. "It's fine. It won't get farther."

"But—"

"It's *fine*," Livia insisted. The stone continued to spread toward her fingers and up to her elbow.

Jessemia let out a sob and immediately said, "I'm sorry!"

"No," Livia said, "it really is fine." She let go of her arm and straightened it. Her entire left forearm, from the tips of her fingers almost to her elbow, was stone. Aderyn's horrified exclamation cut off as she realized that the stone had stopped spreading. Livia raised her left arm and wiggled her stone fingers. They moved a little stiffly, but otherwise as easily as her flesh-and-blood hand did. It looked as if she was wearing a stone glove, though the end of the glove had a ragged edge.

"It's real stone, not unnatural," Livia said, turning the hand to look at it on all sides. "I couldn't fight off the infection entirely, but I could convert it. It feels so strange." She touched the stone, then rapped on it with her knuckles. "Feel that."

Weston ran a hand over her arm. "It's rough like granite."

"I can barely feel your touch." Livia closed her fingers into a fist. "Step back. I want to try something."

With the rest of them out of the way, Livia took a solid stance and punched the wall with her left hand. The slam of stone against stone echoed down the new corridor. Stone chips flew as the wall cracked and dented. Livia lowered her fist. She grinned evilly. "Now *that*," she said, "is something I could get used to."

"So it's permanent?" Owen asked.

"I think so. It feels just as if I've always had a stone arm."

"You're not bothered?" Aderyn couldn't help asking.

Livia watched, not Aderyn, but Weston. "Are you?" she asked him.

"I'm afraid all I can think is that if it had happened to anyone but you, we'd be dealing with a statue corpse of a friend right now," Weston said. "But if you're worried a stone arm will put me off, dearest, I obviously haven't been clear that I will love you whatever comes." He drew her into his arms and kissed her, one hand clasping her stone one. "And if that's the worst this dungeon can throw at us... actually, that makes me even more terrified."

"We have to keep going, though," Jessemia said. Her face was very pale and her pupils dilated, but her chin was set in a determined frown. "There's another door."

"That's right. Let's keep moving," Owen said.

CHAPTER THIRTY-ONE

The door the short hall led to was unlocked. Weston opened it slowly and waited for Livia's lights to fly past. He looked inside and shuddered. "More statues. Sort of."

"What does that mean?" Aderyn asked.

She followed Owen into the room and stifled a shriek. The walls here weren't quarried stone, even rough-hewn, but something smooth and black like obsidian—or like black cloth. Partial human figures emerged from the walls, their hands outstretched as if reaching for something, their faces contorted in snarls or cries of pain. They all looked so agonized Aderyn's heart beat faster in mingled fear and sorrow.

Owen walked to the center of the room and surveyed it with his hands on his hips. "Frozen in carbonite," he murmured.

"What?"

"It's a thing from a movie. Don't worry about it. I'm guessing if we don't touch the walls, we'll be fine." He sounded angry rather than afraid. "I hate this place. Tormenting people to scare others... what kind of sick bastard are we dealing with?"

The others had gathered close beside him. Aderyn couldn't

blame them. It went beyond not wanting to touch the walls with their tortured inhabitants to the desire she shared to feel she wasn't alone. "It hasn't talked to us again," she said. "I don't think I could bear it if it was like Gamboling Coil, always communicating."

"Let's hope it stays that way," Isold said. "That archway is the only way out of this terrible room."

Weston waved them back as he examined it. "I can't help imagining portals to the demon void, or energy fields that turn you to ash when you pass through them. But this one looks clear."

Owen poked at the space beneath the arch with his <**Deadly Blade**> anyway. Nothing happened. He took a deep breath and stepped through. "It's fine."

Once they were all through the arch, another system message appeared.

> *You failed to join the others in their endless embrace.*
> *You can't go forever without touching something.*
> *You have earned [9000 XP].*

Aderyn shivered and kept walking.

The corridor turned a short distance ahead and ended at another closed door. "Writing," Weston said. "It looks like the system notices, but it's engraved on a brass plaque. That same wiggly writing."

"To me, it looks like something out of a horror movie," Owen said. "Like wiggly writing is supposed to be terrifying instead of the sign of someone who never learned good handwriting."

His calm certainty eased Aderyn's mind. She read over his shoulder:

Those who pass beyond this door face torment upon torment.
You will wish you had remained with your lost companions.

"Hah!" Owen said. "It assumes we lost people in one or both of those rooms. It doesn't know everything!"

"I'm more concerned about 'torment upon torment,'" Weston

said. "We've only been in this dungeon for ten minutes and I feel tormented enough already."

"We can do this," Jessemia said. "I know we can. Owen's right, the dungeon thinks we're weaker than we are. But it's wrong. We're going to beat it."

"And it's not like we have a choice other than going forward," Livia said.

"Spoken like a true realist," Isold said, smiling.

"Then what are we waiting for?" Aderyn asked. Her worries hadn't vanished, but they'd faded enough that she could face the thought of more terrible sights and challenges without fear.

Owen nodded and opened the door.

Aderyn braced herself for more horrors. Instead, the door opened on another corridor identical to all the others. With Owen by her side, she followed Weston as he set out down the hall.

For a long time, they walked, never coming to a door or room. The corridor made several turns in unexpected directions, but there were no junctions, nothing but slickly-reflective black walls and rough flagstones. The <**Wayfinder**> would be useless in finding the exit, because there wasn't anywhere else to go.

The world flickered.

Weston stopped. "Something just happened. The corridor changed."

"I didn't see anything," Owen said.

Weston gestured at the corridor ahead. "It took a turn to the left just a second ago. Now it's a straight passage ahead."

The wall to the left looked just like all the others to Aderyn. She almost touched it before remembering the walls in this place could be deadly. Ahead, the corridor ran straight and unbending out of her range of vision. "I haven't seen a long corridor since we went through that door."

"Hmm." Weston waved a hand and called out, "Livia, what do you see back there?"

"A long corridor, and the rest of you, why?"

"So we've all passed through it, whatever it is," Weston mused. "Everyone turn around and go back."

Almost immediately, Livia, now at the head of the group, said, "We came around a right-hand turn, and now the hall goes left."

"Well, we are facing the other way," Aderyn said.

"I know. I accounted for that. The hall is backward. Weston, how far should I go?"

"Stop before you round the corner." Weston crouched, examining the floor and the walls without touching the latter. "Fire and thunder. I can't see what's doing it."

"You think we're being teleported?" Owen said.

"Yes. I think stepping somewhere in this hall triggers the effect and moves us elsewhere in this dungeon." Weston rose and dusted his hands off. "We might never leave this place."

"Let's not think like that," Owen said. "Do you know which part of the floor?"

Weston pointed at his feet. "And it's trickier than simply stepping on it, or we'd have flicked back and forth half a dozen times already."

"Let's be grateful it doesn't send each of us somewhere different," Aderyn said.

Owen drew his <**Deadly Blade**>. The dagger wasn't highly magical, but it kept an edge without needing to be honed. He scored a number 1 deep into the flagstones, sending up a metallic *skree* that put Aderyn's teeth on edge. "It's a start," he said. "Let's head back— at least, what would be back if we were still in our starting place. It might confuse the dungeon."

Aderyn didn't think this was likely, but it wasn't as if it mattered which way they went. Ultimately, they'd run into something dangerous.

After a few more turns, Weston came to an abrupt stop. "There's someone on the floor over there. Looks dead."

Aderyn looked past him at the crumpled form. "Dead? Not asleep?"

"He's not breathing." Weston edged forward. "I don't like this. I doubt he was in here alone, but why would his team have left his body behind?"

A flash of **[See It Coming]** showed Aderyn the moving blade just as Weston stepped on the trigger. She leaped back and yelled, "Weston, *get down!*"

Weston dropped, landing atop the corpse. An enormous scything blade flashed from a hidden slit in the wall and made a sweeping arc across the corridor, narrowly missing Owen's chest and slicing through the spot where Aderyn had been standing. It slipped into a second slot, and in seconds, it had vanished.

"Oh, look," Weston said, his voice higher pitched than usual. "He's been cut in half."

"Weston, don't freak out," Owen warned.

"Freaking out means running around in circles and screaming, right?" Weston pushed himself to his knees. A smear of blood covered his jerkin front, and Aderyn gasped. Weston held out a hand. "I think that trigger is still active. And this isn't my blood. This fellow was killed recently."

"Then there's someone else in here with us," Owen said, sending a chill down Aderyn's spine at the thought.

"Possibly. Unless his team is dead, too." The distant sound of Weston's voice told Aderyn he was concentrating on dismantling the trap. She couldn't stop staring at the bisected corpse of the fallen adventurer in a pool of blood. "I hope—no, it's just the one blade." Something went *clunk*, and Weston returned to Livia's side. "There's another weakness. The dungeon is into blood and horror, but it's not very cunning. I'd have put a second blade perpendicular to the first to make sure nobody got the bright idea of just crawling past the first one."

"That tells me it wants us frightened rather than dead," Owen said.

"I think it wants us dead, too," Aderyn said.

"Yes, but it's trying to do that in a way that terrifies us first. Witnessing the gory deaths of companions so we're too afraid to think rationally, that sort of thing." Owen hesitated. "You're sure the trap is dismantled?"

"Very sure."

At that moment, the system message appeared.

Don't imagine you will survive. There are more blades than this one.
You have earned [8000 XP]

"Then I'll lead the way for a bit," Owen said. "Stay close, just in case."

He rounded a corner, and his steps slowed. "I guess this is the next challenge," he said, gesturing at the door at the end of the short hallway. "Everyone get ready."

"Let me go first after Weston checks the door," Livia said. "I can spray the room with _iron spikes_ if it turns out to be full of monsters."

"The door's not locked or trapped," Weston said. "On my count."

Livia counted quietly with him. "Three... two... one... _now!_"

Weston flung the door open. Livia burst through, shouting the beginnings of a spell.

The sound of screaming filled the air, and someone shouted, "Don't kill us, we're human!"

Livia stopped chanting and stepped to the side to let the others enter. Owen had drawn his sword and was advancing on the huddled figures clinging to each other at the far side of the room. "It's a trap," he said. "Everyone watch for an ambush."

"It's not a trap," one woman said. "We're adventurers. We came in here—half our team is dead—" She burst out weeping, but her sobs sounded dull, as if she'd already cried a river of tears.

Owen twitched. Aderyn, obeying **[Read Body Language]**, hurried to his side with her sword ready. "Keep an eye on them," he said. The set of his shoulders told her he suspected a trick, but she was paranoid enough after half an hour of this terrible place not to need a warning. The "adventurers" were probably disguised monsters, or hiding a weapon, or puppets manipulated by the dungeon to get her and her friends to let down their guard.

The room was as big as the statue room, about forty-five feet on a side. It occurred to Aderyn, thinking back, that all the rooms they'd found so far were the same size. She wished she knew what that meant. Maybe it didn't mean anything, or maybe there was a clue they could use. She glanced around swiftly before returning her attention to the cowering people. In addition to the door they'd entered by, there were two other doors, both identical to... yes, all the doors looked the same, too: plain, deep-grained wood with ancient iron fittings and latches.

Now she Assessed the weeping woman and her companions. After her total failure to see the truth of Sorrowvale, she didn't feel confident in her ability. She reminded herself that **[Improved Assess 2]** was almost always successful, and that she wasn't going to make assumptions about it again. Even so, she opted to use Full Assess in case their skills didn't match their supposed classes or levels.

Name: Meladria

Class: Spellcrafter

Level: 5

<u>Skills</u>: **Assess (5), Awareness (5), Bluff (1), Climb (4), Conversation (2), Intimidate (2), Sense Truth (5), Spot (6), Survival (4), Swim (2)**

<u>Class Skills</u>: **Knowledge: Monsters (5); Knowledge: Magic (5); Imbue Common Item (5); Scribe Scroll, Basic (4); Create**

Common Item (4); Analyze Enchantment (3); Imbue Weapon/Armor, Lesser (3); Disenchant 1 (1)

Name: Ehren
  Class: Stalwart
  Level: 5
  Skills: Assess (3), Awareness (5), Climb (2), Conversation (4), Sense Truth (4), Spot (5), Survival (4), Swim (1)
  Class Skills: Improved Weapon Proficiency (6), Knowledge: Monsters (5), Basic Armor Proficiency (5), Bull Rush (5), Intimidate (4), Improved Bluff (3)

Name: Calista
  Class: Swordsworn
  Level: 5
  Skills: Assess (3), Awareness (5), Climb (5), Conversation (4), Intimidate (3), Sense Truth (3), Spot (5), Survival (3), Swim (3)
  Class Skills: Improved Weapon Proficiency (5), Knowledge: Monsters (5), Basic Armor Proficiency (5), Dodge (5), Parry (4), Improved Bluff (3)

Calista was the weeping woman. She was small, with delicate, petite features and hair cut short to frame her face. The other woman, Meladria, was as opposite Calista as possible, lanky and probably taller than Owen when she was standing. Ehren, on the other hand, looked fat rather than bulky the way a Stalwart should, but having seen his skill ranks, Aderyn was disinclined to underestimate him.

She waved her sword at them. "Get up."

Slowly, the three got to their feet. They stood close together, Ehren with his arms around the women's shoulders. It didn't look like a romantic gesture, more like he meant to protect them. Aderyn still didn't let her guard down. She mentally ran over ways to prove they were what they said they were and came up blank.

She was peripherally aware of her friends examining the room and the doors, though Jessemia had come to stand beside her. Aderyn pointed her sword more directly at the trio and said, "Who's your leader?"

Calista burst into tears again. Ehren hugged her more tightly. Meladria said, "That was Andrus. He's dead. That room—all those people trying to get out—he touched the wall, and it... it sucked him in." Her voice was dull, her pupils dilated, and Aderyn thought she might be in shock. Assuming it wasn't a ruse.

"You said, half your team," Jessemia said. "Literally half?"

"There were six of us," Ehren said. "Andrus was our Pathseer. The walls absorbed him. Gelbin got cut in half—" He swallowed like he was keeping down bile. "The blade came out of the wall and cut him in half. And Doyelle..."

"I killed her!" Calista wailed. "I thought—I believed she was a monster, and I cut her down and then I saw what I'd done and I—" She buried her face in Ehren's broad chest, her whole body shaking.

Jessemia stepped forward and put a hand on Calista's shoulder. Aderyn grabbed her arm, trying to pull her away. "Jessemia! We don't know if they're lying! We don't even know if they're really human!"

"They're not lying. Look at them," Jessemia said.

"But they're level five. There's no way they should be out in the Long Plains. They'd be killed by the first monster that came along." Aderyn tugged on her arm again. "We can't trust them. Remember what this dungeon looked like at first. It knows how to conceal the truth."

"I know. I can just tell." Jessemia's eyes were bright with tears. "Trust me, Aderyn. I can tell."

Aderyn stared at her. Then she let go of Jessemia's arm. "All right," she said. "I trust you."

CHAPTER THIRTY-TWO

Jessemia turned Calista to face her. "What brought your team here?"

Calista didn't answer. Ehren said, "It was a quest. A challenge. Travel from Guerdon Deep to Setter's Valley without encountering any monsters. Andrus was... he was so good at what he did, he was sure we had as good a chance as anyone despite our low level. Because we wouldn't be trying to kill anything, you know? And it was worth so much experience."

"Isold," Aderyn said, "where is Setter's Valley?"

Isold came to join them. "Setter's Valley is the first settlement you come to when traveling west from Guerdon Deep. It's the largest town in the Long Plains."

"I don't suppose you've heard of any quests involving it?"

Isold frowned. "I've never been there, so I don't know what quests are available."

"I mean quests about going there. Delivery quests or something."

"Oh. Well, there was something I heard about in Guerdon Deep, about traveling to Setter's Valley under certain conditions. I don't think it was a delivery quest. It might have been one of those quests where you earn experience for not killing any monsters, or retrieving seven kinds of rare herb. That sort of thing."

"Do you know how far we are from Setter's Valley?" Jessemia asked.

Isold's eyes focused on the middle distance. "Ah... we're at least eight days' travel west of that town. Why?"

"Maybe you're telling the truth," Aderyn said to Ehren, "but that doesn't explain why you're so far west of Setter's Valley."

Ehren's gaze flicked to Meladria. Meladria's cheeks turned a dull red. "We succeeded at the quest," she said, almost too quietly to hear. "I thought we should try it again, going to Misthollow. We did so well!" Her voice turned shrill and loud. "Andrus—we avoided so many monsters, and we were doing fine until we found this dungeon. It didn't look dangerous!"

Aderyn lowered her sword. "I believe you are what you say you are," she said, "if only because this dungeon would spin a better tale. Are you all out of your minds? What did you think would happen when you reached Misthollow? You'd go on to the next village? There's a reason low-level adventurers don't come this way. And now your luck has run out."

"Aderyn," Jessemia said quietly, "enough."

Startled, Aderyn turned her attention on Jessemia. Tears filled Jessemia's eyes. "They know they were stupid," she said. "They can't fix that. All they can do is move forward."

Aderyn didn't know what to say. She and Isold exchanged glances. "I... you're right," Aderyn said. "I'm sorry."

Ehren suddenly said, "No, don't open that door! There's a trap in the room beyond."

Weston, who had his hand on the latch, withdrew it quickly. "There's no trap on the door."

"That's what's so dangerous," Ehren said. "We didn't get very far before we set it off, but we were cautious, so the fire didn't burn anything seriously." He displayed his right hand. The back of it was red and blistered, but not badly.

"What about this other door?" Owen asked.

Meladria shook her head. "We were afraid to try it. This room was empty, and it didn't try to kill us. We were going to rest here and then look for the way out, but this place is endless. We've wandered here for at least two days."

"Did you know about the teleportation traps?"

Meladria's eyes widened. "What does that mean, teleportation?"

"It means a *transport* spell triggered by stepping on a certain flag-stone," Livia said. "The dungeon seems endless because it moves you around."

"Oh." Meladria giggled. "I guess we might have been near the exit a dozen times and not known it." Her giggles turned into hysterical laughter. Ehren shook her until she stopped, then hugged her.

"Well, there's a trap on this other door," Weston said, "and from what I see, the mechanism isn't accessible from this side. Everyone stay well away from the door."

"Then either we go back the way we came, or we figure out this other room," Owen said.

Weston opened the second door. The room beyond was pitch black. "Livia?"

Livia tossed some *orbs of light* into the dark space, and everyone crowded around Weston to look. The room was some fifteen feet wide and extended to the right at least forty feet. It was unexpectedly beautiful, with walls of hammered brass ornamented with large silver flowers that looked like daisies with rounder petals. At the far end, a large lever with a metal handle extended from the wall.

"Well," Owen said, "that looks more like a trap than anything I've ever seen. Complete with off switch. Did the dungeon think we were that stupid? It's beautiful, so we go running into it?"

"The fires shoot out from the flower centers," Meladria said.

"Not every tile triggers them, but we couldn't see a pattern. And we were scared to experiment."

Now Aderyn saw the floor was covered with black and white tiles in a checkerboard pattern. A charred lump of something lay a few paces in. "What's that?"

"A biscuit," Ehren said. "We threw it in there, and it bounced a few times before setting off the trap."

"Hmm," Owen said. "And they shoot fire... could there be a way through that avoids where they aim?"

"Let's see," Weston said. He dug around in his knapsack until he came up with a hunk of bread they'd gotten three days before at the village of Misthollow. He tossed it in his hand a couple of times before lobbing it into the room. It landed next to the burned lump of biscuit.

Half a dozen jets of fire blasted the walls and the floor. The bread caught fire, filling the air with the stink of char and burned yeasty bread. The jets of fire continued for five seconds and then cut off abruptly.

"Well, that's something," Weston said. "The nozzles aren't aimed straight ahead, they point in many directions. So there isn't a way to pass through the room avoiding the fire."

"Plus it's hot enough you'd probably suffocate," Livia said. "I tried using *telekinesis* on the lever, but it must have some kind of locking mechanism on it I can't see, because it won't budge."

"Then I've run out of ideas," Owen said.

"But there's the path," Jessemia said.

Everyone stared at her. Jessemia continued to examine the floor. "It's not very direct, and I can't see the end from here because the room is so long. But it's clear."

"What—" Owen began. "You mean you can see how to avoid the traps?"

Jessemia looked up. "Can't you?"

"I think it's a Pathseer thing," Owen said. "How certain are you? Certain enough to guide Weston through?"

"That's too dangerous," Jessemia said. "I'll go."

"Jessemia—"

"It doesn't matter what level I am," Jessemia said, "or whether I should risk myself. Either we go back the way we came into who knows what kind of danger, or we open that door and set off a trap that could kill one or all of us, or I take this chance. I'm willing to try."

Owen nodded. "You're right. What do we have to do?"

"Stand back," Jessemia said.

She stepped into the room, walking on only the black tiles until she reached the burned bread. Then she stepped lightly onto the white tile next to it. Nothing happened.

Jessemia turned now to face the distant lever. Carefully scanning the ground, she walked forward two squares, then hesitated. She lifted one foot and set it back down. Then she hopped over the next tile and teetered, flailing her arms until she regained her balance. Aderyn grew dizzy and realized she'd been holding her breath.

Jessemia walked three tiles to her left, forward three, then diagonally back one. She still moved cautiously, as if the path wasn't as clear to her as she'd suggested. She was fifteen feet from the lever when she again hesitated. Aderyn bit her lip to keep from calling out questions. Jessemia didn't need the distraction.

Then Jessemia leaped, not forward, not backward, but with one foot on either side of a black tile. Immediately, she hopped off those tiles onto a white one a short distance away and staggered, getting her balance. Her foot neared the edge of the tile, and Aderyn sucked in a frightened breath. But Jessemia caught herself before she crossed the line. She walked confidently, two tiles forward, one left, one forward, and grabbed hold of the lever. She gave it a twist and a tug and yanked it down.

With a sigh of air and the clunk of machinery, all the flowers sank into the walls and disappeared behind brass panels. Jessemia's shoulders sagged. Then she jerked upright, staring at something invisible a foot in front of her face. Owen was already halfway across the room. Aderyn hurried after him.

"I did it," Jessemia said. "I beat the trap. And I'm level eight."

"Congratulations," Owen said. "That was amazing."

"I hate this dungeon," Jessemia said. "It loves hurting people. I wish we could burn it down."

"I agree." Owen squeezed her shoulder in reassurance. "The best we can hope for is to get out of here and spread the word so no one else falls into its trap. So, on that note, let's move on."

"Wait," Ehren said. "What about us?"

"We're not going to abandon you, if that's what you mean," Owen said.

"But won't we get in your way? Your team is so much higher level she's the only one whose level we can see." Ehren pointed at Jessemia.

"Don't worry about it," Aderyn said. "We all stick together. It's not about the experience anymore. It's about getting out alive."

Calista, who'd looked lost in her own world, said, "We're already leaving them behind. Their bodies. This dungeon is evil."

"That is true," Isold said, putting a hand on her arm. "But your teammates would not want you to die as well. You do them honor by surviving."

Calista looked up at him with tears in her eyes. "I don't want the dungeon to win. It feels like it already has. Andrus was my sweetheart, and I saw him screaming for help as the dungeon absorbed him. And Doyelle was my best friend, and she died at my hand. I can't forget."

"I know. You wouldn't be human if those things didn't hurt." Isold put his arm around her and hugged her. "Wait a moment."

They all stood in the now-empty brass room and listened to Isold sing. Aderyn had heard this song before, in the middle of battle. Here, in this dead place where even the walls wanted to destroy them, the music felt different. Isold sang of hard-won victories, of winning at terrible challenges. He sang memories of successes beyond imagining and triumphs of good over evil. Aderyn's spirits rose. She felt confident, not that their success was assured, but that she had the power to beat this dungeon and not let it destroy her.

When the last notes faded away, Calista said, "Thank you. It doesn't hurt so much anymore."

"I'm glad to ease your pain," Isold said. "Now, let's find the way out."

They stepped through the door, and the world flickered.

Owen let out a sharp curse. "It's like the dungeon was listening. It put this thing here on purpose."

"I don't think so, at least not in the way you're suggesting," Isold said. "If the dungeon had the power to move us around at its whim, it would deposit us right where more traps are. I'm certain the teleportation traps, as you call them, are fixed in place."

"I hope you're right," Owen said. He bent and scratched the number 2 into the flagstones with the <**Deadly Blade**>.

Before, the exit to the room had led to a corridor extending to the left only. Now the room was gone, and the corridor extended in both directions. "Which way?" Weston asked.

"I don't think it matters. Left," Owen said.

The corridor immediately turned a corner, then another corner, and stopped at an identical wooden door. Weston checked it over. "No traps."

The room beyond was lit, for once. Cold blue blobs that glowed like moonlight clung to the ceiling and shed their radiance on the room below. The room itself was chilly, too, the chill of an autumn night, and Aderyn shivered.

"I'm not putting up with this shit any longer," Livia suddenly said. She flung her arms wide and chanted. *Daylight* burst above them like the noon sun at midsummer, filling the room with its bril-

liance and warming them all instantly. Aderyn felt better immediately.

"Someone else was here," Owen said. "Look."

Across the rough stones of one wall, many deep scratches made
lines interrupted by the rounded edges of the stones. They lacked the
refinement of the dungeon's writing. Aderyn looked closer. "It looks
like a map. Part of a map," she amended.

"Someone did their best to identify where all the corridors went,"
Weston said. "But they didn't know about the teleportation traps, so
it's all confused. I think over here is the first couple of rooms, the
antechambers maybe if we consider that first door to be the true
dungeon entrance." He traced some lines with one finger.

"Take a look at that other door," Owen said. "Everyone else, be
on guard—"

Aderyn heard his voice give a little hiccup. "Owen?"

Owen stood near the door they'd entered by, facing the wall.
Glowing lines much more finely drawn than the crude map had
appeared in a strange symbol just where Owen was looking. Aderyn
approached him, her heart beating faster. "Owen?"

"Believe in the field or try eating ash," Owen said.

He spoke so normally she didn't understand his words. Then she
realized they made no sense no matter how she thought about them.
"What—eating ash? Owen, what are you talking about?"

"If the dog blows its horn, the elephant cries," Owen said, still in
that same conversational tone.

Aderyn, feeling frightened, grabbed his arm and made him face
her. "You're not making sense." Then she drew in a startled breath.
Owen's blue eyes were nearly black from how enlarged his pupils
were, and within the blackness, silver spirals whirled slowly in opposite directions.

Then Isold was there, drawing Owen aside and peering into his
eyes. He cursed. "That is a symbol of madness," he said, pointing at
the wall. "It's driven Owen insane."

CHAPTER THIRTY-THREE

Aderyn grabbed Owen by the shoulders and shook him. "Owen. Owen! Wake up!"

"He's not unconscious, he's mad," Isold said, gently peeling Aderyn's fingers from Owen's shoulders. "He doesn't see reality anymore. What he's reacting to is the madness."

Aderyn's breath sobbed out of her. "How do we fix this? Healing?"

"It's not an injury, so healing won't do anything. If it's an enchantment, there are items, skills that will reverse it."

"What aren't you telling me, Isold?"

Isold hesitated. "If it's not an enchantment, it might be permanent."

The word sent a jolt of fear through her. Permanent. She realized Owen had wandered away and hurried after him, taking his hand. "Owen, can you hear me?" She knew it was pointless, but if you didn't look at his eyes, he seemed perfectly normal.

Owen fixed his spiraling gaze on a spot above her left shoulder. "The birds, how they soar," he said, wonderingly as if there really were birds there.

Tears filled Aderyn's eyes. Isold put a comforting hand on her wrist. "We can be grateful it's not a violent madness," he said. "Owen is so powerful a swordsman the only way we could keep him from attacking us would be to incapacitate or kill him."

"But he's—" Aderyn wiped her eyes. "All right. We'll figure this out."

"I will have the skill **[Break Enchantment]** at level thirteen." Isold sounded confident, and that eased Aderyn's heart further. "We must be close to leveling now."

The others were gathering around now, and Livia said, "Is something wrong? You're crying."

"That symbol on the wall. It did something to Owen, didn't it?" Weston said. "But he doesn't look—oh, crap, look at his eyes."

"It's a temporary madness," Aderyn said, willing that to be true. "He'll be fine."

"Is it a magic effect? Let me try *dispel magic*." Livia grabbed Owen's chin with her stone hand and made him look at her. He didn't resist. Livia chanted something under her breath and then snapped the fingers of her right hand in front of Owen's mad eyes. Owen blinked.

"Did it work?" Aderyn said. "Owen!"

Livia shook her head. "Just—once more." She spoke slowly and clearly, nonsense words that almost made sense, and snapped her fingers more forcefully.

Again, Owen blinked. Then he said, "Tomato soup and haggis? Thank you."

Livia released him. "I think *dispel magic* is only for magic that's still happening, like invisibility or a levitation effect. I'm sorry."

"It's all right. Thank you for trying." Livia looked so downcast Aderyn hugged her, though her own heart was breaking. "We still have to figure out how to get out of here."

"Um, Owen's our leader," Livia said. "We need him for that."

"Well, we don't have him, and we'll have to make do." Aderyn clasped Owen's hand again. "What else did we find in here? Weston?"

"Until this happened," Weston said, pointing at Owen, "I was going to say there's nothing here. Just that useless map. But I guess Owen found the trap the hard way."

Aderyn swallowed. "Then we move on. Is that other door trapped?"

"No."

"All right. Weston, you take the lead with Jessemia. Isold, behind them with Ehren, Meladria, and Calista. I'll stay back with Owen, just in case he gets confused and tries to run ahead. Livia, you watch the rear." Aderyn tried to project confidence she didn't feel. Somebody had to take charge, and it might as well be her.

They walked slowly, with Weston and Jessemia alert for traps. The pace started to drive Aderyn—well, not crazy, that was a bad comparison with Owen right next to her. But it was so slow she felt an almost uncontrollable desire to run ahead, even if it meant running into a trap. The corridor turned corners and sometimes doubled back on itself as if the dungeon was taking every opportunity to confuse them.

Owen continued to walk so long as she held his hand. When she let him go briefly to wipe her sweaty palms on her trousers, he stopped and tilted his head back, letting his mouth hang open like he was looking at something marvelous. "Bad idea," he said. "The black ooze gets in your mouth and you turn inside out."

Aderyn grabbed his hand again. "There's no black ooze," she said, though he hadn't yet reacted as if he heard anything she said. "It's all right, Owen. We'll fix this."

Ahead, the world flickered, and suddenly Weston, Jessemia, Isold, Ehren, and Calista vanished.

Meladria let out a shriek and darted forward—and she, too, vanished.

"Keep moving," Livia urged. "What if the trap turns off after a while? We can't be separated in this place."

Aderyn dragged Owen forward, the world flickered, and then everyone was together. She let out a deep breath of relief. They had been coming to another turn in the hall, and now the corridor extended in both directions equally. Aderyn took the <**Deadly Blade**> from Owen after a bit of a struggle and scratched an awkward, angular 3 on the stone.

"There's a door up ahead," she said, "and a turn in the other direction. I think we should stay away from doors for now."

They shuffled around so Weston and Jessemia were at the new front of the group and moved on, turning the corner. Immediately Weston strode forward to the new door. "It's all right, Aderyn," he said. "I know where we are." A winding key extended at chest height from the stones beside the door. Weston gave it a few cranks, and the door popped open. "It's where we found our new friends. I told you the mechanism was on the far side."

They all piled into the room. Aderyn told herself not to believe they were safe, but it felt like a reprieve. "We need to eat, and think about what to do next," she said.

The level five adventurers didn't have much food left. "We thought this would be a fast dungeon, so we didn't hunt before," Meladria admitted. Isold shared out grapes and beef jerky from the <**Forager's Belt**>, and Aderyn offered food to Owen only to discover he wouldn't eat. He threw grapes idly at nothing and giggled when they struck the wall. It was so out of character Aderyn struggled not to cry. She ate, and drank her fill, and pretended for a few moments that everything was fine.

"Let's see what we know so far," she said when the last of the food had been eaten. "Isold, you have paper, right?"

Isold removed paper and a stick of drawing charcoal from his knapsack and handed them to Aderyn. Aderyn considered, then passed them to Jessemia. "Do you remember the way we came?"

"Yes, but those teleportation traps make it impossible to keep track," Jessemia said.

"Then we'll focus on the pieces of the map we know. Since that last trap brought us back here, I don't think they *transport* us to different, unconnected areas. I think this dungeon has a single path, and if the teleportation traps didn't exist, we could walk from the entrance to the exit with no trouble."

"Aside from the little trouble that is the many traps along the way," Weston said.

"We can ignore those for now. I mean, not ignore them, but we know they're out there, we don't know how to predict them, and so there's no point in worrying about them. We just have to find the right combination of paths to get out." Aderyn prodded the paper. "Draw what you remember."

Jessemia frowned. She sketched out a squiggly line with a couple of boxes attached that ended at a five-pointed star. "Those are the statue room and the, um, the room Owen said was carbonite. I don't know what that is."

"Nobody does. And that line ends at the first trap. What else?"

Jessemia drew another squiggly line that ended in two boxes side by side. She drew another star outside the smaller box, where she drew a flower. Then she drew another squiggly line from the larger box that ended in another star. "This is where we are now, and this is the teleportation trap that connects to... this other line over here." As she spoke, she drew a third long line with a box in the middle. She hesitated, then drew a spiral inside that box.

Aderyn took the charcoal from her and sketched a quick line connecting two of the stars. "This one leads here. What I want to know is whether the reverse is true."

"We can find that out now," Livia said. "Let's go see."

"Wait," Aderyn said. "Where's Owen?"

The sound of a door closing drew everyone's attention. Aderyn's heart stopped. "He's headed for the swinging blade!"

They all raced for the door. Aderyn got there first and flung herself through it. Owen was already at the end of the corridor, strolling along like this was a pleasant walk through a colonnade. She shrieked his name, got no response, and ran after him.

The grotesque body of Gelbin still lay on the floor, marking the blade's path. Aderyn rounded the corner and dove after Owen, catching him around the knees and bringing him down just as the click and whirr of the giant blade scythed through the air. Owen struggled to get away, kicking Aderyn on the chin and making her eyes water. Then Weston was beside her, wrapping his powerful arms around Owen's thighs and dragging him out of danger.

"I might have known that trap wouldn't stay dismantled long," he muttered. "That was lucky."

Aderyn sat with her knees drawn up, hugging her legs and breathing heavily. She wanted so badly to let Owen hold her—but he didn't know who she was, and she had to pull it together if they were all going to make it out alive.

"Back to the room," she said, "and then we need to find out if that teleportation trap works both ways."

This time, she turned Owen over to Weston and led the way. When they were all grouped together, she put one foot on the square marked 3 and hesitated. Nothing happened, no world-altering flicker. She stepped with both feet. Still nothing. With a disappointed sigh, she walked off the flagstone and waited for the others to follow.

"This is still good information," Isold said. "Triggering one teleportation trap makes that trap inert for a time. Or it might mean it stays inert until we step on another trap. It means, again, that we can't be separated by accidentally setting off the same trap twice in a row."

"We have to move forward," Aderyn said. "Going back means either facing that death blade again or ending up in the same loop that put us in that room with the symbol of madness. Let's see where that door leads." She pointed down the corridor at the door they'd avoided.

"Let me go first," Weston said.

"And me second," Livia said. "I'll use *clairvoyance* to see through the door and pretend not to be embarrassed that I haven't been doing it all along. This place really gets to me."

Weston having declared the door free of traps, Livia stood in front of it, perfectly still. "Crap," she said. "The walls are covered with more of those symbols like the one that got Owen."

"In a rush, the bull hits a pop fly to center," Owen said as if responding to his name.

"More madness symbols?" Aderyn asked, her heart sinking.

"Maybe not that. For one thing, they're all visible, not like the symbol of madness that was hidden until it was triggered. And the symbols are different. It's the lines that look the same, like glowing white ink. Good thing *clairvoyance* isn't the same as natural vision, or I'd have been caught." Livia stepped back. "There's another door at the far side. If we could get through without looking—"

"Straight across?"

"More or less. Straight and to the left a bit."

"We could blindfold ourselves—no." Aderyn watched Owen tie knots in the laces of his shirt. "He can't be counted on to stay blindfolded. And suppose those are symbols of instant death?"

"Maybe we need to knock him out," Weston suggested.

"No! What if it does permanent damage?"

"Not hit him," Livia said. She pulled the <**Wand of Sleep**> from where it rode in a clever sheath on the side of her knapsack. "We'll put him to sleep and carry him."

Relieved, Aderyn nodded. Secretly, she hoped a magical sleep would remove the madness, but that was probably impossible, so she said nothing.

She held Owen's face and made him look at her. "We'll get through this, sweetheart," she whispered.

"I've never seen Paris burn in the starlight," Owen replied with a loving smile, whispering as if he meant some tenderness. Aderyn swallowed tears and held him still while Livia wielded the wand. Owen closed his mad eyes and sagged.

"Let's move quickly," Aderyn said, wiping her eyes. "Blindfolds, and I'll tie us together. Weston, you carry Owen." She touched Owen's head briefly, then pulled rope from the <**Knapsack of Plenty**>. Sentimentality would have to wait.

CHAPTER THIRTY-FOUR

She quickly went down the line, looping rope around each person's waist as they all made makeshift blindfolds. At the head of the line, she tied the end of the rope around herself and waited for Weston to hoist his unconscious burden. Then she opened the door and fumbled through.

The room smelled dank, like there was a stagnant pool somewhere. Aderyn reminded herself Livia would have mentioned it if there were and flung her hands out, feeling the air as she took her first hesitant steps into the open. She saw dim light down the sides of her nose and resisted the urge to tilt her head back to see better. The floor underfoot was as even as it was everywhere else, but with her eyes covered, she imagined she felt the thin threads of the joins between the flagstones.

How long she walked, she didn't know. The sound of her heavy breathing filled her ears, along with the shuffling feet of seven other people. Distantly, she heard the wail of the wind, drawing nearer, and it frightened her into walking faster for a few steps until she felt the tug on the rope that said the others couldn't keep up.

The rope jerked. "He's waking up," Weston said.

"Keep his head down!" Aderyn demanded.

"He's—blast it—stronger than he looks, and he's wriggling like a gaffed fish." Weston's voice was strained with exertion. "We should have—oof—tied his hands."

"Faster, then!" Aderyn exclaimed.

But they could only move so fast. Aderyn stretched her arms as far as they would go, hoping to feel stone. Another step—another— and her fingertips brushed something hard. In that instant, she realized her mistake. Suppose touching the symbols was enough to make them activate?

She jerked her hand back. Livia had said straight and to the left, and Aderyn had aimed for that point. But if she had found the wall, that meant she needed to go farther left—but how much farther? Overshooting would put them all in danger again.

"Hurry, Aderyn," Weston said. The rope jerked again.

Aderyn shifted left and reached again. This time, she found wood.

Gasping in relief, she felt along the door until she reached the latch and could pull the door open. "Everybody through," she said, continuing to walk until the air didn't smell like sewage, then taking off her blindfold. Weston set the struggling Owen down, and Owen backed away from him until he bumped into the wall. His glare raised Aderyn's hopes until she looked into his eyes and saw the silver swirls still gently rotating there.

Weston stood beside the door, his eyes averted from the room, and waited for Jessemia at the end of the line to pass through. He grabbed the latch and swung the door shut, exchanging looks with Aderyn. "I think we're safe."

Fear is the greatest death of all save death itself.
You will not escape its touch forever.
You have earned [10,000 XP]

Welcome to Level Thirteen

Aderyn let out an enormous sigh of relief. "Did you see that? That wasn't Sorrowvale, at least not the level up notice. What does that mean?"

"I don't know and at the moment I don't care," Livia said, ripping off her blindfold with her stone hand. As far as Aderyn could tell, it was just as mobile as her hand of flesh and blood. "Isold?"

"A moment." Isold crouched to sit cross-legged on the floor. He folded his hands in his lap and closed his eyes, breathing deeply. "Have Owen sit here in front of me."

"Owen, sit down," Aderyn said, pressing gently on his shoulders.

"Bumblebee fricassee?" Owen asked.

"No, just sit." Aderyn's eyes were dry, though she wished she could weep for both of them.

Owen squeezed her hand and smiled. "Never a dry seat," he said, and folded his legs beneath him to sit.

Isold took Owen's hands in his. "I can see it," he said. "Like a cloud, or a gauzy blanket. It has no sides to catch hold of."

Aderyn bit back a demand for more information. Her hands clenched so tightly the nails cut into the skin of her palms.

"So I will try another approach," Isold said. He began crooning a wordless lullaby, a tune that crept into Aderyn's ears and wrapped itself around the back of her neck and slid down her spine. It should have been terrifying, but Aderyn felt comforted instead.

Owen closed his eyes and tipped his head back slightly. His breathing grew rapid and shallow until it sounded like a dog panting in the summer heat. Isold sang louder, leaning forward as if trying to keep Owen's attention focused on him.

With a snap, Owen's head whipped forward, almost hitting Isold on the forehead. The song cut off. Owen's breathing slowed until he and Isold were breathing in tandem. Then Owen opened his eyes and said, "What happened?"

Aderyn squeezed her eyes shut and let out a deep breath. Then she dropped to her knees and wrapped her arms around him. "It's a long story," she whispered in his ear, "but you weren't yourself for a while, and you're fine now, and we are getting out of this place."

He returned her embrace. "I feel cold, and sticky," he said. "Where are we?"

"Still exploring," Weston said, giving Owen a hand up. "We found where two parts of the maze connect via teleportation trap, and we're searching for more. If we can map this place—"

"I hope we're not here long enough for that to matter, but I get it." Owen examined the door and then the corridor leading away from it. "Did we just come from there? Then I guess we go this way."

The hall turned a corner, and Owen slowed his paces. "Well, look at that," he said. A flagstone in the middle of the hall had a big number 2 scratched deeply into it. "We've been here before."

"If we're right about how the teleportation traps work, that one will trigger when we step on it because it's the first one we've reached after passing another one," Isold said.

"I can't remember what led to this point, but I'd really like to know where that goes," Owen said, and walked onto it and disappeared.

Aderyn squeaked and hurried after him. The world shifted, and she threw herself at him. "Don't *do* that!"

"Now I really want to know what happened to me, because you're acting like you almost lost me," Owen said, taking her in his arms and kissing her. "It was perfectly safe. And look where we ended up."

The others were all passing into view, crowding the flagstone in front of a door that stood open. Beyond the door, brass walls shimmered in the indirect light from Livia's orbs. "The fire flower room!" Aderyn exclaimed.

"And now we have a link in the chain," Owen said. "The teleportation traps work in pairs. We stepped on this stone, and it took us to number two, and number two brought us back here. Is this number three?"

"Four," Aderyn said. "You missed a lot."

Owen's eyebrows rose, but he scratched a 4 in the stone with the **<Deadly Blade>**. "Let's keep going. I feel certain we're going to beat this thing."

They hurried faster now, barely watching for traps. The corridor twisted and turned like the intestine of some vile beast, an image Aderyn had trouble shaking. But it did feel like they'd been devoured and were desperately trying to find a place they could cut their way free through. She knew she was reaching the end of her endurance that the image didn't do more than leave her mildly nauseated.

"There's light ahead," Jessemia exclaimed. She and Weston were running at the head of the group now. "Natural light!"

"Stop!" Owen shouted. "This is where we need to be careful. If we're near the exit, this dungeon is going to do its best to stop us here. Everyone take a minute to calm down."

Aderyn took his hand for comfort. Owen glanced her way and smiled. "Too pessimistic?"

"No, just pessimistic enough. But... we could be so close!" Aderyn sighed. "I'm done with my optimism jag. We'll be stuck here forever."

"Try to find a happy medium, sweetheart." Owen kissed the back of her hand. "All right. We go in pairs, mostly. Weston and Jessemia, watch for traps. Livia, you keep an eye on our new friends. Aderyn and I will bring up the rear. And... good luck."

Aderyn hated being at the rear. She wanted to see the natural light Jessemia had mentioned. But if the dungeon was going to send something after them, something more dangerous than its many traps, their group needed strong fighters as that line of defense.

"The light's growing brighter," Weston said. "Another turn—"

His voice cut off. Aderyn's heart sank. Another teleportation trap. That was worse than a slicing blade—being so close to the exit and having it snatched away.

"Keep going," Owen said, his voice dull. So he'd been more optimistic than he seemed. The world blinked, and they were all in another of the endless corridors, staring at one another. Ehren and Calista looked near tears. Jessemia had an arm around Meladria's shoulders, comforting her. Livia leaned against the wall and ran her fingers up and down her stone arm, watching Weston pace and mutter to himself.

Owen bent and scratched a 5 on the flagstone. "Okay," he said. "That was the dungeon's second mistake."

All eyes focused on him. "Second mistake?" Aderyn said.

"That was the exit corridor, I'm sure of it," Owen said. He stamped his foot. "And *this* is how we get out. All we have to do is trigger another trap, one we know the location of, and come back here. The dungeon didn't reckon on anyone surviving this long and figuring out where the traps connect. It's going to regret not killing us."

"So what was the first mistake?" Livia asked.

"The first mistake," Owen said, "was luring us in here. Because we are going to tear this place apart before we leave."

A slow grin spread across Weston's face. "I like the sound of that."

"But we're just adventurers," Calista said. "It's a dungeon. You can't destroy a dungeon."

"No, but you can make it damned uncomfortable." Owen tilted his head back and shouted, "You hear me, Sorrowvale? We're done playing by your rules. And when we get out, we'll make sure no one ever comes here again."

Livia shouted something, and a blast of mud smeared the walls and floor. "Let's see what else I can do to mess this place up," she muttered. Another nonsense incantation, and her stone arm glowed with *stone fist*. "Which way are we going?"

"Doesn't matter," Owen said. "Why don't you lead the way?"

Livia took a swing at the wall that wasn't covered in mud and shattered an enormous dent in it. "I bet I can spell out BITE ME."

Calista giggled. The sound was so unexpected Aderyn laughed too.

They followed Livia down the hall as it went through the complicated turns they were all familiar with now. Despite how it slowed them, Livia's explosive lettering was a better boost than anything Aderyn could imagine. For the first time since entering Sorrowvale, Aderyn's heart lightened.

CHAPTER THIRTY-FIVE

They came around a corner into a long, long hallway, and stopped. Pale words quivered on both walls, moving with pent-up energy. "That could be bad," Weston said. "It might be more of those symbols that drove Owen mad."

"I was mad?"

"Not now, sweetheart." Aderyn squinted as if that would stop her going blind or insane from reading the symbols. Nothing happened. She realized Weston and Isold had moved forward. Then Isold waved to the others. "There's another trap here," he said. "Weston's looking for it."

Aderyn joined them. The lettering on the wall, in sentences scrawled well apart from each other and at different angles, read:

This trap will be your doom
You will never see it coming
It is in the last place you look
If you think you've found it, think again

All Aderyn's good cheer evaporated. The idea of an impossible-to-see trap took hold of her imagination. That was exactly the sort of thing Sorrowvale would take despicable pleasure in, watching adventurers search and search and still trigger the trap, which would do something horrible. "Maybe we should go the other way," she said.

"No," Owen declared. "No. This is the way out."

"I don't know, Owen," Weston said from where he was crouched on the ground. "I'm having trouble finding this one, and we can't risk setting it off."

"You can't find it because there's no trap," Owen said.

Everyone stared at him. Owen ran a hand over the shaky letters. "This is Sorrowvale's worst trick yet. It wants us to go crazy looking for something that isn't there and then give up and go back. I'm betting my life there's nothing there but the exit."

"It's too dark," Jessemia said. "It can't be."

"Then there's a door. Or a teleportation trap that takes us to the exit. But I'm certain of it." Owen reached out a hand to Aderyn. "You want to risk it with me?"

Aderyn clasped his hand and nodded. She wasn't convinced, but she'd reached the end of what she could bear. Dying with Owen had to be better than living this half-life of terror.

"We'll be back," Owen promised, and led Aderyn down the hall.

The warning messages grew thicker as they proceeded until their strange white glow illuminated the flagstones. Then they disappeared. Owen stopped. "Everyone all right?"

"We're here," Livia shouted.

"We're past the warnings, and I realized if there's a teleportation trap, we won't be able to come back for you. Come on up. It's fine." Owen squeezed Aderyn's hand reassuringly.

In a little while, they heard the shuffling of feet, and Livia's lights came around the corner, followed by the others. Weston was swearing under his breath. "Stupid dungeon," he muttered.

"Stay close. I know we're near," Owen said.

The corridor made a few turns, but not so wildly as it had before, as if the dungeon was giving up. Aderyn didn't let this lull her into security. Sorrowvale might still have tricks in the walls.

The world flickered. And there was daylight.

Aderyn let out a hiss of breath. Owen, still holding her hand, gripped it tighter in warning. "Don't move, everyone," he said. There were two passages in front of them, both lit by natural light, neither with an obvious exit. "One of these is the wrong one."

"That's the wrong one," Jessemia said, pointing. "It's the hall we were in before, the one we thought led to the exit. We're on the other side of the teleportation trap."

"Are you sure? They look identical to me," Livia said.

"I'm certain. We have to go the other way." Jessemia looked as mad as Owen had, her hair a tangled wreck, her face smudged, one sleeve of her shirt torn. She also looked utterly convinced.

"Then that's where we go," Owen said. "Form up around me, and—run!"

They ran, turned a corner, ran again. The light ahead grew brighter. A roar as of a thousand winds shattered the stillness, drowning out the sound of their heavy breathing and their boots on the flagstones. Aderyn didn't look back. Seeing what made that sound might get them all killed. She heard running footsteps, lighter than their own, and a low, guttural laugh that made her bones weak, but she kept running, because she would not give up—

She burst through an opening into daylight and a grassy hill and stumbled onward a few dozen steps before she dared to look back. An enormous toothy mouth made a hole in the side of the hill, widening and lunging for Jessemia, who was at the back of the group urging Meladria to run faster. Aderyn screamed and raced for her, but she was too far away. She would be too late.

Jessemia flung herself forward. The sides of the hill reared up, and the mouth dropped away into a pit that roared and surged over it. A terrible scream echoed across the hills—and then all was silent. Where the mouth had been, a new hill rose, gently sloping toward the round door set into the earth.

**Congratulations! You have defeated [Sorrowvale].
You have earned [35,000 XP]**

Aderyn collapsed to sit bonelessly in front of the door. "We beat it," she whispered. "But it's still there."

"Like thunder it is," Livia snarled. "Everyone back up." She took a wrestler's stance in front of the door, bowed her head, and began speaking in a low voice. Her words grew in volume as she continued with a string of words that almost made sense.

As they grew louder, the earth trembled, knocking Calista into Ehren and making Aderyn throw out her hands to keep her balance. The ground in front of Livia rose, burying the round door like folding a trinket away into a handkerchief. It continued to shift and flatten until nothing remained of the entrance to Sorrowvale but a plain of grassless earth. The earth let out a sound like a burp, and once more, all was still.

Aderyn got wearily to her feet and reached for Owen. "Is that enough? I can't bear the thought of others stumbling onto this place. You know even if we spread the word, there will be adventurers who think they're immortal and better than it."

**Congratulations! You have destroyed the evil dungeon
[Sorrowvale].
You have received a one-time bonus of [25,000 XP]**

"I guess that's a yes," Owen said.

Thank you.

Everyone froze. "Did you—" Weston said.

"Yes," Aderyn said firmly. "And I'm not going to look too closely at it. We did something impossible, and I don't care how much experience we got, as far as I'm concerned getting out alive was the real reward."

She saw the looks on Calista and Ehren's faces and said, "Oh. I'm sorry."

"No, we agree," Ehren said. "We were stupid, and some of us paid for it with our lives. The others wouldn't begrudge us our gratitude for living when they died."

"I'm glad you can see it that way," Owen said. "Come on. We deserve a rest, far away from this place."

"I'm grateful for our lives, too," Isold said, "but if you don't mind, I think I won't tell this story, not for a long time."

Aderyn didn't know how long they'd been in Sorrowvale, but by the sun, it was midmorning. They made camp anyway, half a mile from the destruction. Livia set up five tents, the most the <**Soldier's Friend**> could manage without producing enough for an army, but Jessemia invited Calista and Meladria to join her, and five became enough.

Aderyn sat by the fire, resting her chin on her knees. She brought up the Codex and whispered, "Advancement."

Name: Aderyn

Level: 13

Class: Warmaster

Skills: Bluff (9), Climb (9), Conversation (12), Intimidate (7), Sense Truth (14), Survival (7), Swim (1), Knowledge: Monsters (9), Knowledge: World Lore (3), Knowledge: Demons (1)

Class Skills: Improved Assess 2 (21), Awareness (14), Knowledge: Geography (9), Spot (13), Discern Weakness (20), Dodge (12), Improvised Distraction (12), Outflank (16), Draw Fire (7), Keep Pace (15), Amplify Voice (11), See It Coming (12), Basic Weapon Proficiency (Swords) (9), Read Body Language (7), Basic Map Access (3), Compel (6), Spot Weakness (2), Secret Message (0)

She focused on [Secret Message] to see what more she could learn.

[Secret Message]: Conveys one message privately to one person under cover of another message.

Aderyn drew in a quick breath. How useful! Or at least it would be if she had any idea how to use the skill. Sometimes she was impatient with how obtuse [Improved Assess 2] could be.

Owen settled beside her and put his arm low around her waist, drawing her close. "You look angry. Something wrong?"

Aderyn shook her head. "Not really. Nothing rational. It's just— my ranks in [Improved Assess 2] are much higher than my other skills, as high as your weapons skill. And yet I couldn't see through Sorrowvale's illusion."

"Ah." Owen rested his head on her shoulder briefly. "Can I offer you a different perspective?"

"What's that?" She didn't really want to be comforted, but that was a stupid, self-indulgent desire.

"Two things. One, I think Sorrowvale was skilled at deceiving even high-level adventurers. Meaning it actively took steps to conceal what it was. You remember Jedrek the Diabolist was the same—he'd had years to learn how to cover his true identity. That's two times in I don't know how many instances where your skill has failed you, and both times it took active malice to defeat you."

That did make Aderyn feel better. "What's the second thing?"

Owen nodded across the fire to where Calista and Ehren sat talking. Neither of them looked cheerful, but they didn't look despondent either. "If you had seen Sorrowvale's true identity, we wouldn't have gone in, and those three would have died there. So your failure, if you insist on calling it that, saved three lives."

"Oh," Aderyn said, feeling awkward. "I hadn't thought of that." Her guilt and anger faded. "You mean it's better to look at the outcome than dwell on the mistakes that led there?"

Owen laughed. "That's one way to put it. I was actually thinking if you keep moping, I'll have to take drastic measures to cheer you up, and you know these tents aren't soundproof."

That dispelled the last of her bad mood. "What if that's what I want?"

"I was going to do it anyway, don't worry."

Aderyn laughed. "Oh, Owen. I was so scared for you."

He took her hand. "You said I was insane. What happened? Did I hurt anyone?"

She put her other hand over their joined ones. "It was a very peaceful kind of madness. You mostly just talked nonsense. But you weren't connected to reality at all, and you nearly got yourself killed by that scything blade trap, and we had to watch you constantly—it was terrifying to be without you, as a leader or as my sweetheart. Especially since *dispel magic* didn't work and we didn't know if your condition was permanent." She discovered tears were welling up and she swiped a hand across her eyes.

Owen drew her into his embrace and held her tightly. "I'm so sorry. I don't remember any of that, just seeing lines swell up out of the stones and then sitting across from Isold. Maybe it's just as well. I don't think I could bear remembering treating you like a stranger."

"It's over," Aderyn said. "And, as you like to say, we move on."

"We move on," Owen agreed. "And I was only partly kidding about sex tonight. I don't like everyone knowing what we're doing, and sound carries an awfully long way on the plains, but I'd like to have something better to think about than those endless dark corridors."

"Hold me tonight, and it will be enough," Aderyn said.

CHAPTER THIRTY-SIX

Traveling to Derry, the next village on their route, meant four days' journey through monster-infested lands. Aderyn welcomed the attacks. They gave her something better to think about than the dark, horrible halls of Sorrowvale. She thought the others felt the same by how enthusiastically her team went on the attack. Killing creatures who were trying to disembowel them was unexpectedly soul-cleansing.

Meladria, Calista, and Ehren stayed out of the way the first few battles, which was a relief. Aderyn couldn't bear the thought of any of them being hurt or killed after everything they'd been through. She wished *transport* was long-range enough to get them back to civilization... though if it could do that, they'd all be in Guerdon Deep already, or worse, have bypassed Sorrowvale and left the three adventurers behind.

But on the evening after they'd fought a bevy of cockatrices, a couple of hulking horrors, and a trio of wylding wolves, when they were sitting around the fire, Jessemia said, "Calista, why don't you and Ehren join us in fighting monsters?"

Calista shook her head. "They're all too high-level. It's better we not get in the way."

"You won't be in the way if you're careful. Maybe not wylding wolves, but we could have isolated some of the cockatrices for you to kill, and hulking horrors are just the right level for you."

The Swordsworn woman reddened. "We don't want pity."

Jessemia scowled. "It's not pity, it's helping you gain experience. I bet you could be level six when we get back to Guerdon Deep, and that will make you more independent."

"She's not wrong," Owen said. "We've been teaching Jessemia fighting skills for the past few weeks, and she's leveled twice."

Ehren and Meladria exchanged glances. "Isn't she part of your team?"

"Well," Owen began.

"I had a bad start to my adventuring career," Jessemia interrupted. "I thought I should gain levels quickly, so I teamed with adventurers much higher than myself so I would get a lot of experience when they killed monsters I couldn't fight. I don't want to fall into that trap again. So no, we're not teammates."

"I've never heard of anyone doing that," Meladria said.

"That's because it's a terrible idea." Jessemia picked up a long, thin twig and snapped it in half, then broke the pieces in half again. "It's how I know the difference between trying to cheat the system and getting legitimate help from... from friends." She gazed into the fire, clearly unwilling to look at Aderyn or Owen.

Owen cleared his throat. "It's true, there's nothing wrong with being guided at lower levels. You would do your own killing, earn your own experience."

"I think you'd feel more confident, too," Jessemia said.

Calista bit her lip in thought. "All right," she said. "If you team with us."

"What?" Jessemia paused in breaking more twigs. "Me?"

"You're only three levels higher than we are. That's within the allowed range. And then, if you help us, you'll gain experience too." Calista sounded more certain the longer she talked.

Jessemia looked at Owen. "Should I?"

"That's up to you," Owen said. "It's not a terrible idea."

"I—" Jessemia turned to Aderyn. "I'm not sure I know enough."

"Your skills are as high as a level eight Pathseer's should be," Aderyn said. "Higher, in some cases. And you know the tactics I've shown you."

"But—" Jessemia's jaw firmed. "All right."

Her eyes glazed over, and she made the gesture in front of her face that said she was accepting the invitation to join an adventuring team. Calista smiled. Ehren clapped Jessemia on the shoulder. "Thank you," he said. "It feels right. Like we're moving forward again instead of stagnating in grief."

"I was thinking," Meladria said. She rarely spoke, and when she did, it was in a thin voice Aderyn had to strain to hear. "None of you wear enchanted armor. I could do something about that. Not much, because I've only had the skill for a few months, and it can't begin to repay you for saving our lives, but it would be a boost."

"We would love that, Meladria," Aderyn said.

Livia checked the kettle and started pouring water over blackberry tea leaves to steep. "We ought to have something to drink to all these resolutions, but there's no wine, so tea will have to do."

Weston joined her in passing mugs around. "Isold," he said, "I think we could do with some music."

Isold nodded. "I haven't felt much like singing, not since Sorrowvale. It's as if it cast a spell over me, something dark that took my desire to make music. But tonight I think I can manage something."

He set his mug aside and broke into a cheerful, lilting song about a girl and the boy she loved and how they defied his father to be together. Aderyn leaned against Owen and closed her eyes to let the music wash over her. For once, the images of Sorrowvale's victims that had tormented her were gone.

Isold finished his song and immediately went into something more melancholy. Its tune was heartrendingly sad, but to her surprise Aderyn found she welcomed the sadness. She felt scoured clean, empty of everything but that wonderful ache. Somehow it made her think of her family, of her parents and her siblings and her grandfather Marrius. She touched the **<Purse of Great Capacity>**, though she couldn't feel the **<Wayfinder>** through it. The idea of it bringing her family back together threaded through Isold's song until despite the sadness she felt hopeful and at peace.

She noticed Calista, who sat next to Isold, was crying, and for a moment her sadness became more personal. Calista had lost her sweetheart and her best friend in the most horrible way possible, and yet she hadn't given up on life. Aderyn hoped Isold's song could bring the woman peace.

At the end of the song, silence fell over the camp. Finally, Calista said, "You have a marvelous gift. More than just being a Herald."

"Thank you." Isold clasped her hand briefly. "I like to think my music brings joy to others regardless of my class."

"It does." Calista let out a deep breath. "I think I'll go to sleep now. Maybe this time I won't dream." She rose and ducked into the tent she shared with Jessemia and Meladria.

"*I wish she could sleep with Isold,*" Aderyn said to Owen. She clapped a hand over her mouth. How could she be so insensitive?

Except... she hadn't said that. She'd said, "I hope she sleeps peacefully," and the other thing had just been in her head. Or not. She was sure she'd heard both phrases come out of her mouth at the same time.

Owen was looking at her strangely. "I agree," he said. "And I think I'm ready for sleep now, too. Good night, everyone." He gave Aderyn his hand, and they entered their own tent.

The moment the tent flap fell, Owen said in a low voice, "What was that about Calista sleeping with Isold?"

"You heard that?"

"Sort of. You said something about her sleeping well, but it was like you also whispered something else to me at the same time."

Aderyn hesitated. "I think that's my skill **[Secret Message]**. I've thought about it since we leveled to thirteen, but I couldn't figure out how it worked. I guess that's it." She stripped down to the shift and drawers she wore to sleep in. "I wonder if it only works on you?"

"You can test it in the morning. For now—" Owen pulled his shirt off over his head. "It's been a long day, and I could use some sleep before my turn at watch. But—come here." He drew her into his arms and kissed her. "Calista's not the only one who's been having nightmares. I keep dreaming of that room with all the people trapped in the walls, and having to walk through it without them touching me, except in the dream they're still alive and moving."

"I'm so glad we destroyed Sorrowvale. Eventually we'll stop remembering it so clearly." She kissed him in return, running her hands over the smooth skin of his back and shoulders. "And I do wish Calista could sleep with Isold. I think it would help. Except I don't know if I could do that only three days after your death, so it's unlikely."

"I hope I'm not that forgettable," Owen smiled.

DERRY WAS A TINY VILLAGE, SMALLER THAN PLENSHOLT, with no inn and no quests available. They ate a good meal, resupplied, and camped outside the village wall. That night, as Aderyn made her watch rounds, she checked each tent as was her habit. She felt superstitious about not making sure all her friends were where they should be. She was about to look into Isold's tent when she heard the murmur of two voices from within. She smiled when she recognized Calista's voice.

After two days of uneventful travel, at midafternoon on the third day Weston, who walked point, called out, "There's a small herd of frill-throat lizards off to the north. Isold, didn't you say those monsters were good for something?"

"They have glands beneath their frills that secrete an oil used by Spellcrafters and Spiritsmiths in their work," Isold said. "It's moderately valuable, though as we have a Spellcrafter with us, she might find it more immediately worthwhile."

"I can use it to add a minor glamour to your weapons," Meladria said. "Something to confuse an enemy's eye, make the weapon appear blurry so they don't know where the next strike comes from."

"I like the sound of that," Owen said. "How many are there, Weston?"

"Looks like seven or eight. They haven't noticed us."

"Do they hunt by sight or by smell?" Livia asked.

"By sight, mostly," Isold said. "We're downwind of them, so we have the advantage."

"I can give us a better one," Livia said. "Everyone huddle round."

They clustered around Livia, who clasped her hands at chest level and threw back her shoulders. "My new sixth-level spell is invisibility for a group. We have to stay close together—all right, maybe not that close," she added as they pressed in around her. "The effect radiates out from me, but I don't know how we look to ourselves. This is a good time to test the spell, when we're facing lower-level monsters." She closed her eyes, chanted a few nonsense words, and threw her hands apart like casting away a handful of sand.

The air rippled like it was water flowing over river stones, an effect that spread outward from Livia until the ripples faded to nothing about ten feet from her in every direction. Livia opened her eyes. "Pay attention to the... I guess it's thickness in the air. Like the air is jelly. Outside that, you're not invisible. And it lasts for about three minutes."

"Sounds good," Owen said. "Let's move quickly."

They crossed the plains at a running jog, then slowed as they neared the herd of lizards. Aderyn counted seven. When they weren't going faster than a slow walk, she Assessed the nearest one.

Name: Frill-Throat Lizard
Type: Magical beast
Power Level: 4
Attack: raking claw x2, tail slap, special
Immune to: none
Resistant to: none
Vulnerable to: none
Special attack: spit (contact poison)
The frill-throat lizard is native to plains and deserts. They are territorial and non-aggressive unless invaded, in which circumstance they will fight to the death to protect their young. Although they are four-footed, they can run very fast on their hind legs. Their spit is a mildly toxic contact poison whose effects intensify over time, going from dizziness to disorientation to the kind of confusion that makes you unable to distinguish friends from enemies. Don't let them spit on you unless you don't like your teammates very much.

"They'll attack us as soon as they know we're in their territory, so watch out for their claws and tail attacks," she told the others in a low voice, though the wind had picked up and was sweeping her words well away from the monsters. "If their spit gets on your skin, wash it off immediately. Have Livia do it if you're close enough."

She examined the way the herd stood and continued, "Jessemia, have your team circle around to the west and cut off the two lizards there. The rest of us, see if we can drive wedges between the other five. If they can get back to back, they'll have a defensive advantage."

"Got it," Owen said. "Everyone ready? Then—go!"

CHAPTER THIRTY-SEVEN

As they moved under cover of illusion, the frill-throat lizards continued to graze peacefully, without showing any sign they knew they were in danger. Then the leading edge of the *invisibility* effect hit them, and they turned, startled, to face the threat. Isold broke into a battle song, and the two groups clashed.

Aderyn ran next to Owen, maintaining her position with [**Keep Pace**] until they neared their target, when she dropped back to let Owen get into place for [**Outflank**]. The frill-throat lizard reared up, screaming a challenge in a voice like a whistling roar. The lace-edged frills on either side of its neck flared out, fiery orange in sharp contrast to its pebbly dun-colored hide, and it opened its mouth to spit.

Aderyn lunged for its unprotected back, though [**Discern Weakness**] had revealed its vulnerable spots to be its belly and throat. She scored a line across its shoulders, making it screech in rage and spin around to attack her. With a quick thrust, she stabbed its belly, and blood poured from the wound. She stepped back just in time to avoid being sprayed with more blood as Owen's sword took its head neatly off.

**Congratulations! You have defeated [Frill-Throat Lizard].
You have earned [300 XP]**

A few seconds later, another system defeat notice popped up. Owen was already moving on to the next target. Aderyn followed, swiping at the next monster's feet to throw it off balance so Owen could skewer it. Again, the system notice flashed.

Aderyn took a moment to survey the battle. Off to the west, Jessemia and her team had surrounded one of the lizards and were slashing at it. Jessemia had paid attention to Aderyn's tactics lessons and was herding the lizard so Calista and Ehren could attack it. As Aderyn watched, the lizard spat a line of gooey saliva that struck Ehren in the face, and then the lizard fell. Jessemia was already fending off the second of their enemies, shouting something Aderyn was too far away to hear.

"Aderyn! Come on!" Owen shouted.

Another system message appeared as Aderyn ran past Weston and Livia, who stood over a bloody body from which a number of iron spikes protruded. Then she and Owen engaged with another of the monsters. This one was bigger than the others and more canny, refusing to be trapped by **[Outflank]**, darting in on its hind legs to strike them with its tail or rake with its claws. One of those rake attacks scored Owen's hardened leather brigandine, but the magic Meladria had imbued it with made the marks seal up after only a few seconds.

[See It Coming] showed Aderyn the monster's tail swinging toward her, but the tail was moving fast enough it clipped Aderyn's shoulder as she dove out of the way. Pain shot down her chest as bone cracked. She lay on her back with the wind knocked out of her, sucking in air and hoping she wasn't about to be trampled.

**Congratulations! You have defeated [Frill-Throat Lizard].
You have earned [300 XP]**

Owen was at her side in the next instant, kneeling and reaching out a hand to help her up. "Are you hurt?"

"Snapped my collarbone, I think." She sat up carefully and tried not to move that side of her body. "Is that all of them?"

Owen nodded. "Jessemia's team just finished their second one off, and I hear they reached level six. So it was a good fight all around. Actually, why don't you sit here, and I'll bring Isold to you."

The healing didn't take long, and when Aderyn wasn't in pain anymore, she got up and hurried to join the others. Ehren was soaking wet, but cheerful. "The spit poison felt like the beginnings of being drunk," he was telling Weston. "Probably would have been less fun the longer it went on."

"Still, as an alternative to drinking," Weston said.

"Don't even think it," Livia warned him. "Nobody's going to be interested in being spat on just to get blissed out."

"And we're level six!" Calista exclaimed. "I had no idea we were so close."

"Meladria, if you wouldn't mind helping me," Isold said. "Harvesting monster parts is a specialization of your [**Knowledge: Monsters**] skill."

"I'm afraid I haven't used it often," Meladria confessed. "We haven't killed many monsters with usable parts."

"Then you'll get practice now," Isold said. "This shouldn't take long, Owen, and then we can move on."

Aderyn joined Jessemia, who stood to one side of the group. The Pathseer looked unusually pensive. "Something wrong?" Aderyn asked.

Jessemia shook her head. "It's just so strange. Six weeks ago I was a completely different person, and yet she's still me. Or was me. I mean, I hate remembering how awful I was, but if I forget, I might end up that way again."

"That's not going to happen," Aderyn said. "How did it feel, leading a team?"

Startled, Jessemia said, "Was that what I did? I guess you're right. I hadn't thought about it that way, just that I was helping them gain experience."

"You showed them what to do, and you made sure none of them were in more danger than they could handle. And you knew how to bring out the best in them. That's being a leader."

"Huh." Jessemia fell silent for a moment. Then she said, "I feel like I owe you a greater debt every day."

"It's not about owing," Aderyn said. "It's what friends do for each other."

Jessemia reddened. "And we're friends?"

"I think so. Don't you?"

Jessemia nodded. "I wouldn't have guessed it. Not with how we began."

"People don't have to stay the same their whole lives," Aderyn said. "I always believed that about you."

Jessemia nodded again. Then she hugged Aderyn, who was surprised but hugged her back. "Thank you. Again."

"You're welcome," Aderyn said. "You want to go watch Isold and Meladria harvest disgusting oil glands? We could help wrap them, or whatever the harvesting requires."

"I guess that's what friends do for each other, too," Jessemia said.

THEY STARTED COMING ACROSS PATCHES OF FOREST TWO days from Setter's Valley, at the tops and bottoms of the hills that were the precursor to the Welterwall's foothills. Aderyn hadn't realized how much she liked forests until she'd spent weeks on the plains. Yes, they were often full of monsters, and she didn't want to be so complacent she ignored that threat, but the smell of the pines and cedars and the cool shade of their branches cheered her.

Despite her fears, they only encountered monsters three times in those days, most of them easy to defeat. They'd fallen into a pattern over the days since Jessemia had joined the other team: Aderyn Assessed the threat and analyzed the tactical situation, directing each team to positions where they could do the most damage, and then Owen's team rushed in, distracting the monsters so Jessemia's team could pick off any stragglers.

At midmorning on the third day, they came out of the trees at the top of a hill to find a wide valley spread out below. Filling most of the valley at this end was a town big enough to be called a city, its many three-story buildings roofed with wooden shingles that absorbed the sunlight dully. Its low wall wasn't more than a token, but it was sturdily built of stone the builders had probably hauled all the way from the mountains.

Outside the walls, extending to the northern horizon, were fields of grain golden with the end of summer and little houses with thatch roofs like the ones Aderyn remembered from her childhood home. Aderyn liked the look of the place. It represented the beginnings of civilization. Not that she didn't love the wilderness, but it was like anything else: she enjoyed a change.

Beside her, Owen stopped to look out over the valley. "Is that a town, or a city?" he asked.

"Oh! I was so busy admiring the view I forgot." She Assessed Setter's Valley.

Name: Setter's Valley
Status: City
Government: Limited-term monarchy
Civilization level: 10
Resources: Spiritsmith x1, Tidecaller x2, Windwarden x3, Flamecrafter x1, Earthbreaker x3, Bonemender x3; Crafters level 9; Hospitality level 10; Food supply level 10
Setter's Valley was founded by men and women from Guerdon Deep, led by a Swifthands called Setter, wishing to take advantage of proximity to the Welterwall Mountains and

to establish a farming community as well. **The city is the last stopping place before embarking on the overland journey to Obsidian, and as such caters to adventurers, many of whom prefer it to Guerdon Deep's less outwardly-pleasing environment. Quests are plentiful, and monsters thrive outside the radius of Setter's Valley's protective field. In all, a very nice rest stop, which is saying something.**

Aderyn read this off to Owen, who snorted with laughter. "It sounds like a travel brochure. Something a city produces to tell everyone how great it is."

"Yes, the system does sound enthusiastic about the place. Usually it's pessimistic about the city's dangers or benefits. Like Obsidian."

"What's like Obsidian?" Jessemia asked as she approached.

"Just saying that **[Improved Assess 2]** didn't have flattering things to say about it. Excited to sleep in a real bed?"

"Always. I'm sure that makes me a terrible adventurer." Jessemia stretched. "Though really—no."

"Really, what?" Aderyn asked.

"It's silly, but I think what I'd like is to do city quests for a while. Fighting monsters is bracing, and it's not like I dislike that, it's just that helping people directly appeals to me."

"I don't think that's silly," Owen said. "You'd be like a private investigator. That's someone who people hire to solve crimes or learn secrets, except you'd solve their problems in the form of taking quests."

Jessemia nodded. "I've been thinking about what I'm going to do when we reach Guerdon Deep and leave this team. I don't know how to find a new one. Papa always did that."

"We'll help," Aderyn said. "There are probably any number of adventuring teams in Guerdon Deep, and some of them will have room on their team roster."

"It's still a little daunting, but it will all work out." Jessemia smiled. "But for now, we can stop in Setter's Valley and have a real meal and possibly a bath. I feel like I've been in the wilderness for months."

She walked ahead down the hill. When she was out of earshot, Aderyn said, "I feel strange about going to Guerdon Deep now."

"You mean because she's no longer a burden?" Owen headed down the hill after Jessemia, with Aderyn at his side. "Yeah. It feels like getting experience under false pretenses. But we did complete the quest. Or will have in a couple of days."

"I know, but it still feels like cheating."

Isold came up beside them. "We are staying here overnight, yes? Not just stopping in? Because it sounds like Calista and the others are considering remaining here."

"I thought they wanted to make it to Guerdon Deep," Owen said.

"Calista told me they want to rest here for a few days and didn't think we should have to wait on them."

"Did she," Aderyn said with a wink.

Isold smiled. "One time," he said. "She needed comfort, and I was happy to provide it. But she's still mourning Andrus, and I don't take advantage of grieving women."

"Isold, you may be the nicest person I know," Owen said.

"You must not know many people," Isold said. "At any rate, they want to pay for supper, as a thank-you—though Ehren said of course there's nothing that really thanks someone for saving your life. But I think it's a nice gesture. Comradely."

"I agree. We'll stay the night. Jessemia suggested baths, which is a great idea considering how ripe we all are."

Isold nodded. "And speaking of Jessemia, what are we going to do?"

"You mean about the [Escort the Spoiled Darling] quest," Owen replied.

"I do. It seems wrong to complete it now, even though it wouldn't hurt her." Isold looked pensive. "Maybe we should discuss it privately. If we abandon that quest, everyone should be in agreement about the loss of experience."

"We'll do that this afternoon." Owen looked as thoughtful as Isold. "It's so strange to think how much she's changed. I didn't believe it was possible."

"Aderyn did," Isold said. "Maybe that belief mattered."

"Well, that and being captured and threatened by Brigands," Aderyn said. She felt uncomfortable at the turn the conversation had taken, as if she was being given credit for more than she'd done. Jessemia had been the one to change herself.

Chapter Thirty-Eight

They gathered at the city gate, which rose well above head height but wasn't nearly so tall and intimidating as Obsidian's. No guards stood outside the wall, waiting to challenge visitors; the gate simply swung open, revealing a man and a woman in leather armor carrying pikes. "Welcome to Setter's Valley," the man said in a friendly tone. "Have you visited before?"

Owen and Aderyn exchanged looks. "No," Owen said.

"Well, we're glad to have you. Don't start fights or we'll kick you out. There are plenty of inns and taverns you'll find hospitable, as well as two houses of negotiable affection—"

"He means brothels," the woman said.

"That sounds so low-class," the man replied. "There are also many craftsmen and armorers and smiths to attend to your adventuring needs. If you're looking for directions, ask anyone wearing a yellow tabard—they'll be happy to help."

"Um, thank you," Owen said, sounding bewildered. "What's the entrance fee?"

"We don't charge for entry," the woman said. "Adventurers spend enough money here it's redundant. Any other questions?"

"*We need to get out of here before I say something stupid,*" Aderyn said, though what came out of her mouth was "That sounds lovely, thank you so much."

The two guards stood aside, and the friends entered Setter's Valley.

Aderyn had forgotten how loud cities were. The streets were thronged with people talking, laughing, bargaining, shouting to friends, and even singing—there was a Herald standing outside a building with a sign depicting a foaming tankard, playing a lute and singing a cheerful song. After the quiet and solitude of the wilderness, it was also almost overwhelming. Aderyn found she was walking closer to Owen out of discomfort.

"I'm glad we're staying overnight," she murmured. "Guerdon Deep will be worse. This will help me get used to the noise."

"I heard your secret message," Owen said. "You still haven't tried it with anyone else, right?"

"I keep forgetting because we don't talk much while we're walking. I should experiment today, when we're in a safe place I won't startle my friends." Aderyn noted a woman in a yellow tabard walking ahead of them. "Should we see what information that woman has?"

"I've never been anywhere in this world more like a city in a MMORPG," Owen confessed. "She just needs a question mark floating over her head for the illusion to be complete."

"That yellow tabard is blinding. I don't think she needs a floating question mark."

Aderyn Assessed the woman as they approached and was surprised to discover she was non-classed.

Name: Betanna

Traits: helpful, loyal, friendly, intelligent

"Hi," Owen said. "We were told we could ask questions?"

"Of course," Betanna said with a smile. "Can I direct you somewhere?" Her smile was a trifle forced, and she looked like she was trying not to wrinkle her nose. Aderyn hadn't thought they smelled that bad.

Owen seemed to see it too. "Bath house, and an inn. Better if they're the same place."

The smile became less rigid. "Of course, sir. What quality of accommodations?"

"Mid-range? Not a dive, but not the most luxurious either."

Betanna's eyes glazed over a bit at the word "dive," but she got it from context, because she said without hesitation, "Traveler's Repose will meet your needs perfectly. The bath house on the premises is well-appointed, and they provide one meal per day free of charge to patrons. If they're full, you might try the Golden Apple, which is farther from the city center if you prefer a quieter stay." She then rattled off directions Aderyn didn't follow past the first two turns, but Isold nodded like he was marking the locations off on his system map.

They thanked Betanna and, following Isold, made their way to the Traveler's Repose. It was smaller than Aderyn expected, with a stable yard big enough for only a handful of horses, but flowers grew in boxes at all the ground floor windows, and the smell of roast beef coming from somewhere inside tantalized her senses.

While they waited outside for Owen and Isold to negotiate for rooms, Aderyn said, "Livia, I want to try a new skill on you."

Livia eyed her skeptically. "Is this the kind of skill that makes me do something embarrassing?"

"Why would it do that?"

"I don't know. 'Try a new skill on you' sounds ominous."

"It's not bad. Just tell me what you hear." Aderyn concentrated. So far, she'd only once used **[Secret Message]** intentionally, and she wasn't as confident as she liked. "*This city is strange,*" she said, and in her public voice said, "I hope the inn isn't too costly."

Livia's eyes widened. "How—all right, it's stupid to ask someone

how they make their skills work. As well expect me to explain
[Tremorsense]."

"What did she do?" Jessemia asked.

"Let's see if it works on someone I'm not teamed with," Aderyn
said. "*You're going to do fine in Guerdon Deep*/I want first crack at the
bath house."

Jessemia looked as startled as Livia. "What *was* that?"

"**[Secret Message]**." Aderyn's excitement grew. How was this
not the most useful skill ever? All right, except for **[Outflank]**, and
[See It Coming] had saved her life and her friends' lives many times...
she had the most amazing range of skills. Too bad most Warmasters
never got this far. She refused to dwell on that melancholy thought.

Owen came outside and beckoned to them all to join him.
"We've got enough rooms for all of us, though Isold will bunk with
Ehren and the women will have to decide who shares. One big bed
per room."

"Fine by me," Ehren said. "Shall we dice for the bath house?"

Everyone groaned. Ehren's love of dice games was by now well
known to all of them. "I'd say you use loaded dice if I hadn't tested
them myself," Weston said. "But it is a fair way to figure it out."

Aderyn managed not to act elated when she won the toss. "I
promise to make it quick," she said.

Weston, who'd won the right to the other bath house, said, "I
don't. I plan to soak for a while."

"That's probably just as well. You're whiffy," Livia said, ostentatiously pinching her nose.

"That's not what you said last night."

"I was being polite. You're ripe as a skunk, dearest."

"Let's go, and save the friendly squabble for later," Aderyn said,
grabbing Weston by the arm and hauling him away.

She scrubbed herself and her hair clean and, true to her word,
only soaked in the gloriously large tub for five minutes. It was

enough to relax her. When she emerged, Jessemia was waiting in the hall. "Sorry, I'm impatient," the woman said. "I feel like I need to shed my skin."

"Enjoy," Aderyn said.

She found the others seated at two tables in the tap room and dropped into a seat by Owen with a sigh. "I feel human again," she said, pulling a hairbrush out of the [Knapsack of Plenty] and working it through her wet, tangled hair.

"Mmm. You smell nice, too," Owen said, kissing her cheek.

"It's too early for food, but the innkeeper doesn't care if paying guests wait here," Livia said.

Aderyn's stomach didn't agree with Livia, but she had self-control. Besides, Owen had ordered her a drink, and the light brew eased the ache of hunger.

She sat back, brushing her hair, and idly surveyed the room. Only a few tables were occupied, all of them by people dressed in the haphazard assortment of clothes and armor that said they were mid-level adventurers, experienced enough to have good gear, but not wealthy enough for it all to match. People just like Aderyn and her team, in fact. Each little group was intent on its own business, to judge by the quiet conversations and lack of loud laughter.

She amused herself making up stories about each one without Assessing them: that group of three Stalwarts was looking for work as caravan guards, the five in the corner were planning a trip to Obsidian where they would pick the wrong faction and get entangled in Obsidian politics, the Swordsworn and Staffsworn were a married couple who were looking to fill out their team...

As she thought this, the Swordsworn woman caught her eye. Aderyn suppressed a blush and nodded politely before turning her attention back to her ale. She hadn't been doing anything wrong, but it was embarrassing to draw the woman's attention after making up a story that probably wasn't true. It was like Aderyn meant to lie about her, which was an irrational thought, but Aderyn was still embarrassed.

She saw the Swordsworn and the Staffsworn were coming their way just as Owen said, "Aderyn, is something wrong?" and she realized she'd conveyed her discomfort to her partner with [**Read Body Language**].

"It's nothing," she said. "Just my imagination."

"Huh. Well, all right—sorry, can we help you with something?" The last was addressed to the Staffsworn, who had come to a stop next to Ehren's chair.

"Not you," the Staffsworn said. "These fellows here. Level six, yes?"

That behavior verged on rude, letting people know you'd Assessed them without giving them the opportunity to introduce themselves first. Aderyn quickly Level Assessed the pair.

Name: Junio
∞ **Renella**
Class: Staffsworn
Level: 10

NAME: RENELLA
∞ **Junio**
Class: Swordsworn
Level: 10

"We are," Ehren said. "And we haven't been introduced."

"Sorry," Junio said. "I'm Junio and this is my wife Renella. We're currently working alone and we have a proposition for you."

"You can't want to team with us. Not at your level," Calista said.

"No. We're talking about a quest," Renella said. She was soft-spoken and had delicate features like Calista, but lines drew down the corners of her mouth so she looked cranky.

Ehren glanced at Meladria. "A quest?"

"We're in the middle of a quest chain that will provide us with a sizable amount of money, which we need to retire," Junio said. "But with just the two of us, it will take forever to complete all the quests. We want to pass one or maybe two of the quests off to another team."

"Is that possible?" Calista said.

"Why don't you have a seat, and explain further," Owen said.

Junio eyed him. "What are you, their boss?"

"A friend who doesn't want to see them exploited," Owen said. He sounded friendly, but Aderyn heard the steel edge to his words.

"It's not exploitation," Renella said. "This particular quest is to retrieve something. Harvest it from a certain monster. We saw you —" She nodded at Meladria— "are a Spellcrafter, which means you have the knowledge to do that. Knowledge we lack."

"So killing the monster isn't the goal of the quest," Aderyn said.

"Right. We need the item as part of a different quest." Renella turned to Ehren. "What we propose is simple. You accept the quest, kill the monster, and bring us the item. You'll get the experience for the quest, plus we'll compensate you for the item."

Ehren looked at Owen. Owen shrugged. "I've never heard of doing it that way before."

"I have," Isold said. "It's not common, but it's not unheard of and it's not a cheat."

"We're prepared to pay two hundred gold for your participation, plus we'll buy the item off you at standard rates," Junio said. "What do you say?"

Ehren again glanced at Meladria. Meladria said, "We'll need to discuss it with our whole team. Can we talk to you about it later?"

"Sure," Junio said. "But don't take too long. It's true we don't want to run all over town searching for partners, but we are in a hurry." He rose, followed by Renella. "We'll be seeing you."

When the two had returned to their table, Livia said, "Discuss with your team?"

"Jessemia's in the bath," Calista said, like this was the most obvious thing in the world. "She'll want to have a say."

"But—" Livia shut her mouth. Aderyn also didn't know what to say. She was pretty sure Jessemia intended to leave her team when they reached Guerdon Deep, but she shouldn't speak for her friend no matter how sure she was. Discomfort made her fidget with the hairbrush. When Calista had spoken, Aderyn had felt the rightness of her assumption that Jessemia should stay, and it surprised her. Their team had come together out of necessity, not choice, but did that mean disbanding it was the obvious answer?

"It's a good opportunity," Ehren was saying. "I'm sure Jessemia will agree."

"You should—" Owen began. He caught Aderyn's eye and fell silent. Aderyn thought about using **[Secret Message]**, but he wouldn't be able to reply to anything she asked. They'd have to wait, and see what choice Jessemia made.

CHAPTER THIRTY-NINE

J ust then, Jessemia appeared, followed by Weston. "Who's next?" Weston asked.

"In a minute," Owen said. "I'm interested in what you all decide."

"Decide what?" Weston dropped into a seat next to Livia and hugged her with one arm. "Now who's whiffy, eh?"

"We have a quest possibility," Ehren said to Jessemia. "Those adventurers over there want us to take on a quest to help them out. It's worth more than two hundred gold and probably a lot of experience. I'm not sure I like the idea."

"Why not?" Jessemia said. "I've done plenty of those kinds of quests. They're usually easy, or at least simple—do one thing and hand the results to the person paying you. So it shouldn't take long."

"I agree," Calista said. "So long as Meladria feels confident in her **[Knowledge: Monsters]** ability."

"I'm sure I can figure it out," Meladria said. "So if you're okay with it, I think we should accept."

"If *I'm* okay with it?" Jessemia said, sounding perplexed. "It's your quest."

"But—you're our leader," Ehren said. "I mean, we all should decide together, but you ought to have the final say."

"Oh." Jessemia blushed. "Um. I thought—well, this was just temporary. Wasn't it?"

Calista's brow furrowed. "You mean you were planning to leave? But we work so well together. Don't you think so?"

"Well, of course, but—" Jessemia looked like she wished she could be anywhere but there. "We were sort of thrown together by chance. I always assumed teams were something you made decisions about after lots of consideration and thought."

"So what?" Ehren said. "Maybe it was random at first. But our team was destroyed by that dungeon, and you brought us back together again. I don't want to lose that."

Jessemia turned a stricken look on Owen. "Is that right?"

"Jessemia, I can't tell you that," Owen said. "But he's not wrong that you've all become a team over the past several days. And Aderyn taught me when you find a team that works that well, you don't abandon it lightly." He took Aderyn's hand. "What do you think? More importantly, what do you feel?"

Jessemia let out a deep sigh. "I've teamed with half a dozen groups of adventurers since I got my Call. None of them ever felt like I belonged—well, because I wasn't really a team member, I was just the useless Pathseer they dragged along with them." She didn't sound bitter, just resigned. "And this—" She looked at Ehren, then Calista, and finally Meladria. "You're right. It feels like a team. Like we're in this together. I don't know why I didn't see it sooner."

"Then we'll take the quest?" Meladria said.

Jessemia shook her head. "I still have to go to Guerdon Deep. We can come back afterward."

"They won't still be here," Ehren said. "And I don't know about you, but none of us have much money. Two hundred gold would help a lot."

"We'll find other quests," Jessemia said.

Owen leaned forward. "No, you won't. You'll take this one."

Jessemia blinked. "I can't do that. Not if you're to complete the quest Eleora gave you."

Owen surveyed his teammates seated around the table. "I think," he said, "we'll be abandoning that one."

"But you came all this way!" Jessemia exclaimed. "What about the experience? You'll have nothing!"

"We'll make it up elsewhere," Aderyn said. "Besides, the quest is already invalid. You're not a spoiled darling anymore."

"I—"

"It's not up to you," Owen said. "Are we all agreed?"

The other four friends nodded.

A message appeared in front of Aderyn's face.

Warning: You are about to abandon the quest [Escort the Spoiled Darling]. This action cannot be undone. Abandoning a quest may negate the possibility of accepting it again later. Do you wish to proceed? Y / N

"That's it," Owen said, and gestured to select Y.

A new message appeared.

Are you sure? [10,000 XP] is a lot of experience to give up. Proceed? Y / N

"Um," Owen said.

"I guess it wants us to be extra sure?" Aderyn said.

Owen nodded. He gestured again.

A third message appeared.

No one would blame you for not abandoning this quest. Don't take this step lightly. Proceed? Y / N

"Oh, for the—" Owen gestured impatiently.

The quest vanished from the right side of Aderyn's Codex display.

"Right," Owen said. "That's—"

Before he could finish that sentence, another message appeared.

**Congratulations! You have completed the secret quest [A Generous Act, A Generous Reward].
You have been awarded [15,000 XP]**

Aderyn, stunned, read the message aloud, and exclaimed, "But—that wasn't the point!"

"Being rewarded for doing the unselfish thing," Livia said. "I could get used to this."

Aderyn hugged Jessemia, who was crying. "We didn't do it for the experience," she said. "We did it for you. For all of us."

"I know," Jessemia said. "And I won't ever forget."

ADERYN WOKE LATE THE NEXT MORNING WITH THE SUN shining directly into her face. She groaned and rolled over, and discovered she was alone in her bed. Pushing hair out of her face, she sat up. "Owen? Is everything all right?"

Owen was looking out the window, the bright sunlight gilding his blond hair. He didn't turn around when she addressed him. "It's fine. I was just thinking."

Aderyn stood and began hunting for her clothes. It had been an active, exciting night. "Thinking about what?"

"About our next step. About leveling to fourteen. I'm having second thoughts about Finion's Gate." Owen turned away from the window. He was fully dressed, though he hadn't put his boots on. "That takes us a long way from the Lonely Tor."

"Level fourteen is just the minimum level for the **[Fire and Ash]** quest, remember?" Aderyn pulled her shirt over her head and joined him at the window. "If we gain more experience, maybe level again after activating the quest, we'll be even more successful. There's no reason we have to rush to the Lonely Tor immediately."

"That's true. Come here." Owen took her in his arms and kissed her, reminding her of last night and how wonderful it had been. "I should probably stop being so anxious about completing the Fated One quests. It's not like there's a time limit. And—"

"And, what?" Aderyn prompted.

He chuckled. "You'll just tell me this world isn't a game."

"It isn't. What were you thinking about that brought that up?"

"In my world, people sometimes play computer RPGs trying to complete them as fast as possible. I guess I still think that way. Anyway, after seven weeks of travel, I'm antsy. But you're right, and I shouldn't alter our sensible plan just because I'm impatient." He kissed her again, slower and more intensely, running his hands down her back to her waist. "With you, on the other hand," he murmured, "I never feel like rushing things."

Aderyn pressed close against him, enjoying the feel of his lean, muscular body against hers. "I overslept. We don't have time if we want to leave for Guerdon Deep before noon."

"Damn." He kissed her once more and rested his forehead against hers. "I love you. I couldn't do any of this without you."

The depth of emotion in his voice made her shiver. "I love you, too. I can't believe I ever thought I didn't want romance in my life."

"I'm glad you changed your mind." He hugged her and let her go. "Finish getting dressed, and we'll get something to eat. We're not in such a hurry that we have to rush breakfast."

Livia was the only one of their friends in the taproom when they came downstairs. She was pouring coffee and smiled pleasantly when Owen and Aderyn approached, so it wasn't her first cup. "Weston and Isold are out picking up supplies," she said. "They should be back soon."

"Where are Jessemia and the others?" Aderyn asked.

"Packing their things to head out. They accepted that quest and Jessemia said they should make a start today." Livia sipped her coffee. "I still can't believe she's a team leader. I would have bet on her staying useless and whiny forever."

"She wanted to change," Aderyn said. "That makes a difference."

The serving boy brought big plates of ham and hashed potatoes flecked with cheese, and Aderyn ate in silence, enjoying how she didn't need to talk to feel close to her friends. Weston and Isold joined them as she and Owen were finishing. "I have recharged the <**Healing Stone**>," Isold said, "and we visited a number of markets, but decided against buying food when we didn't have the <**Knapsack of Plenty**> to store it in."

"That was smart," Owen said, pushing his plate away. "Livia, what time is it?"

"Quarter to ten," Livia said, consulting her pocket watch.

"We should get moving, then." Owen rose and led them from the taproom.

Aderyn settled their bill while the others waited outside. When she joined them, Jessemia and her team were there. They all wore knapsacks and looked ready to set out on a quest. "You look prepared," she told Jessemia.

Jessemia looked nervous, but resolved. "It's a big step, taking on leadership," she said to Aderyn and Owen. "I hope I don't mess up too badly."

"Never forget you're all in this together," Owen said. "And don't dither. Make informed decisions and don't go back and forth over whether they were the right ones. You'll probably make mistakes, because we all do, but being indecisive and uncertain is worse."

"I'll remember. Thank you." She clasped Owen's hand briefly, then hugged Aderyn. "And thank you for believing in me."

"Thank *you* for making that belief justified," Aderyn said with a smile.

Weston and Livia joined them, followed by Isold. "I still can't believe how things turned out," Livia said. "I was so sure you were hopeless."

"That's all right, so was I," Jessemia said with a laugh. "Thank you all for being willing to give me a second chance."

"So, what will you do now?" Isold said. "After the harvesting quest."

"Stay in Setter's Valley for a few days, seeing what's available. Maybe go to Guerdon Deep in a week or so." Jessemia extended a hand to Isold. "You've been so generous, I'm not sure what else to say."

Isold clasped her hand firmly. "Maybe we'll meet again someday. Who knows what the future will bring?"

Jessemia nodded. "I'd like that."

They watched Jessemia and her team head off down the street before proceeding the other way. "Meet again someday?" Aderyn said. "Was that as personal as it sounded?"

Isold shrugged. "She's not who she used to be. I can't help wondering."

"That seems so unlike you," Livia said. "I thought you were committed to living in the moment when it came to relationships."

"I have no intention of pining over lost opportunities," Isold said. "But if our paths cross again someday, well, I see no reason not to consider how our relationship might change."

"Hard to imagine seven weeks ago she was a whining brat with no skills," Weston said. "I can see how your opinion might have changed."

Livia elbowed him. "Are you saying you're interested?"

Weston gave her an innocent look. "Just reflecting on how strange life is."

"Well, you'd better reflect in a different direction, dearest."

Aderyn rolled her eyes. "Can we talk about something else? Where are we going?"

"You said there were a few markets that could supply us, Isold," Owen said. "We need food for two days. Then it's back on the road. Can we do that before noon?"

"It would be faster if we split up," Livia said, "but then somebody would have to wander the streets of Setter's Valley with their arms full of food."

"I don't mind doing that," Weston said. "I can carry a lot in these arms."

"Fair enough," Owen said. "Aderyn and I will pick up meat and bread. Meet at the city gate at noon?"

It was such an ordinary, commonplace conversation, and yet Aderyn was suddenly struck by a rush of emotion. Her team. Her friends. Setting off on yet another adventure. "I'm so glad we found each other," she declared. "Isn't it funny how we were all strangers once? I mean, everybody is a stranger until they meet, but it seems so random in our case. Livia having a quest, and Weston eavesdropping, and Isold coming to Owen's rescue."

"And me being pulled out of my world and dropped right where I could encounter you," Owen said, putting an arm around Aderyn's shoulders. "That's the least likely of all."

"And now it's hard to imagine anything else," Weston said. "I think I see what you mean. We might have done that first quest and parted company."

"So really, it's the Fated One quest we have to thank for what we are now," Livia said. "Which means Isold is responsible for bringing us together, because he knew to recognize what Owen was."

"You're welcome," Isold said dryly, making the others laugh.

"Well, we're back on track," Owen said. "One more level to unlock the next Fated One quest. What do you think will happen next?"

"Something unexpected," Aderyn said.

Owen hitched his knapsack higher. "Then let's get started."

Appendix: Character Sheets

NOTE: These character sheets represent the status of the companions at the end of the book, which means it reveals everything the companions learn about their skills throughout the story. If you haven't finished the book, don't read this unless you don't mind spoilers!

Name: Aderyn

Level: 13

Class: Warmaster

<u>Skills</u>: Bluff (10), Climb (9), Conversation (12), Intimidate (7), Sense Truth (14), Survival (7), Swim (1), Knowledge: Monsters (10), Knowledge: World Lore (4), Knowledge: Demons (1)

<u>Class Skills</u>: Improved Assess 2 (21), Awareness (14), Knowledge: Geography (9), Spot (13), *Discern Weakness* (20), Dodge (12), Improvised Distraction (12), *Outflank* (16), Draw Fire (7), *Keep Pace* (15), Amplify Voice (12), See It Coming (14), Basic Weapon Proficiency (Swords) (11), *Read Body Language* (8), Basic Map Access (3), Compel (7), Spot Weakness (2), Secret Message (1)

*italics are paired skills with partner

Name: Jacob Owen Lindberg
    Class: Swordsworn
    Level: 13
    <u>Skills</u>: Assess (10), Awareness (12), Climb (10), Conversation (12), Sense Truth (11), Spot (10), Survival (5), Swim (10), Knowledge: Demons (1)
    <u>Class Skills</u>: Advanced Weapon Proficiency (21), Improved Armor Proficiency (14), Knowledge: Monsters (11), *Exploit Weakness* (20), Dodge (12), Parry (11), Improved Bluff (11), *Outflank* (16), Trip (4), *Keep Pace* (15), Disarm (4), Intimidate (9), Charge (5), Two-Weapon Fighting (4), *Read Body Language* (8), Basic Map Access (3), Overrun (2), Demoralize (1), Sunder (0)
    *italics are paired skills with Warmaster

Name: Weston
    Class: Moonlighter
    Level: 13
    <u>Skills:</u> Assess (10), Climb (12), Conversation (11), Intimidate (9), Sense Truth (11), Survival (4), Swim (3), Knowledge: Social (11), Knowledge: Demons (1)
    <u>Class Skills:</u> Pick Locks (12), Advanced Sneak Attack (13), Advanced Weapons Proficiency (11), Improved Armor Proficiency (10), Improved Detect Traps (14), Disable Traps (11), Improved Spot (16), Awareness (13), Dodge (12), Stealth (14), Improved Bluff (12), Dirty Fighting (8), To the Heart (12), Hide (8), Improved Thrown Weapons Proficiency (6), Disguise (1), Hide in Plain Sight (4), Evasion (5), Basic Map Access (3), Escape Artist (2), Unarmed Combat (1)

Name: Isold

Class: Herald

Level: 13

Skills: Assess (8), Awareness (11), Bluff (9), Climb (6), Conversation (6), Intimidate (4), Sense Truth (13), Spot (12), Survival (4), Swim (2) Knowledge: Demons (2)

Class Skills: Perform (singing) (15); Knowledge: Magic (11); Knowledge: Monsters (12); Knowledge: History (8); Knowledge: Social (8); Knowledge: World Lore (12); Identify Magic Items (13); Charm (14); Distraction (10); Map Access (13); Inspire Courage (10); Fascination (8); Persuasion (8); Perform (drum) (9); Suggestion (6); Resist Magic (3); Shout (3); Hypnotize (5); Find Object (2); Coercion (0); Break Enchantment (1)

Name: Livia

Class: Earthbreaker

Level: 13

Skills: Assess (5), Awareness (7), Bluff (7), Climb (3), Conversation (8), Intimidate (12), Sense Truth (10), Spot (9), Survival (4), Swim (3), Knowledge: Demons (1)

Elemental Powers: Earth, stone

Class Skills: Knowledge: Magic, Elemental Blast (earth spray, shower of small stones, rain of large stones) (13), Earth to Mud/Mud to Earth (7), Mage Armor (shifting stone slabs) (7), Excavate (5), Summon Elemental Hammer (2), Basic Map Access (2), Tremorsense (2), Sculpt Earth/Stone (2)

Spell List

0-level spells: Daze; Drench; Light; Telekinesis, minor; Mending; Freezing Ray, minor; Root, Spark

1st Level spells

Air Bubble; Break; Force Shield; Grease; Heat Metal (slow); Loose Bonds; Mudball; Sunder Weapon; Thunder Punch

2nd Level spells

Create Pit; Dust Cloud; Earth's Endurance; Thunderstomp; Mirror Image; Mud Minion; Improved Mending; Protection from Fire, Mass (big earth dome); Skip

3rd Level spells

Iron Spike Attack; Thunderstomp, Greater (directed); Clairvoyance; Dispel Magic; Immobilize; Telekinesis, Greater; Daylight

4th Level spells

Stone Ladder; Stone Sphere; Transport, Minor; Invisibility (self); Earth Glide; Stone Fist; Daze, Mass

5th Level spells

Hungry Pit; Dismissal of Demons; Scry; Lighten Object; Darkvision; Passwall; Burrow

6th Level spells

Move earth, major; Stoneskin, Mass; Invisibility, Mass

AND NOW FOR A SPECIAL MESSAGE...

Did you enjoy this book? Want more LitRPG adventure goodness? Then the LitRPG Books Facebook group is for you! Find new recommendations, connect with fellow readers, and more!

About the Author

In addition to the Warmaster series, Melissa McShane is the author of many fantasy novels, including the novels of Tremontane, the first of which is *Servant of the Crown;* The Extraordinaries series, beginning with *Burning Bright;* and *The Book of Secrets,* first book in The Last Oracle series.

While her home remains in the mountains out West, she currently lives in Kerala, India, with her husband and two rambunctious Persian kittens. She wrote reviews and critical essays for many years before turning to fiction, which is much more fun than anyone ought to be allowed to have.

You can visit her at her website
   www.melissamcshanewrites.com
   for more information on other books and upcoming releases.

To subscribe to her newsletter, which is published monthly, visit **www.melissamcshanewrites.com/contact-me-2/join-my-mailing-list**

ALSO BY MELISSA MCSHANE

WARMASTER

Warmaster 1: Dungeon Spiteful

Warmaster 2: Winter's Peril

Warmaster 3: Gamboling Coil

Warmaster 4: Sorrowvale

Warmaster 5: The Glory Games (forthcoming 2024)

THE BOOKS OF THE DARK GODDESS

Silver and Shadow

Missing by Moonlight

Shades of the Past

Path of the Paladin

Bright Moon Deception (forthcoming 2024)

THE LAST ORACLE

The Book of Secrets

The Book of Peril

The Book of Mayhem

The Book of Lies

The Book of Betrayal

The Book of Havoc

The Book of Harmony

The Book of War

The Book of Destiny